PRINCE *of* MISADVENTURE

PRINCE *of* MISADVENTURE

THE CURIOUS CHILDHOOD OF HENRY VIII

BENA STUTCHBURY

Illustrations by Lorenzo Sparascio

*For my husband, Shaun, whose many real adventures
outshine any I could ever imagine*

♥

Author's Note

There is a time for history to be made and a time for it to be written; the first is as a young heart beating, the other, brittle bones covered in dust. Historians can fit together the bones as they must, but the flesh and blood with all its passion has long since gone without a trace. This is a story about that passion, about the early life of a historical giant whose childhood has been overlooked; worse still, forgotten. That boy one day became Henry VIII. This is not history, it is 'his story'.

Copyright © 2022, Bena Stutchbury.

All rights reserved. No part of this publication may be reproduced, distributed, or transmitted in any form or by any means, including photocopying, recording, or other electronic or mechanical methods, without the prior written permission of the publisher, except in the case of brief quotations embodied in critical reviews and certain other non-commercial uses permitted by copyright law. For permission requests, write to the publisher, addressed "Attention: Permissions Coordinator," at the address below.

ISBN: 979-8-8129-7843-3 (Paperback)
ISBN: 979-8-8129-7957-7 (Hardcover)

Any references to historical events, real people, or real places are used fictitiously. Names, characters, and places are products of the author's imagination.

Illustrations by Lorenzo Sparascio Map by the author

Book design by Irissa Book Design on Facebook or LinkedIn

Book interior layout by ThePaperHouse

Editing by Lindsay Henkle, The Blue Pen Editor, and Charlie Wilson, Landmark Editorial.

Line editing and proofreading by Melanie Scott at Reedsy & ThePaperHouse

Published by ThePaperHouse
www.thepaperhousebooks.com

Printed by IngramSpark
First printing edition 2022

South of England 1502

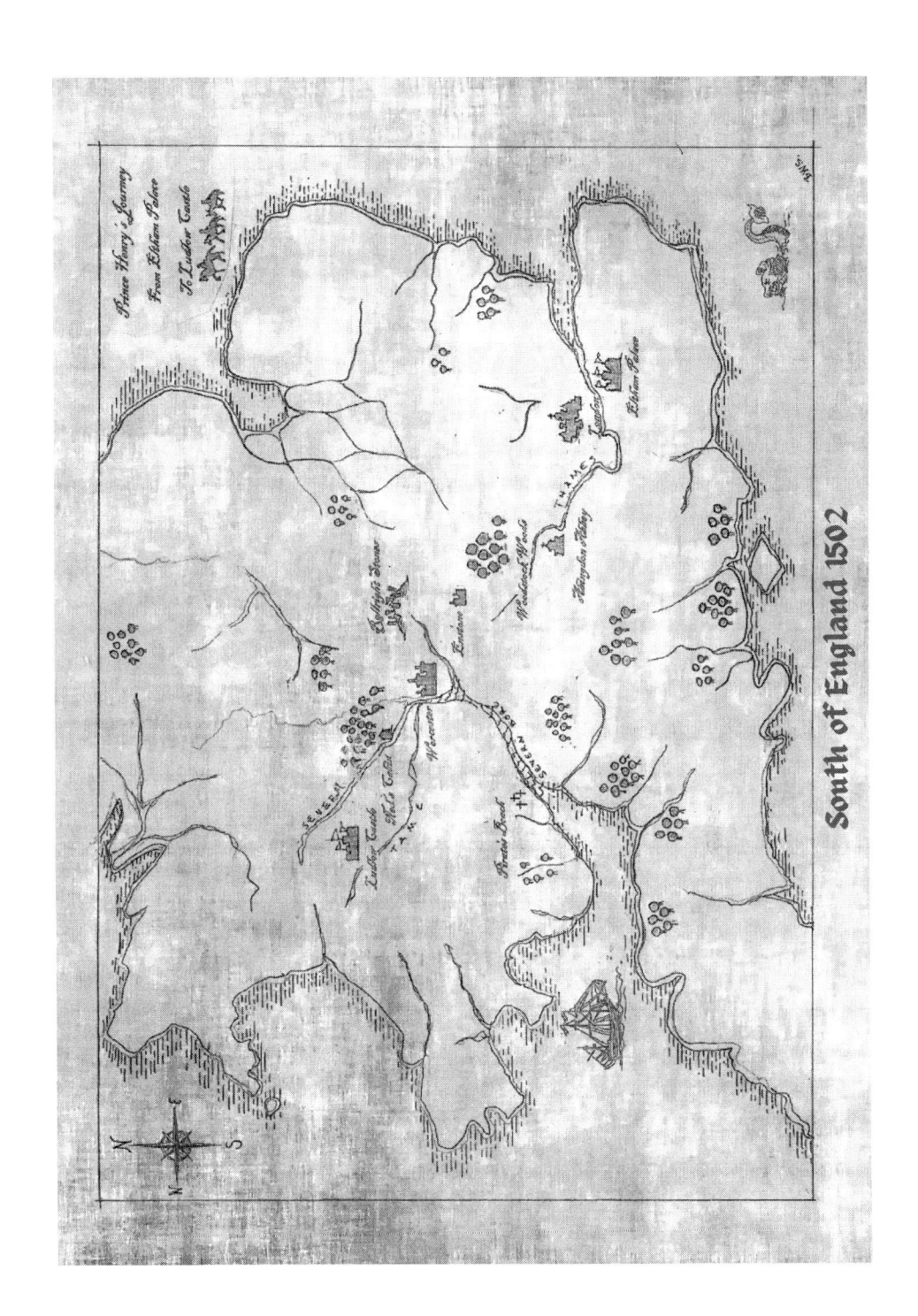

"The World is full of magic things, patiently waiting for our senses to grow sharper."

-WB Yeats

1501

1

13th NOVEMBER 1501

It was the birth of a new century, the dawn of a new era and the eve of the greatest royal wedding to be held in over one hundred years. King Henry Tudor was in his privy chamber, waiting to try on his wedding clothes. Pacing up and down, he confided his innermost thoughts to Denys Hughes, his Groom of the Stool.

"At last, Denys, with this marriage, I can pass on to Arthur some of the responsibilities that weigh so heavily on my shoulders." He halted, his cast eye roaming. "It's years since we threw Richard III's mutilated body over a horse while I set his crown upon my head. Sixteen years, yet I still suffer from the horrors of that battle; the visceral smell of guts, the shattering clash of steel. One roll of the dice and it might have been my body lying over that horse, arse in the air for everyone to mock. That image haunts me."

Denys poured his master a goblet of wine. "It must be t-t-terrible, sire, to be revisited by such memories after all this time. B-but those days are long gone. England is at peace and is p-p-prospering under your rule."

The King twisted the silver goblet around in his hands. "But I still cannot *rest*. I can't sleep in my bed until someone has checked it for knives sticking up that might kill me, nor eat before someone tastes my food in case it is poisoned. Sometimes I fancy that I saw a look of thanks in Richard's eyes as he died, as if he was released from this constant fear and was thinking, 'It's your turn now.'"

"B-b-but you have the Yorkists under c-control these days, sire. They are all d-defeated, imprisoned or... well... dead."

The King grunted. "If I killed *all* the dissenters, I would have no subjects left."

The doors to the chamber opened and in walked the Groom of the Wardrobe. He bowed low. "Your wedding clothes, sire."

"Excellent."

New clothes always put the King in a jovial mood. A cautious man when it came to finance, Henry Tudor understood that appearance mattered. His clothes on, he swung from side to side to see how they moved against his body.

"The Art of Monarchy is Illusion, Denys."

Denys was used to these well-rehearsed truisms. "Yes, my lord."

"I am God's representative on earth. I am no longer a man, but a symbol."

The clothes were encrusted with jewels and pearls, so they shimmered in an unearthly manner. The King was delighted. He admired himself in the venetian mirror. He had kept his figure all these years, riding out every day to do so. He smiled at himself in the mirror, not a pretty sight, as his teeth were yellow, like a wolf.

"You know, Denys, a great king is like a castle: invincible. Yet all castles need a solid foundation, or they will falter, and that is the problem with Henry."

Denys objected. "But he is just a child."

The King swung around; his humour gone in a flash. "Just a *child?*"

"Who has m-m-much to learn, I m-mean." Denys's stammer returned.

"Don't be ridiculous, Denys. Get me out of this… frippery; I must go and check on Henry. Where is Arthur? I want to see him. Now!"

Denys, flustered that the King's good mood had vanished before his eyes, signalled to a guard to fetch the prince immediately. The King never had to summon anyone twice.

Out in the courtyard below, a group of youths were fighting each other with swords of whalebone and wood. The young swordsmen, their court jackets thrown carelessly on the floor, moved back and forth, right arms forward with strong hands holding their weapons and left arms in the air behind them for balance. They lunged forward, then jumped back, hurling insults, and cursing when a blow made its mark. They fought hard, for these boys were fighting not only for their honour, but in some cases for their very positions at court, their being at the Palace of Westminster – the centre of government when the King was in residence.

Among the youths, a ten-year-old boy was pitched against a young man a few years older than him. The younger boy had his sleeves rolled up. His unruly hair, a shining copper colour in the low winter sun, glowed like a halo. Although he was the youngest of all those in the courtyard, the boy was tall for his age and held a presence that was engaging. His blue eyes shone, and his rosebud mouth was puckered, the grin that he normally wore overcome by concentration.

As the sword-master approached, Thomas, the older of the two, was defending himself from a fresh onslaught from the younger boy. As the underdog, the young boy was determined to get past the defence of his foe. Using not only the thrusts and parries he had been taught but also pushing forward, his body seemed to take on a life of its own. Pirouetting on the ball of his foot, he spun round in a full circle before striking at his opponent from a new vantage point.

"Good move," panted Thomas as he blocked the attack. "I didn't know that you took dancing lessons." He lunged forward.

The redhead ducked down, twisted around a second time, and now at knee height against his opponent, he hit him on the back of his leg. Thomas cried out in pain, hopping about, much to the sword-master's amusement. The young boy was proving to be a promising student, using moves that had not been seen in the practice yard before.

"Well done, sire – an unusual method of scoring a blow, but effective," he observed, and then continued, "Where did you learn to do that move?"

The boy shrugged his shoulders. "I didn't. I made it up."

Impressive if true, thought the sword-master, nodding his head. Moments later, a door swung open on the viewing gallery above. A short trumpet blast sounded. The fighting stopped abruptly. The King had arrived, his presence felt. The youths stood panting from their exertions, waiting to be given the order to continue fighting. They looked up at the balcony where the King was leaning on the balustrade, looking down on the scene below. The King had a piercing gaze, the intensity of which bored into the very souls of all who were caught in his stare. Only one boy had the nerve to move: the redhead who had fought with such fervour just moments earlier. He gathered his wits about him, readied himself, then attacked his sparring partner with renewed vigour, coming at him from left and right.

His unruly hair, a shining copper colour in the low winter son, glowed like a halo.

Thomas, caught unawares, fell back from the force that hit him. He lifted his sword, but the boy had taken the advantage and before he knew it, Thomas had fallen to the ground, a blunt-pointed sword at his throat.

"Do you yield, sir?" The boy looked down at his quarry with an intensity that mirrored that of the King only moments before.

Thomas laughed. "I have little choice from this angle." The others in the courtyard also laughed, breaking the tension in the air, for they were all aware that the boy with the red hair was Prince Henry, second son of the King of England.

Up in the gallery, the King turned to Prince Arthur, who was accompanying him.

"See how he behaves?" he asked. "He is an unstable force, a potential threat to your future. We must keep an eye on him and ensure his energy is harnessed before he grows too wilful."

Prince Arthur, a slim, nervous boy with a pale complexion, listened to his father with wisdom that belied his years.

"He is a fine young man, Father. I believe he has inherited your combat skills and will use them to fight for England."

The King grunted. "But what happens if he fights *you* for England, eh?"

"I… I hadn't thought of that. I suppose I would have to kill him."

"What? Before you have had children, a son and heir?"

Arthur began to sweat. "No, of course not. I would have to keep him in the Tower. Except his supporters might free him. Perhaps if you ordered him to train for the Church, Father… that way he would be harnessed *before* he got out of hand, without a weapon other than prayer."

"Good thinking, son." The King pulled a wry smile. Prince Arthur was relieved he had passed yet another test.

He seldom saw the King, having been brought up at Ludlow Castle on the Welsh border since he was a young child. However, these rare visits to court were a test to check he had learned the necessary skills to become a monarch.

The King and Prince Arthur turned away from the scene below and headed towards a pair of oak doors that were opened on their approach by attentive guards. Before he left, Arthur glanced down at Henry and caught the look of anguish on his face. As there was nothing that he could do, Arthur followed his father to pay his respects to his grandmother, Lady Margaret, Countess of Richmond.

Studying all this from a corner of the courtyard was an engaging youth with black hair and a hungry expression. Charles, who at seventeen was two years older than Prince Arthur, watched on. He was surprised the King had ignored such an impressive show of skill by his youngest son. Most parents would congratulate their child for showing such promise – or so he assumed. Being an orphan, Charles had no experience of parental love. He watched as Prince Henry hurled his sword onto the ground before marching out of the courtyard. Charles walked over to pick up the discarded weapon and quietly followed.

Lady Margaret was expecting a visit from her son, the King. She sat on an ornately carved oak chair with a back that was almost as rigid as her own. The chair was small, for Lady Margaret was a small woman, but it was covered in gold leaf and so looked like a throne. Lady Margaret had spent a lifetime plotting to crown her son as King and she had succeeded. It had taken her two marriages, many alliances and at least one heinous crime. The result, however, was that her son was now King of England and the promise she had sworn on her first husband's grave had been kept.

Upon his arrival, the King gave his mother a respectful nod of the head and Arthur knelt, ready to receive her blessing by way of a bony hand on his scalp.

Lady Margaret spoke. "Have you taken Arthur on an instructive tour this morning?"

"I have indeed," replied the King. "His observations have been mature and intelligent. I think he should return to Ludlow Castle as soon as the wedding is over, so that he and Princess Katherine can rule over their own court. He executes his duties perfectly."

"Do you honestly think it is time for them to live together?" Lady Margaret sniffed. "I am not convinced that they should live as man and wife after the wedding. I hardly believe that the two of them are capable of —"

"Lady Grandmother." Prince Arthur's voice trembled as he rose to his feet. "We are quite ready to make the journey to our lands, I can assure you."

Lady Margaret was not convinced. "Well, go ahead then, but I don't expect miracles."

Arthur felt his face turn red with embarrassment. However, this was a subject that Lady Margaret was qualified to speak on with authority. Married at the age of twelve, she had fallen pregnant immediately and suffered a horrendous ordeal when giving birth to her son. The experience had left her barren and no other child was ever destined to form within her body. This made her cherish her only child even more. He was her treasure, her darling, her life.

"Well, we will just have to see how they get on once the ceremony is over," replied the King. "I am sure that Arthur here will *rise* to the occasion."

"Henry, sometimes you shock me with your soldier's talk," Lady Margaret admonished.

Arthur blushed and looked down at his shoes, his heart pounding.

Outside, a cloud was hanging over the head of Prince Henry, who was up on the palace battlements, overlooking the roofscape of London with its many towers and flags. This was his favourite place when he wanted time on his own. *I can accept Father liking Arthur more than me, but not slighting me in front of the other boys like that.*

A bird's nest, tucked up against a chimney breast with two smooth, round eggs in it, caught the prince's attention and he picked up an egg. It was warm to the touch. Henry threw the egg as hard as he could into the void beyond the wall.

Down in the garden below, Charles was wandering around looking for Henry. He still held the sword, his excuse for approaching the prince. He had been waiting for an opportunity to ingratiate himself to one of the princes, be it Arthur or Henry. Charles noted the pain in Henry's reaction when he was ignored by his father. He had something that might appeal to the prince and knew that a distraction from what was making him sad would be welcome.

As Charles carried on searching, a pigeon's egg landed only a few feet from where he was walking. Looking up, Charles decided to go up to the battlements and see if the prince was there. Climbing the stairs that led to the roof, he found the prince sitting hunched up against the base of a tall chimney stack. Henry turned around upon hearing the stairway door opening.

"Who are you?"

"My name is Charles Brandon, sire. I have brought you your sword."

"Oh." Prince Henry looked at the sword with disinterest. "Thank you."

He took the sword and let it fall to his side.

"Oh... and I thought I might come up to have lunch with my friend, Jasper," Charles said, trying to interest the prince. "Are you hungry?"

"I am," Prince Henry acknowledged. "But where is your friend?"

Charles looked down, opened a leather pouch tied to his waist and put his hand in, only to withdraw it while carefully holding a dark-brown mouse with a white tip to its tail. "He is here, see?"

Prince Henry's eyes sparkled. "Is that him?"

"Yes, this is Jasper. Would you like to hold him?" Charles took Prince Henry's hand, opened it and gently placed Jasper on his palm.

Charles was delighted to hear the boy giggle as the mouse tickled his hand. He pulled out a piece of bread and cheese wrapped up in cloth from within his jacket. Breaking off some small crumbs he put them in the palm of Henry's hand and the little mouse began to nibble.

"Here, have some yourself."

Charles offered Henry a bigger piece of bread and cheese, which the prince chewed on as he studied the mouse. The mouse washed his paws without a care in the world.

A conversation sparked and, after a while, Charles asked the prince about the move he had used, twisting around on the ball of his foot when fighting.

"Oh, I do that from time to time. It catches people unawares."

"Where did you learn such a move?" enquired Charles.

"I don't know. I think I made it up. When I am fighting, my body sometimes does things naturally. It's like it has already learned the moves."

Charles was an excellent swordsman himself and recognised talent. "You have a true instinct as a warrior, sire. I would listen to it if I were you and you will soon win every fight you enter."

Prince Henry grinned, dimples appearing on his cheeks. "Are you a warrior?"

"I am training to become a knight, if that's what you mean," explained Charles. "I am entering my first tournament this week in celebration of the royal wedding."

"Well, I will look out for you, Charles. But I must go now, or I will be missed."

"Take the mouse with you, if you like," offered Charles. "Can I? Oh, thank you." Henry's eyes shone. "But how shall I get him back to you?"

"There is no need. Just let him go and he will come and find me."

"Can he do that?"

"Of course he can." Charles ruffled the prince's hair, a gesture new to Henry, but welcome. "Just let him go. But in the meantime, take this box and keep him in there. He might need a bigger box at night. Oh, and don't forget to feed him." Untying the pouch from around his waist where it was held with a thin belt, Charles handed it to Henry, who popped the mouse gently inside and fixed it around his own waist. "I must go. Bye for now, Charles." Henry wanted to find his sisters to show them the mouse. "And thank you, once again." Off skipped the prince, down the stairs as happy as could be. Charles watched him go. His ploy had worked: Henry was happy, and Charles was happy too, for he had made friends with a prince at last.

Prince Henry ran all the way back to the Royal Nursery. He wanted to show the mouse to Princess Margot, his sister, for she loved animals. Margot's real name was Margaret, but it had become Margot when Henry was a baby and could not pronounce her full name. Now everyone called her Margot, although Prince Henry sometimes called her Maggot.

Prince Henry burst into the room to find Margot and their baby sister, Mary, dressed up in an assortment of clothes: Margot as a bride with a veil, a long gown and high platformed shoes known as chopines; little Mary wearing a white chemise and a black floppy hat, with a tartan blanket tied around her waist. Princess Mary was a delightful six-year-old with long auburn hair, sapphire button eyes and a snub nose. Princess Margot was similar in colouring, but a slight difference here and there made her less striking.

"Oh, hello, Henry, you have arrived just in time for my wedding," said Margot with authority. "You can be the King of Scotland and Mary can be the bishop."[1]

"But I want to be the princess," cried little Mary.

Henry was disinterested in being the Scots king; he just wanted to show them his mouse. "Look what I've got," he said, opening the pouch.

"Oh, how wonderful," Margot exclaimed as Mary squealed in surprise and hid behind her sister. "Where did you get it?" She stepped forward, wobbling on her chopines, all decorum forgotten.

"He was given to me by a knight. He is called Jasper, Sir Jasper, and he has come to stay for a few days. Would you like to hold him?"

The siblings crowded around and begged for turns in holding the little brown creature. They played with him for a while before Margot announced, "We are going to need somewhere for him to live."

Looking around, Henry spotted the dressing-up box. It was a massive oak chest with big black handles. "Come on, let's empty the dressing-up box out; it can become his home." Margot rushed to help him turn the chest on its side to empty it of its contents. The children spent the rest of their evening making a home for their new friend. It was as they were leaving the nursery that Henry noticed two rolled-up scrolls protruding from the pile of court jackets, ladies' dresses and other items that had fallen from the box.

"What are these?" he wondered, pulling them out of the pile of clothes.

"Let me have a look."

Margot tried to grab a scroll and caught the faded red ribbon that tied it. It slipped off the parchment, which unfurled. Henry was about to admonish his sister when he was distracted by some small, neat writing that appeared to be in a foreign language.

"I will ask Master Skelton to translate it," Henry announced and rolled the scrolls back up together. He took them to his room and there he folded them inside the prayer roll that he kept in a chest at the end of his bed.

Down in the lower levels of the palace, a dubious duo walked along the corridors with familiar ease. The first strode purposefully, his walking stick under his arm, while the other trailed behind, a black box held to his chest. They reached a turn in the dark passage and the first man pushed a latch with the end of his stick. With a faint click, a door opened, and light flooded in from beyond.

In her private chamber, Lady Margaret had been waiting for the secret door built into the oak panelling that lined her chamber to open. Hearing the telltale click of the latch, she turned to greet the men, her chin lifted in the air. The men entered and bowed: the first, who was rotund, with more of a stiff nod, as if his midriff prevented him from bending; the other, slim and angular, folding into his legs with ease, like a pocketknife.

Thaddeus Fiddle and Nicholas Grope had been in Lady Margaret's service for decades. Always dressed in unassuming robes, they had the art of blending into any scene, be it at court, in an inn or a bordello.

Grope was near bald, with a long wisp of black hair combed and flattened onto the crown of his head to make up for the lack of covering. His walking stick concealed a weapon: he had gouged out a few inches down through the heart of the stick and fitted a sharp gutting knife there, one that could be pulled out quickly, ready for use. The stick sported a few notches carved into it over the decades. Fiddle, his subordinate in all matters, was baby-faced, sinewy and lean. He carried no weapon, for his body was all he needed. Practised in the art of hand-to-hand combat learned in his youth as a sailor, he could break a man's neck with a twist or stun him with a well-placed blow to the head.

"Well? Have you got it?" Lady Margaret's voice cracked.

"We have, Your Ladyship," answered Grope. "The key you furnished us with worked well and we dressed as monks in case anyone challenged us. But there was no need. It was a long night, but we found what you sought. We returned by boat as the chest is cumbersome."

Taking his cue, Fiddle set the solid black box on the table. It was embossed with iron metalwork and had a ruby-encrusted padlock on it in the shape of a heart, although some of the rubies were missing. Seeing that Lady Margaret had noticed this, Fiddle touched the small, hard stones that were secreted in his pocket with sly satisfaction.

Lady Margaret reached out for the box, but Grope put his hand out to stop her. The old woman faltered and looked him in the eye, a moment of hesitation that brought a smile to the man's lips. Opening a strongbox that sat on her desk, Lady Margaret picked up two silver coins, which she placed into his other, outstretched, hand. Grope, one hand possessively on the box, kept his palm open. Lady Margaret sniffed but handed him two shiny gold coins.

"There, that should do you."

Grope released the box, allowing the woman to snatch it.

Lady Margaret stretched to her full height, still having to look up at the two men. She spoke to Grope directly.

"For your next assignment, go to Ludlow Castle. Find employment there. I want to know if there is any intimacy between the prince and princess once they are married. Are they performing? Is there a child in the offing? Send Fiddle to me with a report." She waved her hand. "You may go now."

"Thank you, Your Ladyship."

With money in their pockets, the two men bowed and left.

"What's in the box?" Fiddle asked his colleague once they were safely out of the woman's chamber.

"Never you mind, Fiddle, some things are best left alone. Especially things that have been *removed* from their rightful place. Things with links to the Other Side."

Fiddle shivered. Unsure as to what Grope was referring, he thought twice about the stones secreted in his pocket. They had suddenly taken on a force full of spiritual malevolence. He surreptitiously scooped up the rubies and deposited them on the floor as they walked, whistling as he went to cover any sound of their falling to the ground, in the hope that Grope would not notice.

2

14th NOVEMBER

The Queen awoke to a blackbird singing outside her window and a feeling of trepidation in her heart.

She sat up, her hands to her face, haunted by a dream where her son was washed away in a deluge of water. The Queen was unable to see which son it was, but Prince Henry was a formidable swimmer, whereas Prince Arthur was, well. . . more intellectually than physically adept.

What made it so awful was that she had heard a voice singing the most haunting song, like a siren enticing a ship to sail onto the rocks. It was an eerie sound, one full of foreboding. The Queen was convinced that Arthur was out of his depth and needed her help. Today he would marry the Spanish princess, who had only just arrived after an arduous journey of some five months from her homeland. What was so alarming was the girl could not speak English, not at all. Her French was limited and the Latin she spoke was of a different dialect than that used at court. How the young couple were supposed to communicate with each other was a mystery. It seemed absurd that they had been engaged since they were three years old and yet nobody had thought of teaching them each other's language. The Queen felt that it was her duty to do something to rectify the problem.

She requested a private audience with her son and ordered some food to be brought to her privy chamber. When Prince Arthur came in, she sent her ladies-in-waiting away and fussed around serving him a plate of eggs, butter, sugar and currants, none of which he could stomach.

"Are you ready for marriage, dear Arthur?" she asked. "I am, Lady Mother," he replied. "Only…"

Arthur hesitated, so she prompted him. "Only what?" "What will it be like?" Prince Arthur turned to his mother, his soft eyes pleading.

"Are you afraid?" she asked.

Arthur remained silent. Kings were never afraid.

The Queen gently took the plate from his trembling hands. "It is normal to be afraid when standing on the edge of life, about to step out into the unknown. But once you discover how wonderful that life can be, you will marvel that you ever were concerned. This I promise you."

The Queen looked at her gentle son and, digging deep, spoke candidly.

"Arthur, you are at a disadvantage with Katherine, having no language with which to communicate. She is a brave girl, coming so far at only fifteen years of age. She has travelled through barren landscapes and over tempestuous seas to marry a complete stranger in a foreign land. My advice to you is to be gentle, take your time, treat her like the precious jewel she is and don't try to be a man before the time is right." The Queen sat back and gazed at the fire, remembering how frightened she had been on her wedding day, marrying her father's enemy, the killer of Richard III whom she had been engaged to marry. The King had been courteous but unemotional. His was not the love she had read about in stories of old as a young girl. She so wanted for the Spanish princess to have a better marriage than hers.

The young prince looked at his mother with love and affection. She was wiser than anyone else he knew, even the King, and her words found their mark. He finished his ale, knelt before her and accepted her blessing as she put her hand on his beautiful soft hair. The Queen could smell the crown of his head, as she had when he was a baby. Her baby of just fifteen years. He was incredibly young to be getting married, she thought to herself, barely an adult. He needed time.

※

Prince Henry and his sisters had woken up with only one thing on their mind. Congregating in the nursery, they ran to the dressing-up box to check on Sir Jasper. He needed fresh water and clean bedding, which Margot sorted, while Henry emptied his pockets of various items that he had secreted from the dining table.[2] He had an apple, bread and some cheese, all of which the little mouse took an interest in immediately.

Afterwards, Henry and Margot took the scrolls to their tutor's study. Master Skelton, a priest in his forties who dedicated his life to the royal children in between writing poetry that he hoped would help him rise among the humanist intellectuals at court, looked at the strange writing.

"This is not a foreign language, but a code from what I can make out. Something for you to test your intellect on. When we get back to Eltham after the wedding, I will set you some exercises to help you the code but for now, there is a wedding ahead of us and you must go and prepare for the ceremony." Satisfied that he had dealt with his young charges' curiosity, the poet returned to his writing, leaving the siblings to run back to the nursery.

The scrolls put away once again, the royal children obediently returned to their chambers to have their turn in the large copper bath that was set up by the fire in the royal nursery, in which they were dunked and scrubbed. Next came their wedding clothes, fitted by a host of attendant maids overseen by a fussing matron. Prince Henry was to be all in white, as escort to the bride, and his sisters were in bright crimson dresses cut to the very height of fashion, their hair worn loose around their shoulders as a sign of purity. They had all been dressed to make an impression, for they were the very future of England.

Charles had no copper bath in which to wash that morning, nor a wooden tub. In fact, he no longer had a bed in the Great Hall now that the palace was full of guests invited to the wedding. The guests had been given private chambers, but their servants were now crammed in the hall at night, where the young man and his friends normally slept. Charles had chosen a new bed in the hayloft above the stables, a place where he felt at home, for in his youth he would hide with the horses if he were in trouble for some misdemeanour or another. As he had no parents, nobody bothered to look for him at bedtime and he would lie in the hay with a puppy or two, the aroma of the horses around him acting as a comfort blanket for him, their breathing and occasional snorting a lullaby.

This morning it was not a puppy that was curled up next to him, but a woman. Charles rubbed his eyes and blinked a few times before recalling that he was serving Prince Arthur at the breakfast table this morning. Turning to his companion, he gently awoke her by tickling her behind her ear.

"Come along, sweetheart, it's time to rise. I need to serve Prince Arthur his breakfast this morning. He will need a pep talk and some support, for no doubt he is nervous."

The pretty girl would have none of it.

"There is only one person you must serve right now."

She gazed at his handsome form. Placing her soft lips on his mouth, the girl gave Charles such a powerful kiss that all thoughts of breakfast fell from his mind as he lay back in the hay. The man would have to manage this morning without him.[3]

At Lambeth Palace, Princess Katherine was being cared for by her duenna, Doña Elvira Manuel de Villena Suárez de Figueroa, or simply Elvira, as the princess called her. Of the entourage that had braved the arduous journey from Spain to come to England, Elvira was the one Katherine loved most of all, for she took the place of her mother whom she missed so much.

The princess was changing into a wedding dress made of white satin with tiny gold roses embroidered all over its surface – the same material that had been used for the outfits of both Prince Henry and Prince Arthur, as if to show the world that they were already a united force. While she helped the princess into her clothes, Elvira chattered away to ease the tension that was only natural before a wedding.

"Now, my dear, remember to hold your head high, for you are not only a royal person through your Spanish blood, but you have English royal blood in your veins too, from the same ancestors as Prince Arthur[4]. You are quite the most royal person here today. Not even that dreadful woman, Lady Margaret, has as much claim to the throne as you do, however much she puffs herself up."

Katherine giggled. "I do find her pompous," she said, then added, "I wish my mother and father were here today to enjoy the wedding. Mother would adore this dress."

"You know it was considered too dangerous for them to make the voyage over the sea at this time of year, my dearest," answered Elvira. "Had the ship gone down, Spain would have lost both King and Queen in one tragic accident. It would never have recovered."

"We nearly were lost at sea on the way here. What would Spain have done had our ship sunk?" the princess asked, her blue eyes watery with emotion.

"You know we had God on our side, my angel. He would never have allowed you to drown when he has such an important role for you to play. You are to marry Prince Arthur and make an alliance between England and Spain. A powerful alliance. Your son will become King of England one day and he will have Spanish blood in his veins. England and Spain will defeat the French if ever they try to harm either country. You will bring peace to Europe as the French will be too cowardly to take on either country now."

As Elvira looked at her lovely mistress, she recalled how on the journey they had stopped at the cathedral at Santiago de Compostela. As the princess was kneeling at the altar, praying for a safe voyage across the sea, the smoking silver and gold censer that swung overhead broke free from its chains and came crashing down, breaking a stained-glass window on route. The echo of the precious metal as it crashed to the floor accompanied by the breaking glass that fell around it had been terrifying. That the princess had not been hurt in the accident was sheer luck.[5] Elvira could not shake the idea from her head that this incident was an omen, a sign from God that things would not go according to plan.

Inside Saint Paul's Cathedral the congregation had just witnessed the three-hour long ceremony, in which Prince Henry walked up the length of the aisle with Princess Katherine, only to hand her over to his brother, Prince Arthur, in front of the archbishop and a semicircle of other bishops andclergy who surrounded the altar.

"Mother dear, we have done it," the King announced when a pale Prince Arthur slipped a lavish gold wedding band onto the delicate finger of his new wife. The King slapped his thigh with delight. After months, years, of negotiation with the Spanish, the deal was done, and England was now an ally of the all-powerful Spain. All in all, the King was pleased, especially as the princess had turned out to be so attractive. His son was a lucky boy, for the sway of her hips foretold many a Tudor heir.

Once the bishop had joined their hands together, Prince Arthur could finally raise the veil that covered Katherine's head. As he did there was a gasp from the congregation, for she truly was beautiful. Prince Arthur smiled at her shyly and Katherine smiled back, allowing her lips to politely brush up against his own, their first intimate contact. Then they turned to the congregation and walked back through the cathedral arm in arm as husband and wife. When they stepped out into the sunlight, the roar from the crowd in attendance was deafening, and Prince Henry, who was walking close behind them, regretted that his moment by Katherine's side was over. Instead, he had to accept that he was just the 'spare heir' once more.

The feast that evening was a grand affair, with roast peacocks and swans all decked out with their feathers still in place. There were pigs with apples in their mouths, their eyes staring blindly into the distance. There were sea creatures on silver plates, smaller sea creatures in their gaping jaws. Finally, there were tarts and other pies garnished with exotic fruits and flowers made of marzipan. There was plenty of bread and wine or ale with which to wash the food down. The aroma that filled the massive hall was intoxicating. Even with all the courtiers and their wives in attendance, the amount of food displayed would never be eaten and a long line of vagabonds was waiting outside the kitchen doors to receive scraps at the end of the evening.

The King graced the high table, surrounded by his family. He was now dressed in a black velvet robe lined with white ermine fur over a heavily embroidered scarlet and gold costume that glistened in the candlelight. A diamond-encrusted badge glittered, and a pear-sized pearl hung from the black velvet cap he wore on his head. He was not an ugly man, but his countenance was formal, whether naturally or after years of practice and there was not an once or warmth in him.

"Today we celebrate the nuptials of my son and heir, Prince Arthur, with Katherine, Princess of Aragon and of our esteemed neighbouring country, Spain. King Ferdinand and Queen Isabella, parents of our new daughter, Katherine, are forever in our thoughts and we look forward to a *fruitful* relationship with them in the future, both in trade and in oursecurity. For any enemy of Spain's is now our enemy and any friend of theirs, our friend."The King spoke slowly and clearly so that the Spanish ambassador would understand his words and report them back to his master and mistress.

The King's voice was sharp, cutting like a knife through any festivity. Not a soul moved. He raised a golden goblet that sat on the table in front of him. This he passed to his taster, a man who stood behind him to test all he consumed for poison, and waited for him to sip the wine. It was good, so the King took back the goblet and raised it ceremoniously into the air. "To Prince Arthur and the Princess

Katherine," he announced.

"To Prince Arthur and the Princess Katherine," the guests obediently answered.

The silence was broken as men and women sat back down again. The King leant over to talk to Prince Arthur, who sat at his side. The prince looked so serious. Prince Henry was the opposite. His eyes were bright blue and shining as he chatted to the women around him. Occasionally, when he made them laugh, he looked towards his father for approval, but nothing came. Not a glance, nor a nod or a reassuring smile. The King appeared to ignore his youngest son with studious intent.

Once the feast was over, the tables were cleared against the walls and a dance floor was defined by ribbons laced with flowers that were strewn on the ground. This was Henry's moment. A moment he had been excited about for weeks. Up he jumped and proudly walked into the centre of the room, where his sister Margot was waiting. He bowed most gracefully and offered her his hand. Together, their heads held high and with studied elegance, they performed the first steps of the latest dance that they had mastered.

The music began slowly, but as it sped up, the children picked up the timing of their moves to match the music. The musicians were on fire, and they were spurred on by the sight of the energetic children. Henry was enjoying himself, for he excelled at dancing and knew that he looked good. He danced and pranced and swung his sister around, her long hair sailing in the air. To move more freely, Henry stopped and pulled off his tight jacket, throwing it to the floor in a cavalier manner. The onlookers clapped and cheered, encouraging the prince, who adored the attention. He gave the best performance of his young life and when finished he bowed elegantly. This caused men to throw their hats in the air and women to throw their handkerchiefs on the dance floor, a sign of their favour.[6]

The King, however, went puce red. His eyes smouldered as his mouth pulled tight. He clicked his fingers in the air and a server ran up to him, a handsome youth with a mop of dark curly hair. The King whispered into the server's ear and then waved him away. The young man, who was, in fact, Charles, looked surprised but bowed before making a hasty retreat. Within seconds he reappeared, but this time at Prince Henry's side. He discreetly passed on the message from the King. It had the effect of wiping the joy off the young boy's face, and without further ado, Henry bowed to the wedding guests who had just been applauding him and retired.

After the feast, the Queen visited her youngest son in his bedchamber.

"My darling." She kissed him on the head. "You were the life and soul of the party tonight and I thought you danced so well. But on to more important matters, for your father has asked me to talk to you about your future."

"Really?" asked Henry, his face hopeful. "Am I to get married as well? Has he decided on a wife for me like Katherine?"

The Queen sat down on the edge of the bed and took his hand. "Well, not exactly. He sees marriage for you in the future, but not to a woman, my dearest, to the Church."[7]

Henry's smile collapsed.

"The Church? But Mother, I cannot marry the Church." He bounced out of bed to stand in front of her as tall as he could. "I want to be a knight and fight battles, not marry the Church." He looked so defiant that his mother hardly knew what to say.

"We can talk about it more in the morning," she told him eventually. "Come on, back into bed with you." The Queen stood up and pulled the bedclothes back, waiting for her son to do as he was told. Henry could be defiant at times, but never with his mother, so he hopped back into bed.

"Mother, please don't let me marry the Church. It sounds so cold and lonely. I don't want to grow old like Bishop Warham, all wrinkly with no children of my own and no pretty wife like Katherine. I want to marry and have children. I want to become a champion knight. I can fight battles for Arthur and save England from France."

"Well, there are some bishops in history who also fought wars. Look at Bishop Odo, brother of William the Conqueror. He fought at the Battle of Hastings. You could be like him, perhaps? Anyway, you would be a champion of God, fighting for the Christian faith by looking after the souls of your congregation. You would have many children, for every child would look up to you, and every woman would wish for you to protect her."

"Would they, Mother?" Henry liked this idea and settled back down into the bed. "I would have many children and many wives. More than Arthur." With that, he yawned and closed his eyes.

The Queen kissed him on the forehead and left to report back to the King that she had done his bidding. Personally, she thought the idea flawed, for no Church could ever contain her exuberant son.

※

Towards midnight, after a crowd of courtiers had carried the prince on their shoulders into the bedchamber, making bawdy jokes as they tucked him into bed beside his bride, the archbishop came and blessed the two teenagers, then ushered the wedding guests out of the room to allow the couple to do their duty.

Turning to Katherine, who was waiting there quietly, her long hair brushed over her nightgown like a copper waterfall, Prince Arthur breathed a sigh of relief at their finally being alone. Taking her hand in his, Prince Arthur spoke a well rehearsed speech in Latin.

"Katherine, my wife, there is no doubt that you are the only woman I will ever love. However, before we become man and wife in the way of all men and women, I want to learn Spanish so that I can talk to you and ask questions about your childhood. What games you played and what are your favourite things and… well, learn to truly feel for each other."

Princess Katherine stared at him blankly. The way the prince spoke Latin was hard for her to understand. Arthur had another go at explaining his plan.

"I want us to fall in love, like normal people do. Like the farmers and maidens who work the fields. I believe that love is the most important thing in the world, don't you?"

Princess Katherine looked at him expectantly. Arthur stood again and wandered around the room helplessly. Then he saw some roses in a vase on a table by the window and he plucked out a red rose and brought it back to the bed. With great care, he placed it in her hair and smiled at her shyly. Katherine looked up at him, bemused. She was convinced something was wrong.

She smiled and batted her eyelids, as Elvira had suggested she do.

Encouraged, Prince Arthur continued. "We will be a king and queen to surpass all others in our love for each other and for our subjects. I want to be a just and progressive monarch who cares for his people, and I would like you to be by my side as my consort, my counsellor and my confessor all in one."

"I think… well and want… much… love you… too," she tried in

English.

Prince Arthur was not sure that she had fully grasped his meaning. He would have to show her somehow, but for now, he was tired and all he really wanted to do was sleep.

Katherine felt very tired and emotional. Her eyes pricked before a tear trickled down her cheek. Arthur carefully wiped the tear away with his hand and then kissed the cheek he had so gently touched. Katherine smiled gratefully, her face warming where she had felt his gentle finger.

Relieved that the moment was over, Arthur hopped back into bed, blew out the candles on the nightstand and fell back into the herb-sweetened pillows. Katherine did the same and then it was dark. Neither of them had ever shared a bed before. They were lying in new territory together. As they lay side by side, Katherine slid her hand towards his and he gratefully received it. As the midnight hour approached and all the court were back in the main hall, drinking the last of the wine and joking about the young couple on their wedding night, they fell innocently asleep, holding hands in the dark.

※

Not far from the peacefully sleeping couple, Messrs Fiddle and Grope were practicing the art of mixing with the populace, Grope occasionally grabbing a woman and kissing her before she slapped him, Fiddle rubbing himself against unsuspecting youths who were busy queuing to fill their mugs with the wine that flowed freely from fountains. The King had erected these fountains of wine around the town for the use of the general population to include them in the celebration of the royal wedding. It was a good time for the two men to earn a bit of extra money by picking pockets and to keep their hands in, bearing in mind their nefarious skills.

Fiddle was an expert at picking locks. A quick flip of a window catch and he was in, diving through the smallest gap. Grope would stay on guard outside, for his rotund figure left him at a disadvantage in the burglary profession. Fiddle was good enough on his own and Grope had an ear for advancing trouble.

Having found a house not far from the cathedral, Fiddle pulled out a knife and soon opened a window latch. With a nod of assent from his partner, Fiddle jumped athletically onto the sill and in through the open window. Once inside, Fiddle allowed his eyes to become accustomed to the interior of the room he had just entered. The embers of a fire were glowing in the grate, long abandoned. Fiddle remained silent as he listened for signs that the house was still occupied, but he heard nothing. Moving forward, he tiptoed between two large oak chairs to reach the fireplace. On the mantlepiece he soon found a silver box. Carefully putting it in the large poacher's pocket on the inside of his coat, Fiddle moved on to a side table. There was a drawer, but it was locked. Fiddle withdrew a set of thin wires from up his sleeve, inserted the hooked ends into the keyhole and fiddled about with the wires artfully until the lock clicked. Withdrawing the wires and pushing them back up his sleeve, Fiddle opened the drawer, put in his hand and drew out some papers with heavy seals on them. Stowing them in another pocket, he tiptoed to a sideboard to the left of an oak door that must have led to a hallway. There he found a large brass candle stick, but as he picked it up the candle crashed to the floor. His heart jumped as he heard faint footsteps running from somewhere within the house, getting louder.

The door opened and a young man walked into the room. Fiddle leaped back, silent as a cat, into the shadows. He held his breath as the young man walked about the room, looking to see what might have fallen. Fiddle stood as still as a statue. The man walked to the window, noticed that it was ajar and shut it. He then went to the fire to check a log had not fallen out and onto the floor, for perhaps that had been the noise he heard. The fire was dying and so, with a yawn, he stretched his arms over his head before turning to walk back out of the room. Just as he reached the door, the man thought he saw someone standing there in the shadows. It might be a trick of the light; he could not be sure. It could have been a trick of the light, a distorted shadow – he couldn't be sure. Whatever it was, he never had time to find out.

Fiddle moved like lightning: with the candlestick already conveniently in his hand, he brought it down without mercy onto the man's head. His victim collapsed to the floor as if he were a puppet whose strings had been cut, his handsome face bathed in a pool of winter moonlight.

Fiddle knelt beside him quietly. There was some blood on the man's forehead, so Fiddle took a handkerchief from his pocket and gently wiped it away. Then he rummaged through his clothes, where he found an envelope, and nimbly slipped a ring from his victim's finger – a ring with a large ruby on it. The ruby was dark red, like the blood now soaked into his handkerchief. Fiddle decided that he was going to retain this ring as a keepsake. *No need to tell Grope*, he thought, and secreted it in a pocket hidden in the seam of his jacket, handmade for just this sort of occasion. Patting the concealed ring, Fiddle felt a delicious warm feeling run down through his body. For one last check to see if the man was still alive, Fiddle leaned over him. Their faces were almost touching, and Fiddle could feel the man's breath on his skin. He could not help himself and bent forward to place his lips to the man's own, so soft and tempting – just one kiss and he would leave. In an instant something stirred inside him: the man's aroma triggering a memory, the waft of a boy's hair perhaps.

Without further ado, Fiddle jumped up and hopped back to the window. In a flash, he opened it so that he could slip his skinny bones through and out into the night.

"What's the matter, Fiddle, were you seen by anyone?" asked Grope, who was surprised to see Fiddle emerge from the house so quickly.

"No, no, there was nobody there. Nothing. I'm fine, thanks." Fiddle sounded agitated. "I just saw no point in hanging around when there is a party going on in the streets and we could be enjoying ourselves."

"Let us go now and find a public inn where we can quench our thirst then," suggested Grope. He could see that Fiddle was addled about something but knew from experience that the man was not going to tell.

3

DECEMBER

The King was not a happy man. Spies were coming in from the countryside with talk of a new pretender[8] to the throne, another York ghost risen from the dead. This time it was supposedly Edward V, one of the princes who had disappeared from the Tower of London twenty years before and was presumed murdered by the last king. A man called Perkin Warbeck, who had pretended to be the younger of the two murdered princes, had recently been executed at the insistence of the Spanish King and Queen before their daughter married Prince Arthur. This man was going to end up with his head on the same chopping block.

The King called a meeting with the Royal Council in the Star Chamber – men like Richard Fox, whose long nose made him look like the animal he was named after; Reginald Bray, a long-standing friend to Lady Margaret; and Edward Poynings, who had recently managed to subdue the Irish. The most senior of the group was Bishop Warham, close confidant of both the King and his mother.

The members of the Council were all now in their fifties and sixties. Between them, they had decades of experience in fighting wars and winning battles. They were adept at writing or interpreting laws, so there was not much that they could not handle. They were able to call a spade a spade at meetings and so could get things done. That was what the King wanted, to get things done, and he needed the combined intellect of these men to help him achieve this.

Prince Arthur knew all these men well and respected them. Prince Henry, on the other hand, considered these grey-haired councillors to be nothing other than stale old farts. They had none of the qualities that a young boy appreciated, so they were of no interest other than as a source of ridicule. That was why, as the King was in discussion with his advisors, naughty Prince Henry and his sister, Margot, were hiding under the large table around which the councillors were about to sit. Nobody knew they were there, for they had crept in earlier, Prince Henry gently holding a small leather pouch.

The King called for the attention of the Council so that he could go through the evidence and accounts sent in from his vast network of spies. His mother, meanwhile, stood behind him. She would not deign to sit with the men but hovered over them, her lips taut in concentration. In her statutory black robes and wimple, she had the appearance of a crow about to peck out the eyes of any man who dared contradict her son.

From under the large conference table that filled the centre of the panelled room, there was a stifled giggle as a small mouse ran across the stone floor.

"Christ's bones!" cried Poynings, who, despite having been a heartless tyrant in Ireland, had a horror of mice. He jumped up onto a chair.

"What's that?" shouted Bishop Warham, following suit.

Within two seconds there were two grown men standing on tall-backed chairs in apparent fear of their lives while the others flapped about in total disarray.

"What are you doing, Warham?" Lady Margaret was not amused.

"It was a m-m-mouse, your ladyship," the bishop stuttered. "A mouse?" The scorn in the woman's voice was palpable. "But it could have been…" The bishop was trying to recover his dignity, which was quite hard when he was checking his robes to see if the mouse was inside them.

Lady Margaret strode over to the fire and picked up a coal shovel. Before anyone could stop her, she searched the room until she found what she was looking for.

"Ah, there you are, you little vermin."

With a swift movement that was as precise as any executioner's blow, she smote the shovel to the ground with a vengeance.

"Oh!" cried Henry, a hand to his mouth.

Nobody heard him, for all the councillors gasped at the same time. Henry's eyes were wide with horror and Margot put a hand on his arm to steady him.

"Get out of here, you silly men. Go and run the country. If you can."

The old men climbed down from their chairs and filed out in the most embarrassed of manners, mumbling excuses as they shuffled through the door.

As soon as they were gone, Lady Margaret sat down in the King's chair with a sigh, her shoe tapping on the stone-flagged floor. The children guessed that she was not in the best of moods. Hoping that they would not be found, they kept as silent as they possibly could.

"My son," she began," we have to deal with the facts. Arthur and Katherine are not looking good."

"Mother," replied the King, who was of a different opinion on this subject, "we must give them time. Not all women conceive on the first night. Both you and the Queen were quick to reproduce, but there are others who need time. It is the way of God."

"To Hell with God!"

Lady Margaret smashed her fist down on the table, startling the children underneath. "God has never brought us anything but pain and fear. We need an heir. Your duty is to make sure that your son is performing. We will say no more than this, but the consequences of his failure are devastating to the monarchy."

The King did not want to get into an argument with his mother. Rising from his chair, he kissed her hand and made his excuses.

"Mother dear, I must go and relieve myself. Forgive me."

Heading for the door, he thought he heard a stifled giggle. He could have sworn it was Henry. The boy was eating at his sanity. His good eye twitched, something that irritated him.

A moment later a knock came on the door and a guard announced the arrival of a messenger. In came a man with muddy boots; they were all the children could see of him from under the table.

"Have you any news from Grope?" Lady Margaret's feet moved round towards the messenger.

"I have, Your Ladyship, indeed I have. I have a letter here from my most esteemed partner with the latest report on the matters in which you have instructed us. We are keeping an eye on the subject's habits and his movements since they arrived at Ludlow Castle. Our report is here. Mr Grope asked me to return with your directions."

"Fine. Give me the report. Let me consider the matter and get back to you. Go and find some food and then change your clothes - you smell of horse."

"I do apologize most humbly, Your Ladyship. The journey here was long and hard. I had nowhere to sleep at night other than in the stables with my horse. If I had more coins in my purse, I could afford better lodgings, Your Grace."

"Don't be ridiculous, man, I gave you both enough cash to live like kings. That was only a few weeks ago. Now, be ready to ride first thing in the morning. Go."

Chastised, the messenger headed towards the door and disappeared in a flash.

"Mother dear," began the King as he burst into the room once again, holding a goblet of wine, his nose a little red, "was that one of your men that I saw skulking away down the corridor just then? I must voice my concerns about those two: they are getting above their station. I object to the actions they are taking in my name. They even hung some hunting hounds and said that it was on my instruction. I would *never* give such an order."[9]

The King gulped back his wine.

"What are they up to these days, anyway?" he went on.

"Out collecting taxes, as directed. They are more than thorough, you know. We ought to be grateful for the work they do. The royal coffers were empty when you first took power and these days they are overflowing. You are the richest monarch this country has had for a hundred years, even after the royal wedding and all the other expenses. Do you realize how much money you have spent on your wardrobe in the last decade? You could have built a castle with that money or a fleet of ships. Yet we still have more gold than ever, all thanks to the efforts of those two unassuming men, even if they are a little overzealous at times." [10]

There was not much the King could say to this as it was true, so he broached the other main subject on his mind.

"Mother, I want you to think about where we can send young

Henry. It is time to train him for a role in the Church. I would like your friend Bishop Fisher to look into it. Would you have a word with him, please?"

Prince Henry looked at his sister, startled. She shrugged her shoulders.

Lady Margaret sighed. "Darling, there is nothing wrong with Henry other than a little boyish enthusiasm, which I am sure you had at that age."

"What would you know of such things?" There was a tinge of childish resentment in his voice. The King had hardly seen his mother during his childhood, for he had lived in exile in Brittany. His only contact had been by letter; letters that instructed him never to give up hope, to strive towards the day that he could muster an army and return to England to claim the crown. He had dutifully done this, succeeding on the second attempt.

"Darling, that is cruel. You know that I was desperate to be with you, but I had no choice." This subject always created a chasm between them.

The King remained silent, for he had never really forgiven his mother for abandoning him as a young child. She had insisted that politics dictated her moves, but a little boy does not understand politics and the little boy in him still hurt. There was nothing left to say after this turn in the conversation and so both the King and his mother left the Star Chamber to go their separate ways.[11]

The chamber empty, the children ran back to the royal nursery, where they made excuses to their little sister, telling Princess Mary that Sir Jasper had decided to return home and had asked them to say farewell to Mary on his behalf.

"But I will miss him," she wailed. "Would your nice friend, Charles, have another mouse to give us?" The thought of the handsome Charles coming to the rescue cheered Mary up and she wiped her nose on her sleeve.

"I will ask him for you," Henry agreed, just to keep her from crying again.

Once Mary had wandered off, the mouse already forgotten, Henry and Margot were left alone for a few minutes.

"That was close," admitted Henry. "I wonder what Grandmother meant about Arthur not performing. I thought he was good at everything."

"And why are her servants spying on him?" added Margot. "I don't know, but I don't like it. I would like to see that report that the messenger delivered. I don't suppose we would get a chance, though."

The two children looked at each other conspiratorially.

Knowing that their grandmother would be at mass the following evening, the children decided that this was their best chance to read the report. Margot volunteered to go into her grandmother's chamber, as being a girl, she would not be alien in a female environment while Henry stood guard at the door.

Margot tiptoed into her grandmother's privy chamber, her heart in her mouth. She had been in this room before, but only if invited. It was another matter entering without permission. Inside, all was dark, for the candles were not lit and the curtains were half-drawn to keep the cold winter draughts at bay. The fire in the grate had dwindled to a silent glow, the sea coal having nearly burned itself out.

Margot waited for her eyes to adjust to the darkened room. It looked different when it was empty. Shadows loomed and alarmed her, for they might be servants standing in the gloom. Margot tiptoed forwards to her grandmother's writing desk. There was a drawer in the front of the desk. She pulled the knob and it opened.

Inside was a document written in neat but not elaborate writing, that of an office clerk rather than a gentleman. She began to read:

> *Your most royal Ladyship,*
>
> *We can report that all is in hand here, where we are now living, and that our principal subjects have settled into court life in the countryside. The two appear to spend much time together, but there is no sign of intimacy in the bedchamber. A strange development is that Principal One goes out riding each morning without fail with an ebony-skinned musician from the Spanish court. It might be that an unnatural…*

At that moment there came a faint tapping on the door, one, two, three times. It was the warning signal from Henry that somebody was coming. Margot stuffed the document back into the drawer and looked around for somewhere to hide. There was no large table to duck under in this room, just a small one by her grandmother's chair, where she would be visible. Quickly, she hid behind a curtain in the darkest corner of the room.

Outside the room, Henry was trying to look innocent while a man came walking up to him. It was the servant who had delivered the report the day before, Henry deduced, for he recognized the boots, now quite clean.

"Hello, who do we have here?" said the man in a manner that was a little too friendly for Henry's liking.

"I was looking for my grandmother, but she is not here. She must be at Chapel," was all he replied.

"Can I wait here with you?" asked the messenger, sidling up to him. "Perhaps we can help each other pass the time? Do you roll dice?"

One thing Henry was rather lucky with was rolling dice and in any other situation he would have jumped at the chance to gamble, but all he wanted on this occasion was to get the man to leave so that Margot could make her escape. "I think I ought to go and find my grandmother. You could come with me to look for her if you like." Just as he suggested this and the man took his hand, sending a shiver of discomfort down Prince Henry's spine, a commanding voice called to them.

"What are you doing here?"

The voice was that of Lady Margaret. Henry made his excuses, slipped his hand out of the man's clammy grip and ran off. There was nothing else he could do.

"Do. Not. Run. Henry," he heard his grandmother command imperiously behind him. "Remember who you are and the respect you need to command." Prince Henry slowed down to the most dignified walk he could manage and was gone.

"I suppose you have come for your instructions," Lady Margaret went on to say, more as a matter of fact than as a question to Fiddle, for Fiddle it was who Henry had just met. The tough little woman swept past Fiddle and marched into the room. Her servant followed, going directly to the fire to stoke it up and put more sea coal[12] onto the embers, then lighting various candles. Princess Margot held her breath, terrified that the servant might close the curtains and discover her hiding there, but she could relax. The servant was gone.

Fiddle always felt intimidated by Lady Margaret when Grope was not there to do the talking. She stood facing the fire, stoking it with a poker, for it had yet to come back to life. "My lady, I am ready to take any orders back to my partner at your most gracious convenience, that is."

"I would expect no less of you, Fiddle." The fire burst into flame, turning the old woman into a demonic silhouette and making Fiddle jump.

Lady Margaret swung round to face him. "I can see that things are not going our way at Ludlow, much as I had expected. Therefore, I want you to instruct Grope to take matters into his own hands. He needs to have free rein on this one. I cannot have *any* input into what he decides to do. Like last time, I must remain beyond suspicion for the sake of the family. For the sake of *history*."

Fiddle bowed his head and bowed again. "Yes, Your Ladyship. I understand," he said, and before he knew it, he was backed up against the door, fumbling for the handle, unable to take his eyes off the image of the diminutive woman with the fire raging behind her.

"You may go now," Lady Margaret added, although he was already gone, leaving only a faint smell of stale horse in his wake.

Lady Margaret walked to the door and turned the key to lock it.

Oh God, thought Margot, *why did she lock the door? Perhaps she knows I am here.*

Margot could hardly breathe for fear. She waited for her grandmother to walk over to the curtains and expose her. The seconds on the clock machine that so proudly ticked away in its case, a recent invention that the King had bought his mother as a gift, seemed to pass like minutes, or hours. Margot felt her legs wanting to give way under her but forced herself to remain standing. If she were to be discovered, it would not be as a cowering dog. No, she would stand up and accept her punishment for prowling. She was a Tudor, after all.

Lady Margaret, it seemed, was not interested in anyone who might be hiding behind the curtains, for Margot heard her walk to her chair and sit down. There was a shuffling sound of things being moved around, a key opening something and then her grandmother let out a great sigh.

"Oh darling, how I miss you. It is all I can do to hold you to my heart."

Curious, Margot peered around the curtain to see who her grandmother was talking to, but there was nobody: just Lady Margaret holding a bundle of cloth, which it seemed she had just removed from a heavy black box that sat open upon her table. Margot had not noticed it before.

There was a candle on the table and some other things. A phial of liquid, dark-red liquid. Margot noticed the acrid aroma of herbs burning in the fire. An attentive student, she recognised the smell of mandrake. That perplexed her, for it was an unusual herb to burn on a fire – unless her grandmother was practising the old ways of magic, which seemed most unlikely.

Lady Margaret placed the bundle on a black plate. Or was it a mirror, Margot wondered. It was a round piece of black glass, highly polished and yet with a dullness to it that refused to reflect the object that was now sitting upon its surface. Smoke rose from the dried herbs in the fire, wafting into the room and making Margot's head spin. The old woman gazed reverently at the bundle, then, holding the candle in one hand and moving it over the object in slow circles, she started to chant words that Margot could scarcely hear but for a few words of Latin that she recognised: *'conjuro'*, *'adjuro'*, *'exorcizo'* and then, much to her horror, 'Edmund'. Grandmother *was* practicing some sort of magic. She was trying to summon her *dead husband*. That must be who she was talking to; she was practising dark magic of the worse kind, necromancy.

Margot could feel her heart pumping hard. Her bladder felt weak, and her hands began to tremble. That her grandmother was a witch was not possible. She was a highly devout Catholic who abhorred the old ways. Yet there, in front of her very eyes, the old woman took the stopper out of the phial and allowed a couple of drops of what could only be blood to fall onto the bundle.

Lady Margaret was talking to the bundle as if it were alive. "I have been hearing voices. St Nicholas… do you remember how he spoke to me as a child, advising me to marry you all those years ago?[13] He has come back to me. He tells me that together we will have the strength to do *what is right*. Tell me that what I am doing is the right thing, please. I am so much in doubt. It all seems so sordid. Show me a sign, any sign, my darling."

The old lady had tears in her eyes as she held the object to her bosom and rocked it like a baby. "The signs tell me Arthur will never have issue. I must rid this scourge from our bloodline, or your name will die and my promise to you will be broken. *Please* guide me, my dearest."

Margot could only presume that the bundle represented her grandfather, but what part of him, she wondered. Was it something representative or something *physical*?

Magic was not necessarily criminal, but it was much frowned upon, and had Margot been caught dallying with such things, she would have been severely chastised. Lady Margaret had always been scornful of any mention of the old ways. That made what Margot was seeing so extraordinary. Margot knew that nobody would believe her, not even Henry. So there was no point telling him. She was more interested in how she felt about this new aspect of her grandmother. She was no longer scared but intrigued. Would her grandmother ever let her learn about this new art she obviously believed in after all?

The old woman finally blew out the candle, put the bundle back into the box and locked it with a key that Margot had never noticed before, which hung on a chain around her neck. She tucked the round mirror into a shelf full of books. These too Margot had never noticed before, but now she wondered about their contents.

Grandmother was practicing some sort of magic.
She was trying to summon her dead husband.

Oblivious to the fact that she was being watched, Lady Margaret wiped tears from her eyes and slowly stood up, her old bones giving her trouble. Margot had never noticed before how tired her grandmother looked. She hid back in the shadows and waited while Lady Margaret hobbled to the desk, opened the drawer and then threw what could only be the report into the fire. With that, she unlocked the door and disappeared, leaving her granddaughter weak with trepidation at what she had seen, and what Lady Margaret might have meant about Arthur not having any issues, which did not make sense but at the same time sounded ominous.

"I am so sorry," Henry said when he met his sister later. "There was nothing I could do. First, that creepy man came up to look for Grandmother, and then only seconds after he arrived, so did she. I could do nothing other than hope I had given you enough time to hide."

"That's alright," replied Margot, still shaken, for she had been sure she would be discovered cowering behind the curtains at some point, and God only knows what might then have happened. However, to keep the terrifying truth about Grandmother from Henry, she tried to keep matters trivial.

"I got away with it, but I only read some of that report before I had to put it back when they came into the room, and then Grandmother burnt it in the fire."

"Where did you hide?" asked Henry, who, now that his sister was safe, was beginning to enjoy the conspiracy and could see the funny side of it.

"Behind the curtains. They were so dusty, I had to stop myself from sneezing."

The siblings discussed the contents of the report. Margot explained that it appeared from the report that they were spying on Arthur and that he and the princess were not sleeping in the same bed.

"Well, Mother and Father have different beds, so what's the problem?" asked Henry.

"They have to share a bed to make children," she elucidated, being older than her brother though not much better informed. "I heard one of the maids talking about it."

Prince Henry was bemused, so Margot changed the subject. "She gave a man called Grope free rein to do something. I am not sure what, but she didn't want to be involved, 'for the sake of history'. Those were her words. She mentioned 'last time', whatever that means. I am sorry, Henry. I don't really understand. What we need is for someone to follow that man, Fiddle, to see what he is up to."

"What about Charles?" suggested Henry.

So it was that the young conspirators decided to find Charles and ask him if he had time to follow Fiddle back down to Ludlow Castle to see what he and his partner, Grope, were doing.

4

Since his debut appearance at the tournament on the day after the royal wedding, Charles Brandon had made rather a name for himself, winning almost every tournament he entered. His winnings, a gold crown for every tournament won, allowed him to buy himself his first warhorse, a silver grey with a long mane that hung down his powerful neck. Charles had named him Caesar, after the Roman emperor, and would not let any stable boy go near him. He chose to remain living in the hayloft above the stable and looked after his horse's every need. Caesar was his pride and joy. When Henry and Margot arrived at the stables, they found him grooming the horse until it gleamed.

"That is a fine beast." Henry loved horses too. He wanted to breed them when he grew up, for he thought that the larger the animal, the better the knight who rode him. "Will you breed from him?"

"I have thought of it, but I need to make a name for myself first. We are doing well together. Did you see me at the tournament?"

"I did," Henry beamed. "You are by far the most skilled knight I have seen, ever."

Margot felt that the conversation was going astray. "We have come to ask a favour of you, Charles. Will you do something for us? Please?"

When the royal children asked if he would be able to take a trip down to Ludlow to spy on Fiddle, Charles agreed without hesitation. "It would be a good chance for me to show off my horse to the opposition."

Prince Henry looked alarmed. "The opposition?"

Charles chuckled. "Yes, those who are going to face me at the next tournament."

Henry liked Charles's attitude. There was something infectious about him.

"But you must come straight back to tell us what you see there. We think that the man is up to no good," Margot insisted.

"Of course I will. I will come to you, wherever you are." "And you must not tell anyone else," Henry added. "This is *our* secret."

After Charles swore not to tell anyone else, Henry and Margot left him to his horse, satisfied with what they had done. Charles was fast becoming someone that they both liked and trusted. He had an easy manner. There was no hidden agenda with Charles. He liked them and he wanted to serve them, for they were the royal family, and a courtier is honour-bound to serve his king, so to him it was natural to also serve his king's offspring.

Thinking about Charles, Henry felt an unexpected surge of guilt. "We forgot to tell him about Sir Jasper," he remembered.

Margot comforted him. "Never mind, we will explain what happened when Charles returns. I am sure he will understand that it was a terrible accident."

Charles was packing his provisions for the journey ahead. He had enquired after the whereabouts of a certain messenger called Fiddle and learned that he had left court early that morning. *Time to get going then*, he thought to himself as he forced some extra clothes into his saddlebag. It was going to be a long journey and the weather was breaking. It would rain this afternoon; he could tell by the formation of clouds that were building up like sheep's wool across the sky. The temperature had risen somewhat, but that also hinted at rain. He owned a waxed cloak, but it did not cover his legs and so spare clothes would be a lifesaver.

"Where are you going?" asked a woman who was mooning around in his hayloft. She was a buxom girl, someone from the kitchens, and he had revelled in her sumptuous curves and soft skin the night before. She smelled and tasted of the exquisite fruit tarts and pastries that she made all day long. It was as if her skin had a dusting of icing sugar placed on it. He was looking forward to another evening with her as soon as possible. Right now, though, he needed her gone, for he had work to do.

"I have to head west for possibly a week or two. We will meet again, I promise. There is no way that I will be able to forego another taste of your delectable wares, my dearest."

The woman giggled, kissing him enticingly, before heading back to the kitchen.

Charles tacked up Caesar, who looked resplendent with his wavy silver mane. Life was good to him, Charles admitted as he led the great horse out of the stables. Patting him on the rump, he put his foot in the stirrups and leaped into the saddle before heading out into the first drops of the coming rain.

Fiddle had left some hours earlier and was making good progress. He pulled his cloak tighter around his neck when the wind began to blow and the rain became ever more persistent. Following deeply rutted roads with potholes that were already filling up with water, he rode cautiously, for the horse he had hired was a fine creature and he wanted to keep it for the duration of the journey. Fiddle approved of good horseflesh, and it had taken a lifetime to be able to afford it. In the days of his youth, if he could afford a horse at all, it would be some old nag that was about to be slaughtered for its hooves and hide.

Most days he would have been walking on his own two feet, that is when he was not at sea, sailing in ships that might find new land so that he could make his fortune. That had never happened, but he had learned how to look after himself, how to fight and how to kill. He had also learned how some men liked younger boys and his entry into that secret world had not been a bad one, for he enjoyed the attentions he got from the muscled sailors who approached him. At first, he had been bemused by their needs, but it did not take long for him to enjoy the rough handling they offered. Soon he began to put himself in the way of those men, in the hope that they would drag him into a dark corner of the ship, a storeroom or some such place, for some stolen time together. Fiddle kept himself amused as he rode along, remembering his youth, until he reached a small village on the road to Oxford. There, in the main street, was an inn called the Horseman's Glove, the perfect place to find a decent stable for his horse and a bed for himself. Fiddle gave the stable lad a farthing to rub his horse down, cover him with a rug for the night and give him food and water. He then offered the lad another farthing if he came to see him later, for the memories he had enjoyed had made him hungry for intimacy.

Inside the inn the air was tainted with smoke from a wood fire that was not burning well. Fiddle ordered a meal and a pint of ale before asking the barmaid to find him a room on the ground floor if possible. He always liked to sleep on the ground floor, for it made for an easier escape through a window if there was trouble. Not that he was expecting trouble. When the woman brought him a pint of ale, he drank long and deep, then he ate the sloppy stew with some rough bread before paying for the food and heading to his room. There he pulled back the sheets to check for bugs before stripping off and jumping into bed, and when the stable lad did not turn up, he fell asleep dreaming of his youth.

Charles was still riding Caesar well into the evening. He had no idea which road Fiddle had taken but headed towards Oxford anyway. He stopped outside an inn in one small village to stick his head through the door and ask for some food to be served to him outside, for he wanted to keep an eye on his horse. One look at the handsome man who was refusing to come in to warm himself by the fire and the maid rushed out with a large bowl of pottage along with a free jug of ale. To help keep him warm, she said.

"Has a tall, thin man come to the inn earlier today?" he asked. "He has a funny face, like a baby. Large eyes."

"The only eyes I have noticed this very day are yours." The girl smiled alluringly.

"Then you are a favourite of mine, dear lady. But I need to find this man. Please let me know if you hear of him." Charles winked at the girl, who skipped off back to her work.

She came back later to pass on what she had learnt from serving the other tables.

"I have heard nothing of a baby-faced gentleman, but there is mention of a recent attack on a man who has been staying in a house in London, near Saint Paul's Cathedral. There's a lot of upset about it."

She mentioned the change in the atmosphere of the inn once the news was heard. Groups of men were sitting huddled in corners whispering to one another; what about, she had no idea.

"If you learn anything, I will be out here for a while, resting my horse, so do come and tell me, won't you?"

The girl went back in, determined to find out the content of those conversations so that she could return and give Charles the information he wanted. It was just as Charles had given up getting any further information and so was tightening the girth on his saddle, ready to ride off into the night, that the girl came out of the inn.

"It seems that it was someone of great importance who was attacked and that documents were stolen that would be dangerous to certain persons if they fell into the wrong hands."

"Who attacked him?" asked Charles.

"Well, that is the problem: nobody knows. It seems that this gentleman was staying in the house of a well-known York supporter who has been missing for a good while. His wife and daughters live there in Knightrider Street. He fought for the other side and would be no friend of the King." The girl looked scared. "Please, you won't mention I told you this, will you?"

Charles took her hand and kissed it before bowing to her and promising that he would never do anything that would endanger such a lovely woman.

The girl blushed, curtsied, then ran back into the inn with her heart beating a little faster for having had her hand kissed in such a courtly manner.

64

It took Charles two more days to reach Ludlow, having ridden at a gruelling pace despite the adverse weather. Ludlow was a riverside town lined with merchants' houses with striking black and white timber and plaster facades. The entire town was dominated by the great Norman castle that sat protectively on the hill, its high walls enveloping the stronghold. Thick grey battlements dominated the sky and dared anyone to try to attack them. There were towers and castellations along every length of wall, without a foothold to climb on.

Charles soon found an inn called The Bull and stopped for a quick drink. It had been a long journey and he wanted to quench his thirst before arriving at court. With Caesar hastily stabled at the back of the inn, where a covered stall with clean straw was available for passing horsemen, he felt it safe to leave his prize horse for a short while.

Inside, the inn was empty. A small fire burned in the grate, although it hardly offered any cheer, so Charles ignored it. Standing at the bar, he rang a small bell, and a young woman came to serve him. She was not what another man might call attractive, but Charles was the sort of man who saw beauty in every woman. She had a face full of features that did not quite fit each other, causing a queer smile, but Charles liked her immediately.

"Hello, mistress, would you please serve me a tankard of your best ale and some bread and cheese?"

The girl grinned a toothy grin. "Most certainly, sire," she consented and wandered off to find him some succour.

As Charles watched her walk away, he wondered what it was that made each one of God's creatures different and so charming in their own small way.

When the woman returned, he sat at the bar so that he could talk to her as he ate. It was always interesting what you could find out over a bar counter. Just as he was learning from her the comings and goings of the neighbourhood, a door opened from an interior room and a particularly unsavoury man waddled out. His near-to-bald head had a ridiculous sweep of thin hair plied across it from left to right. He would have looked innocuous but for his face turning red and then purple as he saw Charles talking to the girl.

Coming up to Charles, the man held his walking stick in one hand and pulled the handle out with the other to reveal a sharp knife. In a flash, he stuck it up close to Charles's stomach. "That is my girl you are talking to, 'sir', so stand up, pay your bill and hop it before I stick this knife into your gut. Understand?"

His breath stank and Charles put his head back to avoid the rank odour.

"Look here, man, I do not think that you should take exception to me having a conversation with the lady while I am eating my lunch. We are only chatting."

The girl blushed at being called a lady. "It's true, we were—"

"Shut up, you *slut*," snarled the fat man and he pushed the knife in harder against Charles's body.

Charles realized that the situation was getting out of hand. Glaring steadily at his antagonist, he threw some coins on the counter, knocked back his ale and walked out of the inn, but not before blowing a kiss to the barmaid. Charles was sure that he had seen this man at court before and guessed that he was one of the King's henchmen that he was to investigate. There was no point in making trouble with him from the outset, but at least he now knew where he was staying.

At the castle, the newlyweds were living together in an easy manner now that they were no longer under the scrutiny of the older royals. They were beginning to enjoy each other's company and found that they were flirting with each other more and more. An attraction was developing that was maturing them both at a rate that surprised the two of them. It also surprised Elvira, who was keeping an eye on progress.

Arthur had taken to riding out in the mornings with John Blanke,[14] a black-skinned musician who had arrived in England along with the Spanish courtiers who came to serve Katherine. He was a tall, handsome man who played the trumpet and the flute. It was said that he could play any instrument that was handed to him. The prince had liked him from the start.

John Blanke had learned English when he was young and he was happy to spend the mornings with Arthur, taking him through the rudiments of the Spanish language. Arthur was working on a song in Spanish that his new tutor was teaching him. It was based on a poem he had written for Katherine:

> *As winter is the father of summer*
> *And the flower grows from a seed,*
> *As daylight is the daughter of darkness*
> *And the nightingale hatches from an egg,*
> *Our love will grow from its beginning,*
> *A treaty between two great realms.*

John Blanke was touched by the sentiment of this beautiful poem so had put it to a simple tune. He was now teaching Arthur how to sing the words in Spanish. Arthur was an attentive student and each morning when they rode, he was more fluent in his new language and was retaining more words as he heard them.

Conversation between the musician and the prince had been easy from the start. Having no escort, the prince immediately dropped all protocol and treated John as an equal, which he found easy to do because John was so likable.

"Tell me about Spain. Tell me all you can about how my lovely wife might have lived, the life at court there, what the customs were. I want to learn as much as I can about Katherine's past life so that I can make her future as much like it as I can. She must miss her home very much."

"We all miss our home." John spoke frankly. "But when an opportunity to see the world is offered to you, it would be foolish to turn it down. All the courtiers who came with the princess are grateful for the hospitality you show us, my lord."

Arthur relaxed back in his saddle. "It is good to know this. I want you all to feel at home here. It must be so different."

"I cannot lie, sire. It is very cold here. It can be cold in Spain, but it is a dry cold. Here it is so wet and it gets under one's skin. But winter will not last forever."

Arthur laughed. "No, and we have fires to warm us and music to raise our spirits until the spring come, have we not?"

John knew that the prince enjoyed listening to the Spanish music he played. "I will keep you entertained with music until the sun comes back again, that I promise you, my lord."

In the background, had they not been so involved in their conversation, the prince and his companion might have noticed a rather fat man wobbling about on a donkey following them from a respectful distance, not wishing to reveal himself, keeping to the shade of trees, bushes and other obstacles in the landscape. He was not trying to pass them or go anywhere in particular, he was just ambling along, keeping an eye on them. Had they known, they would have turned around and confronted him, but instead they carried on riding slowly, chatting to each other and laughing, singing and speaking in Spanish so that Arthur could learn more of his wife's language.

Fiddle and Grope had reached Ludlow Castle a while back and had found lodgings and work in the area, despite stopping off along the way to collect a few outstanding taxes for the King. It had been Grope's idea to hang the hunting dogs outside the front gates of the castle belonging to the errant earl. The man loved his hounds more than he did his family. The dogs were his Achilles' heel, and once they had been found hanging from the ancient oak tree in front of the castle, with their stomachs slit open and their entrails spilling onto the ground below, he had paid the outstanding tax by courier the next morning.

When they arrived at Ludlow, Grope had found a position with a local accountant and Fiddle began working as a butcher in the royal kitchens. They shared accommodation in a local inn called The Bull. While Grope learned about how the local economy was growing under the command of the young prince – useful information for Lady Margaret, who would want to know that the prince was learning to be a good administrator – Fiddle was hacking and slicing his way through one dead beast after another, listening to the conversations around him. Loose talk gave way to information. He ate in the kitchens, not wanting to be seen in the dining hall in case the prince recognized him, and it was in the kitchens that he heard all the gossip he needed regarding Arthur and his wife.

"He goes out riding every morning with the black Spaniard. It is most unnatural," one maid said as she kneaded dough on the kitchen table.

"The princess will never become pregnant if he prefers the company of *men* to her; though he is quite fascinating, that black man," said another.

This was all Fiddle needed to hear to set his overactive imagination in motion.

Christmas was celebrated at Ludlow Castle with relish. The mix of Spanish, English and Welsh courtiers was a good one and there was much merriment at court. On Christmas Eve, Arthur was ready to sing his song to Katherine while John Blanke accompanied him on the lute. They had decided to do this after supper when the company were gathered around the fireplace to watch the yule log burn while they sang songs from their different countries. Singing was always a wonderful way of creating competition among their friends. The Spanish and Welsh who attended court were the greatest rivals, for both cultures were well known for their poetry and song.

That morning, Arthur and John went riding as always and stopped at the usual place by the river before dismounting to let their horses graze while they practised the song for the last time. They did not know that they were being watched from a safe distance by Fiddle, for it was his turn to follow them that day. Grope had chosen to stay in bed where it was nice and warm. He had sent Fiddle off with a mince pie for his breakfast and a flask of mulled wine to keep him in a good mood.

Fiddle had drunk most of the wine as he lay in the grass behind a bush, the mince pie untouched. He had cleverly brought a waxed groundsheet so that he kept off the damp grass. Congratulating himself on his forethought, he kept sipping the mulled wine, which he intended to drink before it was too cold. As he watched, he thought how handsome that musician was with his polished black skin and engaging smile.

The two men were in a jovial mood. "I think I am ready to sing to Katherine tonight. Would you agree?" Arthur asked his tutor.

"Sing it to me now; show passion in your words."

Arthur cleared his throat and sang his song. He sang beautifully with a voice that was tuneful and crystal clear, as clear as the running river beside them. John was visibly moved and spontaneously began to dance and jig around the place. Arthur laughed and started to dance too.

"And will you take her in your arms tonight and kiss her?" John goaded him.

"I don't know. I want to, but I am anxious that I will make a fool of myself by being clumsy." Arthur stopped dancing and looked down at his boots.

"That is the most ridiculous thing I have ever heard," said John, and he swept Arthur into his arms and danced with him. "It is simple: you just hold her like this" – he held Arthur with both arms – "you pull her towards you like this" – he pulled Arthur into his arms – "and then you kiss her like this." He pulled Arthur towards him and pretended to kiss him long and slow on the mouth. From where Fiddle was sitting, it looked like a lingering kiss, a forbidden kiss.

Arthur fell over backwards and rolled onto the frosty grass, laughing aloud. "Do you really think I can do that in front of the whole court?"

"Yes, my lord, why not?" John sat down beside Arthur and spoke earnestly. "She will be like melting butter in your hands. She will love it, for she loves you already, you know?"

"Does she really?" Arthur blushed and looked up at John, who pushed him playfully onto the grass.

"Of course I am sure, my lord."

⁂

Nicholas Grope sat by a meagre fire that he had recently poked back into life in his dingy rented room at the back of The Bull. Muffled sounds of daily life could be heard through the thin walls of the establishment. He had enjoyed a lazy morning in bed while Fiddle was out following the prince on his morning ride. He had slept away the early hours of the morning, farted once the clock reached ten and, scratching his scrotum, had finally climbed out of bed close to midday. Grope was hoping that Fiddle would return from his espionage via the palace kitchens, where he might scrounge some bread, dripping and maybe even a few sausages that they could cook over the open fire to enjoy with a quart of ale. A fine feast indeed.

What was on Grope's mind all morning as he lay tucked up under the covers was the letter Fiddle had found in that house they had burgled the night of the wedding. What with travelling down to Ludlow and having to find work and settle in, he had only recently sat down to study the papers Fiddle had stolen. They had sold the candlesticks and other items to a well-known dealer in stolen goods the next day, but these documents needed an enquiring mind to work out the best value that could be wrung from them.

All the documents seemed to point to the same thing. There was a new uprising brewing in the capital city and the York faction had a figurehead this time who they claimed was totally authentic. He was a man who had risen from the dead, for this man claimed to be Edward V, the older of the two princes who had been locked away in the Tower of London and had subsequently disappeared without an explanation. Some thought it was the previous monarch, King Richard, who had done away with the boys and others thought it had been the King himself. Both accusations were absurd, for Grope knew the fate of the children, as it was a subject about which he had intimate knowledge.

But how the older prince was alive was puzzling him. Grope sucked a boiled sweet as he considered the matter. He was at a loss as to how the boy had survived. He had given Fiddle express instructions on how to dispose of the two children and their bodies, although Fiddle had never revealed their final fate. Knowing Fiddle's appetite, Grope had hardly dared ask, for Fiddle never liked to comment on his unnatural urges.

Grope decided that he would have to think about it for longer before he came to a decision. What he really wanted to know was what had frightened Fiddle into leaving the house that they had burgled that night so quickly. Had he seen someone – a ghost from the past, perhaps? Fiddle was like a clam once he had made up his mind about something and it was going to take all of Grope's persuasive skills to get it out of the man. There was something that Fiddle was not telling him, of that he was certain.

That evening the food presented at Ludlow Castle for dinner was a real feast: roast goose stuffed with chestnuts and other delights, mince pies filled with shredded meat and spices, pork basted in thick honey sauce and mustard, lamb covered in herbs and spices, all washed down with gallons of red wine from Bordeaux and delicious manchet bread slathered with fresh butter. Dessert was frumenty pie, served with thick cream dosed with whisky, as well as jellies and small tarts filled with autumn fruits that had been preserved in fortified wine and were richly delicious.

It was a full and happy crowd who gathered around the fireplace after the feast. The men were flushed with wine and were patting each other on the back as they took turns singing. The women blushed and flirted while fanning themselves by the fire, for the yule log was burning brightly. Charles was settled in between two young ladies-in-waiting who were taking it in turns to talk to him, while giving one another dagger glances whenever Charles was distracted. Already well oiled, he was delighted to see the prince and princess looking so relaxed and happy with their lot.

Arthur had already primed his companions to make way for him when the time came, and so he coughed to clear his throat and there was silence. Katherine looked around, bemused, but before she could ask why all were quiet, Arthur came forward and sang his song to her with all his heart.

Como el invierno es el padre del verano,
Y la flor crece de una semilla,
Como la luz del día es hija de la oscuridad,
Y el ruiseñor sale del huevo de la hormiga,
Nuestro amor crecerá desde su inicio,
Un matrimonio diplomático entre Inglaterra y España.

Katherine was delighted with her loving husband, smiling at him sweetly as a small tear trickled down her cheek. Arthur sang faultlessly, not a single word misspoken, nor a note off-key. When he finished, he leant forward while a courtier dangled mistletoe over his head and, gently taking Katherine by the hand he urged her to stand. With his eyes locked on hers, Prince Arthur made his move and kissed her, tentatively at first, awaiting her response. When her lips parted willingly, he kissed her with passion and their companions cheered with delight.

Tragically, Fiddle was not was not invited to the castle that evening to witness the entertainment, for he was just a lowly butcher's boy. Instead, he went back to Grope at The Bull and described what he had seen that morning at the river in salacious detail. Grope was so reviled by the scene Fiddle related that he decided it was time to take matters into his own hands, for it was what Lady Margaret would expect of him. Lady Margaret had specifically instructed him not to involve her in this matter and he would not want to let his royal patron down.

1502

5

JANUARY

Up until now life had been good to Ned. He loved his work on the shoreline, he loved his connection with 'Mother River', and he loved the squelching sound of his high leather boots as he pulled them out of the silt. He loved the sound of the screeching seagulls overhead, the peeping of the oystercatchers as they pitter-pattered over the mud leaving tiny footprints. But most of all he loved his sweetheart, Emma.

Emma was only nineteen, and although he was probably thirty himself, he had fallen for her from the start. He was going to marry her, whatever anyone else had to say about it.

As he sat outside his cottage, cleaning his boots, Emma sat beside him.

"Here we go, my darling." She made a lather of the soap in water and began to rub the foam into the leather with an old cloth. "We will soon have these looking brand new."

Ned loved these moments with Emma. "I missed you, you know, when I was away."

Emma loved to hear this. She had missed him too.

"I feel so bad that I ruined our way out of here," he said. "Without money we cannot marry. But now that my ring has been stolen, my only possession of any value, I cannot afford to buy us a house."

"Then let us run away as lovers and live in a natural state." She looked him in the eye.

Ned was taken aback. "Emma, your parents would never allow it."

Emma had a glint in her eyes as she looked back. "Then we won't tell them."

Ned was even more shocked, for he had been brought up to respect women.

"Let's finish cleaning my boots and say no more for now. You are a temptress and I love you more for it, but I would never take advantage of you before our wedding."

Emma shrugged her shoulders. "Then we will be two old hermits living next door to one another for the rest of our lives, for I will never take another man."

Ned reached out to hold Emma's hand and changed the subject. "Come, we are finished with the boots, so let's go and watch the boats pass by."

Ned sat on a bollard at the edge of the wharf with Emma sitting on his lap. They were just finishing a tender kiss, in which their tongues had delicately explored each other's mouths, when Ned looked up and out over the water just in time to see the royal barge gliding past along with the tide. There he saw the King, sitting inside under a cloth-of-gold canopy on a seat covered with embroidered cushions. The King, who looked deep in thought, was facing towards him, and just out of friendliness and a sort of respect for the man, Ned casually waved at him.

The King, though absorbed by a disturbing conversation he had just had with his councillors about a possible new pretender to the throne, someone they claimed was the once dead prince from the Tower, now risen as Edward V, saw this young man sitting on the edge of the river wharf with his betrothed and was quite taken by them. Normally, the King would have turned away, for to acknowledge a simple commoner was beneath him. But there was something so charming and innocent about the man that he was caught unawares and before he knew it, he was waving back. If only all his subjects could be as loyal as him, he mused.

Ned was delighted. What a charming man the King must be. "Look, darling, did you see that? The King waved at us. Let's wave again."

So they did, both Ned and Emma this time, and the King waved once more before the tide swept his barge further downstream towards Greenwich Palace. There, he was to witness the marriage vows of his eldest daughter, Margot, to one of his greatest enemies, James IV of Scotland. Such was the fate of royalty.

The proxy marriage to the King of Scotland was a private family affair. Margot being so young, the real wedding would take place once she was old enough live with a man. These were modern times after all, not like when Lady Margaret was young, when children were sent into their husband's beds. No. Margot only had to lie in bed while her family watched a hairy Scot climbed in beside her as part of the betrothal. The man, not even her husband, did so with one leg kept on the ground, his bare legs quite the main source of excitement as his kilt fell around him. How many minds were wondering if he wore anything under the kilt, no one would ever know, but Margot was glad that she was too young to marry when she looked sideways at his ruddy face and long straggly beard topped with a tartan cap.

Now that Margot was the Queen of Scotland, it meant that she was now more important than her brother, Prince Henry. Henry, who was used to Margot being his subordinate, was fuming. This was because as a queen, Margot now walked ahead of him in any official procession and sat closer to their father, the King, at any feasts. Henry was in fact so angry that he fell into a fit on the floor, banging his fists and screaming, which, again, only made his father see him as an unstable entity. The boy was still having these tantrums like a babe, when he really ought to have grown out of them. The King thought him spoiled.

To help him recover from this indignity, Henry was given a present by his grandmother. He was to have a new friend to share his days with at Eltham, someone he would have as a subordinate, a 'whipping boy'.

James Worsley was a small, stocky lad of the same age as Henry, with nothing about him that made him memorable. With grey eyes and mousy hair he was able to disappear in any crowd, something he had learnt to use to his advantage. With a smaller brother to entertain, James, commonly known as Jack, had learnt to make all sorts of mischief at home, then to just merge into the background, leaving others to take the blame, or better still, for his tutor to be left flabbergasted.

Jack was none too happy when he learnt that Lady Margaret herself, the King's mother, had chosen him to be Prince Henry's whipping boy. His father said that this was an honour, and that the family would do well out of it. All Jack could think of was how he was going to do badly out of it if the prince were naughty.

Jack arrived at Eltham Palace after a long ride from Lancaster with his father, mostly in pouring rain that he decided was crying in sympathy for him. This was the home of the royal children when they were not at court and a formidable place it was, especially to a little boy.

As Jack and his father, accompanied by their two retainers, rode across the bridge towards the front gates, he noticed the compliment of guards standing at the gates with their halberds at the ready. He wondered to himself if they were to prevent people from getting into the palace or from getting out. If the latter, he was going to have to work out a better way of escaping if things took a turn for the worse.

As it was, Jack was surprised to find a lively welcome from a man dressed in black robes with eyes as large as an owl, or perhaps his round eyeglasses made them appear that way. He stood there, oblivious of the rain that fell on his face and spectacles, waving his arms by way of a salute, surrounded by a brood of well-dressed royal children. There was Prince Henry, adorned with a velvet hat, and his two sisters, one now a queen, or so Jack had been told, the other as pretty as a picture. Jack was so cold that he was numb, but his father was as hearty as ever and broke the silence with his booming voice.

"Ah, you must be John Skelton, the royal tutor?" The owl-like man replied in the affirmative.

"Well, I deliver to you my son, at your service." He turned to Jack, "Jack, get off your mule and show some respect, boy."

Jack did his best to climb down off his mule, but his legs gave way after being all day in the saddle and he collapsed onto the cobbles. Before he could react, there was an arm under his and the prince pulled him back onto his feet. "That was probably not one of your best dismounts."

The prince sounded friendly. He was not teasing Jack but was trying to make him feel at ease. Jack was delighted. He looked up at Prince Henry, who was a head taller than him, and smiled.

"Thank you, my lord, I am James Worsley, at your service, your grace."

The prince looked at the mule. "And who is this, what a strange beast."

The mule, a dappled roan with the largest ears, more like a rabbit than a horse, stared back at the prince and made a whinnying sound.

"This is Bottom, my lord."

"Bottom?"

"He is a good an animal as you would ever find. He is trained to do all sorts of tricks. If I pull his ear, he will kick out behind him with his rear leg *and* I can make him trumpet out of his rear end upon command. I will show you if you like."

"Come on then, show me." Henry's grin gave him dimples.

"I think that can wait for another day, Jack," the booming voice of his father stopped Jack in his tracks.

John Skelton thought otherwise, for he recognised the first signs of a new friendship.

"Sir Hugh, why don't you come in and have some refreshments? We have mulled wine and some pies warming by the fire."

His own comfort interrupting his desire to prevent his son from making a fool of himself, Sir Hugh allowed himself to be enticed into the great hall of the palace, leaving Jack and the royal children to their own devices.

"Your wish is my command, sire." Jack grinned back at the prince.

"And stop calling me 'sire', please. It gets in the way of a true friendship."

"Yes… your… my prince."

"Henry."

To hide his embarrassment at going directly against his father's instructions, Jack jumped onto the back of his mule and with a flick of his whip that gently tickled the mules' side, a gentle dig with his heels and a gentle pull on his reins, the mule did as commanded and trumpeted a bugle salute from behind, much to the giggles of the girls and their delighted brother, Prince Henry.

※

Ever since Henry and Margot had returned from court after Christmas, they had tried, with John Skelton's help, to break the code that would unlock the strange script on the scrolls they had found. So far, they had been unsuccessful, but it was a good pastime on a rainy day.

On one such day soon after Jack had arrived, the three children were lying on the floor in Henry's bed chamber by the fireside looking at the parchments. Henry had explained to Jack that they were looking for a clue as to what the code might be.

Jack, who had a nose for solving problems, a skill he had honed being an older brother and therefore the one who had to have answers to lots of questions, opened his mind. There was a man (or woman) who had created a secret language to hide what they were writing down from the enemy's eyes (whoever that enemy might be). But as his father always said, if a man (or woman, thought Jack, who always tried to be broad-minded) wrote anything down, be it instructions or a diary or even a coded message, they only did so with the sole intent that some other man (or woman) might read it. Therefore, they would make it easy for the right man (or woman) to break the code if they were in the right mind. He closed his eyes and tried to free his thoughts of any barriers or misconceptions. Then, opening them, he allowed himself to focus on the page.

Leaning forward, Jack turned the scroll around and looked at it from every angle, allowing his eyes to roam freely up and down the page, even in between the lines, as if they were roads that could be travelled, or furrows ploughed in a field. Then he turned his eyes to the border that ran around the four edges of the page. It was strange that someone would take the time to draw patterns all along the edges. Then he noticed that the pattern repeated itself again and again. He also noticed that each individual mark, were it not touching the next, looked like the marks in the main body of text.

"That's it. Look at the border pattern. It is made up of the marks in the scroll, only closer together. It looks like a pretty pattern, but it is the key to the code. Don't you see? I bet they are like letters of the alphabet. Look, it repeats itself again and again." Jack felt his chest expand with pride.

"I must be blind," laughed Henry, patting him on the back.

"It can't be *that* simple." Margot was miffed at being outsmarted by a subordinate.

"Well, it is," Henry scoffed. "And Jack cracked the code. Well done, sir."

Jack looked at Margot and seeing her frown, blurted an excuse. "It's just a boy's instinct. We have analytical minds."

Margot gave him a look that, frankly, could kill. "I have no idea what you mean."

"Or… perhaps I was just lucky. And just saw it by accident," Jack tried a new angle.

Henry found himself a pen and began to write out the alphabet, then took a mark for each letter, starting with A and going from there. Noticing what he was doing, the two others buckled down to help. Within an hour they had copied out the marks that were used as a decorative border on the document and written them down next to the letters of the alphabet. They were then able to translate the first few sentences.

30th June 1483 – Tower of London
I have been here for six weeks now and yet my coronation

has not occurred. It has been delayed, yet I know not why.
I have asked my uncle to let me return to my mother, but he tells me
that she has suggested that I remain here in safety. Safety from what?

Henry had a revelation. "Of course. These rolls of parchment were tied with ribbon. Margot, remember Mother always tells us of how Edward and Richard, when they were in Sanctuary at Westminster Abbey,[15] used to play with homemade swords tied with ribbon. I am sure she always said it was red. They must have taken them to the Tower and Edward used the parchment to record his life there."

Henry was delighted, for he now felt he had joined the ranks of 'detective' along with Jack. They had found the diaries of Edward, one of the princes who wicked King Richard had imprisoned in the Tower of London and who had mysteriously disappeared. His mother's little brother and therefore his uncle. Nobody knew what had become of the 'boy king', or his younger brother, but the answer might be in these scrolls if they read all the text.

The children spent the next few hours translating the rest of the scrolls. According to the diary, life in the Tower of London was comfortable but mundane. People came and went. Prisoners were shuffled in and out and onto the hanging platform or to face the axe whenever their time was up. The two boys were kept away from witnessing such unsightly moments and so were happy enough. They missed their mother and wondered why Edward had not been crowned King. It soon dawned on them that their uncle Richard had staged his own coronation and that somehow, they had been forgotten. Edward wondered why they could not go home, for it was not allowed.

2nd August 1483
Things are even worse since the attempt to rescue us. My gentle servants,

Amy and Celine, have been sent away and now I have new ones instead. They are not cruel, but they are not people I know or can trust. There is one man, Thady, who I like. He brings me boiled sweets to suck, as my teeth are sore, and I cannot chew on much. Some are even loose. My hair is thinning too. I will look old before my time if things go on like this. Thady says my hair will grow again. He will bring me a tonic to drink.

The days of playing outside were less frequent. Now, Edward spent his days lying idly on his bed, for he lacked the energy to do more than read or stare out of the window and dream of his mother and his lovely sisters. Richard was at a loss but took to picking at the stone walls to make his mark in case these were the last days of his life. As he had nothing harder than a stick, he made no impression on the hard stone.

It was at this point that the entries became erratic, but the contents were interesting. Thady had told them there was talk of a plot by some bad men coming to do them harm, but that he could rescue them and take them safely to friends of their mother. He just needed to smuggle them out of the Tower. To do this he had modified an old laundry box that was used to bring in clean bed sheets and clothing. By drilling holes in the two ends by the handles he had created air vents, so if a boy lay down and curled up in the box, he could be lightly covered in laundry yet could still breathe while he was carried out of the building. Richard, the younger brother, successfully escaped this way. Edward had insisted his brother reach freedom and safety first.

"Our dressing-up box. It has holes drilled in the sides. Edward must have taken his diaries with him, but forgot them and left them in the box he escaped in."

This was most exciting, and the three children worked away all afternoon deciphering the contents of the diary.

The last entry in the diary was scrawled with a trembling hand. Feeling almost too weak to leave the confines of his chamber, Edward was beginning to mistrust Thady.

28th August 1483

He took Richard away two nights ago and will soon come for me. I asked for proof he was delivered safely to my mother, but Thady would not oblige. I am now scared for I do not know if I can trust Thady. He has a way of looking at me that sends a shiver down my spine.

"That's like what Grandmother's servant does, you know, Fiddle. It gives me the creeps," Henry shuddered thinking about the clammy hand with which Fiddle had held his own.

The diary mentioned that Edward noticed Thady had a tattoo of an anchor on his right arm, and when he asked him about it, Thady told him he had been at sea for much of his life. The prince had heard about sailors and some of their less attractive habits.

Edward was feeble and he was no longer sure he wanted to climb into the laundry box, for he feared that Thady might take him away to another place where Edward might be defiled.

"Oh my God." exclaimed the children when they read about the means of escape and the laundry box. "Did he escape?" That was a question unanswered by the diary.

"I think we should tell Master Skelton," Margot confided to Henry.

"We can't. We can't tell any adults. Not yet. We must find out who this Thady character is," Henry replied.

The children had no way of finding out who the servant with the tattoo might be. It was too long ago, and the man would have since moved on and disappeared. So, the diary was put away as soon as the rain stopped and the sun came out, while they turned to other ways of passing the time, the way children do.

6

When Charles Brandon returned from his Christmas trip to Ludlow Castle on the Welsh borders, he had not come to Eltham Palace to report back to Prince Henry and his sister as promised but had sent them a report by letter instead. This had been delivered along with the royal dispatch bag (he knew a young maid who was able to persuade the dispatch rider to take the letter) to John Skelton, who, as master at Eltham Palace, distributed any extra mail. Skelton had handed Henry this unusual letter with only a slight raise of the eyebrow. On learning it was from Charles, he lost interest. Boys' letters were usually full of silly ramblings about horses and swords and things. He could hardly imagine that Charles, who he considered athletic but a lightweight at any other form of activity, would have anything of interest to say.

As it was, John Skelton was right, for the letter was not that interesting. Charles only reported that the two men in question, although odious in their personal habits and characters, were gainfully employed in the locality. At the most, Fiddle and Grope were sniffing around, keeping an eye out for trouble. Perhaps they had been employed to protect the newlyweds, not harm them. This had allayed any fears with the children that there was malice afoot and they had soon lost any concern for Arthur's safety. Grown-ups sometimes talked in a way that children misunderstood, and Grandmother must have meant something else when they had overheard her conversation. It still rankled Henry that the report back from the two men showed that they were spying on his brother, but perhaps there was nothing in it other than concern for his wellbeing. Children being children, any thoughts about the two servants who were stationed down at Ludlow Castle were soon forgotten and put aside like the diaries.

Cold January turned into wet February and then on to a damp March. Much to Prince Henry's delight, Lady Margaret sent him a present of a new pony as a late Christmas/early Easter present. Henry was growing fast and his legs hung down the sides of his current pony whom he had been riding for the last three years. He was beginning to look decidedly odd on the creature and yet it would be perfect for little Mary to learn to ride on.

The doting grandmother had procured a strong, black Welsh mountain mare that she thought would suit him well. She knew Fiddle was good with horses and so asked him to deliver the animal to Eltham Palace. Fiddle was delighted, as this was a chance for him to ingratiate himself with the young prince, a chance to get to know him at last.

It took Fiddle a long day's ride to lead the little mare all the way from London down to Eltham, and he was tired but happy when he arrived in the courtyard outside the schoolroom. On hearing the horses, Henry bounced out of the schoolroom and ran up to meet the newcomers without pomp or ceremony.

"Is she mine?" he asked Fiddle, knowing full well that a pony was on the way.

Fiddle was beaming from ear to ear. "She is, kind sir, yours for the keeping, with a message from Her Grace, the most royal and reverent Lady Margaret that you are to call her Virtue, by way of reminding you that 'virtue is a quality that outweighs all others'. Those are her ladyship's very words to you, sir, as conveyed by myself to your esteemed self in my own humble manner."

With his speech over, Fiddle bowed with such ridiculously flamboyant mannerisms that Henry almost laughed aloud, but he checked himself.

Henry took the leading rein from the man's outstretched hand, but on seeing his arm Henry froze, for the man had a tattoo of a ship's anchor on his right arm, as did the servant in the diary of Edward V. He had to go and tell Margot and Jack. "Please put the pony in the stable for me, as I have an urgent errand to run that must come first. I will come and see Virtue, as you call her, as soon as I am finished," Henry instructed the man, before turning around and running off as fast as his legs would carry him.

On hearing the news, Jack and Margot were as excited as Henry.

"What's the messenger's name?" asked Jack.

"Fiddle is what Grandmother calls him. That's all I know."

Jack smiled. "Come on, let's go and see the pony. I am going to introduce myself."

The children ran to the stables and found Fiddle chatting to one of the young stable boys.

"I'm back, like I said," chirped Henry

"Hello again, my prince." Fiddle bowed low in his inimitable manner.

"I brought the others to see the pony,"

"Hello." Jack bowed low, just as his father had taught him. He knew that he was bowing too low for a servant, but Jack guessed that in doing so he would be flattering the man into careless talk. "My name is James Worsley, but my friends call me Jack."

Fiddle looked at the short, mousy-haired boy, and bowed back. "Hello. My name is Thaddeus Fiddle, but my friends call me…" Fiddle searched his mind for what he might have been called in the past "…Thady."

He beamed at the young boy, who beamed back, turned and ran away. The others followed, leaving the messenger feeling as if he was missing the joke.

"There you go – he told us himself, he is Thady." Jack was excited now.

"But that means he is the man who tried to help Uncle Edward escape from the Tower. We must ask him what happened." Margot was sure of this.

Henry scowled. "I don't think that would be wise. If nobody else knows the answer to that question, then we, as children, are hardly going to be told, are we? What worries me is that he is now based in Ludlow, spying on Arthur. That's what Charles says, anyway. We need to know what is going on."

The conspirators discussed the revelation that Fiddle was integrally involved with the disappearance of Henry and Margot's two uncles all those years ago.

"It makes sense, because my uncle mentions in his diary that the servant is only around twenty years of age and that would add up, for Fiddle is about forty, I would guess." Margot was always working out things like this.

"It makes him a prime suspect," Jack thought out loud. "Not really," replied Margot, "for he was helping Edward and Richard to escape. In fact, according to the diary, Richard did escape."

"But the diary was written before Edward was rescued—if he was—and he *was* feeling horribly ill. He even suspected he was being poisoned."

This part of the puzzle left Henry at a loss. Thady had been trying to rescue the boys, for he was preparing to sneak them out inside the trunk. Jack listened to his reasoning but had his own suspicions.

"If I were going to murder two children who were fit and adept at swordplay, as they would have been to an extent, just as we are, I would make friends with them first and trick them into a false sense of security. Then I would split them up, take one at a time and do them in."

Margot looked at him in disbelief. "That's horrible of you. But true. Jack is right." Henry nodded his head and continued. "If you tried to attack them when they were together, one would defend the other and it would be more than a handful for one man against two boys of our age."

"Actually, they were older than you, Henry. Edward was my age." Margot was always trying to bring up the fact she was the oldest.

"Exactly." Jack agreed with the two of them. "So, I would befriend the children and take one away with the consent of the other. Maybe drown the first and come back to strangle the other?"

"Jack, stop it." Margot was getting goose pimples.

"Or, you could take one away and poison the other, to weaken him, before putting him in the box and doing whatever you liked to him." Henry shuddered as the words came out of his mouth, his dislike of Fiddle growing. The man was capable of anything, of that he was certain. He totally understood how his uncle must have felt when imprisoned with only Thady around.

The children agreed they could not share their information with any adults, for just like with the diary, nobody would believe them, and if they did, it would only be brought to the attention of the King and Lady Margaret. As Fiddle worked for Lady Margaret, this made any action of his, however treasonous, somehow condoned, or even *ordered* by their own grandmother, the most powerful woman in the land.

"I sincerely doubt that your grandmother would be involved in such dark goings-on." Jack was in awe of the old dame, who had come to visit the children soon after he had arrived. She said that she wanted to see if he had settled in. It was obvious she was more interested in having a look at him herself. His coming to Eltham Palace had been her idea, after all.

"We have no idea what goes on in an adult's mind," Margot heard herself say aloud as she recalled the awful afternoon she had spent hidden behind the curtains in her grandmother's privy chamber, watching her cast dark magic.

"What do you mean?" Henry caught the strange tone in his sister's voice.

"Oh, nothing," Margot sniffed, her nose in the air. "Nothing that *children* would understand."

Her emphasis on the word 'children' annoyed Henry hugely and he punched Margot in the arm. "Just because you are married to a hairy beast of a Scot."

His taunting worked, and Margot went puce in the face as she punched him back. Jack, knowing it was his job to calm the situation down before it got out of hand, pulled the conversation back to the coded scroll. He did not want to be scolded for Henry's poor behaviour.

"Hey, soldiers, pull up the ranks there." This was a saying he had learnt from his soldier father, who had fought in the Battle of Bosworth alongside the King. "Let's agree, we cannot speak of this to anyone and we must not accuse anyone of misdeeds until we are sure of what we have discovered."

This was true so they all agreed. They would only get into trouble if they jumped to conclusions and ran to Master Skelton telling tales. Not even he would believe them, and he was the best adult they knew. They all swore they would deal with this on their own. Any tales about Grandmother's men misbehaving or worse would be dismissed as their childish imaginations. But they had to work out what they could do about it. They were certain Fiddle had been instrumental in the disappearance of the two princes from the Tower of London, so it was sinister that he was now involved in spying on Arthur. Margot was adamant. "Charles said that those men were innocently employed. I mean, working on accounts is hardly the action of a killer, is it?"

Jack pulled a face. "But working in the kitchens is the perfect place for an assassin."

"What do you mean?" Sometimes Margot just could not understand the way Jack thought.

"It's obvious!" Henry's eyes sparkled. "It is the perfect way to secretly poison Arthur's food."

"But what if someone was eating the same food. And doesn't he have a taster anyway?"

Margot was right.

"He must be poisoning him somehow else then." Henry was flummoxed.

"What about in his drink?" Henry suggested. "Or in boiled sweets?" Jack added.

Margot was horrified. "Heavens above. We must warn him. Henry, we need to go and warn Arthur. We cannot send a messenger, for the facts are too strange to be believed, he will have to hear them from one of us. We must find a way of going to Ludlow. Perhaps Master Skelton would take us there for Easter?"

"That might be too late. Time is of the essence." Henry could feel the excitement rising in his throat.

"I will demand that Skelton takes me. I can do that as a Queen." Margot sounded like her grandmother when she spoke with such assurance.

"You can't go, Maggot." Henry used his sister's least favourite pet name to bring her down a peg or two. Margot was now the Queen of Scotland, even if only in name, so her absence from Eltham Palace would be a scandal. "You need to remain here to cover for me. If we both disappear, they will send a search party out for us, but if Jack and I make our excuses, it will be a day at least before they come after us, if at all. We could say we are going out to try out the new pony."

Jack was delighted, for he could smell the beginning of an adventure.

Margot was adamant. "I think I should come too, for I am the oldest. Two young boys wandering around will be spotted as unusual, whereas I can hold an air of authority."

Lifting her head high, she certainly looked like her grandmother. There was no doubt she would one day command universal respect.

The discussions went around and around until Henry had an idea. Charles would come with them if they asked.

"He could legitimately visit Ludlow Castle, like he did before, and we can travel with him as his squires." Henry explained.

"You? Travel as a servant? Henry! You could never pull it off. Your temper would give you away and your red hair will..."

Henry was adamant. "I can cover my hair and I can mind my

temper."

Jack laughed. "I can give him some lessons in how to behave as a grovelling servant."

So it was settled. The matter was closed. Henry knew dispatches were leaving for Westminster Palace, where the King had returned after the Christmas season, and Charles no doubt would be there as his server and ward. Henry wrote a carefully worded note to Charles asking him to come and view the new pony, for he needed his advice about training it. He gave it to Master Skelton to approve, seal and put in the dispatch bag. What Master Skelton did not notice was the second note Henry slipped inside the folded paper of the letter, asking Charles to come immediately, for they had found out something about Fiddle that was a matter of 'national importance'.

In the servants' quarters, Fiddle was sitting supping a tankard of ale. He had been bitterly disappointed that young Henry had not come to admire his new pony. Something must be up for the prince not to want to try out such a fine animal. Fiddle had spent days cleaning the tack so it gleamed and brushing the animal's coat until it shone. He had been delighted when Her Ladyship had asked him to bring the gift down to Eltham. He had so looked forward to giving the handsome youth a leg-up onto the pony's back. It was not often a servant was allowed to stand close to a prince, or to touch him. A shiver went down his spine at the thought.

Now all he had was a missed opportunity, for he needed to head up to Westminster with the dispatch bag before he went back to Ludlow to continue with his espionage. It was a disappointment indeed. Fiddle sunk the ale and asked the kitchen maid for another one. The maid smiled suggestively at him when she returned with the ale, the promise of her breasts showing above her bodice, but he took no notice of her. All he could think of was the young prince somewhere, so close to hand and yet so far out of reach.

※

That evening the three children continued with their plans. Margot saw the benefit of staying behind and keeping up appearances for at least a day, though she had secret plans of her own that she kept to herself.

The two boys wrote list after list of what they might need on a four to five-day journey out in the big wide world. By the following day they had confirmation from court that Charles would come and visit later in the week. So, they began to surreptitiously put together some travel bags filled with the items on the list and more: a flint and steel for lighting a fire plus some charcloth to catch the sparks, a blanket each and a few items of clothing. They left enough room to take some travelling food, like dried meat, hard biscuits, bread and cheese.

Jack also had a couple of packets carefully wrapped in waxed paper. Each was about the size of a man's fist and he packed them right down at the bottom of his saddlebag with some clean shirts wrapped around them. When Henry asked what the packets contained, Jack smiled enigmatically and called them 'insurance'. What he did not know was that Jack had taken these packets from his father's armoury before he left home. His father had fought in the war alongside the King and had overseen munitions. This meant looking after the few hand cannon procured by the young Henry Tudor and his band of hopefuls who had come from France to attempt to win the crown of England. At the Battle of Bosworth they succeeded, although the cannon were only used as a distraction, shot from the sidelines to annoy the enemy forces rather than defeat them. Longbows and swords were the chosen and proven weapons that had actually killed so many of the opposition, being more accurate.[16]

Henry's bedchamber was all awry, with clothes pulled out of their chest and strewn over the floor while Henry chose the plainest shirts he could find. Most of his clothes were discarded, being too rich in material to pass as the clothes of a squire. Margot oversaw all the preparations and watched the others pack. She chose a moment to give Henry a gold ring with a wave-like movement to its design that she had once been given by an aunt.

"Henry, keep this with you at all times, and if you need to sell it, do so. If you still have it by the time you get to Ludlow, give it to dear Arthur for me with all my love."

Henry was taken aback. He knew his sister loved this ring.

It was too big for her to wear, so she normally kept it in her jewellery box by her bed. She had been waiting to grow into it so it could be worn on her finger.

"Thank you, dear sister." He took the ring and quickly kissed his sister on the cheek, a sign of love not often forthcoming. She looked a bit embarrassed but smiled.

"I wish I were coming with you, but I expect Charles will keep a good eye on you both. Please listen to him and do what he tells you. And Henry, remember you need to travel incognito, which means you will no longer be a prince. You will become a commoner and must act so. If you put on airs and graces, you will be discovered and your mission will be in jeopardy."

"I understand. You give me good advice. I hear you and will draw upon your wisdom: I will keep my mouth shut and my eyes open."

With a new sense of honour, Henry knelt, bowing to his sister to ask for her blessing, an action that surprised them both. Without hesitation, Margot put her hand on his head the way her grandmother and mother would do and blessed her younger brother.

Jack, who witnessed this compassionate scene between the recently warring siblings, realized he had seen a rare moment, with both Henry and Margot acting with a maturity beyond their years. He felt privileged to be their trusted friend and made a vow to himself there and then never to let Henry down, even if it cost him his life.

7

Charles arrived to lead the expedition within days of receiving Henry's message with its warning that the mission was of national importance. After an intensive 'war council', the trio of companions were ready to set off on their journey. Before they left, they huddled together with Margot to discuss their plans and she asked Charles to draw a map of the route they were going to take.

"Just tell them we have gone to try out Virtue and will stay away for a day or two. You might have to tell Master Skelton the truth, but I am sure he will understand. We have Charles with us and will only be away for a few days. Charles says it takes him three days to get to Ludlow from London." Henry spoke with authority.

"I am sure I can come up with a good story."

The companions packed up the last of their provisions and were soon mounted and ready to go. Henry has ended up in disguise, wearing the borrowed clothes of a squire whom Margot had befriended. This was topped off with a long woollen cap that covered his head and came down over his ears, covering his telltale red hair, over which he donned a floppy hat for wearing when it rained, with a wide brim.

After the ceremony of the formal blessing the night before, Henry was now feeling somewhat awkward taking his leave of his sister, so he just kissed her quickly on the cheek and told her to look after herself.

"We will be back before you know it. All I need to do is warn Arthur that Fiddle is a dangerous man. Surely he will listen to me." It sounded so simple; Henry was certain it would not take long. The enormity of what he was doing, leaving home without permission and as a prince without a full complement of guards, simply had not occurred to him.

"Don't worry, Henry, I will remain behind to 'hold the fort' and look forward to hearing of your adventures once you return," Margot said, but her fingers were crossed behind her back.

"Farewell, Margot."

Jack kissed his friend, turned bright red and rushed to mount Bottom. He was not used to kissing girls, especially royal ones. He found it easier to wrestle with Margot in the yard or challenge her to archery or a game of tag.

"Look after yourself, Jack. Listen to what Henry says and don't do anything stupid, will you?" Margot had enjoyed putting Jack in a fluster.

"I will take good care of them both." Charles winked as he swept a courtly bow to Margot and then took her hand to kiss it farewell. Even Margot, who was usually immune to Charles's easily spent charm, could not help but smile at his natural grace.

"Thank you, Charles. I will expect you to take good care of them. Though that goes for yourself too. I worry about you all without me there to look after you. Charles, no gambling, and no drink. There will be plenty of time to do so once you arrive at Ludlow." She made herself sound as authoritative as she could.

"Your word is my command, my lady," was Charles's gallant reply, although had he not been holding the horses' reins, he might have had his fingers crossed behind his back too.

There was nothing left to say now, so once mounted up, Charles took the lead and the three companions set off out over the open drawbridge past the guards: a fine white destrier, a beautiful black pony and a mottled mule. Giving a nod to the soldiers standing guard, they explained they were going out to test the new pony and would stay at a nearby castle, so they would not be back till morning.

Margot watched the trio disappear up the road, then turned and went back into the palace to study the map Charles had drawn: Abingdon, Oxford, Woodstock, Enstone, Worcester and finally Ludlow Castle. It should take three or four days at a good pace without pushing the horses too hard. A messenger could do the journey in two days, but that was with constantly changing horses at the coach inns dotting the roadside. The boys would not change their mounts for anything or anyone. Charles loved his stallion far too much to swap him and Henry had only just been given his pony. Even Jack, who had owned Bottom for as long as he could recall, would rather die than swap his family pet for another creature. So, they would be riding at a gentle but consistent pace.

The first stage of the journey was to ride up to London and cross London Bridge onto the north side and then to follow their noses up via the main road out west and towards Oxford. They could have travelled more easily along the south side of the River Thames, via Southwark and beyond, but that would have taken them past both Greenwich and Lambeth palaces and then Richmond Palace beyond. The chance of being spotted by someone they knew was too risky and so they chose the northern route instead, where they would soon disappear into the crowds of the capital city.

The south side of the river was a rundown, unsophisticated area with inns, bordellos and gambling dens built between slum-like buildings where the poorer people lived. Henry had crossed this bridge many times before but had never had time to study the people who lived there as he did now. For the first time ever, he could watch common people doing their everyday things. Normally, if he was riding through the streets, he was in a procession causing a commotion with royal men-at-arms and other dignitaries surrounding him and would have to ride, sitting up straight with eyes held strictly to the fore. Today he felt invisible, riding along in his uncomfortable clothes with his head covered. He could gawp at the ladies who stood outside the brothels, with their low-cut stomachers and bare legs revealed under skirts hitched up in a most unusual manner. He thought they looked enticing at first, until he noticed on closer inspection that some of them were hiding their age under a thick coat of white paste. They looked more like scary clowns in the cruel daylight, and he chose to look away, his face prickling with embarrassment.

Street urchins ran beside the riders begging for money, and Charles threw them a few pennies as they rode up under the towering south gate of London Bridge and onto its crowded thoroughfare. Within a few strides, it was as if they had ridden into another world. London Bridge, with its many arches supporting the roadway, built hundreds of years ago, was sophisticated and thriving. The houses were some three or four stories high, and several were linked with houses on the other side of the road by walkways stretching overhead like bridges in the air. Shops sold fabrics, footwear and anything else a fashionable Londoner might require. There were upmarket inns and hotels offering 'lice-free' accommodation. The location was popular, for the water could be pumped up from the river for household use and the water under the bridge could flush away sewage from the houses above. An astute onlooker might note the water that was pumped up into the houses came from upstream of the bridge and the waste was washed downstream, other than when the tide turned.

Jack was enjoying every moment of the journey. He loved the prostitutes and grinned at them as they blew him kisses and squeezed their breasts provocatively to tease him, something he found strangely exciting. But what he was really looking forward to seeing were the gruesome severed heads that would adorn Traitors' Gate, right in the middle of the bridge where the drawbridge guarded the city. Soon, it stood in front of them with its bloody display of severed heads in various stages of decay sitting on the end of tall spikes for all to see.

Jack was speechless while he took it all in. This was the King's way of reminding all who passed through the gates that treason of any sort would end in death and defilement. Flies swarmed around the dark empty sockets that stared, unseeing, into the distance, buzzing in to eat the remains of the rotting flesh. *It must be difficult to enter Heaven with no head*, Jack thought, and shivered as he walked his mule onwards underneath the gruesome display.

Having crossed the bridge, the three companions headed west along Lombard Street. The streets were teeming with people getting on with their lives, with hand-barrows full of fish heading in one direction and a drover herding sheep in another. Gentlemen rode by on horses and the more fortunate ladies were carried in litters from one fashionable house to another. Children worked delivering messages, and thieves picked pockets, then ran off into the side streets before they could be caught. Few victims would follow them to get their purses back, for the chances were that an accomplice would be waiting there to knock them out with a cudgel so they could rob the unconscious body further as it lay in the filth.

It must be difficult to enter heaven with no head.

Having crossed the bridge, the three companions headed west along Lombard Street. The streets were teeming with people getting on with their lives, with hand-barrows full of fish heading in one direction and a drover herding sheep in another. Gentlemen rode by on horses and the more fortunate ladies were carried in litters from one fashionable house to another. Children worked delivering messages, and thieves picked pockets, then ran off into the side streets before they could be caught. Few victims would follow them to get their purses back, for the chances were that an accomplice would be waiting there to knock them out with a cudgel so they could rob the unconscious body further as it lay in the filth.

Finally, they crossed Holborn Bridge out towards the countryside and the cramped streetscapes of tall houses lined up, pushing and shoving each other for a place to exist, gave way to less crowded lines of smaller country houses. These, in turn, gave way to fields of pasture with sheep and cattle grazing, the animals that made England so rich. They had made it through the city of London without being recognized and now could settle into their saddles for the ride on to Abingdon Abbey, where Charles had decided they were to stay the night.

Once they had travelled a good distance out of the city, Charles decided it was time to stop and give the horses a rest. Unpacking their food, the trio enjoyed their first meal away from home. It consisted of some good fresh bread and delicious cheese, apples Henry cut up using his penknife and some dried meat – chewy, salty but incredibly flavoursome. Jack ate loads.

"How long until we reach the abbey?" Jack asked, food spraying out of his mouth.

Henry spoke, mimicking his sister's stern voice: "Really Jack, you should not eat with your mouth full!"

"Or speak with my mouth open!" replied Jack and laughed, a deluge of chewed morsals flying out in front of him.

Charles was pleased the two boys were happy. They would need to keep their spirits up, as it looked like it was going to rain and they still had a couple of hours to go before they reached the abbey. Henry, as a prince, never carried money, but thankfully Charles still had considerable change from the gold he had recently won at jousting tournaments, so he had enough to provide for the three of them during the journey. This was only fitting as well, if anyone was to believe he was a knight and the boys his squires. It was a small financial sacrifice that would pay him dividends if he saved Arthur's life. Charles had no qualms about being ambitious. With no parents and no family fortune, he had only his wits to keep himself from the pauper's house.

After lunch, he was the first to make a move from where they were resting and hop back into the saddle. The others gathered themselves together slowly, already feeling a little stiff. Jack repacked the food basket and tied it onto his saddle while Henry walked around to stretch his sore limbs. Within a few minutes the companions were back on the road. Less than an hour had passed when it began to rain, so they donned their waxed travelling cloaks and urged the horses into a trot for a while to put some miles behind them. It was good to be out riding, even in the rain, and the boys enjoyed the excitement of the moment and ignored the raindrops.

Night was closing in by the time they saw the welcoming lights of the abbey ahead of them. It was a glorious sight to tired eyes, with the flickering candles in the windows and a brazier by the entrance, where the night watchman stood to keep warm while he guarded the gates, turning away any undesirables who looked like they could not afford to pay for their keep. Henry saw one of these less fortunate folks being kicked away from the gates despite what looked like his begging to be given entry.

"I thought abbeys gave shelter to anyone, regardless of their pocket?"

"They do, in theory," replied Charles, "but then the other travellers would have to share accommodation with the poor and unclean, increasing the risk of fleas and, worse, even sickness."

"That's terrible," Henry exclaimed. "Could they not even let them sleep in the stables?"

Charles grinned. "Not really, for that is where you are going to sleep. Servants are put up in the loft over the stables and the valuable horses surely cannot be expected to share with beggars and vagabonds, can they?"

Charles dug his heels into his horse's sides and called on the others to follow at a respectful pace behind him.

"Hold on!" exclaimed Henry as he trotted to catch up with Charles. "Did you just say I was going to sleep in a *stable*?"

"Henry!" Charles hissed at him. "You are a simple squire to a young knight, and you are not a particularly good one at that. You should be riding behind me and not arguing with… Ah, here is the night watchman."

Charles urged Caesar to get ahead of Henry before he could argue further. He pulled the reins as he approached the cold, tired monk who was standing warming his hands at the brazier. "Good evening, sir, and well met. I am looking for a room for the night and for accommodation for my squires, if you could arrange it for me, please?"

Henry fell back into place behind Charles but was sulking. Things got worse when they were allowed through the gateway and pulled up outside the front door of the abbey. Charles dismounted and passed the reins of his horse to Henry, instructing him to put the horse in the stables and rub him down.

"Don't forget to water him, Robert." he said, using the name they had chosen for Henry, "and make sure he is comfortable before you look after yourselves, lads."

Henry was about to give Charles a piece of his mind when the abbot walked up to introduce himself to the handsome knight. He noted the fine horse Charles was riding. It must have cost a pretty penny, the abbot calculated, and the black pony was a fine breed as well. Too good for a mere squire. But the third beast was a mule. There was a story to this strange group; he would put money on it. Walking up to have a closer look, the abbot caught Henry's eye and Henry, still indignant at having been given the horse, gave him a glowering, challenging glare.

On looking into the angry eyes of the child, the abbot had a flash, a vision. It was these visions he had 'suffered' since his childhood that had allowed the abbot to enter the Church, for the adults around him feared him and decided he was either a child of Satan or of God: they had chosen to help him find God. In a moment of earthly blindness, all he could see was his beautiful abbey being torn down and turned into ruins, with monks crouching in fear or running away holding precious relics close to their chests as if they were little babes in their arms. There were great armed men on horseback, waving documents as if they were swords and giving orders that everything of value should be confiscated, with the rest destroyed. It was only a flash, but the effect of the vision made the abbot sway with shock. Charles put his hand out to steady him.[17]

"Are you alright?" he asked.

"I... I am... fine... thank you, sir. I have just... I mean, I sometimes get these dizzy spells. It's something to do with my ears; they buzz sometimes, and it makes me lose my balance. Thank you for your concern, but all is well."

The air cleared and the abbot shook his head, only to see two innocent children leading the animals towards the stables. The abbot was unnerved but pulled himself together and concentrated on welcoming his guest. He would have to think about this when he had a chance to reflect. There was something significant about the child, something terrible.

"Welcome, welcome, good sir, let us extend our hospitality towards yourself and your entourage. There is room in the stables for your horses and servants and I have a fine room for you. Come and warm your feet by the fire and tell me of your travels."

Charles allowed himself to be led in through the front doors and into the warmth of the rooms inside, while the boys were left to look after the horses and only afterwards themselves.

"Did you see that?" Henry was almost speechless. He was looking back at the front door to the abbey, which had just closed behind Charles.

Jack smiled to himself before quietly taking the reins from his friend and saying with a shrug of his shoulders, "You had better get used to it 'Bob', this is your life now."

"Bob?"

"Well, Robert." With these words of wisdom, Jack went in search of some empty stalls for the animals.

❦

The abbot was still shaken by what he had just seen, but as a master of deception after many years of preaching sermons at the pulpit that meant little or nothing to him, he managed to hide his feelings. Being abbot of Abingdon was not without its comforts, but the company was wanting at this time of year. It was quiet enough this cold night and he would enjoy an excuse to open a good bottle of wine to drink by the fireside while they chatted, hoping that with the wine his companion's tongue would be loosened and he might learn more about the boy.

"Do put your feet by the fire… Charles Brandon, did you say?" The abbot turned on his charm.

"Thank you, kind sir, I am most obliged."

Soon Charles was sitting by a large stone fireplace with a roaring ash fire warming his aching bones as he drank wine with the abbot and shared a few sweetcakes that the kind host had brought in from the kitchens. Charles soon forgot Henry and Jack were outside in the cold and settled in for a night of drinking with the abbot. The man was most hospitable and within a few moments Charles felt quite at home.

Out in the stables, the two younger boys were doing their best to settle the animals as they had been instructed. This was new territory for Henry, for up until now his ponies had been handed to him by a groom and handed back when he had finished riding. He had no idea they needed water and hay, plus a nosebag of oats for each beast as a reward for the long day's work. Once the animals were fed, it was time for the hungry youths to look after themselves, for it appeared they had been quite forgotten.

"Come on," suggested Jack, "let's go and find something for us to eat."

"Where?" asked Henry, who also had no idea how to fend for himself.

"Follow me." Jack smiled wryly, feeling that he was coming into his element.

Jack had a nose when it came to food, even as a baby. When he could not smell it, he could sense it, and without hesitation, he led Henry in the direction of the abbey kitchens. Standing on a woodpile outside the kitchen door, the boys looked in through the high windows that allowed some light into the vaulted kitchen space inside. Even though it was late, there were black-cassocked monks inside, finishing off the day's work, washing dishes and wiping down work surfaces. A massive oak table was being scrubbed clean and the fire was being banked up for the night.

"There, look, on the windowsill, there are some pies left out to cool. They must be fresh out of the oven." Jack nodded to the far side of the kitchen. "If I can sneak in when nobody is looking, we could share one of those."

Henry liked what he was hearing. "Can you really go in there and just take one?" He looked at Jack with new found respect.

"Watch a master at his work." Jack winked at Henry and was gone in a flash.

From his safe viewpoint outside, Henry watched Jack tiptoe in through the kitchen door and merge into the shadows while monks busied themselves all around him. Then, just as Henry thought they would be there all night, the monks disappeared for a few moments through a large door and with lightning speed, Jack burst from his hiding place. He shot across the kitchen, and took not one but *two* pies, making it less obvious by spreading out the remaining ones to fill the gap. As soon as he returned, the boys ran all the way back and up to the stable loft before throwing themselves onto the hay, laughing until they cried.

"Wow, that was quite something! I am in awe, Jack," said Henry while stuffing his mouth. He stopped short. "By St George[18], this pie is filled with beef and mushrooms, yet Lent is not yet over." Henry was most surprised by this, the abbey being a religious establishment.

"Ah, that's nothing." Jack spraying food by talking with it in his mouth for the second time that day.

The pies really were delicious, perhaps tasting all the better for being stolen and eaten in a hayloft. Henry was thoroughly enjoying himself now. Once the pies were eaten, his sense of adventure was fired up.

"Shall we go and have a look around?" he suggested.

Jack did not need much persuading. They crept down the ladder from the loft and slipped back out into the night. It was a dark night without a moon, but the stars were coming out from behind the clouds now the rain had stopped, and the wind had died down. Sneaking around the abbey buildings, the boys saw more than they had ever expected. It being a cold night, most of the inhabitants of the abbey were comforting themselves by fires – that is, if they were not at prayer or in bed. The boys wandered around the place, looking in through windows at the scenes they revealed. The first scene they saw was Charles sitting by the fireside, drinking wine and chatting the night away with his host. He was in no hurry to go anywhere, and the boys moved on into the night.

There was a chapel, with stone walls and plain windows but for a single one of stained glass on the east wall above the altar. Tall candles were burning in brass candlesticks, with the flames flickering on the walls, making the shadows dance. There was nobody in there at all.

"They must be having a break between masses," Henry offered.

Next, they found a library where monks with tonsured heads were bending over large leather-bound books that were larger than any Henry had seen before, studying in the poor light of tallow candles. They were working late.

"How can they work in such poor light?" he wondered. Jack had a twinkle in his eyes. "Perhaps God helps them."

Henry took him seriously. "You might be right."

Jack shrugged to himself. Sometimes Henry seemed so gullible.

Around the back of the building, in the next window they saw that they appeared to be reaching the monks' more private quarters, for the men looked more relaxed and were sitting playing cards, drinking ale and lying on couches, wrestling each other with their legs in the air.

"I never knew monks wrestled," Henry observed. Jack looked and saw they were not 'wrestling'.

"I think they are doing something else, Henry. Perhaps you should look away."

Henry looked more critically and could hardly believe his eyes, for these were monks with women in their arms, enjoying their company without any great show of restraint.

Henry turned around and walked away. "I think I have seen enough of this place."

He walked back to the stable block deep in thought, Jack trotting up to join him once he had torn himself away from the spectacle. He thought it quite funny, but Henry had lost his sense of humour, or so it seemed. Princes were sometimes hard to understand, Jack thought to himself, but he knew when to remain silent.

※

Charles found he had drunk too much and was answering questions that had become uncomfortable, focused on his journey and destination.

"Ludlow Castle, as I am off to see Prince Arthur," he heard himself saying.

"Oh? And what might you be doing there?" The abbot sat upright, his attention fully engaged.

Charles felt the tension in the air. He sobered up. "I… had a bet with Prince Arthur that I could not win at the tournaments and afford a fine horse. I want to go and claim my prize money, for as you can see, I am now the owner of the finest horse in England."

Charles hoped his quick thinking had covered any indiscretions he might just have made in his drunkenness. How stupid of him to fall into a state of false security on the firstnight of the journey. He could feel a cold sweat breaking onhis brow. He took a handkerchief out of his pocket and wiped his forehead before continuing.

"I have always wanted to see Ludlow Castle and have been invited to stay there, so I thought now would be as good a time as any. I have holiday time away from court to use up and my family are all dead, so I have no one else to visit."

Charles was feeling less confident about his situation than he had been when he first sat down in the abbot's chamber, and so he made his excuses and walked, somewhat unsteadily, to his cell. It was a very pleasant cell with crisp linen sheets, a small bed and a table with an ewer of water and a candle. He muttered a quick prayer in deference to his hosts and fell into bed with his clothes on, snoring almost immediately.

Back in his chamber, by the fire, the abbot was turning around in his mind what he had learned over the course of the evening. A young knight from court riding to Ludlow Castle, where the prince and princess were in residence, not with one 'squire' but two, both of whom were more the age of pages than squires. They could be his brothers, although he had said his family were all dead. Furthermore, the abbot had been just told by one of his novice monks who was posted outside as a guard that the young squires had been sneaking around outside during the evening and had even stolen some pies. He would certainly charge extra for the food they had stolen.

Before the abbot retired for the night, he made a note to have someone follow these mysterious travellers. For this, he called upon a young novice monk who had been trained in certain ways that were useful, if not a little distasteful. It was time to let him out for a while and give him a scent to follow.

8

Charles awoke to the piercing sound of birds singing outside his window. He opened his eyes, then closed them again, for his head felt like it had been trodden on by a stampede of wild horses. Rising slowly from his bed, Charles drank all the water that was left in the jug for the purpose of washing. Still fully dressed from the evening before, he brushed himself down, pushed his hair back and smoothed it into place before leaving his cell to find his companions.

Henry and Jack were also feeling dishevelled but rested. A night sleeping in a pile of hay, warmed by the heat from the animals below, was much more comfortable than Henry had expected. While Henry pulled stalks of hay out of his hair and clothing, Jack climbed down the ladder from the loft to feed the horses and tack them up.

As soon as they were able to gather their things together, the three companions said goodbye to their hosts. Charles was handed a long list of what they had consumed last evening, including an account of the wine drunk and the mention of two pies of unspecified filling that had disappeared from the kitchens. Startled at the cost of the first evening of their journey, he paid, but made a note that they would have to choose less fine accommodation in future to make up for lastnight's extravagances.

"Well, I am glad to get away from that place," Henry admitted once they had ridden a mile or two. "If I am to become head of the Church when I grow up, I am going to have to make some changes. You cannot have a priest preaching one thing and then doing another. No more women in the monks' living quarters when I am an archbishop."

Charles spoke in their defence. "I would not judge them so harshly, Henry. You should forgive them the odd trespass, for they are only men. Most of them did not even choose to join an order; their parents gave them to the Church when they were too young to object. Some of those monks have been imprisoned in the abbeys all their lives."

"I think you would like to join them, perhaps, with all those women being so free in their company?" Henry looked askance at his older friend.

"I know I would not like to live as a monk," Jack replied. "Give me the company of girls any time."

Charles looked at Jack with renewed appreciation. "I am with you there, Jack, but let's forget the abbey and keep moving."

The abbot had not forgotten about the strange guests who had sheltered with them the night before. He called for his specialist monk, the one he kept apart from all the others for various reasons.

"I want you to follow the three travellers who stayed last night to find out what they are up to. They are a young man and two boys. I want you to find out the real reason for their journey to Ludlow Castle. Find out more about the boy on the black pony. No, kidnap him and bring him back to me. I will interrogate him myself."

The monk, who was no more than a boy of about fourteen himself, could not reply. Instead, his dark eyes showed cognition and he put his hands together as if in prayer, bowing to his superior. He backed out of the room and disappeared silently into the depths of the abbey to his cell. Later, he mounted his pony and trotted off down the road in pursuit of the three companions: a black monk on a black pony moving like a shadow.

Miles away, in Westminster, the King was feeling lonely. With no children left at court, he and his wife only had each other for company. Lady Margaret was going on a retreat for Easter week to visit her friend Bishop Fisher at Rochester Cathedral, calling in on Eltham Palace to see her grandchildren along the way, which meant it was only himself and the Queen in residence.[19]

"Beth dearest, what would you say to a visit to Ludlow?" he asked the Queen, who was embroidering another shirt for him.

"Oh Henry, that would be wonderful," the Queen replied, putting her needlework down for a moment. "I have some bits and pieces I would love to give the princess."

The King, who was thinking of the princess himself, for he was quite taken by her, mumbled under his breath. "I could think of something to give her myself." He smirked to himself.

"Oh really, dear? What?"

"Nothing dear, I will organize it," he replied and fell into a daydream.

There was Princess Katherine and he was with her, but not as himself, as Prince Arthur. They were standing by a stream and he took her in his arms to dance with her. They danced together to the sound of songbirds in the trees, then he lay her on the ground and....

"Darling? I said it will be lovely to see the newly married

couple." The Queen was looking at him quizzically.

"Yes, yes. I was just thinking that myself." The King shook his head to shake the image from his mind.

The Queen was delighted to do something for Easter, for court was rather dull these days. After the excitement of the royal wedding, followed by Christmas at Richmond and then the proxy wedding of Margot to the King of Scotland, the young royals had been sent back down to Eltham Palace to study and live a quiet life for a few months. She missed her children, but she knew they were in safe hands with MasterSkelton in charge.

The Queen liked Skelton immensely. He was such a positive influence on Henry and Margot. He was even slowly winning Henry over regarding his religious vocation and Henry had written a couple of interesting essays about the importance of faith in choosing a life in the Church. The main thing the Queen so valued with Master Skelton was the patience with which he tutored the children. He never ever seemed to lose his temper.

"What do you *mean* they have gone?" A very startled and agitated John Skelton was glaring down at Margot, who was beginning to think matters were not going according to plan.

"I tell you the truth." She tried to sound calm, but it was difficult when Master Skelton was so upset. "They have gone to Ludlow Castle to warn Arthur about the man who is trying to kill him."

"What man? This is unbelievable!" John sat down with a bump onto his schoolmaster's chair, his head in his hands. They were in the classroom together, where only Margot and Mary had turned up for lessons. Upon interrogation, Margot had admitted that Henry and his friends had set off on some mad epic voyage to go and rescue Prince

Arthur from an assassination attempt. This was because of decoding and translating the parchments that he, Skelton, had told them to break, as an exercise. Never had he thought the contents would be so explosive.

"You could have told me first, before the boys ran off like this. Anything could happen to them. I mean, whoever is possibly involved with a plot to harm Arthur might not like being confronted by two boys and a dilettante knight. They might take it upon themselves to waylay our young heroes or, even worse, do away with them. What on earth were you thinking of, letting them go off like that?"

Margot was feeling out of her depth with John Skelton. He had never lost his temper with her like this before and it frightened her. "But please, Master Skelton, all we need to do is follow them and keep an eye on them. I know which route they are taking, and if we set off straight away, we could catch up with them by tomorrow." Margot looked so earnest and worried that John's heart melted. Sometimes she reminded him of his younger sister, Jane, whom he missed very much, living as he did at Eltham Palace as tutor to the young royals. He relented.

"Alright, my dear, that is what we are going to have to do. We cannot tell anyone, though, or my job will be in danger, possibly my very life. To lose one royal child is careless, but to lose two would be treason and my head would be on the block." John looked terrified.

"Oh heavens." Margot had not thought of how their actions would affect their beloved tutor's reputation, let alone his safety. Without further ado, she pulled out the map drawn by Charles with the route to Ludlow and gave it to him. John pulled at his short beard as he tried to focus on the map and the enormity of the task ahead.

"Come on then, let's get our things together and go right now. There is no time to lose."

Their plan was to tell the royal household they were going to travel to meet Henry and Jack at the neighbouring castle where they were staying, as the new pony had thrown a shoe. Packing the lightest of bags, both master and student climbed onto two fat ponies before trotting out of the palace and onto the road to London.

That same evening, the sound of horses' hooves was heard once again clattering across the drawbridge at Eltham, although this time there were no royal children present to run out and welcome the new arrival.

Lady Margaret was calling in on her way to Rochester, where she was heading for a spiritual retreat. She wanted to talk to Bishop Fisher, her old friend and confessor about not only prince Henry's future, but about the voices she had been hearing of late (though perhaps not about the ones she had been trying to conjure up). She needed reassurance that what she was planning was morally acceptable, bearing in mind it was Saint Nicholas who had come back toher in her dreams.[20]

An evening with her dear grandchildren en route would be a pleasant way to indulge herself and rest overnight, for Eltham Palace was halfway between London and Rochester. She also wanted to see how Henry was getting on with the mare she had given him. It was most inconvenient to find that only Mary was in residence, being looked after by the matron, as the older children had gone.

"Gone?" The woman's voice could be heard throughout the corridors and all the way into the kitchens. "What do you mean, gone?"

The head guard could only stammer that John Skelton had mentioned their staying at a neighbouring castle.

"Where is William?" the old matriarch demanded. "Surely he has not gone too?"

William, Henry's page, was quickly brought forward. Lady Margaret looked down at the young man, who was quaking before her. How a five-foot woman could look down on a six-foot youth was a wonder, but she did it and William felt compelled to kneel before her to help.

"My lady." He bowed as low as he could, hoping the ground would swallow him.

"Where are my grandchildren?" The question cut like a knife. It did not take long for poor William to admit the children had set off to Ludlow. To deny Lady Margaret the truth was like trying to make water run up a hill.

"William Compton." Lady Margaret spoke like a judge about to condemn a criminal. "It has come to my attention that you owe over one hundred pounds in gambling debts. Is this true?"

William was astounded that this was known by anyone in authority. He was a keen gambler and often lost to Charles when they played in the evenings at court, but her only ever borrowed from this closest friends. "Madam, I have only borrowed –"

"Is. This. True?"

"It is."

Lady Margaret sniffed. "Well, let me strike a bargain with you. Go and find Henry. Bring him back to Eltham. Do not allow him to reach Ludlow Castle. If you cannot find him by the time you get there, you must go and see my agent Nicholas Grope, who is staying at The Bull. Report to him and let him know that the prince and his entourage are coming and he is to 'call it off'. Use these words and no others, and do not remember this conversation once you have passed on the message to Grope. Understand?"

William looked up at her fathomless black eyes and nodded wordlessly.

"Do this and I will pay your debts for you. Fail and you will be brought up before the courts for embezzlement."

"Embezzlement? But ma'am, I am going to repay the loans," William insisted.

"Embezzlement, for which you will be thrown into the debtors' jail for a very long time."

William's jaw dropped, but this was not seen by the diminutive woman, for as soon as she had finished speaking, she swung round, her black silk dress rustling like leaves in a winter's wind, and left the room.

Grope was in The Bull gazing proudly at his book of secrets. The book concealed a nest of drawers that were full of treasured secrets, and it was always locked with the key on a chain around his neck. He would not like Fiddle to get hold of the herbs and potions all neatly labelled inside the small drawers: *Hyoscyamus Niger*, *Papaver Somnif*, *Aconitum Napellus* and *Bryonia Alba* being just some of them. No, these were his special possessions, substances that gave him ultimate control over anyone he chose. It would not do to allow Fiddle to take people's lives into his own hands, other than when given express orders to do so. Fiddle was a weapon, a tool, not a mastermind like Grope.

Grope had been studying the effects of his different poisons for weeks in order to choose the right one for removing the heir to the throne in a flawlessly unsuspected manner. His relationship with the innkeeper's daughter was going well and she had given him a key to an empty room down in the cellars – a cold, damp room with water dripping from the ceiling, possibly from the latrines above, the smell of the place indicated as such. There, he had set up a dozen cheap birdcages and inside each cage was a hapless mouse. None of them looked well; all had a dull glaze over their once shiny black eyes. Some writhed in their straw beds, others did not move at all. Flies hovered around opportunistically, buzzing in anticipation of a corpse from which to suck the juices, for these mice were being poisoned, one by one.

Grope smiled and whistled to himself as he looked in each cage, prodding a few of the more lethargic creatures to see if they were indeed still alive and writing notes in his little black book. He had considered the various symptoms of the different herbs and powders that could be introduced into the food that was served to the prince and had been perfecting the doses by feeding such foods to the mice.

Just as Grope was writing in his book with his small but neat letters, the door opened and he turned around quickly, grabbing his walking stick in defence. Seeing the innkeeper's daughter enter the room, his expression went from one of determined malice to one of lecherous delight.

"Ah, Mirabelle, my pretty one. Have you come to see your Uncle Grope?" His smile was as ugly as his intent, but the silly maid thought this a romantic expression and she giggled. "Oh 'Uncle', I came to bring you a pint of ale and to see if you needed anything."

"You know what I need, you little vixen." Grope's voice went down a pitch as he put down the book and walked over to the girl, grabbing her by her rump and pulling her towards him. He had done this for the first time the day he arrived in Ludlow, fully expecting to be slapped in the face, but instead the woman had thrown herself at him and slobbered wet kisses all over his face. He could not believe his luck.

"Oh, Uncle Grope." She giggled again as she kissed him with a mouth both warm and wet. So inviting, he thought, as he held her warm body against him. Sometimes one's professional duties just had to wait. While she shuddered with abandon, Grope seduced her with urgency and little finesse. If a passer-by noticed the grunting and squealing noises exuding from the grille set in the pavement, they would have thought that the slobbering and giggling was the sound of a pig being slaughtered for the pot, down under The Bull.

After Mirabelle had left, Grope got back to business. Over the last few days, he had been lacing the prince's food with a lesser poison, to weaken his immunity. Grope had also been sending him a 'tonic' in a blue bottle that counteracted the poison. This ensured the prince began to rely on the tonic. He was saving the fact that Prince Arthur was learning to trust the liquid in the blue bottle for his coup de grâce. Being somewhat of an artist – no, he corrected himself, a *great* artist, Grope had chosen Easter Sunday to be the day of the prince's assassination. Prince Arthur, like Christ, was being made a sacrifice for the common good of mankind, or more specifically the Tudors. Grope liked to be specific, for it was more scientificic and he was a scientist, a leading scientist in the art of clandestine murder. Easter was an appropriate date and one Grope secretly commended himself for deciding upon. It was poetry.

Prince Henry was hungry and his backside was sore after a second day in the saddle. He wondered how the Crusaders had managed to ride day after day. Jerusalem was weeks away by horse. They must have had leather behinds by the time they arrived in the Holy Land.

"Charles, when are we going to find somewhere to stay?" Henry's earlier self-confidence was waning without the familiar surroundings of Eltham Palace and all his creature comforts.

"We have accommodation you will love tonight." Charles grinned wryly.

A few miles later, as the open rolling countryside was beginning to close in with more and more trees surrounding them, Charles pulled up at a tiny stone cottage with chickens scratching in the dirt around it, jumped off his horse and knocked on the door. It was such a small cottage it could only have one bedroom, and Henry was alarmed that they might be staying in such a hovel. There were bound to be bugs in the beds; that is, if there were any beds at all.

The door opened slowly and a timid old woman stuck her head out. "What would ye be wanting, my lord?" she asked Charles. "I 'ave little to offer ye and my husband, 'e died a few years back. We've no riches 'ere for ye, me lord, and I pay my taxes, I do."

Charles smiled his most charming smile. "Dear lady," he explained, "I was only hoping to trouble you for a few provisions. We are travellers and need to camp tonight. I need an onion and some carrots – spare me that might go into a hot stew. I will pay you handsomely." With this, he produced a shilling and offered it to the woman, who had not seen so much money since the death of her husband. She looked at the silver shilling again then looked up at Charles and down at the shilling. It was still there in his outstretched hand.

"Wait a minute, sir. I will bring ye some bits and pieces."

She disappeared into the gloom of her cottage and all they could hear was crashing and banging as tins were opened and objects were thrown about inside. After a few minutes, the woman came back out holding a sack full of indeterminate items and handed it to Charles, who had a cursory look inside. He was happy with the transaction and handed over the shilling.

"I thank you, dear lady," he said, taking the old woman's hand and kissing it while looking in her eyes. "You are most kind."

The woman bobbed a curtsy, something she had almost forgotten to do over the decades, but this handsome stranger had awoken old feelings from her youth and a tear came to her eye. "God bless you and your companions, me lord. God bless ye."

Charles said no more but hopped back into the saddle with the sack in one hand and urged Caesar forward.

"Did you say we are camping tonight?" asked Henry. He liked camping, for Master Skelton would take them out to camp in the woods sometimes, but mostly in the summer. It was only March at present and the nights were cold.

"We are entering Woodstock Forest and can make for ourselves a shelter of sorts. I am going to catch a rabbit, and now this kind lady has provided us with the ingredients, we can cook ourselves a fine rabbit stew."

"I love rabbit stew," piped up Jack, as it was one of his favourite treats. "Come on, let's go." He kicked Bottom and trotted ahead.

Henry, not liking to be second, set off quickly to catch up and Charles sighed in relief. One shilling was a better price for a night than what he had paid that morning for all the excesses of the evening before, and the kind woman had popped a bottle of what looked like alcohol into the sack to help him relax at the end of the day. He trotted after the others, and they soon disappeared into the trees.

What none of them had noticed was the black-cloaked youth on a pony who was travelling along the same road, studiously keeping a half-mile behind so as not to be noticed by his quarry.

They had ridden for a good while into the dense coverage of the royal forest before Charles was satisfied that they had found the right spot in a clearing for a campsite. Henry took charge of making them shelter and a fire, while Charles and Jack went to set up some snares Charles had packed in his bag. Both Charles and Jack had spent many a night poaching in the past and they set off, a professional team with nothing other than victory on their minds.

Henry found some dead branches and began setting up a frame to hold the other branches and moss with which he was going to create his shelter. Using strips of inner bark from a nearby elm tree, he tied the corners of the frame together, remembering the special knots Master Skelton had taught him so patiently. He then laid branches at a slope to the back and sides of the shelter, leaving the front open. This was where he was going to build a long, narrow fire. Skelton had taught them to build a fire that was wide, so it kicked more heat towards the full length of the opening of the shelter. He then dug out a small pit inside the shelter, just to clear it of any damp debris, and collected as much dry matter as he could to lay in its stead as a bed on which the three boys could lie. He did not forget to clear the ground between the fire and the shelter and lay a row of stones in between the two areas so no stray sparks could set the ground in between alight. Fire was a good servant but a bad master, Master Skelton always drummed into them.

Henry thought about Master Skelton and wished he was there with him now. John Skelton would have enjoyed this journey. He was a brilliant teacher and Henry admired him even more for having had the foresight to teach him the skills to make a shelter and light a fire. For that was his next task. Fire.

Lighting a fire was simple enough if you constructed the timber in a pyramid shape before collecting birch bark and dry leaves as tinder. Then, all you needed was charcloth, flint and a striker, all of which they had packed. Henry wandered into the woods searching for dry leaves, twigs, bits of lichen he knew would burn and whatever else he could find. Ash trees were always useful, for their wood would burn even if green.

It was difficult in the ever-encroaching darkness to recognize which tree was which, as their leaves were not yet formed, or in some cases even visible. He could make out the last of the catkins and pussy willow that were out. However, as it was getting dark, he could also see strange shapes and shadows that spooked him to the point where he began to wish he had brought his dagger with him. He was just thinking about this when he heard the distinct crack of a twig or branch breaking. "Who's there?" He waited for a reply but was disappointed as none came.

Only a few yards away from the boy picking up sticks in the wood, the shadow monk had made a terrible error, for he trod on a dead branch on the forest floor and it cracked loudly in the otherwise quiet woodland. He seldom made a sound when stalking his prey, but it was almost pitch black at this stage and difficult to see. He heard the boy calling out names, *Charles* and *Jack*. The assassin memorized these names. But for now, he must not be seen, so he used the art of camouflage he had been taught and imagined he was a tree. Tall, straight and silent, nothing of him would move, not a finger. This was how to remain as still as possible and to disappear, merging into his surroundings: in a wood, become a tree; on a mountain, become a rock. He used his imagination and concentrated on his feet becoming the roots, his torso the trunk, his arms the branches and his head the crown of a tree. It worked.

Henry could see nothing but trees all around him. He was beginning to panic. He felt as if he was lost in a crowd of tall, uncaring giants who had no interest in his wellbeing. There were no guards with halberds here to stand between him and any threat; no teacher, no dukes, knights or earls who would lay down their lives to save him. He was alone and he had forgotten his dagger.

"Where are you? Whoever you are, if you stand up and come forward, I will not harm you." He spoke with as much authority as he could muster although his voice quavered. Nothing happened. Nobody revealed themselves. Henry was not sure he was in control of the situation.

It could be an animal, like a deer or a hog or a badger, but it could also be a poacher, a vagrant or, worse, a spirit of some sort, a magical creature or a ghoul. The forest felt claustrophobic in the dark, with branches hanging down as if they were trying to grab him and roots billowing up as if they wanted to trip him up.

Henry was scared but took a deep breath. He held his panic down and forced himself to believe it to be a deer or some other woodland creature. He kept still for a short while longer and soon convinced himself he had imagined the cracking sound. There was no echo from it. There was nothing out there. An owl hooted. This familiar sound made Henry feel more at home and he decided to get back to camp and light that fire.

Moving with as much dignity as possible, just in case he was being watched, Henry picked his way back to the campsite, hoping his friends would be there waiting for him. The shadow monk held his breath as the prince walked straight past him, his hand brushing against the monk's clothes as he passed by. *I am a tree, I am a tree.* It had worked. He was safe from being exposed this time, but he must be more careful in the future.

Henry arrived back at the camp in the pitch dark to find the others were not there. Fumbling around, he returned to preparing the fire. Kneeling, he struck a spark, caught it in the charcloth, which glowed red, and with careful and consistent blowing, he managed to get a flame to light the tinder. Thank goodness for the fire, for now there was light and he could see once again. If it had been an animal, the fire would keep it away. But if it had been a man? Henry searched for his dagger in his pack and held it close.

Soon the fire was roaring brightly, helping to guide the others back from their foraging. They had only caught one small rabbit; however, the old lady had put in enough vegetables and barley to bulk up the stew, and within an hour the food smelled wonderful to the hungry travellers. The woman had also given them a loaf of rough country bread and some dripping. Then there was the bottle of homebrew and Charles opened this while Jack served up the potage. Having taken a large swig, Charles lurched forward, coughing and spitting the drink into the fire. The flames jumped up as they were ignited by the liquid.

"Good God," he spluttered. "That is the strongest brew I have ever drunk."

Charles could feel his throat on fire and his stomach warming up. After a while he passed it to Henry, saying, "You know, it isn't half bad, and if you take just the tiniest sip, it will warm you up."

Henry tentatively wet his lips with the liquid, testing it before he took the daintiest sip. He passed the bottle on to Jack, who knocked it back and choked as a result. But the liquid had made its way down Henry's throat and he giggled. The companions continued to pass the bottle around and, after a while, Henry felt relaxed enough to bring up a subject that had been worrying him.

"Charles, would you help me? I need to do my business and William is not here."

Charles was puzzled. "You can pee against a tree at the edge of the camp."

Henry stood. "You don't understand. It is more than just a watering I need."

Again, Charles was slow. "Then you go out a little further, clear a space and crouch down. Surely you have had a shit in the woods before now?"

Henry cringed at the coarse word. "You should never use that word. It rhymes with 'hit'. That's how I am to refer to it. That's what William tells me."

Tall, straight and silent, nothing of hims would move, not a finger.

Charles grunted. "But I am not William."

"But William was always there to wipe my bottom." Henry had sounded confident at first, but now urgency was creeping into his tone. "I don't know how to do it on my own."

Jack giggled when he saw the expression of horror on Charles's face.

"You want me to wipe your arse?"

"My backside, of course. I always have to have someone clean it for me."

Charles could take no more. He grabbed the bottle and had another swig. "Well, you are not royal right now and it is time you learned to live like a normal human being. Pick up some leaves and wipe yourself with them, and do it well, or you will get sore."

Now it was the prince who looked incredulous. He was about to complain, but the need to go and empty his bowels was too great. "Well, at least keep an eye out for me. I heard something out there earlier, I really think you ought to at least stand on guard."

Henry grudgingly stomped off into the trees, turning to make sure that his companions were keeping an eye out for him. Sure enough, Charles was watching him, although he was still sitting there with no intention of helping with the event. After a few moments Henry was back, whistling to himself, and sat down looking somewhat pleased with his accomplishment. It was proving to be quite an education, travelling without his usual entourage. While they sat together watching the flames, the boys passed the bottle around, Henry becoming a bit braver every time until he felt courageous enough to speak up again.

"You know, you might think me mad, but I am really sure I heard someone in the woods a while back, unless it was a deer."

"I doubt it was a man. Not unless he was after rabbits, like us," Charles reassured him.

"But that would be poaching." Henry sounded indignant.

Jack spoke up this time. "We trapped a rabbit. What do you think we were doing?"

"I do not consider it poaching when we are in a royal forest and I am the King's son. I think that leaves us in a secure position, legally." Henry was feeling a little wobbly.

"My father was caught poaching once when he was a lad," Jack expounded. "He got twenty lashes from the landowner for his troubles. He never told them he was the son of a knight and that, by right, they should have let him go. He did not want to bring his father's name into disrepute."

"That was brave of him," said Henry.

"I think it was stupid of him," said Jack. "Unless he had some leather stitched into his pants."

Sitting on his haunches, so close to the small group of friends, so close he could almost have joined the conversation if he'd had a tongue, was a slightly saddened man-child. Covered in his black cloak and settled for the night, the shadow monk was living up to his name by blending in with the ark shadows. He listened to the companions' tales of family misdemeanours and wondered what it must be like to have a normal life. He would not have cared if he were a prince or a pauper. Money had no value to the monk, for he had never touched it before, never held even a farthing in his calloused hands. The only items he knew how to hold were a knife, a rope, and a bow and arrow. Things which brought death, not happiness. He listened to the stories and a small spark of warmth came into his otherwise frigid heart.

The red-haired lad seemed to be some kind of prince. He could not truly be the King's son, or he would have an entourage of guards and other attendants travelling with him, but he was interesting. He held an air of grace about him and the others, though not fawning over him –

they wouldn't help him with his ablutions – showed a certain deference. As for the others, who were they? The monk did not want to just grab the prince and go, he wanted to follow the companions for a little longer. Then he might hear a few more stories of what real life was like. He waited, as still as a stone, until finally the three boys stumbled into their makeshift bed and fell asleep to the crackling of the warming fire.

Just before he crept away, the monk noticed that the bottle of liquid that the boys had been drinking was not quite finished. Without daring to breathe, he crept up to the bottle and took it. Back in the shadows, he tried a swig, letting it burn his throat and fill his empty stomach and move on to his heart, where that first little bit of warmth had started. Like blowing on a spark, the liquid acted as breath on charcloth, and a flame was lit. One more swig to finish the bottle, which he then carefully replaced. The shadow monk crept off into the night to make a nest for himself in some bracken and sat brooding all night long, thinking about the childhood that he might have had, had the abbot not taken him from his family when he was but a babe.

9

Lady Margaret arrived at Rochester to be greeted by her confessor and friend John Fisher. Fisher was a busy man, for he was head of St John's College and Christ's College, Cambridge, both of which Lady Margaret had founded using her incalculable wealth. He was never too busy, however, to greet his benefactor. He welcomed her with a gracious bow, much diplomacy and the offer of a chair by the fire in his private chambers. He had not seen Lady Margaret for a good while, and nor had he heard her confessions, his primary role, and so he was looking forward to what she might come up with this time as her most reprehensible deed. Lady Margaret was always good at inventing some great sin or other for which she would need a good few 'Hail Marys' to cleanse her soul, even though they both knew her real sins would never be confessed. Fisher was too intelligent to be ignorant of this and too dependent on her wealth to mention it. Instead, they chatted about family and friends, court and Kings, and all sorts of frippery before Lady Margaret felt ready to begin her debate on when it was acceptable to 'play God', as it were.

"Well, Your Grace, there is but one God and no man on earth has the right to take his place. However, there are times when it feels God is guiding us to act on his behalf. We both know about Joan of Arc, and we both know you have been visited in the past by Saint Nicholas, for he spoke to you when you were a child. The saints hardly visit one on a whim, do they? It must be that they have been sent to pass on a message or an instruction from a Higher Authority."

Without knowing what specific matter the woman was referring to, Fisher felt he had answered her question to the best of his abilities. He knew well that Lady Margaret was looking for assurance that her political decisions were acceptable to God, for she had a mortal fear of ending up in Hell for some reason known only to herself. It was not his duty to pry into her soul. It was his duty to support her.

The old woman hesitated before asking the question she really wanted answering. "Tell me, Fisher, what if it is not a saint but a deceased relative who has spoken to me or might speak to me? What if they are telling me what to do? Is that a sign of God?"

Fisher was a little surprised by this question. A saint was a run-of-the-mill way of communicating with the Almighty, but he had yet to hear of a deceased relative being the conduit. "Would the said relative be perhaps on the path to sainthood? That would give him or her the authority to ask you to do God's work." Sometimes he thought himself quite brilliant at coming up with workable solutions. Lady Margaret's face lit up in a way he had never yet observed. *Goodness*, he thought, *I might be in the presence of something quite remarkable here.*

"I would say your Hail Marys tonight in homage to his giving you such favour by these visitations. If your instructions work and God's will is done, we might have the makings of a saint in you after all, dear Margaret."

Only Bishop Fisher knew of Lady Margaret's childhood dreams of becoming a saint. She had once confessed this to him and he had entertained the idea that there was no pride in such yearnings, just the rather charming wishes of a devout and religious child. He had forgiven her these youthful aspirations decades ago.

Feeling uplifted by the direction of this conversation, Lady Margaret bit into the delicious, sweet buns her confessor had offered her along with some mulled wine. She was beginning to warm up and felt quite at home. She led the conversation like a pretty dance, stepping lightly over the area of dark deeds she was in the process of developing, painting a picture of the lighter side of royal life, like a skipping stone flying swiftly over dark waters. Fisher, like the good friend he was, kept her spirits high, defending her right to act on God's behalf had she been given directions from him through her prayers, and she felt much better than she had for weeks.

Once settled in her own private chambers by one of the many servants of God who worked at the cathedral, Lady Margaret was given a letter sent by Nicholas Grope. He informed her he had some interesting information regarding a certain York figurehead who appeared to have risen from the dead to lead a new uprising that was brewing in the capital city. The man claimed he was in possession of documentation that might be of interest to her. She could tell by the tone of this letter that Grope was up to his tricks again and was looking for money. She would send their usual go-between, the rather unpleasant Fiddle, to tell Grope to name his price.

At the same time, a Mrs Lovell of Knightrider Street, London, had received an anonymous letter telling her that her harbouring of a certain 'aristocrat' had come to the attention of several nefarious agents who might be loyal to the King, and that if her party were interested in this information being diverted, they were to reply by return by giving the messenger waiting outside a specified amount of money.

Grope was a happy man. Fiddle had gone back to London and on to Rochester to deliver his letters, and was waiting for a reply from each of the persons to whom he had written. This meant Prince Arthur was being given a few days' respite from his poisoning regime, but it would be worth it if the money came good. An uprising would be more valuable to the two henchmen than the death of a prince. Grope was even wondering if he should approach the King to see if there was more money to be had in saving the prince than there was in killing him. However, double-crossing Lady Margaret would leave him open to the old witch double-crossing him in return. She could do this by revealing his part in the deaths of young Edward V and his little brother, Richard, who had been kept in the Tower all those years ago. But then, Grope was now unsure as to whether Edward was even dead; it seemed not, miraculously. He was going to have to sit down with Fiddle and get to the bottom of this mystery. Had Fiddle cheated on his partner, he wondered. His instructions had been simple enough: smuggle the boys out of the Tower, murder them and dispose of their bodies. Even Fiddle could manage this simple task without bungling it, or so Grope had thought until now.

Back to thinking of his current project, Grope knew the prince had to go. He absentmindedly scratched his arse as he mused upon the fate of princes and how vulnerable they were, like young fawns hiding in the woods. Vulnerable, that is, until they were crowned, when, like powerful stags with massive antlers, they became dangerous to approach and ruled their domain with a ruthless force to be reckoned with.

※

One young prince who remained unnoticed by Nicholas Grope was waking up to find himself in strange, wooded surroundings, cold and damp, with the strong smell of a spent fire smoking at his feet. He noticed the telltale odour of strong alcohol on his breath and on that of his companions. His head was all fuzzy.

"If this is how you feel each morning you wake up after a drink, I cannot understand why you bother." From now on he would leave strong brews alone, or at least treat them with suspicion.

"That's funny," said Charles, who was up and poking at the fire to see if he could get it going. "The bottle is empty. I am sure we didn't drink it all last night. Did you finish it off, Henry?"

Henry chuckled. "Not likely. Jack might have, which could be why he is still snoring."

Sure enough, Jack was still happily asleep. Charles continued to try to get the fire going while Henry realised that he needed to relieve himself. He felt nervous, remembering the sound he had heard the night before in the dark, yet he did not dare ask Charles for his help anymore, so he stepped boldly, but not without trepidation, towards the trees at the edge of the clearing. *It surely must have been a deer or some other animal*, he thought.

But then, just as he was relieving himself against a tree trunk, Henry notices the grass and earth in front of it had been pressed down as if someone had been sitting there. Looking more closely, Henry could swear there was the imprint of feet. He searched the area some more and noticed more footprints. He ran back to the campsite to warn Charles. "I think someone was here last night after all. Look." He took Charles back to the footprints to show him.

Charles shrugged. "But didn't you walk around looking for timber last night?"

"I did. Yes, I suppose so."

Henry kept his thoughts to himself. Although he could not prove it, he was certain he had walked in the other direction, and he wore boots, whereas these were footprints without shoes. Still unsettled, Henry decided it was time to wear the dagger his father had given him for Christmas rather than just carry it in his bag. He took it out of the cloth in which he had so carefully wrapped it and fixed the dagger's sheath onto his belt, feeling much safer with a weapon near at hand. Standing with his feet apart as if ready for action, Henry practised pulling out the dagger as if he were defending himself from an attacker. He did this a couple of times, swiping at the empty air to make sure the sheath was fixed in the right place on his left side. It felt reassuring and he decided he would not go anywhere unarmed from now on.

"If you are going to wear that dagger, you had better be able to use it," Charles warned.

Henry answered by pirouetting on the ball of his foot in a full circle while bending his knees. He ended this move bent with his dagger at knee level.

"Oh, that's right - I had forgotten that move." Charles laughed and Henry, feeling that he had won a point, smiled as he fitted his dagger into its sheath.

Jack awoke, and the three friends drank some hot water flavoured with pine needles from a nearby tree, giving it a refreshing taste. A slice of cheese, some dried beef and the last of the bread and dripping was their breakfast. After clearing the camp and putting out the fire very thoroughly, something John Skelton always insisted upon, the boys tacked up their mounts and climbed into the saddle. Henry was learning how to saddle his own pony, for Charles was not going to have Jack doing everything, and Henry was beginning to enjoy the work. He had never thought much about how one tacked up a horse. Normally, they came ready fitted. As the weather was cold and damp, they wanted to get some miles under their belts, so the boys trotted off into the forest without further ado. Despite the cold, the birds were singing with an optimism that was catching, and before long the boys were laughing as they rode along without a care in the world. The leaves on the trees were budding, the moss and ferns on the ground were green, life appeared to be ready to burst forth with optimism and the mood was infectious. Though it was a misty morning, a feeling of warmth pervaded the air, and the sun would no doubt soon burn its way through the haze. Henry quickly forgot the mysterious sounds of the night before and he and his companions were feeling good with food in their stomachs and a day of adventure ahead. What they did not expect was to come across an adventure so early in the morning.

Much to the three travellers' surprise, as they came around a corner where they had not been able to see the road ahead, they were confronted by a band of what could only be described as scoundrels, rogues, opportunists, men of the road. Four of them. Four big, scary-looking men. The boys were outnumbered. The leader of these men had his sword drawn, and as the three companions reined in their horses, the group of vagabonds surrounded them on all sides.

"Well, what 'ave we got 'ere?" taunted the leader, a gruff-looking man with a stubbled face, thick eyebrows that met in the middle and a gravelly voice to fit. "It looks like we might 'ave found ourselves some breakfast pickings."

Charles drew his sword. "Get back, I warn you. We mean you no harm. Just be on your way and there will be no trouble." He sounded calm, though his sword hand trembled.

"No trouble, 'e says?" scoffed the leader. "Well, that's mighty noble of you, young sir, but you are wrong there, for you are in trouble deep. Unless, that is, you want to 'and over your purse to see your way out of trouble?" He leered at Charles. "There is a toll to be paid if ye's want to travel safely through these 'ere woods."

"What are you talking about, man?" demanded Henry. "These are my father's woods…"

But before he could say anything more, Charles, taking advantage of Henry having distracted the ringleader, kicked Caesar and pulled the reins at the same time, and the mighty horse reared up and struck a blow to the leader's head with its flailing front feet. Down the man went like a stone. At the same time, Charles took a swipe at the head of the next man and opened a gash in his cheek. Henry was left speechless, which was probably a good thing, but then, seeing his chance, he pulled out his dagger and charged at the third man.

"For God and for England!" he cried as he stabbed the man straight in the gut. The thief was so surprised at being attacked by a ten-year-old that he had not raised his own sword. He doubled up in pain and Henry, seeing he was now at an advantage, hammered the man's head with the butt of his dagger. The man lost his balance and fell to the ground, where he looked dazed.

"Come on," cheered Jack, "two down and two to go!" He backed Bottom toward the fallen man and pulled the mule's ear. Bottom swiftly kicked the thief in the stomach. The man collapsed further, crying out in pain.

Hearing this, the man with the wounded face kicked his pony and ran away, mud flying from the beast's hooves in its haste. The fourth man was now in desperate combat with Charles, who really was an excellent swordsman. The thief had little fear, yet he did not stand a chance. Charles was a champion tournament knight, and within a few moments, he had dealt a fatal blow and sent the man tumbling to the ground, the wound to the back of his neck so deep that his head lay at a disturbingly crooked angle.

"By God, Charles," exclaimed the young prince. "You were incredible."

Charles was panting like a dog, eyes ablaze and his hands shaking with battle fever. All he could see for a short while was red, but he soon calmed down and patted his destrier. "He is the most wonderful beast. Well done, Caesar, well done, boy."

The leader of the bandits groaned. He was not dead, and nor was the man whom Henry had stabbed, but they were both wounded. The other, however, was as dead as could possibly be.

"We had better bury him," stated Henry.

"Nah, just leave him to his friends to bury." Jack was not feeling very charitable.

"I agree with Jack. Let's tie them up and leave them here to rot." Charles spat blood from his mouth. He must have bitten his tongue when Caesar reared up.

Henry prevailed. "I will not have a dead man's soul on my conscience," he told his friends. "If I am to lead the Church when I am an adult, I must act like a man of God even now. I cannot let this rogue die without a prayer over him to save his soul."

The wounded men were made to dig a shallow grave and put the dead thief in it, then cover his body with stones so no wild animals could scavenge it in the night. Afterwards they were bound and gagged while Henry pulled out the small cross he had packed and held it over the grave as he said a prayer. The two wounded thieves watched on, wondering who this child might be who had so much gravitas at such a young age. He was no normal child; they were sure of that.

The three companions turned back to the road and walked on, with the thieves thrown onto the back of the mule led by Jack, who sat doubled up on Virtue with Henry. Charles rode behind, to keep an eye out for the missing thief in case he tried to rescue his friends, but he was nowhere to be seen.

"We will have to take them to the next village and hand them over to whoever is in charge," Henry said with an unquestioned authority that was beginning to emerge naturally. At his command, when they arrived at the village of Woodleys, the brigands were deposited with the local bailiff before the travellers made their excuses and moved on.

"I hope they get a few days in the stocks at least," laughed Jack, who was feeling both relieved and exhilarated by their recent exploits. "Henry, you were really brave. You pierced that man like he was a piece of meat."

"Well, he was, really. It was hard to pull my dagger back out of him and I thought I would lose it for a moment." Henry's stomach turned at the thought, the taste of bile rising in his mouth. He had carefully washed from his dagger all traces of blood after they handed over the outlaws. "Charles was the real hero," he added.

"Actually, it was Caesar who won the day," ventured Charles, for he was incredibly proud of his horse. He had never fought in anger before and was taken aback that he had caught the battle fever so quickly. His hands were still shaking involuntarily, for he was in shock. He would have killed all four men rather than let them harm Henry. However, in truth, this was his first kill and it bothered him that he had taken the life of a man who might have been someone's husband or father.

"Henry, I am humbled by the way you conducted yourself today," he went on. "You were right to insist we buried the dead, and you were right to make us take those rogues to the authorities. May they rot in prison. Imagine if it had been a small group of women out riding in the woods. Anything could have happened to them."

Henry, who had taken control of the moral and legal decisions without any drama, took the compliment with nonchalant grace. The others were beginning to see qualities in him they had not noticed before.

<hr />

Things were not going so well for Margot and John Skelton. They had ridden their fat little ponies hard the first day and managed to reach Oxford. There, they stayed with an academic friend of John's who willingly put them up for the night, despite wondering at John's choice of companion, bearing in mind her age. Understanding it might look odd, a forty-year-old man travelling with a twelve-year-old girl, John quickly explained Margot was his student and that he had been entrusted with getting her safely to her brother's house. He omitted to mention who her brother might be. His old friend, knowing that John was a devout clergyman, relaxed and put them up in the guest rooms of his house. He was married to a woman who had not yet conceived, so their large house could accommodate the travellers in comfort.

The next morning, not long after they had set off from the beautiful city of Oxford, with its ornately carved university buildings and stone houses, Margot's pony cast a shoe and they had to walk until they found a blacksmith in a small vilage. There, they happened across a great big farrier with a mop of curly hair and laughing blue eyes who homed in on every woman who passed by. John Skelton kept Margot close by his side while the man showed her how the new shoe was heated up in the hot fire and pummelled into shape on the anvil before it was set against the sole of the hoof. The burning smell of the hoof tissue, the sound of the bellows and the roaring fire were all intriguing to the girl, who had never watched a horse being shod before. Her eyes were lit by the flames and the farrier enjoyed showing off his sculptural muscles as his bare arm smote the malleable shoe on the anvil and sparks flew into the air. John did not like the effect all this was having on the young girl. He could feel her trembling as she leaned against him. John tried to lead Margot away, but she was transfixed. Next, the blacksmith slid his hands suggestively down the back leg of the pony and, as it lifted its foot in response, he artfully slipped its hoof in between his thighs. With his back to the pony, he held the shoe to the base of the animal's foot. That burning, acrid, singeing aroma filled the air yet again. For all his faults, the man was a good farrier, John admitted to himself, and he was as captivated as Margot watching the shoe being nailed onto the foot.

Paying the blacksmith, the schoolteacher thanked him and asked him if there was anywhere he and his charge might eat some lunch. "There is a small inn on the crossroads about half a mile ahead. You will not be overcharged there," was his answer.

John Skelton thanked the man and ushered Margot back out of the smithy and onto her pony. Within minutes they were back on their way.

"You didn't like that man, did you?" Margot was puzzled. The man had done no harm and they had never met him before. She looked at John, wondering why.

"I have no complaints, for he did the job well enough. I just didn't like the way he was looking at you, that's all." John felt it was appropriate to mention the man was not a natural gentleman and that young ladies like herself should be wary of men who had wandering eyes as he did.

"Wandering eyes?"

"Oh, never mind." Skelton just did not know how to explain this matter to the innocent girl. He kicked his pony in the ribs and it trotted ahead, with Margot doing her best to catch up with him.

Lunch was a good idea. They could talk about it then, or not at all. Margot was not interested anyway. She had liked the man who had shod her pony for her: he had been nice and friendly, and he had the largest arms she had ever seen, like Hercules of legend, but now he was forgotten.

That was the problem, according to John. He had noted the princess was on the verge of womanhood and she was noticing the opposite sex in a new way. With innocent inquisitiveness at first, but that could lead to all sorts of dangerous liaisons. He might be here to protect her right now, but in the future, when she was sent to Scotland all on her own, she would be at the mercy of the Scots and her own growing sensuality. He shuddered at the thought and decided he would avoid blacksmiths from now on when Margot was around.

They found the inn and went inside for a well-earned meal. It was only after they walked inside and allowed their eyes to become accustomed to the light in the dimly lit room that they saw a familiar figure sitting at the counter, looking at them with a satisfied grin on his face. William Compton, Henry's page, was enjoying a tankard of ale with his eyes on the door, waiting for someone. It turned out they were who he was waiting for.

"Good day and well met, William," John began. "What on earth brings you to this neck of the woods?" He was most certainly puzzled.

William shrugged his shoulders and smiled. "Well, you, of course. I could hardly leave you and young Margot here to ride around the countryside on your own without protection. I am here, at your service, along with a horse, saddle and my sword, for what it is worth."

Margot was delighted. "Oh William," she gushed. "Thank you so much. How very thoughtful of you. We did not think of troubling you to come along with us as our guard, but we are delighted, for dear Master Skelton could not be expected to fight if there was any trouble."

John was decidedly put out by this comment. "What do you

mean? I am perfectly able to defend you, Margot, if the need arose. I might not be accustomed to wielding a sword, but I can throw a punch as well as the best of them. I spent my youth fighting, you know."

William stood up and put his arm around John in a friendly manner. "I am sure you could beat me any day, Master Skelton, but with a sword in my hand, you would not be able to get close enough to me to use your fists. Trust me, I am here to defend you both and to be of whatever service I may. I understand the nature of your journey and want to help."

There was no more to it other than to allow William to join up with them. "I suppose three heads are better than two," John admitted, perhaps even a little relieved he was no longer solely responsible for the safety of his royal ward.

They found themselves a table in a quiet corner and settled down to a bite of lunch while they whispered conspiratorially about their mission: to find and keep young Prince Henry safe and to rescue Prince Arthur if it was true that he was in danger. This was a tall order for a poetic page, a chalk-covered schoolteacher and a young princess, or rather, queen, but they were excited about the possibility of their succeeding.

Back in London, at Westminster Abbey, the King was sitting in the Star Chamber, with Bishop Warham and his other councillors around the table discussing the news. It was being reported by various spies that the new pretender who styled himself as Edward V had definitely disappeared and that both Look loyalists and those of the King were looking for him in vain. An 'Edward V' had appeared in a house in London and was being readied to front a new uprising. The problem was the pretender had cleverly slipped their spies' net and now nobody knew where he was.

"He cannot have gone far," said the King, annoyed as he had been looking forward to a break from ruling the country over Easter and going down to Ludlow. "Surely one of our men can track him down."

"We thought this might be possible, but the scent has gone cold," answered Warham. "My spies had solid proof of the man being groomed: he has receipts for new clothes. In addition, he has been seen at various secret meetings over the last few months, talking of his childhood and his life before the Tower. Nothing that could not be made up by anyone who was given the correct information. Nothing *genuine*. But he has convinced quite a few Yorkists into action. And now he has walked off the face of the earth."

"Could he have gone abroad, or to Ireland?" was one suggestion.

"No, Warbeck went there and since we executed him, the Irish are still smarting, as we also beheaded some of their own."

"Perhaps he lost his nerve and ran away?" was another, which sounded more plausible.

The fact was, nobody knew what had happened and why the supposed uprising had simply dissolved.

"Well, all we can do is keep our spies out there and hope we pick up the trail somewhere," suggested the bishop.

"That suits me," stated the King. "Send me a messenger if you need me, but in the meantime I am going to take a few days off over Easter and visit my son and his wife at Ludlow."

Sitting by the River Thames, Ned was thinking about his situation. Although he had forgotten much of his royal past, the knock on the head with the candlestick had jolted his memory and now he knew that he was indeed the man they claimed he was. When the political people had first questioned Ned about his earliest recollections, he had pushed out any earlier memories on purpose.

But since he had been concussed, a flood of sorts had entered his head. Days at court as a toddler, laughing at the jesters who played so skilfully with skittles. Moments with his big, old, bearded father, sitting on his knee and playing with the ruby ring on his finger, pushing it round and round while his father said to him, "When you are King one day, this ring will be yours." Sitting quietly with his mother, who was crying so sadly upon his father's death. Even hating living in the cold basement of Westminster Abbey when they were seeking sanctuary with his brothers and sisters, all locked up without anywhere to play. Oh yes, he remembered it all now, as clear as day. But there was no way he was going to admit this to anyone, not even Emma. No. Ned had decided he was going to play dumb until they left him alone. Then, he and Emma would escape. Up the river. Mother River would look after them.

Ned remembered the stories his mother used to tell him when they were in sanctuary about the river goddess who was their grandmother. That was why his uncle was called Earl Rivers. Ned remembered it all. He felt the river was in his blood, in his soul, and it would take him back. The river goddess would welcome him and Emma if only they gave themselves up to her like he had the night that strange man, Thady, must have given him a second chance by lowering him carefully into the water and pushing his wasted body towards the shore. Ned remembered the finality of that moment, when he thought he was going to drown. Instead he heard the serene song of the river goddess as she enveloped him in her arms and carried him to the shore, gently lying him on the muddy surface for his new father to find, giving him his new life.

10

Unseen, unheard, unloved by anyone, the shadow monk looked on from the sidelines, deep in contemplation. He had just witnessed two children and a young man fight against four woodland thieves. Not only had they fought together, but the young boy called Henry had shown extraordinary compassion towards his enemy's broken body. The shadow monk had never thought of caring for the remains of his victims. He might cut off their head and hands to prevent them from being recognised, or throw their chopped-up remains to swine for breakfast, but to bury them with a prayer? This generosity of spirit had raised questions in his mind. He rode on, thinking about the effect this strange boy was having on him. He tried to imagine what sort of life he could have, were he not an assassin – some other life, whatever it might be.

Prince Henry was not impressed by anything. He was feeling saddle-sore and hungry, and longed to reach the next place where they were planning to stay the night.

"Are we nearly there yet?" he whined.

Charles was exasperated, for it was the fifth time he had heard this question. "If you ask me that again, we will stop right here and sleep on the ground!"

Henry looked peevish. "I am sorry, Charles, but I am tired."

"And I am starving," piped up Jack, his stomach rumbling loudly.

Charles had had enough. With an ill-humoured nudge to the flanks of his horse, he took off up the road, leaving the two hungry boys to catch up with him.

It was not long before they all pulled up in a village called Enstone, the horses covered in mud and sweat. There, they found an old stone building with a rickety sign swinging above the door: the River Crossing, with the sound of laughter coming from within. It looked so welcoming, with light shining through the windows and smoke billowing out from the chimneys above, that Henry was ready to jump off his pony and run inside. Charles, however, was quicker than him, and before Henry could make his move, Charles dismounted and handed him his horse.

"Here you go, Robert," he said. "Walk him around for five minutes to allow him to cool down, then find him a stable and feed him his supper. Oh, and don't forget to rub him down with some clean straw. I don't want him covered in cold sweat. You might even ask for a rug for him tonight. It will be cold later."

Turning his back on the prince, Charles walked through the welcoming door of the inn.

Henry gawped at the doorway with his mouth open.

Jack continued the charade. "Come on 'Bob', you are going to have to get used to it someday. The sooner we get going, the sooner we can go inside."

"Bob?" Henry glared at him.

"Get used to it."

Jack took Virtue and Bottom before walking off towards what looked like some stables. Henry was about to follow him when a middle-aged knight rode up to him on an old horse. Jumping off cleanly with an energetic vault, he handed the reins of his horse to Henry and said, "Rub him down and feed him some oats, boy, and I will give you a farthing."

"Excuse me, but you can feed your own horse," retorted the indignant prince.

Jack had caught this moment from the corner of his eye and he hastily ran back to take the knight's horse from him, kicking Henry in the shin at the same time. "Forgive him, please, sir. He is a truculent imp, the son of an important knight but left with his mother too long. I do apologize, and *you do too*, Jack!"

Henry's shin was stinging with pain. He bit his lip, for he understood he had acted in a dangerously confrontational manner, bringing unwanted attention to himself. "My lord, forgive me, I will do as you ask. Please forgive my impertinence, but it has been a long day and I am both tired and wanting in manners."

The knight looked bemused. First, he had been insulted and now this odd creature had apologised. Then he noticed a curl of Henry's red hair that had fallen from under his cap. He regarded the petulant child before him.

"Ah, I see you have some Celtic blood in you, young man. Your topping gives you away. I would be fearful of such a man as you, were you ten years older. I accept your apology and will say no more. Make sure you look after my horse well, mind you. I expect you know how to do so, for that is a fine creature you are holding. No man would leave such a good horse in the hands of an imbecile." The knight looked covetously at Caesar. "Is your master inside?"

This was a rhetorical question, for the knight's interest in the fine destrier left him disinterested in anything more, andhe walked off.

On entering the inn, the knight looked around him. It was a typical low-ceilinged room with oak beams and an open fire with a large cooking pot on a crane, simmering away. People sat around tables drinking tankards of ale, or if of a more refined level of society, sipping wine.

Charles looked up and noted the newcomer. He was sitting at a table close to the welcoming fire and was holding a goblet of spiced wine. He recognized this was a man of quality and thought he had found some good company with which to pass away the evening. Charles was sick of listening to the complaints of his childish companions at this stage. As soon as the knight saw him, Charles smiled and spoke with confidence.

"Well met, good sire. You look as if you need a warm cup of wine. Come, join me here by the fire if you wish. It is a cold enough evening."

The knight had no further need for persuasion, for he guessed this road-weary gentleman was the owner of the fine creature he had just spotted. Introducing himself, he sat opposite Charles while a serving maid came and brought him a mulled wine. They were soon in deep conversation about the fineries of horse-breeding, for the knight had already mentioned his interest in Caesar.

"That is the best-looking horse I have seen in a while.
Where did you find him?"

Charles explained how he had recently started his career in jousting and that, with his winnings he had gone looking for the best horse money could buy. As he was talking, in through the door came two tired, hungry boys. Seeing Charles had settled down for the evening with the man he had insulted only a short while ago, Henry decided it was best if he and Jack went to sit at their own table. Charles saw them do so but said nothing.

The knight told Charles he had fought in several wars on the Continent, and they found they had much in common. He was keen to play a round of cards with Charles, who was never one to shy away from an opportunity to earn some money. Although Charles had yet to fight in a war, he had just killed his first man and a distraction was what he needed to rid him of the haunted feeling he was suffering at the enormity of what he had just done. The knight had slaughtered many foes in his past yet still had a smile on his face. Killing was a knight's duty and Charles was on the verge of knighthood; he needed to get used to it.

Charles had generously ordered some food and drink for the boys, leaving them to their own devices. Henry could hardly complain, and in truth did not want the knight to tell Charles of his recent outburst, so he and Jack tucked into their food as they watched the flames of the fire from a far corner in the room, dancing in a hypnotic manner. Once they had eaten and drunk their fill, there was not much else to do than to ask the landlord where they were to sleep that night, fully expecting to be sent out to the stables. Surprisingly, the man led them down a long, dark corridor to a room with two narrow beds in it. Charles had been generous. The boys asked where Charles would be sleeping and were told he had a private chamber next door.

Inside their room there was a bedside table with a lit candle, and a table with a bowl and a ewer of water. After a quick wash, as only young boys can get away with, they stripped down to their underclothes and gratefully climbed into their narrow beds, enjoying the sensation of soft sheets, so welcome after the last few days of sleeping rough.

"Goodnight, Henry." Jack could tell Henry was out of sorts after the run-in with the knight. "Don't mind men like him. You have to remember that without all the trappings, you just don't look like a prince anymore."

If that was meant to cheer Henry up, it had not worked. "I was not thinking about him," he replied haughtily, although he had been. "I was wondering if Charles was ever going to go to bed early for once. He always gets drunk and makes a fool of himself."

⁂

Outside, in the shadows, wrapped up in a cloak that was as black as its surroundings, was the near invisible form of the shadow monk. He was watching to see which room the boys were going to sleep in. He was wondering if he could climb into their room in the night, cover his prey's face with a handkerchief covered in a liquid that would render him unconscious within seconds, and carry him away without his friend awakening. It would only work if he put the liquid-soaked kerchief over both boys in case the other one awoke. He was not sure he wanted to waste so much of his precious potion in this manner and so he considered his options. He wondered if he should even kidnap the boy at all, but if he did not take him back with him, the monk would be punished. This was never fun and could go on for weeks. No, that was not an option, so he dithered, something he had never done before.

It must have been the wind that woke Henry up. It was the middle of the night and all was quiet but for some object banging against the wall of the inn. He had heard a sound just now, which was what had awoken him, like someone trying to flip the window catch. The candle had burned low and the flame was dancing in a draught. Henry moved the candle, for he did not want to lose the only light in the room.

As he was doing so, Henry thought he caught a movement outside the window in the corner of his eye. He froze and waited. Nothing.

Back in his bed, Henry sat for a while, wondering if he was imagining things again. Last night he had heard someone in the woods and in the morning he had seen footprints. Now he was sure he had seen someone outside his window. He was convinced someone was following him.

The banging stopped outside, although the wind had not died down at all. Blowing out the candle, Henry cautiously crept up to the window and peeped outside. He could see nothing but shadow upon shadow and they all looked like the outline of a person in a cloak. Here, there and everywhere. How foolish of him. There was nobody there.

Henry felt his way in the dark back to his bed and crawled under the covers. He lay there thinking about home and his bedchamber with its warm fire glowing and William always sleeping on a cot at the end of his bed. William, who had been his page ever since Henry was born, a constant figure in his life. Henry had never known a life without this kind and gentle man being there for him. He had never felt scared when William was around; even when he snored after a night out with Charles, Henry knew he would wake up and protect him were there an intruder.

Thinking of William made Henry feel homesick. For the first time since they had set out on this journey, he began to think about the seriousness of his actions. He had left a safe and happy home in order to travel through dark and dangerous countryside with only a young trainee knight and a friend.

His father would be furious with him if ever he found out what they were doing and for once he would have every right to be. Henry now understood that for a prince he was particularly irresponsible. As the second son of the King and the only 'spare heir,' for him to go gallivanting around England without a proper escort of guards was unbelievably stupid. Henry began to doubt himself and what they were doing. Anything could happen to them. The inn could burn down and they could all be killed without anyone knowing it was he and not 'Robert' who had died in the fire.

As he lay with the covers up to his nose, thinking about his situation, Henry looked back over to the window and saw, without a doubt, a face peering in. Henry wanted to grab his dagger, but it was out of reach. The window was locked, for sure, as he had made certain of this before he went to bed. But the man might have managed to unhook the latch. That must have been the sound he had heard when he first awoke.

"Jack, Jack!" he whispered. Jack groaned. "Jack, wake up but don't move. There is someone looking in through the window."

"What?" Jack sat bolt upright and knocked the candle onto the floor. "Where? Who?"

The face disappeared in a flash.

"You fool, you scared him away!" Henry exclaimed. He jumped out of bed, ran to the window and opened it, shouting, "Come back! Who do you think you are? I can see you!"

It was pointless, for the figure had gone.

"What's going on?" asked a bleary-eyed Jack, still fumbling around for the candle on the floor.

Henry came back and sat on his bed as he started to dress, pulling on his tunic. "There is someone following us; I just saw him looking in through the window. I think he was spying on us last night in the woods. I saw his footprints, but Charles didn't believe me."

Jack rubbed his eyes and yawned. "Well, there is not much we can do about it now, Henry, so go back to bed."

"I am going to go out and look for him." Henry was up again and about to rush out through the door, but Jack pointed out that this was not advisable, for the main doors of the inn would be locked. If he got up and walked about in the middle of the night, he might bring attention to himself.

The boys agreed to take turns on guard for the rest of the night. Henry took the first watch, for he was wide awake. He rummaged around in his backpack until he found the flint and strike and, using some charcloth, was able to light the candle once more. Blowing out the charcloth created a lot of smoke and the two children started coughing and then laughing. It helped to break the tension in the air and soon Henry was more relaxed, sitting on the bed, while Jack lay curled up under his covers. Before long Jack was gently snoring.

At what must have been about two in the morning, Henry heard the staggering steps of someone coming in from the parlour and crashing into a bed next door. Charles, most likely. He would be sleeping soundly for a good while, so there was no chance of their setting off at a reasonable hour in the morning. Henry wondered if he had chosen the right guardian after all. Charles was a nice enough chap, but that was all he was. A nice chap who drank, gambled and chased women.

As he sat on his bed thinking about Charles, while keeping an eye on the window, the door from the parlour reopened and he heard someone tiptoeing in soft shoes or even stockings, coming down the hallway. Pulled out of his reverie, Henry grabbed his dagger and unsheathed it. Jumping off the bed, he faced the door, ready to confront his pursuer. Whoever this man was, he would soon be on his knees with a dagger through his heart.

The footsteps came closer and then stopped. Henry felt the sweat on his palms and hoped the dagger would not slip when he thrust it forwards into the man's chest. But then there was a knock on a door that was not his, and the sound of that door opening and closing. He listened. There was the muffled sound of talking, then giggling, before he realised a woman had just crept into the room next door to spend the rest of the night with Charles. Honestly, the man was incorrigible.

Jack awoke the next morning and realized he had slept through the rest of the night undisturbed. He sat up to ask why Henry had not woken him up to take his turn as lookout, but soon saw why: Henry was sound asleep himself, still leaning against the wall, a dagger in his hand. Well, had there been a spy outside, he would not have seen much, just two children sleeping. Jack wondered if Henry was not just a little paranoid.

Jack started to dress, and his movements awoke Henry. Within a short time, they were both up and out looking for food in the parlour. The fire from last night had burned itself out; the aroma of smoke and stale alcohol filled the room. A maidservant was sweeping out the embers of the fire into a metal bucket and a young boy was carrying in more timber with which to revive the fire. A wonderful smell of fresh bread came from the kitchen beyond, and Henry asked if he and Jack could have some breakfast.

"Wait there and I'll bring ye something to eat. Your master said to give you some gruel and for you to feed the animals then ready them for the journey, for he is to be woken up at ten with a good meal." The girl smiled at the two boys, poured them both a mug of light ale and went next door to sort out their breakfast.

"Gruel?" Jack hated the stuff. "I would rather starve," he muttered, so Henry decided to order something a little better. He followed the maid into the kitchen and politely asked if they could have some ham and eggs instead.

"Will your master pay for such a fine breakfast?" she asked. "Of course he will," Henry replied convincingly.

Within a few minutes the two boys were tucking into a royal breakfast.

Later, as they were still waiting on Charles, Henry suggested Jack go and pack up the bags in their room while he readied the horses.

"I would like to do the animals myself this morning. Just to see if I can."

Jack was impressed that Henry felt confident enough to prepare the horses on his own, so he agreed to pack their bags and went back to the room.

Now he was alone, Henry decided to walk around to outside the bedroom window to see if he could find any evidence of their stalker last night. He stayed close to the edge of the building, checking before he came around each corner to see that there was nobody in sight. Finally, he was standing outside the bedroom window where, sure enough, there were footprints, just as he had seen them in the woods. Turning around to go and find Jack, to show him the prints, he just caught sight of a figure standing behind him before someone threw a sack over his head and lifted him up into the air, his legs kicking wildly.

"Let me go!" Henry screamed as he pummelled his fists into his assailant's body. "Put me down. You do not know who you are dealing with!" was all he could say. But his efforts were without any success, for even as he struggled, Henry was thrown over the back of a pony and tied down, and the pony lead away with him on its back like a sack of turnips.

"Put me do-o-o-o-w-n! Let me go-o-o-o-o-o!" It was impossible to be coherent while bouncing on the back of the animal, so he kicked and wriggled to free himself instead.

Jack, meanwhile, had packed the bags and carried them out into the stables, only to find Virtue had gone and Henry too. Running outside and looking around desperately, Jack thought he could see someone in the distance, disappearing down the road on a pony and leading another pony with a sack of something on its back. Something wriggling.

He ran into the inn and down the corridor to where Charles was sleeping, but the door was locked and there was no answer despite his banging hard. Not daring to lose any more time, Jack ran back to the stables and pulled Caesar out of his stall. Throwing a bridle on the beast and himself onto his bare back, Jack kicked the animal's sides and held on for dear life.

"Come on, Caesar, you must go like the wind, for we have to save Henry," he said, urging the beast into a canter. Caesar was massive, much bigger than any horse Jack had ever ridden, but there was no point taking Bottom if he was to catch up with whoever had kidnapped Henry. Jack had not believed Henry earlier and now he would repent at leisure. He would have to catch up and rescue his friend. Caesar understood the urgency of Jack's voice and galloped off with the boy desperately hanging on to his mane.

About half a mile up the road, Jack had a change of mind and asked Caesar to stop. The destrier was the most incredible animal. He almost read Jack's mind and had pulled up before any pressure was put on the reins. Jack, even in this moment of emergency, had the sense to realise he was riding an extremely well-bred and well-trained horse.

"Thanks, friend," he muttered, half to Caesar and half to Charles for having trained the creature so well. "We have to find a way of overtaking them without being seen." Again, it was as if Caesar understood, and without further instruction, the horse took off in an arc, down a side-track and into the woods. The main road would eventually swing in through the trees and on toward Oxford, for the kidnapper was heading back in the direction they had come the evening before. Jack recognized the woodland.

"Good thinking, Caesar," Jack encouraged his companion. They were in this together and two heads were better than one. Having been brought up on Bottom, Jack recognised a smart animal when he rode one and Caesar was smart. Leaning down right against the horse's neck, Jack loosened the reins and allowed the horse to find his own way through the trees. If he looked up, there was a chance a branch would knock him clean off the animal's back. Jack just held on and prayed.

"We have to find a place where we can ambush them," he said, sharing his thoughts with Caesar at this stage, for his trust in him was complete. "Find me a good spot, old boy."

Within minutes, the horse slowed down. Jack had no idea if this was the right place to stage an ambush, or if Henry would be brought down this track, but he had to trust in fate. So, he jumped down, falling onto his back, for he had forgotten how high off the ground he was when on Caesar's back, and hitting his head hard against a rock.

"God's teeth!"

There was no time to lose. He took the long reins off the bridle so he had something to tie the man up with, then shooed Caesar away. Jack climbed a tree over the country road and waited. With a better view of his surroundings, he looked about to see if there was any place from which he could make his attack. There was not. However, he noted Caesar had kindly only gone a few yards and was waiting quietly for him to call him back. What a horse. Soon there came the sound of hooves thudding against the dirt road, at least two animals trotting briskly, and a lot of muffled sounds, like someone coughing in a distant room. Then, as luck would have it, the very duo he had been waiting for came into view: a cloaked man on a horse, leading Virtue, who had what could only be Henry thrown over his back. Henry's legs were flailing around and he was coughing and spluttering, probably as the old grain sack and the husks inside were hindering his breathing.

"You will hang for this," he heard Henry shout. The otherman said not a word. Jack got ready and then, just as the two ponies passed beneath him, he readied himself and jumped.

The shadow monk was taken totally by surprise. He struggled, but with the weight on his back he lost his balance and the two youths fell to the ground.

"Got you, you bastard," shouted Jack as he picked up the stone that had wounded him earlier and used it as a weapon, smashing it down onto the cloaked man's head. There was a chilling, crushing thud and then silence.

Jack had not meant to be so violent. He sat back, panting. The pony on which the monk had been riding, frightened by the sudden pounce from above, had bolted, with Virtue following it in flight with a terrible nauseous sound coming from the sack on her back.

Damn, thought Jack as he stood up and brushed himself down. "Caesar, where are you?" Nothing. Jack whistled, like he did with Bottom, and within seconds Caesar came crashing through the trees. Jack patted him, climbed onto a dead log and jumped on his back, without the reins this time. "Go, Caesar," he shouted, "catch them!"

Again, he had hardly needed to ask, for Caesar was on the chase already. Clinging on for dear life, Jack soon overtook the two bolting ponies, and once they had a leader, they slowed down. Caesar slowed to a trot and then a walk, and finally swung around to nip any pony that tried to pass him. They saw his teeth and stopped abruptly.

Jack jumped down and ran to Henry. "Are you alright?" he asked as he hurriedly worked to untie the bundle that was his friend and help him down.

"Jack, oh Jack, my saviour," cried Henry. "I thought I was going to die. I can hardly breathe – please, get me out of here."

Within a few minutes Henry was removed from the sack and put back on his feet. He bent double with pain. It had been a rough ride on his stomach, especially after a hearty breakfast, some of which had come back up and was now all over his face.

Jack could not help but laugh. "You do look awful, and you smell even worse." Jack was nothing but truthful here.

"I am lucky to be alive. Where is the scoundrel who kidnapped me?"

"I think I might have already done for him, but let's go back and see who he was." Jack was convinced he had cracked the man's skull.

After Henry had taken a moment to straighten out his clothes and rub his face as clean as he could with a handkerchief Jack had lent him (he made it clear he did not want it back), the two boys collected the reins of the frightened ponies and rode back to where they had left the body, Jack riding Caesar once more, for he had rather taken to the beast. The monk was not dead, but he was in a bad way. He was unconscious, and the boys decided they would rather not be around when he awoke. They agreed the best thing to do was to make him comfortable but tie him to a tree, where he could remain until a passer-by let him loose. They did not want to steal his pony, or his belongings, and so they left them there beside him. Whoever untied him would decide what to do with the man.

As they pushed him up against a tree trunk, the monk's hood fell away. The boys looked in wonder at his exposed features. He was only a few years older than the boys, fifteen years at the most. But that was not what fascinated them. What struck them both was that the monk looked like an older version of Jack.

"He could almost be your brother," Henry ventured. "Well, he's not quite as good-looking as me, but I see your point." Jack felt almost sorry for the boy now that he felt something in common with him, even if only his looks.

Having checked that his head was not bleeding too much, they tied up the unconscious would-be kidnapper with the rope he had used on Henry, and left him there with his pony tethered nearby.

"Come on," urged Henry, for Jack was standing looking at the youth questioningly. "We have to go and wake Charles. I hope he's sobered up by now."

Jack fitted the reins back onto the bridle and hopped back onto Caesar, and they made their way back to the inn to find Charles before heading on their way.

Jack was puzzled. "I cannot think why he tried to kidnap you."

Henry felt only chagrin towards the boy. "I don't care. All I want is to get away from here before he tries to find me again. That was the worst thing that has ever happened to me. I hope he rots in Hell."

11

Charles woke up bemused. Looking around, he saw he was in a strange room and that his bedsheets were all a-tumble. Remembering the two boys, he knocked on the wall behind the bed to awaken them, but they did not respond. Pulling himself out of bed, he stretched a long stretch of contentment and donned his breeches before walking barefoot along the corridor to knock on their bedroom door. Again, there was no reply, so he turned the handle and peered inside. The room was empty. There were no bags or any sign his companions had stayed there all other than two unmade beds. At first, Charles thought he had the wrong room, but looking up the length of the corridor, he saw there were no other bedrooms off it. Confused, Charles went to look for the boys in the parlour.

There, washing down the countertop, was the pretty girl he had been flirting with the night before. She looked up at him and smiled on seeing him only half dressed. Her skin glowed and flushed a little with embarrassment. Her smile brought back sweet memories, but it also brought other images flooding into his mind. Bad ones, for he had spent the evening gambling with the knight, and he had lost everything. His money, his sword and, worse than that, finally his horse, Caesar. He had made one last mad bet to win back his purse and sword and had gambled his horse away. His pride and joy.

Oh God, forgive me, he thought to himself and then he asked the girl where his friends were.

"I don't rightly know," was all she could say. "One minute they were here and then they were gone, horses and all. They left in a terrible hurry."

"Horses? What do you mean?" Charles was in a panic. Where was Caesar? Surely they had not taken *him*. He rushed out into the stable to find his worst nightmare. Caesar was gone, although the ugly mule was still there.

He raced back into the parlour. "Where did they go?"

He could not believe it: they had left without him. At first he was furious, but that feeling was soon overtaken by concern for Henry. It was unlike him to rush off and leave – unless he was in trouble. However, Charles's first problem was that the knight would be coming to collect his debt in the form of the horse. He had taken the money and sword last night, leaving Charles enough to pay the inn for the three companions' stay. The knight was going to think Charles had hidden Caesar rather than hand him over. This would be a most unknightly thing to do and would be a massive stain on Charles's character.

Hastily paying the bill, including two large breakfasts that left him penniless, Charles stole a last kiss from the girl and gave her a note explaining the circumstances to hand to the knight when he arrived, then he set off to find the boys. The only transport left for him was the mule. So, with a groan of disbelief, he tacked up the odd-looking creature and set off at a brisk trot up the road towards Worcester with his long legs dangling either side of its body.

By the time the boys had returned from their adventure, Charles was gone, instead there stood a very angry knight with his arms folded, tapping his foot impatiently as they rode up to him.

"I don't know what game you're up to, but you boys have caused your master a lot of distress this morning. What on earth were you doing, taking off on the destrier? Are you mad? He could have killed you, and anyway, he belongs to me now."

The knight showed the two boys a note saying, much to their surprise, that Charles had sold the horse to him. Henry noticed Charles's signature was shaky and erratic as if he had been drinking heavily and he gave the knight a calculating glare.

"It appears your documents are in order, sire, so I must hand this fine horse over to you," he began. "But I question what state my master was in that he signed the documents so poorly and I wonder if this acquisition would hold firm in a court of law."

He looked at the knight accusingly, without flinching. The knight, unused to being confronted by a mere boy, a lowly squire, was unnerved by the air of authority the boy exuded and began to stammer an excuse.

"I am not interested in your excuses," Henry continued, "for I have far more urgent matters to deal with. Take the horse but remember this: I never forget the face of someone who has crossed me."

Standing there with his feet apart and his hands on his hips, Henry looked quite imposing, despite his tender years. The knight hastily took possession of Caesar and rode away, Caesar throwing his head around in trepidation as he was led away from the people he thought of as his own.

After begging some food from the girl and asking her to tell Charles if he came back that they were heading towards Worcester where they would look out for him, they set off up the road, two boys on one pony. It was lucky that Virtue was a strong mountain cob. They reckoned they were at least an hour behind Charles and sharing a pony it would take all day to catch up with him.

William was the first to find the shadow monk, for he was acting as the advance guard while Margot rode in the middle and Master Skelton kept a lookout from behind. They were walking under some trees along a woodland road, coming up to the village of Enstone, when William came across the sorry figure of the monk tied up against a tree.

"What have we got here?" he asked and jumped down to release the cords that tied the hands of the bedraggled heap that was the shadow monk.

"Aggha whawa," was all the monk could say.

John was the next to dismount and he quickly weighed up the situation. The stranger had been attacked and hit on the head. But that was not why he had trouble talking. As John examined his patient, he realized the monk could not speak, for he had no tongue. Peering into his mouth, he assessed that it had been removed a long time ago. Skelton was appalled.

"Can you hear me?" he asked the monk, wondering if he also deaf, but the monk nodded in the affirmative.

"Can you write?" he further enquired. The monk shook his head. No.

"Maybe he can do sign language?" suggested Margot, to which the monk nodded again.

"What use is that to us?" pointed out William. "We don't know it."

Skelton contradicted him. "Well, actually I do. I had a friend at Oxford who taught me the basics."

He signed to the monk and the monk carefully signed back that he understood, but he could also understand normal speech.

The first thing John Skelton wanted to know was if he was alright. Looking at the wound on the monk's head, he decided it was a hard knock, but nothing fatal.

Had he fallen from a horse? *Yes.* Was he attacked? *Yes.*

Through questions and answers, the monk indicated he had been jumped upon by a thief who was hiding in the tree above the road. The thief had hit him on the head with a rock, tied him up and then run off, leaving him unconscious and helpless.

"Did you come across a young knight travelling with two young squires along the road?"

At this, the monk looked startled, and his eyes shot from one companion to the other.

No, he signed. *I have met no one on the road but the thief.* He could say this truthfully.

Skelton then handed the monk some wine to quench his thirst and some bread to eat and offered that he could travel with them for safety, but the monk signalled that he was travelling in the other direction. He thanked the trio for rescuing him by bowing with his hands together as if in prayer and, climbing unsteadily onto his pony, waved farewell and disappeared in the opposite direction, swaying somewhat in the saddle as he went.

William watched the monk leave. "He was an odd fellow," he pondered out loud. "He claimed to have been robbed, yet his pony and his bags were all intact. What could they have taken from him, and why did they tie him up if he were unconscious when they left?"

Margot looked puzzled. "He looked strangely familiar to me."

"Did you notice how he looked when we asked if he had seen the others?" William had not missed the obvious discomfort of the monk when asked this question.

"He was lying, I am sure." Skelton hated liars. "We are better rid of him. I wonder where he is going?"

"Heading to Oxford or London, I'd guess," William ventured.

This was probable, but as it was, truthfully, none of their business, they remounted and went on their way. They did not need to get distracted.

William was proving to be somewhat of a boon, for he had keen eyes and an observant mind. When they were riding through the royal hunting woods of Woodstock, it was William who had spotted a recent campfire and shelter built a few yards off the beaten track in a clearing. Skelton had immediately recognized the work of one of his pupils.

"Henry has done this. I taught him these knots," he told them proudly.

Skelton had always thought it might come in handy for the prince at some point in his life to know how to survive in the woods, like his father, the King had once done as a teenager running from the York King Edward IV's troops,[21] although he had hardly expected it to be so soon. The good news was that they were behind Henry and his friends, and if they rode hard, they would catch up with the others by the end of the day, or the next at the very latest.

At Westminster, the Queen was in a reflective mood as she thought about her upcoming holiday at Ludlow. Opening a chest kept under the window in her privy chamber, she began to sort out some small smocks and shawls she had saved from when her children were babies.

"Do you remember little Lizzie and dear Edmund wearing this?" she asked her lady-in-waiting.

"Oh madam, yes. You made that dress Prince Henry, didn't you?"

"I think so, but it fitted Mary too. It would still be useful for Arthur's child. I love the tiny Tudor roses we embroidered."

Both Lizzie and Edmund had died in infancy and were now in the arms of God. But even knowing this was not enough to prevent the Queen's heart from hurting. Everyone knew only around half of all children born survived childhood to become parents themselves,[22] but it never made the pain of losing a child more bearable. Every woman of her age had lost at least one child, maybe more. Rich or poor, it did not make any difference. God was indifferent to riches when it came to taking these little ones as his angels. Oh, but goodness, how it hurt, for a mother loved her child, be he ugly or beautiful, sick or healthy, and even the frailest of babies whose life slipped away took a little piece of their mother's heart with them. A piece that left a wound that never healed.

As the Queen reflected on her losses, a tear found its way from her sad blue eyes and rolled down her cheek. She wiped it away. It would not do for anyone to see her weak like this. She turned away from the woman sitting with her. Now Arthur and Katherine were married, her days of having babies were over, thank God, and she would never again have to go through the terrible trauma of giving birth to a child or, worse, of losing one. The marriage of her son had given her a gift nobody else had considered: of no longer having to give birth to another heir.[23]

The King was delighted with himself. He had ended the lastest council meeting by ordering his councillors and their spies to track down the new pretender. He insisted they bring the man to the Tower to quell any rebellion amongst the population, using force if need be. A stint in the Tower of London usually took the wind out of any imposter's sails, a job in the palace kitchens or, if that did not do the job, the axe.[24]

The King was back in his private chamber, attended to by the ever-faithful Denys.

"Denys, I am going to visit Arthur and Katherine this Easter. Would you like to come to Ludlow with us or would you like a few days with your family?" he asked.

Denys seldom saw his family and so jumped at the chance. "That w-would be wonderful, sir – to see my w-wife, that is." He hoped the King would not change his mind.

"That's settled then. I expect you to pack for me, however, with some hunting clothes and some clothes for the evenings. I would like to think that with a younger generation in attendance, we might have an evening or two of dancing, so put in some lighter clothes for me – ones you know will flatter my figure."

He would enjoy taking his wife away for a few nights of intimacy. Perhaps they could even try for another son. Elizabeth was only thirty-six and had great child-bearing hips. To think he and his wife could sire a son at Ludlow while Arthur was siring their grandson on Katherine was quite titillating.

"You had better put in some of my finer nightwear too, for I will be visiting my wife at night. Know what I mean, Denys?" The King was feeling skittish these days.

Lady Margaret was back at Westminster, ensconced in her private chamber with the door locked again. The curtains were half drawn, and the fire had been banked up with sea coal and had the glow of a blacksmith's forge. She had already taken off one robe, but the instructions in her book of ancient lore had insisted on a hot fire. She wondered if she could open the window, but then the aroma of the mandrake wouldbe diluted by any fresh air.

Looking at her side table, the old woman smiled a crooked smile of satisfaction. There was the dark mirror, highly polished, surrounded by a ring of chalk with a pointed star drawn from side to side to side. There was the candle, made of the finest beeswax, and there was the phial of blood. Not chicken's blood like last time, but human blood, she had been assured. She had added to this some hair clipped from the head of a newborn babe and the fingernails of a dead priest. It was lucky Grope had told her where one could procure such things, for they were not easy to find in a palace. Sometimes it was necessary to don her maidservant's cloak and to walk through the streets of London to the poorer part of town south of the river. In between bear-baiting arenas and drinking dens whose windows were adorned with prostitutes, there were narrow streets filled with debris and stray dogs where you could enter the most disreputable of shops; if you could call them shops, that is.

The shop Grope had told Lady Margaret about was run by an old woman with warts all over her face, a disgusting creature of an indeterminate age, a real old hag. Strangely, that was exactly the opinion the old hag had concerning Lady Margaret. Despite their natural inclination to criticize each other's appearance, money talks, and when Lady Margaret asked for the hair of a newborn babe and the fingernails of a dead priest, all the old hag had asked was, did she want just the clippings, or in fact the entire nails, pulled from the fingers of the man as he died?

This detail threw the otherwise hubristic woman. "I... I am... not quite sure. Is there a difference?"

"Well, madam, it's all down to quality of product. Quality is everything, you know." The shopkeeper warmed to the subject, rubbing her hands together. "You see, if a man is clipping his nails before he dies, he is probably in an absent-minded frame of mind, so the potency of the product is questionable. I mean, he might be thinking of his dinner, or the itch on his nose... or... women... But if his fingernails are being pulled out while he is being held down by villains using pliers, well, then he is concentrating on the pain; it makes sense."

Lady Margaret was feeling uncomfortable. "And the quality of infant's hair?" she dared to ask.

"Oh, you don't want to know. But I can give you the best, the *very* best..."

Now shuddering, Lady Margaret prevented her mind from wandering. Quality comes from concentration. She had learned that from the old hag, if nothing else, as she scurried out of the shop holding her goods. The goods had included fresh blood 'of the highest quality'. Lady Margaret had refrained from asking where it had come from.

"Stop it!" she told herself. "Concentrate on your work."

So far, Lady Margaret had failed to contact her dead husband by dabbling in the dark arts. It could not be that difficult, she kept trying to convince herself as she opened the page of the old book which normally sat on the bookshelf behind her favourite chair. The book had not mentioned the nails or the hair, but Lady Margaret had heard tell that these were potent additives. Out of sheer desperation she had added them, fixing the stopper back in the bottle to prevent the blood from spilling as she gave the concoction a shake.

Once the dried herbs were burning and the candle lit, the hopeful apprentice sorcerer, for that was what she was becoming, reverently took the bundle out of its black box and laid it ceremoniously on the glass. She then mumbled the same charm as before three times before she broke down.

"Edmund, oh Edmund. Come to me. Come to me, my darling. I have need of your wisdom and your assurance. Am I doing the right thing? You did not show me a sign. Are you displeased with me?"

At this point, her hands now shaking, Lady Margaret removed the stopper from the phial and poured some of the fortified top-quality human blood onto the bundle that contained the remains of her good husband's heart. It landed on the dried blood from the last attempt, now black. The red blood dripped over the black and then ran down the sides of the bundle and onto the dark glass. Lady Margaret was sure she heard a hissing sound, although it might have come from the fire. Her heart was beating fast; she clasped her breast to try to control it. It was horribly uncomfortable, and she began to pant like a sick dog.

"Edmund, Edmund. Where are you? I can't feel you! Have you abandoned me? Oh, woe is me! I am the most wretched —"

At this point, the old woman felt the most searing pain in her chest. It was as if her heart was being constricted and yet torn apart at the same time. "Oh darling, I love…!" she gasped and then dropped to the floor like a deer with an arrow shot true to its chest, her old heart pitter-pattering like that of the infant whose blood she had just unwittingly used.

Charles was riding along on the ambling mule, wondering how he had got into this mess. Whatever had made him think he could safely escort a couple of immature infants around England as if they were sensible adults like himself?

"Tell me, Bottom, did you see the boys take Caesar? Why on earth did they do that, I wonder?"

Bottom almost seemed to listen. He had a habit of moving his two ears independently of each other. They turned this way and that as if they were hearing everything at once, including himself. Bottom let off a long fart as he walked along that sounded like a bugle playing the same note againand again.

"I see. Well, that was most illuminating of you." Charles laughed and patted the mule on his shoulder. He was not a bad creature at all really.

Talking aloud, Charles continued to question why the boys had run off with Caesar. Although it still angered him whenever he first thought about it, he kept coming back to the fact that Henry would never intentionally steal anything, let alone his friend's most treasured destrier, meaning they had done so as a last resort and were therefore in deep trouble. He needed to find them.

Charles urged Bottom onwards. Once one got used to his mulish stride, the creature was really quite comfortable. Charles was as surprised about this as he was about the fact that he was riding him. He truly hoped he did not meet anyone who knew him, and on thinking that, he pulled the wide-brimmed hat he normally only wore when it was raining, further down over his head.

Henry and Jack were also wondering about friendship. Their friendship with Charles was up for debate, and he was getting something of a verbal bashing in the open courtroom of the country air as the two lads walked along on Virtue. They could go a bit faster from time to time in order to catch up with Charles, but they did not want to wear the pony out either, so when they walked, they talked.

"I wish I had asked William to accompany us instead of Charles," Henry admitted. His earlier musings about his loyal page were still fresh in his mind. "He is good with a sword, you know. And he would look the part." William was older than Charles by a few years. "He also would not be distracted by women and gambling," Henry added.

"I am not so sure about that." Jack mused truthfully. "William loves losing at cards and he writes poems about women all the time. I know because I read some of them."

"Really?" Henry was surprised and wondered who it was that William wrote poems about. He changed the subject.

"I am still mystified as to who that monk was and why he kidnapped me," he went on. "There is no way he could have known my identity, and he never said a word or mentioned my name or asked for a ransom or anything."

Jack laughed. "Well, we didn't really give him time to talk, did we? Perhaps we should have brought him with us, as our prisoner?"

"A fat lot of good that would have done – we can hardly look after ourselves, let alone a mad monk, if he was a monk. Perhaps I was just a random target. Or perhaps it was a case of mistaken identity and he was really after *you*."

The boys were so deep in discussion at this point that they did not notice they had come to a fork in the track. There stood an ancient milestone, partially hidden in the spring grass, pointing in two directions, left to Worcester and right to a place called Birmingham. As they ambled along, oblivious, Virtue was left to take whichever road she saw fit. Being an animal, she took the one to the right, as that appeared to have more grass along the edge of the road, a common-sense decision for the pony.

It was an hour after this that the boys decided to stop and have a bite to eat. They pulled up and dismounted, taking the bit out of the pony's mouth so she felt she had been happily rewarded for choosing the right path.

"I cannot see any sign of Bottom's hoof marks along here," Jack pointed out.

Henry was not convinced they would see them among all the other marks from horses, cattle and sheep that would regularly be taken along this ancient path. "It doesn't mean he wasn't here."

"True, but it doesn't mean that he was, either."

The journey was beginning to feel like a holiday, and with some food to eat and a sip of ale, they could go for a good while yet and hopefully reach Worcester before dark. Only then would they put their minds to finding Charles.

"What do we do if we don't find him?" asked Jack.

"I have the ring Margot gave me, and she said I was to sell it if need be. I think we would get a fair price. I would rather pawn it and have the chance of buying it back on our way home." Henry felt grateful that Margot had been so generous in giving him the ring and he would like to repay her by not losing it.

"That's settled then," said Jack. "We aim to reach Worcester in a couple of hours' time, then we can look for a place to stay. There is bound to be an abbey somewhere."

Henry agreed. "You know, we were safe at that abbey, den of iniquity that it was, for there was no one spying on us there. I only saw that man the night in the woods and last night. We might be safer if we sleep at night within the confines of an abbey's walls."

Their friendship for Charles was up for debate as they rode along sharing a pony.

"But I don't think we are going to find Charles in an abbey. I would say an inn is more his style. Let's look in any inn we see, but head for the abbey afterwards, once we have pawned the ring," Jack suggested.

Henry thought Jack had a better head on him than he had ever noticed before. Generally, Jack was a clown, to be enjoyed at every turn. But here, he was speaking sense. They would check the inns for Charles but sleep within the safety of a religious establishment. Henry did not want to have to sleep outside again, for he certainly wanted to avoid being kidnapped again, ever.

⁂

The monk was desolate. He did not dare go back to the abbey and yet he had nowhere else to go. He meandered aimlessly on his pony, the bump on his head throbbing and making his thoughts muddled. Eventually, he decided the best course of action was to turn around and keep following the boys he was meant to spy on. He might learn information of great importance, with which he could safely return to his superiors. Failing that, perhaps he could be of use to the travellers themselves and they might let him into their group. He did not *have* to go back to the abbey. It was the only life he had ever known, but the boy Henry had opened his mind, giving him a glimpse of a better life, a better world. And there was something about the boy that intrigued him.

Turning his pony around, the shadow monk made up his mind: he would catch up with the three companions and trail them from a safe distance. Urging his pony into an easy canter, the monk felt a thrill of excitement. He was going against all his training, for he was using his initiative to benefit himself and not his master.

12

The two associates, sticklike Fiddle and rotund Grope, sat together in a dark corner of The Bull, habitually merging with the shadows that surrounded them. They had a few empty tankards in front of them and were now drinking brandy. Grope needed to discover from Fiddle what had happened the night he was sent to murder the two princes in the Tower. Up until now the man had refused to go into any detail as to how he had disposed of the young bodies. This was unusual as Fiddle normally enjoyed revealing his ingenuity when on such missions.

Grope got straight to the point. He could see no benefit in beating around the bush. "So tell me, dear Fiddle, what did happen that night? Your instructions were plain and simple. Was there a problem, a change of plan?"

Fiddle fidgeted nervously, sitting on his hands as he looked this way and that and stretched his neck till it clicked in either direction, playing for time.

"Well, Grope, it went like this. It was a beautiful evening when I took the first child, Richard, out of the Tower. It all went to plan, but I could see no point in killing the younger prince, for he was just a babe and no threat to anyone. You had only told me to 'get rid of' the boys, and I did. I arranged to have a childless couple meet me further down the river and I sold him to them. They came all the way from Flanders to buy him, so I knew they were keen. They paid me seven pounds and took him away."[25]

"Seven *pounds?*" Grope was impressed that Fiddle had made such a bargain all on his own. That meant Fiddle owed him three pounds and ten shillings. Grope would make sure this discrepancy was evened up next time they made any money. He kept quiet about this for the moment, though, for he did not want to stop the flow of talk. "Go on."

Fiddle felt pleased with himself for having proved to Grope that he was as good a businessman as he. He was about to continue his tale when he stopped.

"I want you to tell me where Edward V is living now, for that is our bargain and we like to keep a bargain, don't we?" He peered at his partner.

"Well, I have to admit, that is the problem, dear Fiddle." Grope stared into his drink. "He was living at Knightrider Street, but they have moved him now. He was injured somehow and lost his memory. A nasty bump on the head, I have been told. They have sent him away to convalesce. But I don't think he is far. I have been told he is in hiding disguised as a mudlark."

"A mudlark?" Fiddle knew where to look for him now.

"Come on, Mr Fiddle, do tell me what you did to young Edward V?" Grope had always had his suspicions about Fiddle's sexual orientation.

"It was midnight when I left the Tower with the second prince. I had drugged him, like you said - he was hardly breathing. It was a full moon, and once I had crossed the river, the moon came out from behind a cloud. I opened the laundry box to throw the body of the prince in the river with a stone around his neck. But you know, Mr Grope, I couldn't do it. He looked so innocent. He was ill, close enough to death, for he was all skin and bone with teeth missing. He was barely breathing. I lifted him up and he was as light as a feather. *He won't need a stone around his neck*, I thought to myself, *I will just lay him in the water and the tide will take him away. I will let him float away.* So that is what I did. I watched him, and he looked like a little angel on his way to Heaven, just like an angel."

Grope leant back and adjusted his position. "An angel, well how about that? A bleeding angel!" He slapped his hands down on the table.

"No, he wasn't bleeding. I did him no harm." Fiddle's eyes were bulging. "I would never harm a child, you know that. I just laid him in the water."

"Ah, now that explains things somewhat, does it not, dear Fiddle? That must be how he floated away. Someone must have rescued him, perhaps even a mudlark. He was taken in by the river rats."

Fiddle did not like this term for the people who had to work along the shoreline.

"It isn't their fault that they have so little, Grope. They work hard like anyone else for their living." He felt protective of the poorer population of London, having come from similar circumstances himself.

"Well, we will not fall out over a few miserable rat folks, will we?"

"No, not at all, Grope; we are good friends. But I wish you would not use the word 'rat' in such a way. Shall we have another round?"

"Well, Fiddle, perhaps you ought to go and talk to your 'river' friends and see if you can't track down our little angel, eh?" Grope leant forward and his pungent breath, spiced with the odour of a rotting tooth, filled Fiddle's nostrils so that he had to lean backwards.

"I will, I will," he promised. "Perhaps we can help him get away, protect him. That would be a fine thing, would it not?"

"For sure it would, dear boy." The expression on Grope's face told another story.

The King and Queen had packed lightly, with only four cartloads of possessions, including some barrels of exceptionally good wine, a few chests of baby clothes, their everyday wardrobe and the possessions of the courtiers who had been chosen to come with them. The men-at-arms who were to accompany the royal couple were carrying their own possessions, with an oxcart between them to bring their weapons and armour. For travelling, they wore their leather jerkins and shiny helmets. With their halberds gleaming in the sun on this crisp afternoon, they looked particularly fine, their streamers and banners flying in a gentle breeze.

At the head of this band of yeomen-of-the-guards was a chisel-faced man called Captain Cripps, a thirty-five-year-old professional soldier who loved to lead his men, for he knew they were a handsome sight, with their matching uniforms and their well-groomed horses. With dark hair and deep brown eyes, he had a proud expression, topped off with a beautifully manicured moustache that was as straight as the rest of his attire. The King looked upon him and chuckled to himself, for he had handpicked these men and Cripps was the figurehead that the King admired most of all.

"Ready, Cripps?" he demanded, mainly just to show he was the head of this smart collection of soldiers and Captain Cripps answerable to his every whim.

"Ready, sir!" Cripps snapped to attention, a pristine toy soldier in front of his toy army.

The King was excited. He had chosen to ride for some of the way, but to ride beside the Queen, who was settled in a carriage. He enjoyed the feeling of spring in the air, the sound of the birds in the trees. Horses loved riding in convoy, he reflected to himself. As did men. The sound of the harnesses clinking and the snorting of the many animals around him only added to the sound the people of the city made as they either watched on in wonder at the sight of their monarch orslunk away to get on with their lives.

✿

Ned was on the run.

It was old Jim, a mudlark, who had found him all those years ago on the riverbank. Lying unconscious, his torn shirt splayed around him like the wings of an angel. Jim had taken him in and brought him up as his own. An old bachelor, he had enjoyed the company of the young boy, who had soon learnt how to scurge the riverbank for treasure alongside his new father.

It was hard saying goodbye to old Jim, but it had to be done. Old Jim had wished him luck and given him his blessing when Ned knelt before him just moments before. Ned had then donned his long leather boots and slipped over the side of the wharf. Now he was walking along the shoreline, below the waterline of the rising tide so as not to leave any footprints. He was walking along towards where Emma lived with her parents, for they had agreed to meet up and take flight that night. He was so excited. They would make their way out west, where he knew of a tiny cabin by the river where he used to play as a child. He was sure that the King's son would not mind him living in the tiny cabin. It was hardly fit for swine, and nobody else would want it. They would move there and start a new life. Ned knew he could make a living as a fisherman there, and Emma would be his wife, for they would marry along the way. All he had to do was wait for Emma outside the back door of her house and carry her bags for her. His few belongings were already packed in the bows of the small riverboat he had procured, which was hidden upstream among the other boats tied up against the wharf.

Ned knocked on the door of the house and waited. Nobody came, so he knocked again, harder this time. The door opened and a very flushed woman appeared. It was Emma's mother. Her hair was all in a mess and her eyes were red.

"What has happened?" asked Ned, for there was obviously something wrong.

"Oh Ned, those people came and took Emma away," she sobbed.

Ned's blood went cold. "Who has dared touch my Emma?" he demanded.

"I don't know. But they told me to explain that you would know where she was. It was those people you went to stay with, I think."

Ned needed no more information. He told Emma's mother not to worry, but not to open the door to anyone other than him. Then he walked all the way to Knightrider Street, all six miles, with his boots covered in mud, though they dried off soon enough and the rubbing of the leather made a swishing sound as he strode along. He let nothing get in his way. His face was red with fury, and his determined stance made everyone turn to look at the resolute man as he marched up the street. He had no idea what a stir he caused: he looked like a warrior heading off to war.

"Who is that man? Doesn't he look familiar?" said one bystander.

"He does; he is a good-looking fellow. He looks like old King Edward."

"Edward IV? By God, he could be his son, he is so like him."

"That's Edward of York," people began to cry as they saw him coming up the street.

Soon men dropped whatever they were doing and fell in behind him – stoic Yorkists at first, but soon the crowd was so large that other men fell into line out of magnetic force. They could not help but join the march. Women began to shout and throw flowers at the men as they strode past, soon walking in step with each other, turning a mob into an army. Rats ran ahead of the crowd, unsure of what was happening, scuttling into gutters and squealing with fear. Children chased the rats with sticks, the sound of their laughter adding to the cacophony as they cracked their sticks down onto the cobbled street to crush a rat skull or two.

"To Edward, to York!" came the cry from the crowd, which was growing all the time. Ned said not a word, but marched straight on.

The King and his company were coming along in the opposite direction.

"What is all that noise?" asked the Queen.

"I have no idea," replied her husband, but he did not like it.

Soon they found out a mob was coming their way. Children were running ahead of the impromptu army, shouting, "Here he comes, here he comes!"

"Here *who* comes?" asked the King, who was beginning to feel very vulnerable. He looked around for assurance, but his companions were none the wiser. When the crowd came around the corner, led by a single man wearing the oddest boots ever, the King realized there was trouble brewing. Turning to the captain of his guards, he shouted, "Cripps, do something! Get us out of here!"

"Sire, turn around. We will protect you and the Queen," the brave captain replied.

Within seconds he had arranged his men in a circle around the courtiers and their King, who pulled his horse around, its legs stumbling in confusion. The royal procession turned on its heels and rode back to the palace with as much decorum as they could muster, notwithstanding the fact they were running away from an angry mob.

There was an uproar from the crowd, who were now running riot and throwing their hats in the air. They were not sure if they had won a victory, but whatever had just happened felt good. Ned purposefully blocked out the commotion around him and kept on marching until he reached Knightrider Street and banged on the door of number thirteen.

A man opened the door. "Ah, Ned, we thought you might come calling. We have been talking to your friend Emma and she has accepted it is time for you to reach for your true destiny and—"

Ned knocked him out cold with one blow. The crowd cheered, but Ned did not hear them. He stepped over the fallen body of the man and walked into the hallway of the house he knew so well. Pushing the door into the living room, he demanded to know where Emma was.

"Now look here, Edward," another man began, trying to reason with him, but within seconds, he was on the floor as well.

Edward left the living room and went into the kitchen.

There was his loved one, sitting at a table, crying.

"Ned, oh Ned!" She jumped up upon seeing him enter the room and ran to him, despite the mistress of the house trying to prevent her. "They told me you were going to have to become King and I was never to see you again. Oh, my love, my love." She fell into his arms.

Ned was red with rage. "Now look here, all of you: this is my Emma," he said to those left standing in the room. "We are going to get married and there is nothing you can do. Look outside. You have your uprising. Go and deal with it. I am through."

Leading Emma gently by the arm, Ned left the house through the kitchen door, and slipped away without another word.

Outside the front of the house, the army of Londoners became impatient. They had marched for miles and wanted action, but it had come to nothing. Someone threw a stone at the front window of the house and soon everyone was throwing stones, jeering and shouting. Men were shaking their fists and jeering until their women pulled at their sleeves, saying it was time to go home to have their tea. There was no revolution happening here today. It was a false alarm, a shambles.

Ned heard nothing of this. He saw nothing. He held his arm protectively around Emma's shoulders and led her through the back streets until they were well clear of the masses.

"I will never live in this godforsaken city again," he swore. "Come on, darling, the boat is ready and our bags are packed. Let us leave and head west, as we planned, before anyone has the thought of coming after us."

The couple hurried back home, and Emma grabbed her few meagre possessions. After explaining to her parents what had just happened, Emma told them she was leaving with Ned before the plotters could come after them again. Her mother cried and her father looked sombre, but gave his blessing. He could see now that Ned was a good man and he loved Emma. That was good enough for him.

"Off you go then, children, and you behave. Come back and see us when the heat has died down. We won't be telling anyone where you are going. God be with you and safe journey. Slip out the back and down to the river. We will keep an eye on the road and will delay anyone who might be looking for you."

After a tearful farewell, the two sweethearts cautiously stepped out of the back door of the house and climbed down onto the shore.

The King and Queen were hastily ushered back through the entrance of the palace and the heavy gates were closed firmly behind them.

"That was too close for comfort," exclaimed the King, who was happy to put down rebellions, but only when he had the upper hand. A mere handful of soldiers was not enough. "We must call out the troops and send them into town to break up that mob before it gets any larger. It was just a spontaneous gathering. There was no real organisation to it. But who was that man in the boots? He looked so familiar."

The Queen had never seen him before, or so she thought. But there *was* something about the man in the fancy boots, something uncannily familiar. She felt a shiver down her spine for some strange reason. Memories flooded in, overwhelming her completely.

"You don't think he was the pretender?" she suggested, for the man had looked like her father, Edward IV, the York King. Her husband shook his head. "No, surely not, out in the open air without an army. That was just a mob of common people. People as common as he. I mean, he looked like a mudlark in those long leather boots!"

The royal couple were shaken and so went straight to their private apartments, where they felt safe. The yeomen-of-the-guard were all around them here, one on every door.

"Double up the guards on each door and then call Bishop Warham," ordered the King. "I need to talk to him, now."

Something had to be done. This rebel must be caught and brought to justice. They could no longer travel safely in their own kingdom, their own capital city. This was a national scandal, and the man must be caught and thrown into the Tower.

※

Emma stopped for a moment and, turning to Ned, she kissed him passionately, allowing him to engulf her slim and supple body in his muscled arms. They were both so excited at the audacity of what they were about to do, running away together and starting a new life in the countryside, leaving in the quiet of the evening to escape by boat and be so far away by dawn that nobody would find them.

"Come on, my love," whispered Ned as he lifted her bags and took them with him to the river. "We will have to be quick, or the tide will rise too high for us to escape along it. It is a spring tide tonight and the water is coming in fast."

Emma was wearing leather boots, but they were not as high as Ned's. They only had to go a few hundred yards more, however, before they reached his boat. Keeping their footsteps in the water, the two lovers worked their way up in the failing light until they found the spot where the boat lay hidden. Ned threw the bags into the boat, hauled it out in one fell swoop and turning to Emma, swept her up in his arms before planting her safely into the boat. Next, he waded out into the water and pushed the boat off as the strong tide started to pull it away into the current.

He climbed up and into the boat. It was not an easy thing to do, and the fragile vessel tipped over dangerously as he hauled himself over the side, making Emma nervous. Within moments they were both sitting comfortably aboard, and as the current pulled them out into the middle of the river, Ned steadied it with his oars, rowing steadily out towards the distant sea. As they sped along in the current, going faster and faster, he watched the wharf, his father, his home and all his memories slipping away into a diminishing speck in the landscape. Waterscape perhaps was a better description, with ships and boats all hunkered up together against the quayside or out on moorings, waiting for orders to sail back out to sea to trade with other countries or to move closer to land to be overhauled.

The river was Ned's mother; he felt the water running through his veins. He was never happier than on the water, and as he rowed along, he flexed his strong back muscles with ease. The sound of the water lapping against the sides of the boat and the rhythm of the oars as they stretched forward, dipped and then drew back was like the rhythm of his heart. He and Emma would head west, where nobody knew them, and would start a new life together.

13

Charles was looking for Henry and Jack, but they were nowhere to be seen, so he decided the best thing he could do was to keep going. He would head for Worcester, stop at the nearest inn and wait to see if the boys were smart enough to find him there. Bottom would need a rest and a good feed, while he could do with a drink. The problem was, he had no money. He decided he would have to sell the mule's saddle in order to pay for a place for the night. Jack might not be pleased, but he would buy him another one. If he was lucky, he might find someone who would play a game of cards or dice with him, so he could win some money.

Feeling better now he had a plan, Charles kicked Bottom into a brisk trot, and within an hour he had found a roadside inn where, after a quick negotiation in the stable yard, he sold the saddle. There, to his delight, was a group of men rolling dice. Soon Charles had introduced himself and he began amassing a small fortune.

Henry and Jack were having less luck. They were lost. The countryside had opened into a massive landscape of rolling hills covered with sheep, but each time they rode up to a cottage to ask for directions, it was derelict. The roofs were good, but the doors were ajar, with the interiors stripped of furniture and abandoned. Afraid there had been a plague here, they chose not to touch anything and to leave as quickly as they could. But they were still lost.

"I know." Henry's eyes lit up. "We can go up to that ridge and look from there. The sun is heading west at this time of day, so we know we are going in the right direction. It is just a matter of seeing where the next village might be. People will be lighting their fires soon and we ought to be able to spot chimney smoke or some sign of life."

Jack agreed, and so Henry turned Virtue towards the hilltop. But what they found up there took them both completely by surprise.

"What sort of place is this?" asked Henry, for they had found themselves by a circular arena marked out with large erect stones standing like sentinels. Neither of the children had ever seen anything like it. There were a few trees, but no buildings other than a lone windmill on stilts that looked like a man waving his arms in the air. Except it was still, there being no wind. The stones were all different shapes and sizes and there was a strange atmosphere about the place. There was also no sound, for the birds were not singing, as if they revered their surroundings.

"This is a magical place," Jack said with wonder. He slipped from the back of the pony and wandered into the circle. It was a perfect circle. Jack counted his steps as he paced from one side to another. "It must be one hundred feet wide," he marvelled. "And some of these stones must weigh over a ton. Look, this one is huge. It must be nine or ten feet high."

The stones were all different shapes and sizes.

"I wonder who put them here and how they managed to lift them into position," Henry thought aloud. His engineering mind was calculating how many men it would have taken to move these massive stones, let alone set them on edge.

Jack replied, "I have heard there are stones arranged in a circle in Wiltshire that were built by giants in ancient times.[26] They are meant to be as tall as a church roof and as heavy as all the congregation put together. The priests say it was pre-Christians who set them in place in a time when giants roamed the earth. People were killed and sacrificed there to their gods."

"That's stuff and nonsense!" Henry did not want to think about sacrifices while they were here all alone.

Just as he was beginning to wish someone were here with them, Henry heard the distant sound of the prettiest kind, along with the faint sound of music. Turning around, he stared down the road that passed the stones and saw, approaching from the direction from which they had just come, a caravan of people with the most colourful clothing, wearing large hats and lots of silver that glinted in the evening light. They were accompanied by wagons, along with horses, donkeys and dogs that ran along beside them. He could hear children singing, and an uplifting tune played skilfully by a man on a flute or penny whistle, amplified by the jingling of the horses' harnesses, which must have had bells attached.

"Hey, look, we have company!" he shouted, and waved to the people as they came up the hill.

"Careful," Jack warned. "We have no idea who they are. Whatever you do, remember you are called Robert and you are the son of a knight. Okay?"

Henry checked himself. He also thought it prudent to hide his gold ring in his boot in case these folk were less friendly than they appeared.

The music was a welcome sound to Henry who missed his music at home, so he ran up to greet the man at the head of the caravan of travellers.

"And what do we have here?" asked the leader of the caravan in a thick accent that was foreign to Henry's ears. He was a handsome man, with a twinkle in his dark eyes and a smile on his face. He sported a thickly grown moustache, almost like a living thing that wiggled when he spoke. He was missing a tooth and in its place was a replica made of solid gold. Henry warmed to him immediately.

"We are travellers who have lost our way and the rest of our company, so we came up here to find our bearings. Who are you, kind sir?" he asked, using his courtly manners.

"Well, well, we have come into fine company," laughed the leader on hearing the cultured voice of the prince. "We are a humble troupe of travelling actors and musicians just making our way to the next town, where we will earn some money entertaining the honest people who live there. If you are lost, you are welcome to join us for some of the way. We are heading to Worcester."

"So are we," Henry admitted, delighted to have found a potential way back to civilisation. "Can we really join you and your company, sir?"

"Well, for a start we will have none of that 'sir' stuff, young man. You can call me Lorenzo, and these here are my wife and children, our family and friends. We are going to camp here for the night, in the stones. We do so every time we pass here, for it is a good place and we enjoy the protection of the King's Men."

Henry was alarmed to hear this. "The King's Men?"

Lorenzo laughed. "Yes, that is the name of this ring of stones. There are more over there. The whole collection is called the Rollright Stones, after the local village, but they are not all friends. There is a story about them, but I will not tell you now, while we are all standing here cold and hungry. You are welcome to stay with us, my friends, but first you must introduce yourselves, and then you can help set up camp and light the fire. We have food to cook and tents to erect, or some of us will be sleeping under the stars tonight." He held out his hand to Henry.

Henry grabbed it willingly and shook it. "I am Henry, and this is Jack, my friend." Jack looked alarmed at Henry using his real name, but it was too late to do anything about it, so he came forward to shake hands as well.

Soon, the boys were being introduced to the members of Lorenzo's extended family, including children of all sorts of ages. There must have been twenty souls in total, of every colour, shape and size. Within minutes Jack and Henry were being treated as members of the family and were given tasks to complete before the company could settle around a brightly burning fire that had been built right in the centre of the stones.

These newcomers were a happy bunch with gold rings in their ears and bracelets on their arms. The children ran around doing somersaults and backflips and walking on their hands, and some had a go on a pair of wooden stilts. The oldest group of them was very good at juggling balls and threw them high up in the air before catching them. It was difficult to keep an eye on any one ball at a time, there were so many of them.

Jack immediately struck up a friendship with the younger members of the family and was soon learning how to juggle, a pretty girl with black hair teaching him. He picked it up quickly. Henry, who was more used to adult company, found himself drawn to Lorenzo, who was a natural leader. Under his command, the camp was set up and running within a very short period of time.

As the sun went down behind the landscape stretching out before them, Lorenzo poured a cup of brandy and gave Henry a watered-down version to sip. "It will keep you warm, son, so don't turn it down."

Henry felt compelled to do as he was told. Sitting there with the head of the family, he felt a bond growing between them.

"Tell me, if you know this area, why are the houses all empty and abandoned? Has there been a plague here?"

Lorenzo looked pensive and gazed at the fire for a while before he answered. "The land here has been requisitioned for the farming estates of Eynsham Abbey, not far from here. At first, they allowed the tenant farmers to remain in their houses, but since the wool industry has become so lucrative, the abbey has taken the land off the farmers and used it for running sheep. They evicted the villagers last year, so all their houses stand empty. It's a terrible crime on humanity, for where can those poor people go to find new lives? It's not easy to move on and find other land to farm or other houses to rent.[27] You displace people, and they end up becoming vagabonds and thieves, roaming the roads. I know because we come across them." He spat into the flames and it sizzled.

Lorenzo continued to philosophise. "If I were king, I would look after my people better than this, and I would lessen the power of the Church. Bishops and abbots are becoming too rich and independent. If a man of the cloth does wrong, he is tried by members of the Church, not the judiciary like the rest of us, and is more often than not found not guilty, while a layman would be found as guilty as hell. That is not a fair system of government."

Henry was surprised at hearing a common man speak so freely, criticising the way of the King and of the Church, but the man's words hit home, and he did not wish to stop him talking.

"I have to say that some of the places we have stayed have left me wishing the abbeys were better managed. I am sad people are suffering from their greed. I must talk to my father about it when I see him. I mean…"

Lorenzo looked at Henry. "Your father is in government?" His raised eyebrows showed he was impressed by this.

Henry covered his tracks as best he could. "He is an important man involved in important decisions. He seldom discusses matters with me, but perhaps if I showed interest, he might."

This thought had never occurred to him before, for Henry had never taken an interest in government or anything his boring father made such a fuss of doing. Perhaps he should try to take an interest in his father's work. He had never thought of it that way before. Henry liked the concern Lorenzo had for his fellow countrymen. He was speaking for the good of others, not on behalf of himself. He was a selfless man. "Tell me about the stones," said Henry to change the subject, for it was not good to be listening to a man speaking treasonous words, however well intended.

"Ah, well, that is a story. You see, this circle of stones is the King's Men and then there, over the road, is the King himself." Henry looked, and sure enough, over the roadway was one solitary stone, large and contorted, about twice the height of a man. He must have been a tall king.

"Even further along the road, you can see another small group of stones, and they are called the Whispering Knights. The story goes that in ancient times, when this land was divided into many small kingdoms, one of the many kings, a man who had ambitions to become the overlord, the great King of England, was marching along the ridge with his men when they stopped to rest. While the king went ahead to survey the land, a group of knights stepped aside to plot against the king and they were immediately turned into stone for their disloyalty."

"Who turned them into stone?" Henry asked.

"Well, of that I am not sure, but the story continues. For while the king was surveying the scene, a witch appeared from nowhere. The witch made a bargain with him:

>*'Seven long strides shalt thou take;*
>*if Long Compton thou canst see,*
>*King of all England thou will be.'*

"The king, being ambitious and thinking this an easy bargain, took seven long strides, but his view was blocked by a mound that magically rose up between him and the landscape So, the witch triumphantly announced:

>*'As Long Compton thou canst not see,*
>*King of England thou shalt not be.*
>*Rise up stick and stand still stone,*
>*For King of England thou shalt be none.*
>*Thou and thy men hoar stones shall be,*
>*And myself an elder tree.'*

Henry was captivated. "What happened next?"

"They all turned into stone, there and then, so maybe it was she who had turned the treasonous knights into stone earlier. She obviously had strong powers. As for what happened to the witch, well, we will never know, for there were no witnesses to record her next move and there is no elder tree here today." He looked down and smiled at the boy.[28]

"But you don't really believe in witches?" asked Henry, looking up at this wise, well-travelled man.

"I would be a fool not to believe in them, son," was Lorenzo's reply as he stared into the flames. "There is many a man who did not believe in witchcraft to their detriment, sometimes even their demise. I know of men who bowed with respect in the presence of such sorcery and became rich and prosperous for doing so. I have been the recipient of the beneficial powers of witchcraft. My wife would not be alive now had a local witch not come in her hour of need and helped her when her baby was misplaced inside and would not come out of her belly. The witch applied her sorcery, and the child was born and my lovely wife saved."

Henry looked at Lorenzo in wonder. If witches could do such things, why were they not treated with better respect? This was a thought that stayed in his mind all evening, while he watched the women and children dancing and singing around the campfire. He wondered which child it was who had been brought into the world in such a manner.

Later, when the men were playing on their flutes, Henry asked if he could have a go. They were delighted and handed him an instrument. As he had been learning music for several years now and was a talented pupil, Henry delighted his audience by playing one joyful tune after another.

One of the women came up to him and smiled as she spoke. "You play like an angel. Where did you learn to play so well?"

"Oh, I have a friend who has taught me for many years," Henry replied nonchalantly. "We often pass the time together making up tunes. I love music."

So, with Henry and the other musicians sharing their music the company whiled away the hours, until hot minced meat on a bed of strange slippery string was handed around by the women.

"What is this food?" asked Henry.

"Ah, that is "itriyya."[29] It comes from Sically, where I used to live, but its origins are Arabian. We eat it as we can store it easily. It is a traveller's companion."

"It's delicious," Jack spoke with his mouth full, as usual, much to the delight of the dark-haired girl who laughed. It was a jolly atmosphere. As the others disappeared to their beds, Lorenzo and Henry were loath to end the night. Lorenzo had taken a shine to the red-haired boy. There was an intelligence to him that was rare.

"You know, I would never pry into another man's life, but it seems odd to me you two boys are wandering in the middle of nowhere without any adults. Have you run away from home?" He noticed this question made Henry look uncomfortable, so continued. "You do not have to answer if you do not want to. It is just that, if you like, you two could stay with us. What with your musical talents and Jack's natural ability to learn juggling, we could find a place for you in our troupe. You would get paid and you would have food and company." Henry was taken aback by the man's generosity and, strangely, a part of him wished he could say yes to the offer. A life on the road without a care in the world sounded most attractive, Jack would love it too. But it could not be. Ever.

"There is nothing I would love more, and your guess is not far from the truth. We have left home without permission, and we will need to keep going, for we are on a journey to visit my brother to give him an urgent message. But I truly regret not being able to stay with you for a short while. You are a good man, and your family is both large and fruitful."

"Oh, they are not all my family," laughed Lorenzo, "only my wife, Stella, and our little girl; the one with the long black hair, that's my Lydia. The others are people we have met along the way, people who needed a home and some love. I call them my family and you are always welcome to join in the future. We are heading to Ludlow, to see the new prince and princess, in the hope we can spend an evening or two entertaining the court over Easter."

The two friends sat in silence for a while staring at the fire, each enveloped in his own thoughts. After a while, and with another glass of brandy in his hands, Lorenzo turned to speak again. Henry was still sipping the watered-down drink he had been given earlier. Though he disliked the taste, he could feel the effect of the alcohol warming his thoughts.

"Your father will surely be worried about you once he finds out you are missing."

Henry thought about this for a moment. "He doesn't even know. I don't see him much, as I live in the country. He is far too busy to take much notice of me or my sister."

Lorenzo noticed a trace of bitterness in the boy's words. "He must be a very important man, to stay away from you."

"He is," Henry agreed, "and I have an older brother who takes up all his time. My father much prefers him to me, much as I try to impress him with my studies and everything."

The two companions stared into the dying embers of the fire.

"You know, Henry, a father being distant doesn't necessarily mean he does not love you. Sometimes men find it hard to show their feelings. We are all brought up to be strong and brave, and as a result, showing our feelings does not come naturally. Do not take your father's apparent distance to heart."

Henry liked the sound of this, although he was not convinced this was the case with the King. It was kind of Lorenzo to give him such warm words of comfort and Henry decided to let him think he had spoken well.

"You make me feel much better, sir – I mean Lorenzo. I will try not to judge my father by his lack of interest in me. He is a busy man. I will endeavour to grow into a man worthy of his admiration, if not his affection."

Lorenzo looked at Henry for a long while. "I am not sure you sound convinced. But trust me on this. Any man would be proud to have a son like you, Henry. Maybe one day I will meet your father, and if I do, I will tell him he is a lucky man." Lorenzo swiftly swallowed the last of his drink and, unfurling himself, rose to his feet.

"Come on, son, it's time for bed."

Henry also stood. "Before we retire, do please show me the village the king could not see, the one in the story."

Lorenzo laughed. "Well, he would have seen it from where he stands now, for that is where he was turned to stone for failing."

The two friends walked over to the King's Stone, and Lorenzo pointed towards where the village lay, but as stated in the legend, a small piece of ground was in the way.

Henry looked and saw, as clear as day, the twinkling lights from the windows of a village in the distance. He stayed silent but stared. Lorenzo looked at him.

"You can see the village?"

Henry silently pointed out where the village would be, were the ridge not in the way and were the houses not empty and the people gone. Lorenzo stared at him long and hard.

"Boy, there is something you are not telling me. Something about you. I am not going to ask, but just let me say this: if ever you need my help, I am here for you." He put his hand on Henry's shoulder in a gesture of comradeship.

"Thank you," Henry replied. "There is one thing, actually. I haven't mentioned it until now, but I think we are being followed by someone, a man in a black cloak. Do you think the dogs will keep him away?"

Lorenzo laughed. "The dogs will bark if they see anyone, and they will bite if that person tries to enter the camp. Don't you worry, young man. You are safe while you are with us."

Lorenzo bid Henry goodnight and went to his wagon, where his wife was warming up the bed for him and his young daughter was already asleep in a small cot by their side.

Jack had arranged a place to sleep for himself and Henry in among some of the other children at the camp. The children had made a pile of blankets on a soft bed of cut ferns under a cart and told each other ghost stories until, one by one, they fell asleep together in a muddle of limbs. Henry and Jack were the last to give in to their fatigue. They carried on talking after the others fell silent.

"Tell me about your father, Jack."

Jack looked up at the timbers of the cart over their heads and let his thoughts drift back towards his home life.

"My father is a hard-working man. He has always served his king and he has always been faithful to his country. But therein lies the problem, for he cares so much for everyone else, he seems not to care much for me."

He paused for a while. Henry kept quiet, for he knew that to try to contradict Jack at this point would be crass.

"But he is not a lucky man. His own father died in debt, leaving him nothing, and he never managed to save his money; it always was spent on the family, or on works to the buildings, or on more stock. We had a bad harvest followed by a run of illness amongst our cattle and they aborted their calves. The hay was rained on and rotted; the barn caught fire one night. The list of miseries goes on and on."

Jack rolled onto his side and looked at Henry. "You know, I heard him talking to my mother one night. They mentioned a brother I had that I never knew about. An older brother called James. I wonder if I was named after him. He would be four years older than me. They lost him. I am not quite sure I heard them right, but it seems they had to give him away in to pay a debt to an abbot before I was born. They had no food. I often think of him and what it would be like to have an older brother, not just a younger one."

Henry was shocked. "They gave him away? Oh Jack, I am sorry. I had no idea. Do you know where he is now?"

Jack lay back down and looked up at the timbers again. "No. I don't. But sometimes I like to imagine we will bump into each other one day. Perhaps he left the abbey and became a knight after a long apprenticeship, or maybe he went into the Church as a scribe. One day, when I am able, I will ask my parents about him. But not now. Not until I can do something about finding him."

Henry lay back beside Jack. "You know, when this journey is over, maybe we could go and look for him together. You are helping me save my brother. If we succeed, then I should help you find yours in return."

"That would be good. Thanks." Jack smiled in the dark. "That's alright. Goodnight, Jack."

"Goodnight, Henry."

Turning over, Henry snuggled under the blankets. He was not used to being in such proximity to other children, especially at night. This was a new experience for him, and he quite liked it. He felt safe, for nobody would dare to kidnap him here, as to reach him they would have to tread on a handful of children, who would surely wake up and cry out, bringing all the adults out from their wagons to see what was going on. He fell asleep and dreamt of playing in the garden at home with all his siblings, including the babies who had died. They were all together, healthy and happy, juggling red, yellow and green balls that fell around them – as they fell, they turned into musical notes that played tunes until they touched the ground and burst like bubbles.

Only a few yards away from the camp, a dark figure was creeping around looking for an opportunity to settle. The shadow monk was still in a quandary. The recent attack on him, including the bang on his head, had left him unable to think as clearly as he once had. He knew he must capture the red-haired boy and take him back to his master, but the further he travelled from the abbey, the less inclined he was to return there at all.

Sleeping in a barn or under a raised windmill like he'd just found was better than a night locked away in his dungeon, the groans and cries of tortured inmates around him a sad lullaby. Here, he could only hear the night owl crying and the occasional scream of a fox. He knew if he did not kidnap the prince and take him back to the abbey, he could never return safely: it would be him on the rack screaming out loud. But if he could be of some use to the boy called Henry, he might become a friend to him instead.

Settling down under the cover of his cloak, the monk started his night's vigil without a single dog barking at him, for he had used his powers and the dogs stayed quiet.

14

The next morning, Henry felt strangely optimistic about the future, while Jack felt dizzy with love. He followed Lydia like a foal follows a mare while she did her chores, helping whichever way he could.

Henry washed his face in a bucket of water and then went to explore the strange windmill on stilts that stood so upright near to the stones. After a while, Lorenzo came to join him.

"The windmill. What is it for?" he asked Lorenzo.

"It would have been used by the people of the village for grinding their corn for bread, but the people are now gone and the windmill is empty."[30]

"That's funny." Henry observed footprints and a nest in the grass under the body of the mill. "Did you see anyone sneaking around the camp last night?" he asked the older man, feeling a little less secure after all.

"The dogs would have scared away any trespassers, that I promise you. There was nobody here last night. This could have been made by one of the children playing house. Or maybe your Jack went there for a little private time with his sweetheart?" Lorenzo chuckled at the thought of the two innocents holding hands under the windmill.

"By the way," Lorenzo said, changing the subject, "I am not sure what happened last night, but I do believe you to be gifted in some way. We will do whatever we can to help you. We travel to Worcester today, then through a few villages to Leominster and on to Ludlow in about a week's time. You are more than welcome to travel with us, and share our food and our company. You know, I never had a son, but if I did, I would want him to be just like you."

Henry's eyes watered. Lorenzo's words had caught him unawares; he wished much the same. He controlled himself as best he could.

"I thank you, Lorenzo. I cannot express how much that means to me," he said, smiling. "For the moment, we must find our friend, Charles. He should be in Worcester, waiting for us. But if we cannot find him, and even if we do, we would love to spend more time in your company. I can see it would suit Jack. Look over there."

Jack was carrying buckets of water for Lydia, who was accepting her suitor's help with a coy smile. She could only have been around ten years of age, but she already knew how to hypnotize a boy.

Lorenzo laughed. "She is just like her mother, you know." The troupe tidied up the camp, ensuring the fire was put out properly and they had left nothing behind, no rubbish and no possessions. With their carts loaded up and the few men who owned horses on their backs, the caravan began to move slowly forward with Lorenzo at its helm.

Charles was feeling pleased with himself. He had played cards well the evening before, having been careful this time about how much he drank, and he had won a serious amount of money. Had the inn been less reputable, he would now be worried about those he had beaten wanting their money back and mugging him as soon as he left the inn. But this was a respectable establishment and the men who had lost last night could afford to do so. They would have gone home to their wives with lighter purses but with no great loss to worry about.

Another thing he had won last night was some information about the knight to whom he had lost so badly the evening before. The man was well known for playing cards and he was not entirely honest. Many a man had been stripped of his belongings in a game with him, and the men with whom Charles had been drinking had been all too happy to inform him of where the man lived. His castle was not far from Worcester, and Charles now had a plan as to how to get him back,. Charles went to the stable and bought back the saddle he had sold the night before, put his purse into his boots, just in case he was wrong about the customers who used the inn, and mounted Bottom. He was in a joyful mood as he bounced down the road in a rhythm with Bottom's gait, whistling a tune as he went.

Only an hour after Charles left the inn, William, Margot and John turned up, exhausted after many hours in the saddle, for they had left Enstone early and were now ready to eat a hearty breakfast. John ordered ham and eggs on thick bread to be washed down with some fresh ale, and Margot tucked into her food with the appetite of a boy. William was not hungry, so to pass the time he wrote some thoughts in a book he had on his person.

"Goodness, Margot," scolded John in a singsong, lighthearted manner, "if you don't slow down, you will choke."

His words had little effect on the girl. She just looked at him and smiled over a large chunk of bread into which she was biting. He could not help but grin back. Soon he forgot all decorum and tucked into his food with the same gusto.

"Riding always makes me hungry," she admitted once she could speak again. "I think it's the fresh air. Shall we ask if the innkeeper has seen the three boys?"

John Skelton enquired of the innkeeper if he had seen a young man with two young squires passing through recently, as this was the only inn in the area, but the man said no. A few travellers had stayed last night, but they were all single men, except for one married couple. There were no young boys around at all. This was not encouraging news. They had ridden hard all day yesterday and since dawn this morning to make up ground and catch up with the others, but to no avail.

"Never mind," said the ever-optimistic Margot, "we will catch up with them by this evening, of that I am sure. I feel it in my bones that I am not far from Henry. It's a family thing."

As Margot said these words, she heard the jingling of bells as a large caravan of travelling folk passed through the village. They could just see the wagons and the legs of the riders who rode past the windows of the inn. The sound of someone practising a tune on a penny whistle could be heard over the clattering of the horses' hooves as they passed on by.

"That's funny." Margot sat up, her ears cocked. "Henry plays that tune all the time. How odd that it can be heard this far from Eltham. I thought he had composed that tune himself. I must be wrong. They are not playing it very well."

William looked up from his writing. "I remember Henry playing that often. Maybe we have found him?" He was rising out of his seat to rush to the inn door.

Margot called him back. "Henry would play it far better than that. This man has the timing all wrong. He has no flair." William sat back down again, disappointed.

"They will be playing in Worcester tonight, no doubt," John guessed. "In other circumstances, I would love to take you to see their show. It is quite different to see the travellers perform in a town than it is at court, you know. The audience is a lot more colourful and the interaction between them and the performers can be quite entertaining."

Margot's eyes lit up. "Oh John, that would be wonderful. Perhaps we could sneak into a show just for a short while?"

"I don't think going to the theatre is appropriate in the circumstances," warned William.

John agreed. "Let's wait and see. Maybe they will still be in the area on our way back from Ludlow. We should be there in a few days. I wonder where the others have gone?"

Saying this, Skelton arose and went to pay for the meal while Margot finished her ale. William wrapped up his book and collected his belongings.

Inquisitive, Margot asked him, "What are you writing?"

"Oh, just thoughts and things." William blushed. William was shy about his creative side. "I like to capture them before they blow away on the wind."

Margot was sensitive enough to know when not to push her curiosity too far. Perhaps he would read her some of his thoughts another day. She was enjoying William's company on this journey. He had a dreamy air about him she found compelling. She wondered if he had a woman back at court, anyone for whom he was writing his thoughts down in his closely guarded book.

Henry was riding at the head of the caravan, alongside Lorenzo and his wife. Lydia was in the wagon just behind them, with Jack at her side, holding the reins of the two horses that pulled the wagon. He looked quite at home with his girl by his side. He was humming along to the tune that the musician whom Henry had taught his ditty was playing on the tin whistle.

"Henry wrote that song himself, you know," [31] he told her. "If he wasn't a pr…" Jack stopped himself from saying 'prince' just in time. "I mean, I think one day he might become a great composer."

Lydia looked up at Jack with her large brown eyes. "You always talk about Henry. 'Henry this and Henry that', like he is someone special. You are just as special as he is, you know." Jack looked at her and saw she was smiling. Her words were not malicious towards Henry; she just wanted to reassure Jack that he was special too – to her, at least.

"Why, I don't mean to… I mean, Henry is special. He is my best friend. He means the world to me. We have been friends for a while now and he always shares all his things with me. You should see the trouble we get up to together at Eltham." Jack was blushing with the exertion of sticking up for his friend yet not giving his identity away, while at the same time enjoying the idea that he was special in some way. He had never seen himself as his friend's equal before and yet here was a girl who did. His chest filled with pride.

Lydia looked at him earnestly. "Perhaps we will come your way someday and I can see you again." Her eyes were full of hope.

"I would like that," Jack admitted shyly.

As they rode along in the wagon, Jack noticed the birds seemed to be singing all the louder and the first spring flowers that adorned the country lane appeared all the brighter, primroses and celandine. The pony that pulled the cart threwits head about to shake off flies, and as the reins jingled, it sounded like music to his ears. He began to hum along with the penny whistle. As they moved slowly along, he daydreamed he was married to Lydia and that they were living a life on the road like Lorenzo and Stella.

"Would you continue a life on the road once you were married?" he asked Lydia and then blushed again.

She laughed, and her laughter sounded like the clearest spring water to his ears. "I would if I were with you."

Jack felt so happy, he wished this moment would never end. With his heart leaping inside his chest he turned to Lydia and shyly kissed her cheek.

Charles was plotting his next move. He had to make sure Henry was safe, but once they were reunited, he would go to retrieve his horse. In all the years since his parents had died, Charles had never allowed himself to love anyone. Not even his grandfather, any more than a grandson ought to out of duty. He had good friends like William, with whom he drank and gambled. He had had some success with women, but to him they were dalliances. Nothing serious. If ever he felt a relationship was turning into something serious, he felt trapped. His instinct, which he followed without fail, was to run away. If you do not love, then you cannot lose that love. His earliest memories were of crying his tiny heart out when he had lost his mother, who had been the centre of his world. His later memories haunted him, of being passed around like a parcel from one nurse to another, nobody loving him like his mother had, with her soft brown ringlets of hair that fell into his face, tickling him and making him giggle and reach up to play with them. No, he would never allow himself to love like that again. But then he had bought Caesar, a horse.

To Caesar he had lost his heart, and he wanted to get him back at whatever cost. And he had a plan.

Margot had no plan at all. She was at the mercy of John Skelton, who had taken matters into his own hands from the start, and of William, who had joined the group with ideas of his own.

"We could go cross-country and head straight for Ludlow. That way we could rescue Prince Arthur at least," suggested William, who, not having found Henry, was thinking of reporting to the man called Grope to repay his 'debt' to Lady Margaret.

"No, we must find Henry first," argued John. Henry was his charge and he needed to know he was safe before he pushed on to rescue Arthur.

"Arthur is our future king," William replied. "We will be guilty of treason if we do not do our best to warn him of this plot against him."

Margot agreed with this, but at the same time, Henry was her little brother and he was out in the wide world with only Charles as his guide. Not that Charles would let him come to harm, or so she hoped.

John Skelton had had enough. "Look, we are on this wild goose chase in order to find Henry, and Jack for that matter. They might have Charles with them, but he is hardly my idea of an upright and moral character. He has probably taken them into a gambling den, for all I know."

"Charles would give his life for Henry, you know." William felt the need to stick up for his friend.

John Skelton had never taken much notice of William before, other than noticing that he had an interest in writing poetry, which, as a fellow poet, had originally made him like the affable young man. But in close quarters, riding together as they were now, John had had time to study his companion, and what was more, to study the effect William had on Margot. He did not like what he was seeing. William was slim, tall, almost reed-like in stature, with pale skin and pale green eyes. His golden locks fell about his forehead in an unruly manner, flopping over his face, so he had to sweep them aside with a shake of his head or a flick of his hand. This should have looked idiotic, but in truth was an endearing habit and it was working on Margot. She had even offered to lend him her comb earlier. It seemed Margot was hanging on his every word.

"Perhaps William is right, John," she said as she trotted to catch up with his pony. John had urged his animal on in his tetchiness. "There is not much trouble Henry cannot wriggle out of with both Charles and Jack as his companions. There is nobody threatening them, whereas Arthur is in real jeopardy."

John pulled the reins and drew his pony to a halt. "Look, William, you can go off to Ludlow to warn Arthur, be my guest. But Madame Margaret here and Prince Henry are my responsibility; I will not let either of them out of my sight. Once I find Henry again, that is. We were doing quite well without you to start off with."

William was taken aback by this outburst. "Sir, I do not intend to create discord here; I just want to do the right thing. Arthur is the Prince of Wales, and his very existence is possibly threatened by the doings of persons known only to us. We need to act. Henry is in the good hands of Charles, a devoted friend and protector. I cannot see him coming to harm while Charles is there. I just feel honour-bound to go and warn Prince Arthur."

"Then go," ordered John, "and I will stay on course to track down Henry and his friends. We will meet again, no doubt."

William had no choice. "I will go with all haste and will see you both when you reach the safety of Ludlow."

With little else to say, he turned his horse and headed off in the direction that would take him soonest to the castle, where the young prince and his court were settled.

"Please send Arthur my love," Margot called after him. "And… take care, William. Keep yourself safe." She knew she would miss him, but Henry was uppermost in her thoughts. "Come on, John, let's keep going until we catch up with them. They cannot be much further ahead of us at this stage." With all her thoughts concentrated on finding Henry, Margot had no time to look back at William as he rode away. She broke into a trot and then a canter, with her pony swishing his tail in delight at being given his head. John Skelton followed her as best he could on his rebellious mount, who bucked as he jumped to follow his friend.

William turned to watch as the young girl and her chaperone disappeared in a disorderly manner over the horizon and on towards Worcester.

Only a few miles further along the road, Lorenzo and his troupe had finally arrived at that very town and were settling into a field they had rented from a farmer allowed them to setup their camp there every spring. A gang of youths was using the field as an impromptu football pitch, kicking around a massive, heavy leather ball. They sometimes caught it and threw it to a friend before being pummelled by the other 'team', who would stop at nothing to get their hands on the prized ball. With hats and scarves flying behind them, the mass of humanity flowed around the ball, fists flying as they flailed aimlessly, hoping to hit flesh of some sort or other. Nobody knew the rules of the game, and few even knew where the ball was. Sometimes it sat silently on the sidelines as the group fell into a heap of laughing lads. The aim was not to win the match, but rather to settle old scores and have a bit of fun. Eventually, Lorenzo and his troupe's arrival slowed up the game and the crowd began to disperse.

"Look, it's the actors come to town. Give us a penny, mister, and we will help you put up your tents, mate."

The largest of the boys took off his hat and held out his hand. Lorenzo obliged, handing out a scattering of coins, which the boys scrambled to grab. Then they took off their coats and started to unpack the tents and other items on the carts. These boys were used to the travelling folk coming to town and had probably just been playing football to kill time until the troupe turned up and they could earn a penny or two.

This was the moment for Henry and Jack to say their farewells and to carry on with their journey on their own once again.

"Travel safely, my friends," said Lorenzo as he shook hands with the two boys and then, spontaneously, he gave them both a big hug. "It is a dangerous world and I only hope you find your way safely to your brother's house. Remember, you are always welcome wherever we are and we will do all we can to help you."

Henry thanked him emphatically and then bowed to Stella and said goodbye. Jack was saying goodbye to Lydia, who had tears in her eyes.

"I will come and find you once this journey is over. I promise you," he told her.

Henry also said goodbye to Lydia. He gave her a short hug and promised he would look after Jack.

"We will come and find you all. Your friend's tin whistle is loud enough for us to hear from ten miles away, so we only need to follow the music."

This made the mood of the parting a little lighter, and the two boys jumped onto Virtue's back to begin their journey down the road to look for Charles, with a huddled group of friends waving after them.

Worcester was a busy town with lots of shops and a massive cathedral that appeared to be having alterations done. A swarm of stonemasons sitting on stools were crafting stone into parts of the massive Gothic front doorway. Carpenters were assisting them, making wooden arches for the stone to be built upon to maintain a true shape to stretch over the doorway and rest on the pillars already in position. Henry had always wanted to visit this cathedral, for he knew it to be the chosen resting place of King John and he wished to say a prayer for the man.

King John had not been a popular king, but he had signed the Magna Carta, as produced for him by his nobles, and this had been the beginning of a more just system of rule in England. John Skelton had taught Henry that a king, although chosen by God, should allow his subjects to feel they had some say in government, or else they would become restless and revolt against him. Henry's father had begun his rule in this manner, but over time he had become more autocratic in his handling of affairs and John Skelton considered this an error, without saying as much. It would be treason to speak out against the King, but Henry knew John well enough to be able to read between his words.

"Wait a while for me here, will you, Jack? I want to go in and light a candle at the altar," he said to his companion.

Jack was still in the habit of doing whatever Henry asked and so he patiently held Virtue, who rubbed her itching head against Jack's body, almost knocking him over. He rubbed the pony's forehead and scratched her in between the ears, something he knew all ponies adored.

"I will stay here and keep an eye out for Charles," he replied.

Henry hopped up the front steps, past the stonemasons and in through the cavernous doorway. The cathedral was enormous inside, with a roof that seemed to be as high as Heaven itself. He wondered at the skill of the architects who designed such buildings. They must be truly inspired by God. He knew the building had been under construction for over three hundred years and wondered how the men of the old days had the skills and the knowledge to build such a marvellous and awe-inspiring space. God had a hand in this, for sure. Henry felt as if he were inside the ribcage of an enormous animal and yet it was light, not dark and oppressive as he had expected it to be. There were enormous windows everywhere, with light spilling in from all sides. At the end of the aisle was the altar, all in gold with steps up to it. Where was King John's tomb, Henry wondered. It was no surprise he had wanted to be buried in this amazing place.

There were Franciscan friars at the front of the cathedral, so Henry decided to remain quietly where he was, for he had a healthy suspicion of monks after Abingdon. He knelt in the shadows beside one of the carved pillars that held up the main roof and prayed to God for guidance. He was four days into his journey now and had lost his protector, Charles; plus he had no money and only one pony between himself and Jack. Jack was in a dreamland now; all he could think about was the girl he had met. Henry could tell his friend was in love. It was almost as if he was only half there, and Henry felt abandoned.

"Please God," he whispered into his clasped hands, "give me the strength to find my brother and warn him of his plight. Help me find a way to convince him that there are men around him who wish to do him harm, and help us both survive the conspiracy against us."

Against us. Henry thought about this for the first time. Up until now, all he had thought about was saving Arthur, not why he was being targeted or what the outcome would be if they succeeded in poisoning him. It was obvious: Arthur would die and then he, Henry, would become the Prince of Wales instead. He would be destined to become the next King of England. He would have a role in life after all and an important one at that. In fact, it would be the most important role in the kingdom. Only second to God himself once his father had died, and his grandmother too for that matter. Who would he have to support him in such an enormous role? His darling mother, of course, for she would become the King's mother and would stand beside him.

This was the first time Henry had thought about himself this whole time. He was rushing to save his brother, while his grandmother was making way for him to become the heir to the throne, and would have all the attention he craved from his father. There would be no uncertainty about his future, no future as a bishop, a prospect that made him shudder.

Looking up at the golden altar, Henry could almost see himself sitting there, ready to be ordained, with a crown held over his head by the bishop and all his courtiers around him. His subjects. He would be the most powerful man in the kingdom, perhaps even Europe.

He could even make war on France!

Just as Henry was kneeling there, imagining his future, the sun came out from behind a cloud and a shaft of light shot in through the stained-glass windows and lit up the centre of the aisle. It was as if God had been listening: God knew he was there, and God was signalling that his future was set out ready and waiting for him. All he had to do was allow things to happen and to stop trying to change the course of history by interfering with what was happening. His grandmother and her allies were manipulating history, he knew this, but perhaps they were doing so for the greater good, perhaps they knew something he did not know. Henry questioned whether he was old enough to understand the politics of the adult world. In truth, he had never considered them much at all; he had only ever thought about himself and what he wanted in life.

He must have been kneeling there for a long time considering this new train of thought, for a concerned friar came up to him and spoke.

"You are a most devout young man to pray for so long, my son. Is there anything on your mind you would like to talk about? Can we help you in any way?"

Henry was just about to make his excuses and leave when he heard shouting outside.

"Stop, thief! Stop the boy on that horse – catch him. That is a royal pony he has stolen!"

There was only one boy outside and only one pony that belonged to a royal: Virtue. Without even having time to excuse himself, Henry jumped up and over the pews, ducking past the friar and out into the open. There he saw Jack being attacked by a tall, angular man in dark clothing. Fiddle. Fiddle the horrid henchman who worked for Lady Margaret, the one who was going to poison Arthur.

"Run, Jack, run!" shouted Henry, and he ran at Fiddle and tackled him, charging with his head down so he hit him in the stomach and bowled him over. Jack disappeared down a side street, leaving Virtue standing there, her reins loose to the ground.

"You… little… tyke," whispered Fiddle hoarsely, completely winded by the attack. He sat up but could not move until he caught his breath.

Henry had to get out of there before Fiddle recognised him. Without further ado, he leaped onto Virtue and kicked her into an instant gallop. His legs flapped while he found the stirrups and the reins dangled about until, by lying forward, he was able to catch them and get them under control.

Fiddle stood and shouted, "Come back, you vermin! I say halt, in the name of the law!"

Looking around in desperation, Fiddle saw a man on a horse walking along past the cathedral. He ran up to him and dragged him to the ground, before jumping onto the man's animal and quickly chasing after Henry while shouting after him.

"Stop! Come back in the name of the King, come back!"

Henry chose not to obey and rode blindly through the streets and into a market, knocking over anything in his way – crates of apples, fish, vegetables, a milk churn. He was causing havoc and leaving behind him a crowd of cursing stallholders, servants, ladies and gentlemen. He did not care and would stop for no one. The wind was rushing past and before he could stop it his cap had blown away, the cap that hid his russet locks. He was certain Fiddle would recognize him were he to catch him and would try to take him home, so he urgently pushed Virtue onwards, not caring what street they took or which direction they went.

Fiddle was furious. A great lover of horseflesh, Fiddle could recognise a horse anywhere and for some reason, Virtue, the pony he had delivered to Eltham Palace, some two hundred miles away, was here with some young lad riding him. How the pony had travelled so far was anyone's guess, but she was a royal pony and the lad was obviously taking her to the market to sell. He would catch the little thief and have him strung up for this on a pole for all to see what happened when you stole a horse from a prince. He would open his gut up before the scoundrel died and burn his entrails on hot coals. That would teach him a lesson, and everyone else who was there to watch.

Kicking the horse that he had 'commandeered' onwards, he jumped over a sea of spilled vegetables and cleared sacks of turnips. He jumped cleanly over a handcart in his attempt to cut a corner. He chased the thief on the pony right through the town and back again, twisting one way and then another, until finally he clattered over the stone bridge past the tower and onto the other side of the river. Behind him came a crowd of furious stallholders and other folk shaking their fists, spades, hoes and other tools at the two riders.

Some men mounted their own horses and joined the chase. It was becoming a massive manhunt and Henry was the prey. Virtue was faultless, not missing a foothold or turning a corner too slowly. She was like quicksilver, throwing herself around blind bends, changing legs as she swerved down one street and up another. Street urchins cheered her on and threw rotten apples at her pursuers. Men congregated on street corners and put bets on which rider would fall first.

Henry thought his heart was going to burst with fear. He could feel it pounding in his chest and hear the blood running through his ears. Fiddle was relentless in his pursuit. Henry took a sharp right turn down a side street, hoping he would cut through to a parallel street that might lead him out of the maze he was lost within, but it was a hopeless dead end. What was worse was that he could hear the advancing army of men who were chasing after him, for the clatter of what must now be at least twenty horses was coming closer like an advancing thunderstorm.

"Oh God, help me!" he shouted in despair, at which point, much to his surprise, a voice answered.

"You called?"

Henry looked up to see who had spoken.

"'Tis not God, but I," came a thin, quaking voice and, looking around him, Henry saw a door that he had not noticed before in the alleyway was open and an ancient man was beckoning him to enter. He did not hesitate but ducked down as he pushed the pony through the door, forgetting all decorum in his haste. Once he was inside and the door firmly locked, he could breathe again.

"Thank you, old man. I don't know who you are, but I know you are a friend. You have saved me from an unjust hanging by a lawless mob."

There was a loud banging on the door, but the old man did not answer it.

"Come, we must be quick; they will not give up, but I can help you," said the man, and without acknowledging that it was somewhat odd to have a boy on a pony ride into his shop via the back door – he led him into the main part of the shop, which was full of hardware, hats, ironmongery, tools, coffins and rugs.

"Who are you, sir?" asked Henry.

"Sadly, we do not have time to introduce ourselves to each other, but I know who you are and your red hair is going to give you away, so put this on." The old man handed him a soldier's helmet; it looked almost Norman it was so old, but it covered his hair.

The old man opened the front door of his shop, and the boy and pony trotted out and set off once again before anyone could catch up with them.

"Thank you, Thomas!" Henry found himself shouting as he waved to the old fellow who stood by the door, and then wondered how he had known the old man had never mentioned it.

Meanwhile, once Jack had realised he was no longer the quarry, he had slowed up and crept back to try to see what was going on. He could hardly take in that Henry had saved his life by taking Virtue and leading the irate man away from him. A prince saving a mere whipping boy and putting his own life at risk instead! He was astounded, and his heart leaped with joy as well as fear. Henry cared for him. He must do.

But he also understood Henry was now in mortal danger: since he was not dressed as a prince and if caught had nobody there to prove he was one, he could be strung up on the spot with no trial with which to redress the situation.

As Jack stood there, taking all this in, he heard someone call out his name:

"Jack!"

He turned around, his heart even more in his mouth, for he recognised the voice of that errant knight-in-training, Charles.

"Charles, thank goodness we have found you at last. I mean… where have you been? Henry is in danger – quick, we must help!"

Charles, lost for anything more constructive to do until he found Henry and Jack, had been dallying with a woman on the top floor of a nearby inn. Hearing a commotion in the street, he had hopped out of bed to see what was going on and witnessed Henry with his telltale red hair galloping on Virtue right under his window, with a man on a horse chasing him, and catching up by the looks of it. Charles had grabbed his breeches and hopped around the room as he pulled them on, followed by his riding boots. Leaving no time to put on his shirt and jacket, he had run out and down the stairs onto the street barechested, and that was when he had seen Jack.

"What the hell is that rogue doing chasing Henry?" he asked.

"He thinks Henry's a thief, the bloody fool. He thinks Henry has stolen Virtue. We have got to do something, Charles." Jack went red with emotion.

"Jack, we only have Bottom, but you are welcome to have him back. I think he misses you."

Jack ran to the stables and was delighted to be reunited with his mule, who seemed equally pleased to see his master and farted loudly.

Charles paid the stable boy to loan him an old nag and, after tacking up quickly, the boys chased after the 'hunt'.

Soon after he left the front of the shop, Henry had taken a route he hoped would lead him away from his tormentors, but by this stage the entire town was after him. Wherever he rode, screams and shouts rose around him.

"Here he is – get the scoundrel!"

The posse of riders headed by Fiddle, now foaming at the mouth as much as his horse was, came after him and Henry rode blindly, as fast as poor Virtue would take him. The chase had now entered the countryside. Poor Virtue was on her last legs, for she had been running at full speed for over half an hour at this stage. As soon as he had left the shop, despite taking a road he hoped was clear, Henry's tormentors were soon back on his tail and the man on the horse behind, though also tiring, could not be shaken off. Henry chose a road that ran along the winding river but then branched uphill. He thought the incline might slow down the horses behind him. Quickly glancing behind, Henry could count more than twenty horses of different shapes and sizes coming up the hill. Fiddle was in the lead by far, for he had a swift horse, but there were other men joining in the chase, although Henry could not think why. He had not done anything to harm them. It was so unfair. He felt like a fox being chased by hounds and it was not a good feeling. His heart was about to burst with pumping and a cold sweat was pouring down his back. If ever he had been closer to death, Henry could not recall it. This was as bad as it got. Digging his heels into Virtue's lathered side, he spoke almost in prayer.

"Come on, Virtue, you can do it," he encouraged the pony, whose flanks were covered in frothy sweat. "Come on, my girl. If ever I needed you, I need you now." It was as if the pony understood, and she gave one last burst of effort as they turned into a field and headed up over the horizon.

Fiddle followed relentlessly and, seeing them, pushed his mount further by hitting it on its backside with a whip. "Come back, come back, I've got you now," he shouted, but Henry looked at him one last time and then pushed Virtue upover the hill.

He had come to another dead end, for there was no way out of the field and Fiddle and the other riders were right behind him. Henry had to make a split-second decision: stop and face his pursuers or jump the hedge and pray there was a soft landing on the other side. He made the decision to jump, for whatever was on the other side of the hedge could not beworse than being caught by Fiddle.

Digging his heels once more into Virtue's sides, Henry readied himself to spring forward, throwing his heart over the hedge in an old trick a soldier had once taught him as a way to get a horse to jump anything. "Throw your heart over and the horse will follow," the old man had told him. Henry did this and the pony was compelled to follow. With fear in her eyes and all her instincts screaming, "Don't jump, don't jump!" the brave black pony sprung her flanks like a clock's springs and, letting go, she leapt into the air, over the hedge, and saw nothing, nowhere to land, nowhere to reach with her front legs, no field, no earth, nothing.

15

That Henry survived the fall was a miracle. Jumping over the hedge in a desperate attempt to flee from Fiddle, he discovered no firm turf on the other side, just a void that ended in the river with nothing for him and his valiant pony to land on. Down, down they fell, parting company, and as Henry landed, he hit his head on the rocks, and even wearing the Norman helmet, that was that.

The current tossed him to and fro, sometimes slipping past a rock, other times dashing him against a fallen tree or dragging him underwater along the gravel bed. As he travelled along the river like a rag doll, the very essence of the river seemed to cradle him and protect him from fatal blows from rocks and pull him away from the arms of murderous branches that might hold him under water for too long. Floating and unconscious, Henry dreamed that he was floating into the arms of the most beautiful woman he had ever seen, with long black hair and the palest skin, like porcelain. The woman held her arms out to welcome him as she sang to him a hauntingly beautiful song. Even in his state of near death, Henry listened and thought it the most captivating sound he had ever heard. The temptation to give in to her was almost too great to bear, but something in his heart urged him to resist. At last, as if tired of playing with his lifeless form, the river carelessly washed him ashore on the outer edge of a wide bend, where it left him, bedraggled but not drowned.

Walking along the edge of the river to relieve himself, a fearsome brute of a man came across Henry's body. This man was a giant oaf, a muscled, tattooed, ear-pierced monster with bloodshot eyes and bad breath after a night of heavy drinking. He leant down to peer at what he thought at first was a dead child and, kneeling, he searched the body, finding the chain around Henry's neck that held the wavy ring Margot had given him. Without further ado, the man yanked the chain so that it broke and put both the ring and chain in his pocket. The tug of the chain against his neck made Henry jolt with pain. Noticing that there was a glimmer of life left in the child, the ugly man tore Henry's shirt apart and laid his hands, one over the other, on his chest. Knowing how to pull a soul from death, the man pumped the young chest until Henry spewed water, coughed and opened his eyes.

"What...? Where...? Who are you?" Henry croaked in a voice raw from river water.

The man looked at him and then barked back in a language that sounded unlike any he had heard before. More wild-looking men walked up the beach to have a look at what their master was doing, for the large man was the captain of a crew of opportunistic Welsh sea-dogs, miscreants and rogues, otherwise known as pirates.[32]

*Henry dreamt that he was floating into the arms of
the most beautiful woman he had ever seen.*

This was a group of villains hiding away upriver for the winter months in a haven that they had used for years and that all local folk knew to keep away from if they cared for their freedom. Each and every one of them had an unkempt beard, missing teeth and a weatherworn face. The exception was a boy who looked to be about the same age as Henry. He stood on a rock above the beach, watching silently.

Having established that Henry was alive, the captain roughly dragged him up off the ground and passed him to a little man with a bulbous stomach. He spoke again in that strange guttural language and the man took hold of Henry in an iron grip. Henry was alarmed, for he did not know where he was other than that he was among strangers. He had no weapons, no friends, and nor could he understand the language these men were speaking.

"Let me go. Leave me be. I am Prince Henry Tudor, son of King Henry VII, your monarch, and I demand your help," he asserted, no longer thinking of pretending to be anything other than the son of the King.

The jolly man held him in a not-so-jolly grip, his arms around Henry's neck. They were not responding. Henry decided that the men were foreigners.

"Hablais español?" No response. So, they were not from Spain.

"Loquiminine Latine?" Henry asked, for many travellers used Latin as a common language. But this was no good either. The sea-dogs ignored his words, for they did not speak Spanish or Latin – or French or Greek either, both of which Henry also tried. At this point, to his relief, the handsome boy, who was still watching, was moved to join in and help him. Jumping down from the rock on which he stood, he spoke in French.

"Bonjour. Je m'appelle Balthazar," he said, and he bowed low in a

courtly manner, his hand sweeping the air with graceful ease. "At your service."

"Je m'appelle Henry." Henry spoke French well, but it was courtly French, so he doubted this ruffian would understand him if he conversed in the language.

He studied the boy who stood there so confidently, with a red scarf tied loosely around his neck and his white cotton shirt open halfway down his chest, its sleeves billowing like sails in the wind. He was tall and slim with fair curly hair and intelligent brown eyes. Henry was suitably impressed.

"You note I speak right English too," Balthazar boasted with a winning smile. "You land your feet in stupid shit, *non*?" Henry, not so impressed by the boy's English, was relieved that at last somebody understood him. "Look, I have found myself in an impossible situation due to circumstances quite out of my control. I trust that you will assist me in telling this man to let me go." He tried to speak with as much authority as he could muster.

Balthazar smiled an infectious smile. "I think you have wrong contemplation here. These men have you much captive now."

"Captive? But I can't be – I am a prince, and I am on an important mission. You must tell them to let me go!" Henry struggled to free himself as he spoke, but the jolly sea dog just held him all the tighter. The man's breath stank, as did his sweating body. Henry felt weak with foreboding.

"Please help me, Monsieur Balthazar, I need your aid," he implored. "Can you please explain to these gentlemen that I am *Prince* Henry, son of the *King* of England, and that I am on an important mission to rescue my brother, *Prince* Arthur Tudor, from an attack on his life."

Balthazar smiled and looked at Henry as if sizing him up. "You say you prince but look like wet dog."

Henry looked down at what was left of his clothes, torn from being swept along in the river. His shirt was in pieces, his shoes lost, his breeches torn and frayed, and there were cuts and bruises all over his body. Henry felt more vulnerable than he ever had before. But even if he had no fine clothes, he believed that his manners would show him to be of royal blood. Also, there was his ring. Henry felt for the chain around his neck with the ring on it. It was valuable enough to show he was a gentleman. But to his dismay, it was gone, fallen into the river, no doubt, just like his connection with his past. He tried to hold up his spirits.

"I agree with you there. I do look like a ruffian, but I *am* a prince, a prince of England. This is of the greatest importance. Please explain to them that, if they help me, I can bestow great riches upon them in return, riches that they will never have seen before."

Balthazar looked askance at him, then shrugged and said, "So be it – if you might wish."

He turned towards the group of men, who had been watching the two boys while they spoke in English to each other. Balthazar thought for a moment before speaking to them in Welsh. His words caused an eruption of laughter from the sea-dogs. The joker of the sea-dogs set his hands in a mock-feminine manner and wiggled his hips. The others laughed heartily at his mimicry. There followed more raucous laughter from the men.

"What are they saying? What language are they speaking?" asked Henry, who was not at all sure that the conversation was going his way.

"These men are Welsh, and in, how do you say, 'a nutshell,' they not believe you, that man says if you prince, he be Queen of Sheba," Balthazar explained. "The man in charge is King of sea-dogs here, so I suggest you bow to him. His name is Morgan, Llewelyn Morgan."

Henry bowed stiffly towards the captain, but just a small, polite bow, not a subservient gesture. "But I am a prince – Prince Henry. My grandfather was Edmund Tudor. He was a Welshman and half-brother of Henry VI. Surely they must know of him?"

"I ask them," said Balthazar.

Turning back to the sea-dogs, Balthazar asked them if they had heard of a man called Edmund Tudor, who was a brother of a King called Henry VI, for this boy was his grandson. The sea-dogs knew of the Tudors, but as renowned soldiers who had fought in the Welsh rebellion against the English. The Tudors were Welsh heroes and any of their offspring would speak Welsh, not English.

Llewelyn Morgan asked a question. Balthazar translated. "They want you speak Welsh."

Henry thought hard. Although his fine education had given him fluency in Latin, Greek, French, some Spanish and a little bit of German, he had not been taught one word of Welsh. This was a disaster. He was the grandson of a Tudor, yet he could not speak Welsh. The only Welsh he could think of was a saying that one of his earliest nursemaids used to say.

"Bwrw hen wragedd a fynn?"

This caused an explosion of laughter from the band of wild men.

"What does it mean?" Henry asked Balthazar, who was also laughing.

"You not know? You say, 'It rains old hags and walking sticks.'"

The sea-dogs had wasted enough time. Llewelyn Morgan spoke and his men stood up. Before Balthazar could translate the captain's words, a second pirate walked up, picked Henry up by his feet and, with the jolly man, carried him away. Morgan watched Henry fighting all the way to the cave where the sea-dogs kept all their booty, including prisoners, whom they sold as slaves. Then he turned to Balthazar and spoke quietly, telling him to keep an eye on the prisoner, for he was a spirited child and was bound to be trouble.

Sure enough, Henry struggled and fought to free himself, cursing at the sea-dogs using the worst language he could possibly use. For the first time in his life, nobody could understand what he meant and so he allowed himself complete freedom of speech.

"You pigs, let go of me, you turds, you bloody dogs, you damnable heathens!"

Then he changed tactic, pleading, "You have to believe me. I *am* Prince Henry and I must rescue my brother. You have to let me go – please!"

A quiet voice came from the darkness into which he had been thrown unceremoniously by the sea-dogs. "There's no yelling at them. They don't understand English."

Henry looked around him, letting his eyes grow accustomed to the darkness. He was being held in a cage, like a wild animal, one of his father's lions or bears. The door was locked, and the bars went from the floor to the ceiling in one corner of the cave. He held onto the rusty bars and shook them to test their strength. They rattled but did not give way.

There was someone else in the cave-prison, a huddled mass in a corner.

"And who are you, may I ask?" he enquired.

"My name is Rosalind and I am happy to meet you, my prince." There was a touch of irony in her voice, but she was not being unkind.

"You don't believe me either, do you? What am I going to do?" Henry flopped down on a wooden bench. Rosalind seemed happy to sit on the floor in a dark corner.

The girl felt his despair and waited a while before adding to his woes by saying truthfully, "Right now, probably not much. They are a filthy bunch of animals and they will not listen to you even if you shout all night and all day. I have tried."

"Really? This is impossible!" Henry sighed in desperation.

A thought came to him. Master Skelton said that there was always a solution to a problem; you just had to give it time to reveal itself. Henry sat motionless, deep in thought, waiting for inspiration to come. Perhaps Charles or Jack would come searching for him? Only if they did not think him dead, which they most likely did. Nobody would think that he could have survived that fall. But then, Jack and Charles were his sworn friends. They would surely look for him along the river until they came to the encampment. Then, they would come and enquire of the men if they had seen his body in the river, and the sea-dogs would ask for a ransom and then set him free once they knew he was really a prince. A ransom! That was a good idea.

"Hey, you, Balthazar," he shouted out towards the group of sea-dogs, who were now settled around a fire, drinking and singing. He kept shouting until Balthazar finally came up to him and spoke.

"I think to speak not so loud. Captain Morgan is sleepy of your fat face, my friend," was his advice.

"It's you I want to talk to," insisted Henry. "Look, if you can get them to believe me, I can arrange a massive reward for my release. I will pay you handsomely if you could get a message to my father, the King."

"That is one kind offer, my friend, but how anyone believe me? Do you have a, how do you say, big truth that you are big prince?"

Henry racked his brains. Everything that he held dear had been lost when he fled from Fiddle. It was all in his backpack, which had been tied to the saddle of his pony, but he had lost her in the fall.

"Look, Balthazar, I have lost everything. I have no proof, other than…" Henry thought hard. "There must be some way I can convince you. How about you ask me any question you like about my royal life, and I give you an answer."

Balthazar considered for a moment. "There is nothing I can think asking you. Sorry."

He threw Henry a piece of bread that he was holding and sauntered back to sit with the sea-dogs. Henry picked up the bread, took a bite, then threw it on the floor, for it was a rough bread that peasants ate, not what he was used to.

"I wouldn't waste food if I were you," warned Rosalind. "They don't give away much. He's not a bad child, but the pirates order him to keep our rations short so that we don't get too strong and fight with them when they move us."

"Move us where?" Henry asked.

Rosalind looked at him with pity. "Don't you know? Welsh pirates are famous for trading in slaves. They take prisoners from here and sell them abroad. We could be in some strange far-off land by next week. I will be sold to a harem; you will become a house servant or a farmhand. If you are lucky, as you seem educated, you might be taken on as an apprentice to a scribe or an accountant."

"A slave?" Henry was horrified. "I can't be sold as a *slave*!" Blood boiling, Henry stood up again and shouted for

Balthazar. The boy returned, somewhat irritated. "What you want now?"

"*Please* help me!" Henry begged with as much dignity as a prince could muster in this situation. "You are my only hope. Please tell them that I could even get them knighted, if they will only let me go."

"I think not that they have interest in rantings," said Balthazar. "You have no proof if you are born of king." He was about to walk away when Henry saw the sword he wore and had an idea.

"Look, Balthazar, I am well trained with a sword. Only a noble would be able to sword fight. It is not what peasants do. Let me show you my sword skills. Will that make them believe me?"

Balthazar thought for a moment and then turned and walked back to the sea-dogs. After a conversation with the captain, he returned with a couple of the men and a long chain.

"The men are happy at you to show your sword skills but you wear chain on leg." He pointed at the chain, which Henry now noticed had a shackle at the end of it.

There was no point in arguing, so Henry allowed a man to put the shackle on one ankle and then he was led to an open space near the fire that the sea-dogs had cleared as an arena. He was given a somewhat blunt sword, but that did not matter, for it was his skill that he wanted to show off; he was not about to try to fight his way out. That would be sheer folly as he was outnumbered.

Henry was wondering who he would be allowed to fight when Balthazar stepped forward. He was a good match, about the same height as Henry and probably the same weight too. The two boys squared up against each other and Henry scored the first point by bowing with great dignity. No mere peasant would show such etiquette. Balthazar followed suit, being a natural gentleman, smiled a confident smile, then quickly took his stance. He looked well-schooled and nimble, Henry thought. He would be fun to fight. Henry gracefully fell into his first position, arms held, right to the front with his sword and the left hand behind in the air for balance. He adjusted his feet to find the correct position and gently bent his knees, ready to begin.

Within moments, the two boys were dancing while circling each other, hopping from this foot to that, their weight distributed evenly so that they could move with speed, with the occasional thrust and stab at each other, weight thrown onto the front foot as they lunged and then back again. They were evenly matched, but Balthazar had more experience, so although Henry had been taught by his sword master, one of the best swordsmen in the country, he was at a disadvantage: he had never fought to the death as Balthazar had on his ship. Balthazar had the edge: he attacked with more gusto and his sword hand was deadly. With a lightning strike, he knocked Henry's sword out of his hand and, stepping back, he laughed in a good-natured manner.

"Pick it up, boy. You give three lives," he told Henry, who, keeping his eyes fixed on the pirate boy, bent down to pick up the sword.

Without saying a word, Henry prepared to fight again, and before long the two boys were battling in earnest. The seadogs watched, at first with lazy amusement; however, the fight was so compelling that they were soon standing around the two combatants, shouting encouragement and laying bets with one another. Some of the men even chose to bet on Henry, not that he knew this.

Balthazar, who at first had taken Henry to be a young upstart with ambitions above his station, soon realised that he was a well-taught adversary. He doubled his efforts and, in a quick dash for glory, thrust forward too hastily. Henry, who was waiting for such an error, sidestepped and spun around low, and his blunt sword caught Balthazar on the back of his knees, which buckled, leaving him prone on the ground. His signature move had worked, and Henry felt triumphant. He gallantly stood back to give Balthazar time to recover.

The sea-dogs were cheering with enthusiasm, but as Henry could not understand them, he ignored their cries, for they might be hurling insults to try to distract him. He took up his position, sweat pouring down his brow, and faced Balthazar once again. Balthazar was somewhat shaken at having hit the ground. His blood was up, and he was no longer smiling at Henry but was gritting his teeth, preparing for a strike. Henry could see his anger and stepped back. He needed to wear the boy down rather than attack for a while.

"The men are happy at you to show your sword skills but you wear chain on leg."

Balthazar came again with more determination than ever. Henry danced like he had never danced before, spinning, hopping, bending low to miss some blade swings and jumping high to avoid others.

"Ne bouge pas, tu petit singe!" (Keep still, you little monkey!) Balthazar cursed at him as he thrust his sword forward yet again. Henry hopped backward and smiled to himself for the first time, for he was beginning to learn his opponent's mindset, his tactics and his modus operandi as if they were written on a page, things he had studied for years – a trick not learned by pirates, or so it seemed.

Just as he was about to make his final move on Balthazar, Henry slipped in the mud. As he fell, he saw the flash of a stick or whip under his foot. Someone had tripped him, but there was nothing he could do. As he hit the dirt with a wet thud, Balthazar jumped forward and put a foot on his back and the tip of his blade against his neck.

"Voila!" he cried out triumphantly, with a flourish, and the crowd of onlookers cheered.

Henry knew he was defeated, but his quick mind realised that he would win even more favour if he took his defeat with good humour, so once he was allowed to get up from the ground, he bowed before Balthazar, handing him his blunt sword with both hands, gracefully admitting defeat. He was now even dirtier than ever.

His audience loved this gesture and cheered, while Balthazar nodded acknowledgment. Turning to the pirates, he told them that he thought that Henry was at the very least the son of a gentleman. It seemed that they agreed, but only thought that this would make him more valuable as a slave. A couple of them came up to him and dragged him back to the prison in the cave, where they at least removed the chain and shackle.

"But wait, please, can't you see that I am who I say I am?" he cried hopelessly.

The sea-dogs had lost interest in him, for they were settling bets between themselves. As the evening wore on, Henry was left to sulk in the prison while they drank and sang songs before slowly, one by one, nodding off or crawling to some pile of blankets under which to sleep for the rest of the night while the fire burned low.

"Come on, cheer up, love," the woman said after a while. "It won't be that bad. I hear that the weather is beautiful over on the other side and they treat you well if you work hard. I know of some slaves who have risen to respected positions at foreign courts. With your manners and knowledge of languages, you ought to do well."

This was certainly of no comfort to the prince, who wondered at the fact that only a short while ago he had been thinking of his future coronation if his brother died. Now, owing to unforeseen circumstances, he had lost everything, even his freedom. To go from potentially ruling the country to losing control of one's life so suddenly seemed almost ludicrous. This could not be happening to him. It just was not possible.

"They can't be allowed to just *sell* somebody, like a dog or a horse!" He sounded incredulous.

Rosalind came out of the darkness to comfort him. All he could see in the dim light of the dying fire was her face. She was beautiful, like a Madonna, with soft skin and sparkling eyes. Henry guessed that she must be as old as Charles, but not as old as his mother, certainly no more than twenty-five at the most.

"My dear little prince, you have no idea what they can do to us. They have complete control over our lives now. This cage is strong, and we have no way of escaping. They will keep us under control by taunting us and only feeding us bread and water until we are too weak to fight. When the moon is full and the tides are high they will shackle us and take us onto their ship. They will then slip out of the estuary into the seas, and from there we will be taken to a country where we cannot speak the language so cannot ask anyone for help to escape. We will become slaves in a strange world, with no friends and no money of our own with which to bribe someone to help us. We will be stripped of our pasts and become tools for someone to use as they wish. I know this, for I have been warned about straying into the arms of a pirate since I was young, but I was tricked."

Henry was intrigued. "How could you be tricked into walking into this horrible situation? Surely you could tell they were sea-dogs by the cut of them?"

Rosalind smiled one of the saddest smiles that Henry hadever seen. "It was not as simple as that. I was young and foolish. I am a glove-maker by trade and lived just outside of Worcester with my widowed father. The overseer of the glove-master took a shine to me and kept pestering me for my hand in marriage. He used to go at me all the time. When my father died a few weeks ago, the overseer made his move. He came to my house and tried to seduce me. When I refused his advances and slapped his face, he swore his revenge. That night, when I was asleep, some men came and burned down my house. As I ran out into the night, one of them caught me, threw a sack over my head and tied me up. I was thrown over the back of a pony and brought here, where I was sold to the pirates for a few pennies. I have been here ever since, and I have no family left to look for me. I am doomed."

Henry was appalled. "But that is criminal. This surely cannot happen in England. Not in my father's country. We live in civilised times. There are judges and courts that are meant to stop such things happening."

Rosalind looked at him with the kindest eyes. "My dear child. Your father, if he really *is* the King, would do well to teach you the truth about his wonderful kingdom. There is law for the rich, but none for the poor. There is not a soldier in the land who would bother to rescue a poor woman like me unless he wanted me for his own amusement. I am not worth them risking their lives, for I have nothing to offer in thanks other than myself or a pair of gloves."

Henry realised that he was powerless. "Then I am doomed. Nobody knows where I am, and my friends who were travelling with me think I have drowned. My father does not know that I have left home and would not know where to look for me even if he did."

Henry was desolate, the grim truth of his situation laid bare before him. Life as a slave, if he survived the voyage in the bowels of a rat-infested ship, was becoming a terrifying possibility – worse, a certainty, for he could see no way of escape.

Rosalind truly felt for the boy, who was only young despite being tall. She got up, sat down on the bench and put her arms around him, pulling Henry gently towards her. She felt soft and warm, with a sweet yet musky scent that brought memories of his mother flooding into his mind that overwhelmed his senses. Henry allowed himself to sink into the comfort of her embrace and cry. She would not mind, as she did not believe he was who he was, he thought. Anyway, it no longer mattered, so he sobbed uncontrollably like a baby, until, at last, he fell asleep in her arms.

16

Anxious over the safety of his best friend, Jack was not giving up. He and Bottom were traversing dangerous paths, sticking to the edge of the river into which Henry had fallen. He was sometimes forced to find his way back up along a country road until he could pass this obstruction or that, but he returned to the riverbank as soon as possible.

Jack was furious with Charles for abandoning Henry. Once they had caught up with the mob who had chased Henry, only to learn that he had fallen to his death by jumping over a hedge into the water below, Charles had insisted on heading to Ludlow Castle. Now that Henry was dead, he declared that his duty was to rescue Prince Arthur, the surviving son of the King. This had been their original quest and he would make sure that they succeeded, honouring Henry in this manner. Jack admitted that this all sounded noble, but he suspected that Charles was looking to cash in on the glory he would receive if he saved Prince

Arthur from his assassin.

"I always thought he was no good," Jack muttered angrily. "He is too fond of money and glory to care for Henry. He will do better for himself at court by saving Arthur. He will gain fame and fortune. But what about Henry?"

Bottom shook his head up and down, snorting and spraying spume from his mouth.

"Exactly my point," Jack replied, and Bottom trumpeted out of his backside in reply.

The going was hard, but Bottom walked carefully, picking the best route through the mud and sharp stones. Then they heard the not-so-distant sound of cheering and shouting, plus the clangour of swords clashing. Bottom stood still and would go no further. Jack slipped to the ground and gingerly crept forward. There was a craggy outcrop of rocks on the bend of the river and the sound was coming from the other side.

Jack lowered himself to the ground, moving as stealthily as he could. Peeping over the rocks, he saw a gathering of the wildest-looking men he had ever seen, the ugliest misfits he could have imagined. Tall and short, fat and thin, they all wore the same brightly dyed scarves either around their necks or tied as caps on their head: blue, green, yellow and red. The bright colours somehow brought them together as a group, who otherwise were in dirty old jackets and breeches. Armed with knives that were tied to their legs or on belts, with the last rays of the dying sun reflected on the metal, they certainly looked menacing to the young boy.

Studying the scene more carefully, Jack noticed that the men were cheering on two figures who were sword fighting. The men were shouting in a strange language. Were they French? Dutch? What were they doing here in England? At first, Jack thought he had stumbled across some sort of invasion and wondered if he should go and raise the alarm. Then one of the combatants bent his legs and turned on one foot, hitting his opponent on the back of his legs so that he collapsed. Jack knew that to be Henry's signature move. Nobody else did that. He had found Henry!

Ecstatic, Jack was about to jump up and run over to Henry when he noticed that his friend wore what looked like a shackle and chain around his leg. What was that for? Was he a prisoner? *Goodness.* Jack watched the fight through to its conclusion, when Henry bowed before being led off into what looked like a cave. Jack could not see what was in the cave, but he doubted that it was anything good. He kept vigilant. The wild men appeared to be enjoying themselves, but as the evening wore on, the campfire died down, so they each found a place to recline and fall asleep.

Jack crept back to Bottom, who was standing patiently while eating a nearby bush, thinking the situation over. He could go and get help. He *should* go and get help, but help was not close at hand; in fact, Jack was miles away from anywhere or anyone he knew. So, all he could do was creep into the cave and see what was there. It was dark enough for him to do this, for the sun had now disappeared completely and a waning moon was slowly rising into the sky. A light wind was blowing in his direction, which would help disguise any sound he might make. It also brought the smell of the dying fire mixed with the less savoury aroma of unwashed bodies and rum-powered breath. He could hear the odd grunt as the slumbering men slept soundly.

Having tied Bottom to an overhanging branch that stuck out over the muddy bank, Jack took off his coat and shirt. That done, he carefully slid over the rocks. There might be a guard on duty, so he moved as slowly as he could, breathing deeply to calm his racing heart, a trick John Skelton had taught them.

Closer and closer he wriggled along the bank, mud sticking to him everywhere. With a flash of inspiration, he rubbed mud all over his face as well, to make himself appear part of his surroundings. Master Skelton would have given him a pat on the back for that. All he could hear was the crackling of the last few sticks in the fire, trickling of the river against the bank and the odd cry of a night creature, a curlew, fox or some soul, floating on the light wind. A man was snoring. Jack kept on going, staying as far from the men and as close to the edge of the river as he could, pushing against the brushwood that grew there. He stopped every now and then when he thought he saw a man moving. At one point a pirate woke up, stood over by the water and noisily relieved himself before lying back down to sleep. Jack lay for a good five minutes after that to ensure the man was unconscious again before he crept onwards.

It seemed to take forever, but finally Jack reached the cave. He stopped and listened. He could hear the gentle breathing of someone asleep.

"Henry?" he whispered and waited for a reply. Listening, he could hear the drip, drip, dripping of water from within the cave. It sounded like a drum beating.

He took a chance at speaking a bit louder. "Henry!"

"Hello?" a woman's voice whispered.

Oh no, thought Jack, holding his breath, staying as still as a statue.

"Is anyone there? I am a friend of Henry's," said the woman's voice. "He is sleeping next to me. Shall I wake him?"

"Please," Jack answered. If she was not telling the truth, he would soon know.

There was a bit of movement in the darkness before him and all Jack could hear was mumbling and then, "Who's there? Charles? Jack?"

"Second time lucky!" Jack was somewhat disappointed that his name came only after Charles's.

There was the sound of someone jumping up and Henry appeared, as close as the prison bars would allow him.

"Jack! By St George! Come, let me out, quick, please!" Henry sounded elated and desperate at the same time.

"Hush," warned the woman, who was obviously a friend. "They will wake up if you are not careful."

"Sorry." Henry was elated. Never in his life had he felt so low, so vulnerable and in need of a friend, and here was Jack, as faithful as ever, come to rescue him.

"Jack, you have to get me out of here. The cage is made of rusty old iron. I have studied it. The bars are drilled into the rock overhead, but they twist, so I think they are single bars and are just dug into the beach. I would have started digging, but the sea-dogs would have seen me."

"Sea-dogs? Do you mean pirates? Oh my God!" Jack nearly passed out at the mention of such cut-throats. They were renowned for their ferocity, and he was breaking into their camp. He gulped. "How many of them?"

Henry had done his homework. "There are eight adults and a boy my age. He is French and has been civil to me. But the others are animals."

Jack sat back in the darkness and thought for a while. "If we had some rope, I could get Bottom to pull the bars out, but you will have to run like hell in order to escape if the bastards wake up." He was imagining the scene as he spoke.

The woman pointed. "They keep their rope in the back of the cave," she told him.

Jack felt his way into the cave and, after what seemed to Henry like a lifetime, came back with a long coil of rope.

"If you do this, I will be in danger too," said the woman.

Henry felt responsible for her. "You had better come with us then."

The woman shook her head. "No, that would be folly. We would all be caught. I will run in the other direction and create as much noise as I can. They will catch me and do their worst, but I can take it. I want you to escape, for if you are who you say you are, then your safety is of greater importance than mine. Come and rescue me later, if you can – after you have rescued your brother, of course."

Henry was startled at the bare courage of this peasant; no, she was more than that, this woman who would put her King's son before her own safety. "I will find you and rescue you, that I promise," he said, and with that, he took her hand and kissed it, before turning back to Jack.

"Here, give me the rope to tie to the bars while you go and fix the other end to Bottom's saddle. When you break the bars, I will follow you by holding the rope. Be ready to flee," he commanded, back in his usual state of mind.

"I will - but take this." Jack pulled a packet out of his pocket. It was one of the mystery packets wrapped in waxed paper that he had stored so carefully into his saddle bag at the beginning of the journey. Henry wondered if it had anything to do with gunpowder. That would be typical of Jack... He held it in his hand, weighing curiously.

"Throw it into the fire to create a diversion. But for God's sake, run as fast as you can afterwards, for it will cause havoc." Henry was about to ask why, but before he could open his mouth, the intrepid Jack had disappeared into the night.

Henry clung to the packet, determined to use it if he could get close to the fire.

Henry's mood was lighter already. He and Jack had been in all sorts of trouble during their time together, and apart from the obvious extra danger of there being pirates in this instance in this instance, tonight was just like any one of their escapades.

"He is my best friend, you know. I trust him with my life," he told Rosalind proudly.

"That's lucky, for you are going to need all the help you can get, young man. If they catch you, they will kill you, you know," Rosalind warned. "They always do."

Henry was alarmed. "Will they kill you then?" he asked, ready to insist that she came with them rather than act as a decoy.

"They will do worse. But it is something I can survive." Henry was not quite sure what Rosalind was referring to,

but the tone of her voice painted a picture of so much suffering that he almost refused to leave her.

However, Rosalind was insistent. "You are our only hope," she reminded him. "Come back and get me if you can. I will only remain here until the spring tide in a week's time. Then they will set out to sea in their vessel, and I will be chained up in the hold. If the voyage doesn't kill me, I will become the plaything of a sultan out in some distant land."

Her words sent a shiver down Henry's back. They were in serious trouble, he knew.

Jack crept his way back across the length of the beach and trembled as he tied a firm knot to Bottom's saddle before leading him away from the beach, where the sea-dogs were sleeping. If the bars bent, they would pop out without too much noise, but if they cracked, being old and rusty, it would make a loud sound and mayhem would be let loose.

Slowly, Bottom leaned against the straining rope as Jack urged him onwards. The mule was primarily a working animal, used to pulling a plough, so he took the strain with ease and began to pull against it. At first, nothing seemed to happen, but then, just as Jack thought that they were going to get away with a silent, secret escape, there was the mighty crack that echoed across the river and back. The sea-dogs jumped out of their slumber and fumbled around to find their boots and swords.

Up jumped Captain Morgan, shouting orders to the waking men. His strange words, although unintelligible to Henry and Jack, could be understood as his calling his men to arms. Had the boys had time to watch, they might have found the scene quite comical. The men were in were in a state of startled chaos. They had taken off their boots to sleep and were hopping about on sharp stones, cursing and swearing as they leaped from one foot to the other then the other while pulling their boots on. At the same time, they were waving their swords in the air at nothing and anything as if they were being attacked by ghosts.

Balthazar immediately thought of the prisoners and ran to check on them just as Henry bolted out of the cave. The two boys crashed into each other and fell to the ground. Henry tried to get up and run, but Balthazar grabbed his foot and pulled him back down, whereupon the two of them fought like common street urchins. The stakes were too high to allow for courtly manners now, and Henry sank his teeth into Balthazar's hand to make him let go.

"Ouch! You little monkey!" he cried out in pain.

Henry jumped up and managed a few steps before a large pirate charged him, grabbing him around the waist. Henry's feet were lifted right off the ground and he kicked his legs furiously while he struggled against the man's bear hug.

Rosalind chose this moment to bring part of the broken prison bar down on the sea dog's head. He collapsed onto the ground. Henry landed back on his feet and turned to see who had saved him. Seeing Rosalind, he smiled, blew her one last kiss and ran like he had never run before, while she ran in the other direction, shouting some of the rudest language Henry had ever heard a woman utter.

Henry ran towards the fire and threw the packet into its midst before sprinting up the beach to find the rope, then he followed it, hotly pursued by a gang of men. There was a flash as bright as the sun and all shadows became nothing but memories as the whole world went white. A millisecond later, an explosion shook the ground Henry was running on. He slipped and fell, the impact of the soundwave making his ears throb with pain, warm blood emerging. His head was ringing. Men were screaming.

Bottom hollered and reared, knocking Jack to the ground as he bolted into the darkness. Henry stumbled on and reached Jack, who was lying on his face, whether stunned by the explosion or by falling and hitting his head, he did not know.

"Jack, Jack, can you hear me?" Henry shook his friend desperately.

"What happened?" asked Jack. Both boys were talking, but neither could hear.

Henry looked back at the fire. He could see nothing, for the fire had gone. "We had better get out of here." he suggested. Jack did not need to hear him to have the same idea.

Up the beach the pirates came. The boys ran, but without Bottom, they had no fast means of escape. Their legs were like jelly with fear and the terrain was slippery and almost impossible to run on. Jack fell and Henry stopped to pull him back to his feet.

"I can't run, Henry, go on without me. Bottom will not be far." The boys could hear once again.

Henry was resolute. "I am not leaving you – come *on*!" He grabbed Jack by the arm and tried to lift him onto his back.

But he was too late. The two boys clung to each other as the sea-dogs bore down on them. They kicked, bit and punched anything they could, arms and legs flailing, but they were no match for the massive, muscled men who held them. They were carried, kicking and screaming, back to where the fire had once been before it was blown to kingdom come. There was a crater in the beach and all around it were men lying in the moonlight. Three were corpses and two were badly wounded, one with a foot missing. He would not last long unless someone stopped the flow of blood that was coming from his stump of a leg. This was a terrible scene, with blood everywhere, a blackish colour in the half-light. Knowing that he was responsible for this carnage, Henry felt sick and emptied his stomach in the darkness.

Captain Morgan called out for Balthazar, who had not been hurt, for he had been standing near the cave when Henry threw the packet into the fire. Balthazar was in shock but did what he was asked. With the help of one of the surviving men, Balthazar ensured that the two boys were tied up.

Soon, out of the gloom came another pirate holding Rosalind. He threw her forward in a rough manner while barking out orders. The boys were none the wiser about their fate, for the sea-dogs only spoke Welsh, but Rosalind understood. As her hands were being bound, she warned them.

"They are going to kill us. It is an old pirate law. When they capture you, they treat you well enough unless you try to escape. If you do so and fail, the punishment is death."

Henry could hardly believe his ears, which were now covered in dried blood. He was the son of the King of England, for God's sake! He could not be killed like a common criminal! There must be somebody who could stop this, someone who would vouch for him. Where was Charles? Where was John Skelton? Where was his father? He would never know what had happened to his younger son. Realising how reckless he had been to think that he could travel across England without a full escort of soldiers, Henry understood why his father thought him a poor candidate for kingship or any other ship.'

"Balthazar!" he shouted, thinking that he had to up his game. "Where are you?"

A very frightened Balthazar came out of the shadows. He suspected that the boys were magicians after what he had witnessed. He had just seen five fully grown men blown up into the sky, and only two were still living, although probably not for long, their wounds were so awful.

He looked at Henry angrily. "You are in for it now, 'Prince'. They will not forgive you for this. There is nothing that I can do to help you." He stared at Henry accusingly and then walked away.

The night was old, and the half-moon had travelled its arc across the sky. There was the faintest touch of light coming from the east and a solitary blackbird began to sing its welcome to the dawn. The wind had died, as had all feelings of hope for the captives who were tied together sitting on the beach: Jack and Henry were in shock, and even Rosalind was at a loss as to how to comfort them.

The sea-dogs began to dig graves for their comrades. Once the dead were in the ground, covered by stony mounds, they cut down some young trees from a nearby wood and dragged them onto the beach. Henry wondered what they were making from the timber, for they were strapping shorter pieces across the longer tree trunks at a right angle. One of the men then dug three holes in the ground and the timber was dragged over to the holes. It was as the three remaining seadogs hauled the end of the larger timber into the hole and raised it up that Henry understood what they had been making: three crosses. Crosses that overlooked the graves of the dead men below. Perhaps they were to mark the graves.

Llewelyn Morgan then approached Henry and gestured that he

should stand. Balthazar was made to translate the captain's harsh words, increasingly unhappy though he was.

"You call yourself a prince; then you shall be crowned as one." Morgan produced a crown made from a thorn bush and placed it on Henry's head. "It is Easter this week. Just as Jesus claimed to be the son of a King, so do you, so you can enjoy the same fate as he, King of the Jews."

Henry wore the crown with as much decorum as he could muster and looked the captain in the eye. "You are making a grave mistake," he said slowly, so that Balthazar could translate, "for if I die, my father, the King, will stop at nothing until he has found you and hung, drawn and quartered both you and your men. Your heads will end up on spikes at Traitors' Gate."

He then stood quietly, wondering if God would accept him into his realm now that he had killed three men, however unwittingly. "Forgive me, Father, for I have sinned," he whispered under his breath again and again as the pirates hoisted him up to one of the crosses and tied him to it, his arms out to the sides. Rosalind was tied to the middle cross and Jack to the third one. At least they had not used nails, just rope tied tightly around their arms and wrists, their waists and ankles. They were doing to leave them to die slowly as they looked down on the graves of the men they had killed. This was good, for it would take days to die of thirst and somebody might find them and save them in the interim. Henry held his head up and allowed hope to bolster his spirits.

The captives then watched the sea-dogs collecting something – their possessions, he assumed – as they prepared to leave camp. But when they turned around, he saw with horror that they were collecting driftwood and bringing it back towards Henry and the others. As he blinked in the hope that he was seeing things, the men began to build a pile of kindling under their feet. They were surely not going to burn them, for that would be murder.

"Balthazar!" cried Henry. Surely they would not be so cruel? "We are *children*!"

Balthazar was horrified, but as a young pirate, he had had to learn to have a strong stomach. "I am sorry, friend, but you killed our brothers with big magic. For all of you it is death. There is nothing I can do to help. I am badly unhappy." Then he walked away, for he did not want to witness what would happen next. He wanted to get far away from the smell of burning flesh and the accompanying screams that were bound to occur.

"Where's Charles when we need him?" joked Jack, there being little else he could think of saying. "Always look on the bright side: we won't need coffins for our bodies after this." Jack was not frightened of death, but he was frightened of the pain of burning. He would prefer hanging, or at least at that very moment, he thought he would.

※

Thankfully, Charles was not that far away and had been wandering along the river's edge for hours now, looking for Jack. After they had argued and parted company, he discovered he could not bear the thought of Henry being in trouble if he was actually still alive. The last that he knew, Henry had fallen off his pony into a river and had probably drowned. But then Jack believed that he was still alive and had chosen to go and save him. Jack had a connection with Henry that was undeniably stronger than anyone else's, and if he thought that Henry was alive, there was a good chance that his instinct was correct. And if Henry *was* alive, then he was most likely in trouble without someone to look after him. He was not used to the real world; he was used to the life of a cosseted prince.

Jack was not frightened for death, but he was frightened of the pain of burning.

He would be like a lamb to the slaughter without Charles and Jack as his protectors, and Charles had sworn to protect him. He *must* find Henry to keep this promise.

"You are a bloody fool," Charles berated himself as he walked along in the dark. "If you had not been out drinking and gambling, this would never have happened."

Charles walked on through the night until dawn, almost delirious at this stage, both from worry and weariness, searching for the hoofprints of Bottom, which he had followed to the best of his ability. It was then that he heard the trotting of an animal on the beach below and soon was met by a frightened Bottom, with his saddle on and his reins hanging down. "Oh my God," Charles said to himself. "Jack must be in trouble."

Having caught the mule, Charles quietened him down by patting his neck and talking to him. "And where have you been, my friend?" The mule looked lost without Jack. "Come on, let's go and find your master. Show me the way."

Charles heard voices ahead.

"Is this where you left the others?" he asked him. Bottom turned to lead the way. Charles took the hint and followed him. He could see the beginnings of smoke from a newly lit fire.

Then he heard screams. Terrified screams.

Charles could not walk fast on the slippery beach, but a mule is more sure-footed. Climbing onto Bottom, Charles urged him to go as fast as he could. The mule understood. Mules are extremely intelligent creatures. Bottom could smell the fire and he could smell fear. All living creatures give off an acrid aroma when terrified and the mule could smell it strongly. It was a mixture of sweat, urine and hormones. When Bottom knew that there was imminent danger ahead, he came to a halt.

Charles was not having dissension at this point, and he jumped down, took the mule by his nose and faced him head on he spoke with determination. "Bottom, this is not the time to behave like a coward. You are coming with me, whether you like it or not. This will be our finest hour, I promise you. Just trust me."

Looking around him, Charles was surprised to see a Norman helmet floating up against the edge of the river, bobbing gently in the breeze. This gave him an idea. He picked it up and drained it of water before putting it on his head. It was a little on the large side, for the lining inside was missing, but it would do. Next, he needed a weapon. Spotting a fishing boat under a tree, he looked to see if there was anything useful inside. The boat had seen its day on the water, there being a large hole in its bow, but there were some oars that looked sound enough.

I could use an oar as a lance, he thought to himself.

Charles picked up first one oar, then the other, and hefted them about to feel their weight and balance. They were similar, as oars are meant to be, but one was a little bowed, so he left it behind and chose the other.

Hauling himself into the saddle, Charles patted the mottled mule in a gesture of solidarity.

"Come on, my friend, it is time for us to show our mettle." He spoke with resolve, although his guts felt trepidation.

He then decided that being quiet was not the way to build up momentum. He needed to employ a full-frontal attack, as he would on the battlefield or in the lists.

"Okay, let's go. Bottom, our prince is in need of us, for you and I are the only men here who can save him."

As Charles urged the mule into a fast trot, he shouted to bolster his courage. He felt that his mount needed a rallying cry as much as he did, so gave full vent to his voice.

"For God And For Henry!"

There were three large, angry, red-eyed men standing on the beach, fanning the fires under three crosses and laughing as their captives screamed with fear. They were the ugliest adversaries that Charles had ever come across and he knew that he was outnumbered. But Henry was in danger, so Charles charged in a one-man assault, his 'lance' held out before him.

"FOR GOD AND FOR HENRY!" he cried out again.

The sea-dogs heard his battle cry and turned to see a strange apparition charging at them: a man in an oversize helmet, riding a mule and pointing an oar at them with the long rabbit ears of his odd mount seeming to keep time with the man's flapping legs.

Bottom traversed the muddy beach with his teeth bared and his backside blowing the bugle salute. With the blade of the oar levelled at the first sea dog's head, Charles urged his loyal mount forward. He knocked the man over, splintering the oar, then charged the other man and ran him through, the splintered blade piercing the pirate's chest, who fell to the ground, dead. At the same time, Charles knew that he had to find a moment to kick the fire away from the crosses. This was impossible while mounted, so he threw himself down from Bottom, who, understanding the gravity of the moment, went around causing chaos in his own right, kicking and biting pirates wherever he could.

"Charles, it's Charles!" yelled Henry. "Please, Charles, HELP US!"

Charles did not have time to reply. He had killed one man, but the one he had knocked over had risen again and, with the captain, was coming at him with murderous intent. With the remains of the oar Charles thrust forward into the armpit of the first of his assailants, who screamed in pain. Falling back, the man dropped his sword to put his hand under his arm. Blood spurted out from his armpit and covered his hand with a crimson river.

Morgan was the only pirate left standing. With his crew dying or dead around him, he was ready to fight to the death. But in all the chaos, the large helmet on Charles's head had slipped over his eyes, so that he could not see anything other than his feet, and he was going around in circles. He could not see Morgan, who was looking at him with a bloodlust that would have turned anyone's blood cold.

When Llewelyn Morgan had first seen this apparition come charging across the beach on a mule, he had noted the oar being used as a lance and the Norman helmet too big for his head and he had laughed to himself. But this knight had just killed the last of his men and he had witnessed the courage in the young man's eyes before they had been covered by the helmet. Now those eyes were blind, and the captain began to laugh in an ugly manner, for he was about to reek his revenge.

Charles tried to push the helmet up, but he could not let go of the oar, his only weapon, and it was too awkward to push the helmet back into place with his sleeve. All he could do was square up to face what was coming to him, and what was coming was death. However, by laughing, Morgan had given away his position, and, looking down while tipping his head back, Charles could see the captain's feet dead ahead of him. Raising the remains of the oar, Charles prepared to fight, even if he could only guess where Morgan's blade might come down on him. He swung the oar first one way and then the other but hit nothing. The pirate was an old hand at fighting and could jump out of the way with ease.

"HELP! Charles, help me!" cried Henry in desperation as the flames began to take hold. His friends were also screaming in terror at the enveloping flames. They were not yet as high as the captives' feet, but they were high enough to scare anyone who was about to be roasted like a pig on a stick.

Balthazar, meanwhile, had been watching from the shadows, witnessing his world crumbling around him into violence. This brought back memories of the blood and terror he had suffered years earlier when his ship was attacked by the seadogs. He remembered how the callous pirates had laughed as his father fell to his knees. "Look after my son," he had begged before falling onto the deck, never to rise again. Balthazar felt a surge of fury towards the sea-dogs, who had stolen his childhood from him, and he could take no more.

"I AM BALTHAZAR!" he cried as he ran recklessly to the stack of wood that was now burning well. "My name means the protector of the King! I will help you, Prince Henry!"

Grabbing a spade that lay near the graves, he took his blind rage out on the flames that were licking at the base of the crosses and stamped on the timber, burning his bare feet as he trampled the hot embers. Henry had no idea why the pirate boy had suddenly taken his side to rescue them, but he was not going to complain.

"Balthazar, *please* help me – cut me down. That man is my friend and I need to help him."

Balthazar pulled out his sheath knife and cut the ropes that bound Henry to the roughly made cross, then supported him as he climbed down, after which he set about releasing first Rosalind and then Jack.

Henry hardly had time to thank Balthazar, for he had to run to help Charles, who was facing a man Henry knew was deadly. Balthazar followed him, sword in hand, to protect him if Morgan got the upper hand. Balthazar had made his decision: he was now for Henry.

Henry was considering his strategy. He was only ten, and although he was big enough, he was hardly a match for a massive man like Llewelyn Morgan, so he would need to use his brains as much as his brawn. But then he saw the man attack Charles and all his planning disappeared. With brute force and a primal scream, Henry ran across the muddy beach ready to tackle the sea dog's legs. He was about to dive when Captain Morgan stopped dead in his tracks. The great pirate, with sword held high in preparation for his final death blow against the blinded Charles, came to a stop like the end of a book. He looked down in surprise at the arrow protruding from his chest.

It had struck him in the back and come out the other side, a red tinge to its head. Eyes wide and startled, the massive captain fell to the ground without further ado. He was dead.

Looking up, Henry saw a figure standing on the other side of the river, dressed in black robes and holding a bow. He was in the stance of an archer who had just shot an arrow, which he had, right through the heart of Llewelyn Morgan. It was the man Henry called the 'mad monk', who had been following them for the last week, hiding in the dark.

Henry was stunned, for this was the very person who had tried to kidnap him only days before. Now he had saved them. Henry waved, and after a moment, the shadow monk reacted by tentatively raising his hand in a salute.

Henry hailed him, as he wanted to talk to him, but it was too late. The monk had gone.

17

Balthazar stood staring at the body of the man who had been the greatest influence in his life since his father had died four years earlier. Captain Llewelyn Morgan. The man who had killed his father, then replaced him, but who had also put the fear of God into the young boy.

"Charles, Balthazar! Thank you for saving our lives," Henry spluttered in relief, running up to hug Charles before patting him on the back. "Where did you find my helmet? I lost that in the fall."

"I found it upstream. It came in handy." Charles took it off and ruffled his hair, which was wet with sweat. "You can have it back now. It doesn't fit me. My head is not as big as yours, my prince."

Henry was about to object at the insinuation, but then laughed and patted his friend on the back. "Thank you again, Charles. You saved my life. I will never forget that."[33]

Then he turned to Balthazar and solemnly shook his hand. Whatever had made the pirate boy change sides had just saved their lives, for within a few moments the fires would have burned them to death.

"Thank you, my friend, for what you did. I thought I was about to be roasted like a pig, and to be honest, I would not have had a brave death."

"I hope it is true that you *are* a prince, and you give me best friendship for life." Balthazar joked lamely. "I have no family now and no home." He was in shock from seeing his entire pirate life disappear in a matter of moments. All the pirates were dead. In a strange way they had become his family. Now he had no one.

Henry spoke in earnest. "Balthazar, you saved my life. Come and live with me at Eltham Palace. You can be my bodyguard and I will pay you well. I owe you my life." Balthazar was delighted.

Rosalind wanted to thank Balthazar, for he had saved her life too. Afterwards, she turned to the handsome man who had also come to their rescue and curtsied before him. "I don't know who you are, but you have saved my life and I am grateful, sir."

Charles smiled and bowed low before her. "It is my pleasure, dear lady, and I am only sorry that I was not here earlier to have saved you from this ordeal altogether. But we are all safe now – assuming these dead men have no other friends, that is?" They all looked at Balthazar. "There are no other pirates, are there?" asked Henry, for he had not given this a thought until now.

"No, they are all dead now. I am not unhappy. I was their prisoner too, but I had nowhere better to go, so they softened toward me and treated me as one of their own."

Charles offered Rosalind his hand and suggested that she bathe to wash away the smoke from her hair while he washed it from her clothes. He had quietly noticed that in her fright when being burned, the girl had wet herself, and he wanted to discreetly wash away the evidence. She took up his kind offer, and while she waded into the frigid water in her underclothes, Charles carefully washed her skirt and hung it out to dry. He then found a blanket and held it until Rosalind came out of the water, then wrapped it around her shoulders.

Meanwhile, the boys lit a fire, using the timber that only a short while ago had been set around their feet, and before long the small group was sitting around the fire, getting warm and eating what food they could find. Afterwards, Charles took himself off into the river to wash away the blood and sweat that covered his body.

Later, Charles took control and called a meeting, checking what they had lost and what they still had among their possessions. Though they had lost their other mounts, they still had Bottom. They also still had two swords, although Henry had lost his dagger. Balthazar then pointed out that the sea dog's swords were there for the taking, and so Henry soon found a dagger that felt comfortable in his hands. In return he left the Norman helmet in amongst the pirates' possessions for, in truth, it was a little too large even for him and he saw no reason he would need it again.

The sea-dogs had a stash of money and other loot, but this, they all agreed, belonged to Balthazar. Considering this, Balthazar took a beautiful gold cross on a chain, set with diamonds, and gave it to Rosalind.

"This is for all the horrors that you suffered," he told her. Rosalind was delighted with the gift and kissed Balthazar on the cheek, which made him blush.

Then, much to Henry's delight, Balthazar produced the wavy gold ring on its chain that he thought he had lost in the river. "I saw Captain Morgan take it from you when you were dead on beach. It is right yours."

Henry was delighted and hugged Balthazar, which took the pirate boy by surprise, making him smile happily. It was not often that he had been given a hug since his father died. Sea-dogs were not normally demonstrative.

Getting back to business, they knew what they did not have was time. Henry was concerned that they might reach Ludlow Castle too late. Balthazar came up with a solution that beggared belief. "I know clever ride to travel upstream fast by sea-dogs on a magic wave. If I find the paper they wrote out, when the wave comes, we ride the wave together."

Henry did not understand what Balthazar was talking about, but Rosalind did and she laughed. "You are talking about Sabrina."[34] she exclaimed. "My brothers used it too, just to play on. It is a mighty wave that travels up the river at certain tides. It is simple enough to predict if you have the tides and the moon worked out. It's a common event. Some call it the Servern Bore."

Balthazar went to rummage around the sea-dogs' possessions, pocketing a few items along the way. Finally, in a ditty box, he found what he was looking for.

"*Voilà*. It is tonight at four bells."

"We must give it a try, boys," Henry urged his friends. "We have to get to Ludlow Castle as soon as possible to save my brother."

Balthazar went back to the ditty box that had belonged to the Captain, or so he supposed, and brought out a map.

"That would be good to have," Charles pointed out. A map was a rare thing. This one looked as if it had been compiled by the owner through his knowledge of the area rather than having been prepared by a proper cartographer. The writing was uneven and smudged in places, but it was readable.

"See here, the river walks up Worcester and more." Balthazar ran his finger up the course of the river.

"That's where I fell in," said Henry, pointing on the map, and a shiver ran down his spine. He never wanted to go through that trauma again.

"Ha! You come long way; you must float like turd!" Balthazar's sense of humour had returned.

Henry insisted that they bury the bodies despite Charles arguing that it would take up valuable time.

"You know my feelings on this." He stared Charles in the eye, who backed down, shrugging his shoulders. "Anyway, these men were Balthazar's companions, even if he was captured by them too. We ought to respect that."

Jack had kept to himself all this time, but now he spoke up. "Look, a few hours ago this boy was happy to have us burned at the stake and now you two are best friends!" he complained.

"He is trying to help us, Jack." Henry was disappointed in Jack, although he could see his point. "There was not much he could do when there were many pirates, but let's face it, he saved our lives."

Jack stood up and walked away, kicking at the pebbles that lay on the beach. Walking to the river's edge, he picked up a handful of flat stones and began to skim them across the water.

"Your fat friend not like me." Balthazar pulled a face.

Henry shrugged his shoulders, but it was Charles who came to the rescue.

"You must give him time," he told Balthazar. "We three have been travelling together for the last few days and it has been an intense journey. We have already lost Henry twice –the fool – so Jack is just being protective. I am incredibly grateful that you saved my friends' lives. Jack will soon grow to understand that you are a friend. Just give him some time." Rising to his feet, Charles brushed himself down and went over to the bodies of the men, which were attracting the first few flies of the spring, for they smelt sour, as dead bodies do.

"Come on. It is time to bury these men."

The boys found the spades that had been used by the seadogs to set up their crosses and began to dig graves for the last of their adversaries. It was long and arduous work, but once the holes were dug, the boys dragged the corpses into the graves and covered them over. The three large crosses that towered over the set of graves, so recently the place where Rosalind, Jack and Henry had been about to die, would have to do as markers for all of the dead men, and also to mark the passing of an era where they brought terror to the land.

Henry put his hands together in prayer and spoke. "Forgive these men for all they might have done in their lives and please accept them into Heaven, dear Lord. Amen."

"That was quick mass," Balthazar smirked.

Rosalind went over to Jack and spoke to him quietly. He looked at her and shrugged his shoulders, then went to help her with something. Henry, who was concerned about his friend, wondered what it was that Rosalind had persuaded Jack to do. The pair of them were searching through all the possessions of the dead sea-dogs.

By the time that the others had gathered themselves together, Rosalind and Jack had made several piles of objects, useful items like clean clothes and food. They set them out for Balthazar to check, then asked him if he would allow them to take some items. He happily agreed.

The companions wolfed down all the food as they could, which was not much, as everything had been spoiled during the fighting. Jack also took a cleanish shirt, as his was ruined after crawling around on the muddy riverbank the night before. Henry chose to keep the few clothes that he had rather than take any that had belonged to anyone from the pirate gang. His shirt was torn and his breeches were without buttons, but he would rather these clothes, which his sister had given him, than any from a suspect source. He did take a belt, however, to keep his breeches from falling around his knees.

Finally, having taken what they felt they needed, the group discussed how to disperse. Balthazar showed the others some coracles, small walnut-shaped boats made of a timber frame with canvas stretched over like skin and then painted with pitch. He had three of these and thought that if they tied them together with a rope, he could lead them by controlling one boat.

As there were only three coracles and he was too large to attempt to share one with the boys, Charles chose to ride back to Worcester on Bottom, taking Rosalind home to her burned-out cottage along the way. He looked happy to do so and wondered if she might not have some cousins to stay with until her house was rebuilt.

Henry said his farewells to Rosalind. "Thank you for being so kind to me when I was at my lowest ebb," he said.

Rosalind looked at the young boy and then hugged him. "I don't care if you are a royal prince, you will always be my Henry," she teased him. "Take care of yourself, young man, and maybe one day we will meet again."

Henry thought this unlikely, as from now on their paths would take very different directions and, not only geographically. He did make her one promise, however. In front of the others, as witnesses, he promised that whenever she married, he would send her a present, be it money or whatever she would ask for, so long as it was within his power to do so.[35]

Rosalind knew the boy meant it with all his heart and she thanked him with a kiss on his cheeks and a smile. "I will hold you to that promise, my dear prince."

With that, they parted, and Henry, Jack and Balthazar went down to the river to wait for the magic wave.

After Charles and Rosalind left the beach, the boys headed for the coracles and pulled them down to the water's edge.

"I am not at all sure about this." Jack was terrified of water, and water that contradicted itself by going upstream when it should be going the other way seemed unnatural to him.

Henry looked at him. "For goodness' sake! Where is your sense of adventure, Jack? We are literally being invited to live life on the crest of a wave!"

"I think that I have had quite enough adventure for a while now. Father says that adventures can turn into calamities if you don't pick them carefully," Jack retorted.

There was no denying that this was a great moment of discovery, but Jack had a feeling in the seat of his pants that all would not go well. Henry was genuinely excited. Never had he heard of such a thing as a magic wave coming up a river. He had seen large waves on the sea, but they were many, coming one after another, and were soon washed up against the shore. But according to Balthazar, all they had to do was paddle out into the middle of the river and wait, then this huge wave, defying all the laws of nature, would come up against the current and carry them upstream. If it were not for the fact that he instinctively liked Balthazar so much – they were very alike, the two friends – he and a disgruntled Jack would not be paddling out now, into the middle of the river, in a craft that was more like an over-sized eggshell. The coracle was only the length of a man its width was half that. It weighed next to nothing, allowing Henry to carry it over his head before he lowered it into the water, where it sat on top, hardly making an impression on the surface. Balthazar carried one too and led the expedition with aplomb.

"This is sheer madness!" grinned Henry as he jumped into his boat and it spun round and round.

Balthazar, who had boasted earlier that he could manoeuvre these boats, was having problems too. He had seen the pirate crew travel in the fragile crafts with the greatest of ease, using a sculling movement that he could not master, much as he tried. The result was that the boys got the giggles as they splashed about, spinning in circles and nearly tipping over if either of them tried to change position in their boat.

All Henry wanted to do was to enjoy the moment. He was alive and he was free, two things that only that morning had seemed like impossibilities. The last few days had gone from bad to worse, ever since he had had that vision in the cathedral, and now all he wanted to do was get back home – after saving Arthur, of course. Arthur should become the next King of England after their father, so he, Henry, could become a carefree boy and spend his days with Charles and Jack, andnow, Balthazar.

Henry took a moment to look around him in wonder. He was sitting in a tub in the middle of the river, the early signs of spring evident all around him, as the young leaves were just starting to unfurl in the trees while the pussy willow and catkins hung over the water. The water was deep, so that although the current was strong, he felt truly at ease, at peace. The world was a beautiful place, and as a fish jumped and then splashed back into the water, and Balthazar turned around to look out for it, making his tiny boat rock, Henry felt truly happy.

"Come, take this rope, 'Jacky'," Balthazar grinned while throwing Jack a rope.

"My name is Jack, not Jacky," Jack frowned but did as he was told.

"Now tie it to you boat and throw end to Henry."

Jack wrapped the middle of the rope to some pegs that stuck up in the stern behind him, if it was the stern, then threw the remainder of the rope to Henry, who also secured his boat to the rope. The three boys were now tied together in a line with Balthazar in the lead.

"That's funny." Henry pulled out of his reverie and noticed a changing feeling in the air. There was an eerie silence. The birds had stopped singing and the wind seemed to have died. A distant rumble could be heard downstream, a sound that was alien to the prince's ears. It was unearthly, not quite like thunder, more like the underworld coming to the surface. Looking at Balthazar to see if he felt the same, Henry noticed that his hands were gripping his one oar firmly. Balthazar was looking downstream with a serene smile as if he were waiting for a lover. He was not frightened, so neither was Henry, but this false sense of security was short-lived.

Without further warning, the river seemed to rise up like it was trying to swallow the little boats. The water was black and smooth, almost mirror-smooth, the colour of agate. It rose like a monster and the boat began to tremble. Henry was no longer sure that this was going to work. Just as he had survived being crucified and burnt to death, he had allowed himself to be cajoled into being swallowed by a great wave.

Just at that moment, Henry felt a tug on the rope that secured his boat to the one that Jack was in. His boat in turn was being tugged by Balthazar's, which was getting sucked along by the crest of the wave

"Row, row hard as you can!" shouted Balthazar as he desperately paddled with his oar to catch the crest.

Henry thought that Balthazar had changed his mind and was paddling hard to get away from the wave, but then Balthazar shouted out again: "Now can stop, just your oar to direct." For now, the row of boats took on a life of their own and, as if they were being pulled by a team of horses, they found their way right over the great wave and soon they were running just ahead of the mass of water.

"Here we go!" shouted Balthazar over the sound of the water. "Hold on. Now we sit on wave."

Just as Balthazar had promised, the coracles sat atop the marvellous wave and danced on the crest, with white water breaking to one side of them as they were carried along at what must have been the speed of a charging horse. It was exhilarating. Henry could feel the wind in his hair, being upon the crest of the wave and open to the elements.

"It's wonderful!" Henry cried, and he saw Balthazar laughing with glee. He had never experienced anything like this before, and watching Balthazar steering his craft with his oar, Henry followed suit, and it kept them right in the optimum location so that the experience just kept going.

"Goodness." Jack had gone green. "Give me a bucking mule any day."

Balthazar laughed. "You look like a jack-ass."

Jack blocked his ears to any more insults from the French boy. He would seek revenge once they survived this devilish wave.

The banks of the river rolled past: trees, bushes, then open fields with sheep grazing who took no notice of the huge wave as it slithered past. They had seen it all before. A few farmhands turned to see the boats riding the wave, but they too had seen this before and went back to their work.

After what seemed like only a moment, they saw a bridge and a tower in the distance, coming ever closer, and Balthazar started to paddle frantically with the oar towards the riverbank. Leaving the wave called Sabrina was easier said than done, he discovered, for the tiny coracles wanted to stay where they were, on the crest of the wave.

"Paddle to the bank," shouted Balthazar, who had never done this himself, although he had seen the sea-dogs manage easily in the past. He had not realised how difficult it was to change course. In fact, tied together, the manoeuvre was impossible, and before he knew it, they had missed the bank where boats were normally landed and were heading dangerously close to the bridge.

"Paddle yourself, Frenchy," Jack sneered. "You said you knew how to ride this damnable wave. Get us out of this one, if you can."

"Jack, Balthazar. Stop arguing and get us out of this mess!" Henry shouted.

"Hold on to life," Balthazar cried as the massive wave carried them towards the arch under the bridge.

The boys' shouts died a death as they looked ahead of them and realised the gravity of their situation. They had a fifty-fifty chance of being smashed against the massive stone pillars that supported the bridge or of being sucked through the arch in a swirl of fast-running water. Neither option was going to be comfortable. A group of townsfolk standing on the bridge had stopped to watch the wave advance. It looked as if they might be washed away with the boys, or so Henry thought. One of them looked just like his sister and another like John Skelton. Henry had heard that you see your life flash by just before you die. He was imagining things now, which was not a good sign. Perhaps these were going to be his last moments alive. Why dream up those two though? What about his mother or father?

Just as the boys found themselves being sucked under the bridge in a maelstrom, one after the other, all through the middle arch in the bridge so that the three coracles were still attached to one another, Henry thought he saw a shimmering, sparkling dust fall from the sky creating a shiny net of calm seemed to level them up and the three small, walnut-shaped boats made a safe passage through to the other side.

18

It took three days for Lady Margaret to get over her heart attack, for that was what she had suffered. She had lain on the floor for over an hour before she regained consciousness to the sound of someone banging on her door. It was Captain Cripps, who had been notified by one of the guards when Lady Margaret had not answered an earlier call. Captain Cripps had knocked down the door and, on seeing the woman lying prone and barely moving on the floor, had called for the court physician. Recognising the smell of mandrake and seeing the shenanigans that must have been going on by the fireside, he had not allowed any of his guards in until he had hidden the various items around the room. It was only then that he had allowed the doctor to attend to Lady Margaret. She was cold, but they called for her chambermaids to come and put her to bed, where she was kept until her temperature was normal and she could eat some chicken broth.

Now the woman was up, still bemused by what had happened, especially how nobody had found out her secret. It was the captain of the guards who had found her. Was her necromancy paraphernalia still on the table when he came into the room? She could not remember.

Mulling it over, Lady Margaret called Captain Cripps in to see her.

"Your Ladyship." Captain Cripps saluted smartly.

Lady Margaret looked into his eyes, searching for a sign that he had seen her secret experiments, but his eyes gave nothing away and nor did his expression. She was going to have to dive into unchartered waters.

"Captain, I need to share something." Nothing; he did not flinch. He was good.

"Ma'am?"

"Can you keep a secret?" This was a question that Lady Margaret knew was irresistible to anyone.

Cripps looked at her questioningly. "Do you want me to speak off the record, ma'am? If so, what I cleared up the day you fell was only seen by me and I have wiped it from my memory. I am at your service, my lady."

"A good answer and you will be richly rewarded for your loyalty. I will see to that."

An unwritten contract had just been invisibly signed by the two people standing face to face in the room, no witnesses necessary.

"I need you to get a message to my man Nicholas Grope, staying at an inn called The Bull in the town of Ludlow. Do not tell anyone else, do not dally along the way, and if you report back to me with confirmation of your success, you will not be wanting. Ever."

"It is a two to three-day ride, your ladyship. Can I suggest a carrier pigeon? We use them for messages, and I can send one to the captain of the guard at Ludlow Castle. He would be happy to deliver it straight to the inn in question. I am sure he would like to wet his whistle there, if you allow it? Prince Arthur need not know that the message was not royal business. But then, of course, it would be, were it sent from you, madam."

Lady Margaret smiled. She liked the way that this man used his head. She nodded her assent gracefully. The matter was sorted.

She went to her desk, withdrew a small piece of parchment and wrote just a few words: *Urgent. Change of plan. Call it off. LM.* The heart attack had been a warning from God to change her plans; a sign. Arthur was saved. She rolled up the piece of paper and sealed it so that it could not be read. The finished item was small enough to fit in a pigeon's leg ring, in the clip where a message could be attached. Lady Margaret had used this method of communication before, Captain Cripps noted. The captain, delighted to have been taken into the confidence of the most influential woman in the land, the power behind the throne, saluted smartly, clicked the heels of his highly polished boots and left the room without a moment to spare.

Margot and John Skelton arrived in Worcester to the gossip of how the most terrible accident had occurred when a thief who had stolen a horse had jumped over a hedge and fallen into the river beyond. They had no idea that this awful event had anything to do with their search for Henry and so they booked into an inn, then settled down to a hearty supper.

"I am sorry to have lost William," Margot ventured, feeling that some of the romance had gone from their journey without the quiet, dreamy-eyed man.

"He had his priorities and we have ours," John Skelton stated factually. "This is the first town we have come across, and while we look for any evidence of Henry being here in the last day or so, we should also start looking for the ingredients we will need to make the Nine Herbs charm,[36] that which will act as an antidote to any poison that might be in Arthur's digestive system – if, indeed, he is being poisoned. There are many ways of disposing of our future monarch and it is only my guess. You can help me look in the market tomorrow. You know your herbs, I believe?"

"Of course," replied Margot, forgetting William straight away, which was Skelton's intention. "You have taught me all of the main ones. What are we looking for in particular?"

John settled them down in a corner by the fireside and brought out a notebook with some neat writing in it. "We need all of these herbs: mugwort, venom-loather, crab-apple, plantain, camomile, chervil, lamb's cress, nettle and fennel. This is the task we have ahead of us: tomorrow we go to the market to search for the ingredients and instruments with which we can make it. There will be herbs sold at the market, or there will be an apothecary within the town where we can find them."

Margot studied the list. "Some of these might be just beginning to grow in the wild. If only we could go and search for them. They would be more potent if they were fresh, wouldn't they?"

John was delighted that he had caught Margot's attention and that her interest in learning had brought back the banter that they usually shared together. Life was better without William.

"They would be, but the question is – do we have time?" This was a rhetorical question, for it was his decision to make, not his pupil's. "I think that we should get up early in the morning and take the ponies up into the Malvern Hills to see what we can find. Morning is a good time to pick, and we are bound to find nettles if nothing else."

They were sitting huddled together, discussing the ins and outs of potion-making, when a conversation was struck up beside them.

"I say it was a royal horse he was riding. That fellow who purloined my horse told me later, when he brought the poor brute back to me half-dead. He said that the thief had stolen one of the King's horses.

He gave me a florin for Flyer. Said he wanted to buy him, he was such a good'n."

"It looked a bit on the small side for a King's horse if you ask me. More like a prince's pony," one of the men joked.

Margot's ears pricked up.

"A fast one too – a mountain pony, I would guess. My Flyer is a speedy creature when it is asked of him, but he could not keep up with the little blighter. I would say that the boy was a natural rider, the little vermin."

"A terrible tragedy. The boy could not have been local, or he would have known the river was on the other side of the hedge. No local lad would be so foolish as to jump that bloody hedge. It was a death sentence, to be sure," the man wheezed.

The horse owner's reply made John and Margot's hearts lurch.

"You know, there were two of them. One got away. I saw the gentleman confront a boy who was holding the pony outside the cathedral. Then another boy came and attacked the gentleman. He floored him, then jumped on the pony and fled."

John Skelton was unable to keep quiet anymore. "Excuse me, kind sirs, but what happened to the other boy? Do you know? And what colour hair did he have?"

The old fellow looked alarmed at their conversation having been overheard by a stranger. It was dangerous to be caught talking about the King or anything to do with him, possibly even a stray pony. "What is it to you, if you don't mind my asking?" he challenged.

John grasped at straws, unprepared to answer questions when he was asking them. "Well, I am looking for a couple of lads who were on the road and who passed us. I have lost my wallet and it might be that they took it as they rode by."

Margot looked at him accusingly. If the boys were caught, they could end up being charged with two crimes now. She was not amused but could think of nothing to add that might mitigate matters.

The old man looked satisfied at John's answer. "A right couple of vagabonds, I would say. The sooner the second one is caught, the better. Put him in the stocks for a few days or send him to prison for a few years' hard labour. That'll teach him a lesson."

The horse owner had been quiet for a few moments, trying to remember the colour of the boys' hair. "The one who ran away had brownish hair, but the other, you couldn't tell, for he had a woollen hat pulled right over his ears!"

Margot froze – she had given Henry a long woollen hat with flaps that covered his head and ears.

The horse owner thought for a moment and said, "The woollen hat had flaps on it to keep his ears warm; I remember that, as they flapped up and down like a dog's ears. Funny to watch, although it was not funny in the end."

That was all they needed to hear. It was obvious to both Margot and John Skelton that Henry had been the 'thief' riding the pony, who was most likely his own Virtue, and that he had met a watery grave at the bottom of the River Severn. Margot looked so distressed that John paid their bill and led her back out into the street for some fresh air.

"I can't bear to think of Henry having fallen into the river. Oh John!" she cried and buried her head in his robes. "Now, now, my dear." He leant forward to pat Margot on the knee. "We do not know for certain that it was the boys, so there is no point in getting upset. Henry is as resilient as a Welsh cob himself and can bounce back when others fail to do so. Mark my words."

This cheered Margot up somewhat, so the tutor and student went back into the inn and up to their two rooms to bed for the night. John warned Margot to be ready for a ride before breakfast the next morning.

As Margot lay in bed that night, having already said a prayer for Henry's safe return, she looked back on all the fun that she had enjoyed in his exuberant company. Master Skelton was right: nothing could kill Henry, for he simply had too much life in him to give up. He would have swum ashore without any trouble. John had taught them all to swim in the palace moat and they often went swimming in the rivers with him. Having convinced herself of this, the young girl closed her eyes and quietly sobbed herself to sleep, for she missed her little brother very much and wished that she had never let him out of her sight. Now she was not sure if she would ever see him again.

✿

John Skelton knocked on Margot's door before dawn broke the next morning and they crept out to the stables to pick up their ponies and ride out into the Malvern Hills. It was the most beautiful morning, and the ponies were fresh after a night in warm stables with plenty of hay. As the mist began to clear, the stunning views from the hillside opened before them. Margot decided to search for the necessary herbs to distract herself but could not keep back the tears that ran silently down her face. She hoped that Master Skelton had not noticed.

John had noticed, but as he could think of nothing helpful to do, other than to keep his young charge interested in their task, he only called Margot whenever he found a herb. Then the two of them would jump down from their ponies and they would laugh as they tried to prevent the naughty animals from eating the herbs before they had a chance to pick them themselves. Margot did sound very much like her grandmother at times.

Later that day, the two companions were back in Worcester looking for a shop from which they could purchase the rest of the herbs that they had not found on the hillside. Asking a few passers-by, they soon learned that there was an old shop up the main street where the owner made medicines and potions for a fee. He was an eccentric creature, they were told, but mostly harmless and he did know a lot about medicine. Some said that he dabbled in alchemy too. It was a hardware store, apothecary and hatter's, as well as a funeral parlour. He also sold an extremely strong homebrew that they were warned not to try for fear of it knocking them out.

When they found the shop, Margot gaped in wonder, for on every beam going all the way to the back of the shop there were hooks with hats hanging from them. There were also hats on shelves, hats on hatstands and stacks of different-shaped hatboxes, presumably with hats inside. Then there were coffins stacked upon other coffins in a dark corner. In between the beams were hooks with herbs hanging upside down, drying. There was a counter in the corner with a wall of small drawers built into it, each with a name scrawled on a label in Latin. Also behind the counter was the oldest man that Margot had ever seen, with sunken eyes, wrinkled skin, a white tuft of hair on his forehead like a quiff and a long beard that was plaited at the bottom into a thin wisp. He held a withered arm under his chin. Margot wanted to ask how he had injured himself, but at the same time, she did not want to be nosey.

"Good morning, sir," started John Skelton, peering at the man, who seemed to be asleep, but then again might be dead, he was so ancient and lifeless.

"Eh?" was all that came out of him, proving that he was alive, which was encouraging.

"We are looking for some help with the production of an antidote to poison and wonder if you might have the necessary ingredients." There was no point beating around the bush. A small fire was burning in an enormous fireplace beside the counter. Hanging over it, on an iron hook, was a black cauldron that was simmering away, giving off a pungent aroma. "What have you got cooking there, my friend?" John tried again to strike up a conversation with the owner of the shop, who seemed totally disinterested in communication.

"We need your help, sir," piped up young Margot. At the sound of her voice, the old man became animated.

"Is that a woman I hear?" he asked.

"It is, and I need your help." Margot walked up to the counter so that she was more visible. The old shopkeeper slowly stood up, not that he seemed any taller for it, and shuffled forward. He leaned on the counter and looked at her closely, peering through thick glasses, before he spoke again.

"I can help you both, but only if you tell me what it is you are after." His voice was thin and stretched as if his vocal cords would snap at any moment.

Margot explained that her brother was being poisoned by an unknown adversary and that she had to go and rescue him. That her other brother had already tried and failed. That she and John were all that was left between her older brother and death. The old man listened carefully and once she had finished he asked a question. It was not about the antidote that they wanted to make but about her brother, the younger one.

"He is called Henry. He was here, but he was mistaken for a horse thief and chased out of town." Margot choked on her words and broke down thinking about Henry.

But the old man surprised her with what he had to say next. Resting his wrinkly old hand on her shoulder, he looked her in the eyes. "Your brother Henry is still alive," he told her with authority. "He came here, and I helped hide him for a while, but when he left, the man chasing him came after him again. You are right in that he fell into the river, but he is still alive. He will return; of that, I am sure."

John and Margot looked at each other in disbelief. How could this old man know that Henry was alive?

"Some things cannot be explained in words. You will just have to trust me and have hope. He will return on the crest of a wave. I will show you, but first let us make this potion that you seem to be in such a hurry to conjure up."

Margot jumped about. "So, you know Henry is alive! We must go and find him, now."

The old man waved his good hand to slow her down, "No, not now. Henry is safe and will come soon. We must try and save Arthur now, not that his future looks good."

How did he know her older brother was called Arthur, Margot thought to herself. She looked at John Skelton, who just shrugged.

The shopkeeper poked around in his drawers until he had produced the herbs that they were after. Next, the old man swung the crane on which the cauldron was hanging over the fire out into the room, whereupon he swapped the bubbling cauldron for an empty one.

He then turned to John. "You know how to make this potion?"

John, who was good at nearly everything that he tried his hand at, was worried for once in his life that he might not be able to manage this task on his own and he decided that he would ask for help. It was the right thing to do, for the old man smiled a toothless smile and spat into the palms of his hands, which he then rubbed together.

"I haven't made this for many a long year, but I think I can remember the chanting," he muttered as he busied himself around the back of the counter, digging out wooden spoons, knives and a chopping board, as well as a pestle and mortar.

Margot raised her eyebrows. This 'chanting' seemed a bit too like witchcraft, just as her grandmother had done. Was it not such a frowned upon discipline after all?

"Chanting?" she whispered into John's ear. "What is he talking about?"

John put his finger to his lips. "Hush! Don't say a word to distract him. Watch and learn." This was something John would often say when the children kept asking him questions back in the classroom and he did not want to give them the answer that easily. It meant, take note of this – it is important. Margot kept quiet and watched.

As soon as the old man, who introduced himself as Thomas, began to work on the potion, the years fell from his countenance and he hopped about on his old pins, cutting up ingredients and grinding them in the pestle and mortar. He whispered a chant as he worked, an old charm that fused the ingredients together as the words floated like a scent over the concoction. He recited the charm three times over each herb that was to be used, perhaps to intensify its individual qualities:

"Now these nine herbs have power against nine evil spirits, against nine poisons and against nine infections: against the red poison, against the foul poison, against the white poison, against the pale-blue poison, against the yellow poison, against the green poison, against the black poison, against the blue poison, against the brown poison, against the crimson poison, against worm-blister, against water-blister, against thorn-blister, against thistle-blister, against ice-blister, against poison-blister."

He then added each herb to the cauldron with a base of the clearest spring water, sourced, he told them, from a secret spring up in the hills, a special spring. Margot was beginning to relax, as John had indicated that what they were witnessing was not a dark art after all. She could not help but become fascinated by the goings-on by the fire.

However, she would never have thought that John Skelton would approve, let alone get involved in what could only be some form of witchcraft, even if it was benevolent.

The liquid in the cauldron started to bubble and spit. The steam that rose appeared to emit a glow, almost like vaporous sunlight and Margot was convinced she could see faces emerging from the steam, people from another world perhaps. Their mouths moved in time with the chanting of the spell, as if they had been chanting it for generations. Her hands began to tingle, she felt a warm fuzzy feeling in her body and her hands started to tremble. The old man continued with his chanting:

"If any poison comes flying from the east, or any from the north, or any from the south, or any from the west among the people. Christ stood over diseases of every kind; I alone know a running stream, and the nine adders beware of it. May all the weeds spring up from their roots, the seas slip apart, all saltwater, when I blow this poison from you."[37]

Finally the light dissipated, the faces melted away and the steam died down along with the fire under it. Thomas stirred the liquid that remained in the bottom of the cauldron. He then picked up some soot from the dying embers of the fire, mixed it with some water and a beaten egg, then added the paste to the liquid to thicken it up. When the liquid had cooled down, he added some juice from an apple to make it more palatable and bottled the potion, stopping it with a cork and some sealing wax.

Margot was convince she could see faces emerging from the steam.

"Give this liquid to your brother, make him drink it all and sing the same charm that I sang into his mouth and into both his ears. Keep chanting until he begins to respond. He will survive."

Old Thomas had sunk back into his chair and the years piled back onto him as he settled down. "Now, put the kettle on, make us a herb tea and I can teach you the words of the charm while we wait for your other brother to return. He is on his way; I can feel him."

John and Margot looked at each other. There was not much that they could do, other than sit and memorise the charm that Thomas had recited. They went through it again and again, with Thomas correcting them if they went wrong. Margot was a quick learner, and John, as a poet, found it easy to commit verse to memory, so within an hour they were word-perfect.

Their task complete, the cooks were sitting down to enjoy a nice brew of reviving herbs in a tisane when old Thomas jumped up and waved his hands in the air.

"Quick, quick, they are coming!" he said, donning a hat and coat, then hobbling out of the back door of the shop with John and Margot hot on his heels.

They walked down the street and towards the bridge that crossed the River Severn. There, Thomas stopped and waited, searching down along the river. People crossing the bridge looked askance at the old man as he stood there, checking the wind direction and the position of the sun in the sky, and then looking out over the water downstream. He held a finger in the air, having licked it, and then he cocked his ear, cupping it to improve his hearing.

"Here he comes, here he comes!" The old man was as animated as a child. He even began to jump up and down a little, not that his old bones ever left the ground.

John and Margot looked at Thomas and then followed his gaze to where the river disappeared around a bend. They saw nothing at first, but then they noticed that birds who had been nesting in the trees along the riverbank were flying up into the air as if they had been disturbed. It was then that Margot heard a rumbling sound, like distant thunder brewing up a storm. In the distance, she was amazed to see a huge black mark coming towards her like a wall of darkness, night coming to overtake the day. It was a wall of water flowing against the current, and on the top of it was what looked like bundles of flotsam and jetsam all tangled up together, riding the crest of the wave.

As the wave approached, people started to stop and stare. The 'bundle of something' came closer and transformed into three tiny boats, like corks, floating right on top of the highest tip of the wave. As they came towards the onlookers, it was obvious that there were three tiny figures hollering and whooping as they rowed with single oars that caused them to spin around in tight circles.

Henry, Jack and another boy, a tanned foreign-looking boy, were tied together as they raced along, totally without any form of control as to where they were going, which was, at this very moment, right under the bridge where Margot and John were standing.

"Jump, jump!" shouted John, but the boys couldn't hear him, and they could hardly jump into such a maelstrom of water. Margot saw Thomas throw something over the boys as they passed under the bridge, just before they disappeared. It was as if he had thrown an invisible net over them, and she could just see it shimmering even though there was nothing there.

"What was that?" she asked, but John had not seen anything.

"You must have seen it, it was the same shimmering light as what we saw in the cauldron."

John looked at her. "What shimmering light?"

Margot sometimes found adults so dense. "Oh, nothing. It doesn't matter."

The old man, who had been listening to the conversation, winked and answered her with an enigmatic smile. "I threw them some protection. They will be safe now. It is a charm that guides a person to their family without fail, a sort of magnet effect that will help Henry find his brother, even without a map or knowledge of the region. He will be like a homing pigeon flying back to his nest, except it will be to his nearest family, which in this case is his brother. Simple. Unless, that is, it makes him turn back to find you… I had not thought of that." He grinned in an impish manner.

"But we must go after them!" exclaimed Margot. John held her back, for she was about to run off after the boys along the riverbank.

"Margot, we will never catch them up. We need to stick to our plan to go and rescue Arthur. Henry is safe, sort of. He is with Jack, and it looks as if they have found a most enterprising friend. The wave will die down eventually, though I have never seen anything like it before in my life. They can both swim, thank goodness, and the direction they are heading is not far off the beaten track when it comes to meeting up at Ludlow. The most important thing is that Henry is still alive. Sometimes I am in awe of that child."

Margot turned to look at her tutor and saw that there were tears welling up in his eyes. She quickly turned away and ran to the other side of the bridge to watch the strange wave bearing her precious brother 'safely' upstream.

"Well, at least he is heading in the right direction," she said. "I wonder where Charles is, though, and where are all their horses?" Thinking of Virtue, Margot decided to leave the conversation as it stood and just gazed after her brother, muttering another prayer under her breath.

Charles and Rosalind had not found it possible to say goodbye after they had finally reached her burnt-out cottage. The place was black and sodden, with an acrid aroma that would take years to dissipate. They had searched through the wreckage to find a stone by what remained of the hearth, which Charles prised off the floor to reveal a hidden compartment. There, Rosalind retrieved a small metal box.

"My father was saving this for my dowry," she explained.

"Well, at least the men did not find it. They have ruined your home but a house can be rebuilt. Do you want to stay here and start your life anew?" Charles was hoping not.

Rosalind found the place eerie. "I would rather leave, in case the overseer comes back to look for me if he learns I escaped from the pirates."

"That settles it then." Charles gave her an encouraging smile. "You can come with me to Ludlow Castle where I am certain Princess Katherine will find you a place to stay. If not, perhaps you can come with me down to Eltham Palace, for Henry will look after you, that I know. He never forgets a friend."

Charles said this despite the fact he hardly knew Henry, but from what he did know of him, he thought he spoke true about the prince. There was something about Henry. He would find her a position with him somehow.

Within a few hours they were back in Worcester, where Rosalind found an inn where she could rest while Charles went out looking for any sign of his friends. They had agreed to meet at the bridge, but the three boys were nowhere to be seen. Charles decided that it was time to go and have a drink and get something to eat. Killing people made one hungry and thirsty. He had still not gotten over the murderous battle on the beach.

Out on his own, Charles was just about to slip through the doorway of an inn when he had second thoughts. This was how he had got into trouble in the first place, when he went on a drinking binge after killing the robbers in the woods, so instead he turned around and walked up the main street to see what he might find. It was just as he was giving up on finding anyone that he saw the strange hardware shop with hats and herbs in the window. Henry had mentioned hiding for a while in this shop and that the man inside was special. He had suggested that they call in on him when they reached Worcester. Charles decided that this was a good place to look for Henry and so he entered the shop.

Margot and John were sitting around the fire talking to Thomas.

"That was strange. Jack was with Henry and the other boy in the boats, but there was no sign of Charles. I wonder where he has got to?"

"He is closer than you think, and you will be reunited before you know it," said old Thomas enigmatically.

"Is this more of your magic?" asked Margot, who was beginning to enjoy the company of the old rogue.

"Not really," he replied, smiling at her. "Turn around and you will see."

Both John and Margot turned to see the silhouette of a man standing in the doorway.

"Charles, oh Charles!" Margot jumped up and ran to him through the herbs and hats. She threw her arms around him, nearly knocking him clean off his feet. Then she pulled back and put on her sternest voice.

"Why aren't you with Henry? You promised me that you would not let him out of your sight."

Charles was just getting over the surprise of finding Margot and John Skelton here in Worcester when he had last left them down at Eltham.

"More to the point, what are *you* doing here?" he replied.

After Charles was introduced to Thomas, the four sat around the fire and told each other of their various adventures, and Charles told of Henry's plan to reach Ludlow by hook or by crook. He also mentioned that he was travelling with a woman, something that caused a few raised eyebrows. "You will like Rosalind. She is different. There is something special about her," he found himself saying, much to his surprise.

"Well, to have another girl on our side can only be a good thing," Margot pointed out, her nose in the air. "I miss the conversation of an intelligent woman."

Charles smiled, his eyes looking softening. "Oh, she is very intelligent, and well, different. Special."

Margot looked at Charles quizzically, but chose not to speak further on the subject. She looked forward to meeting this mysterious woman who had so quickly gained the admiration of the champion knight.

"But where is Henry?" Charles asked, as if the others might know. To his surprise, it was the old man who answered.

"He is well on his way," stated Thomas, "so you had better get going if you want to catch up with him. He will succeed in reaching Ludlow, but will he be in time? I think it is imperative that you keep on the move and attempt to get there as soon as you can. Just promise me one thing: you will call in on me once your work is done. I must talk to Henry."

This request seemed more like a demand, for the old man would not accept payment for the work he had done that day, saying that talking to Henry was all he wanted. He shooed the tutor, his pupil and the young knight out of his shop, saying that if they wasted any more time, they would be in danger of failing in their quest.

The last that Worcester saw of the reunited friends was their riding away from the city on two fat ponies and a mule who carried an extra passenger on his back, her arms wrapped round the body of a very happy and contented Charles.

19

As soon as the three coracles had passed under the bridge at Worcester, Henry felt that he had passed into another world, a world where he saw his situation in a different light to before – a shimmering light, in fact. It was as if he had had a flash of inspiration, an uncovering of the truth. This was a family affair, and it was for him alone to solve it: to find his brother and save him from harm. Henry felt the most incredible urge to get back to his family, to leave his friends and be among his own flesh and blood. Friends were good, but blood was thicker than water and it was blood that was calling him now.

As much as he loved Jack and liked his new friend Balthazar, Henry now understood that they were no longer supposed to be with him on his journey, for it had become his own personal quest, his odyssey. What he had to do was of his own volition and he knew it. As the day was coming to its end, so was his time with the others. So, while the coracles were transported up the river on the wondrous wave, he took the decision to cut the rope between his craft and the next, which held Jack, allowing his coracle to fall back and drift away. Jack and Balthazar were so distracted by the moment they were experiencing that they did not notice.

Henry lost momentum as his coracle slid off the back of the wave and left him in the stillness of the river, where neither wind nor wave had formed. All he could hear was the last of the evening birdcalls and the lowing of cattle in the fields. The coracle was as useless a craft as he had ever come across. Henry tried to paddle, but it just seemed to go around in circles. Splashing about uselessly, he felt giddy as he went around and around. He was about to throw the paddle in the water and use his hands when a voice called out to him.

"That's not the way to do it, son. Put the paddle out the back, behind you, and make a motion like two circles flowing against each other and it will propel you towards the shore."

Henry looked towards where the voice was coming from, but as it was getting dark, all he could see was a black figure holding a lamp of some sort. He did what he was told and soon found a way of propelling the boat, but not well. Within a short while, with some adaptation and experimentation, Henry found that it worked, and he was able to move up closer to the man to thank him. For some reason he was not at all afraid of the stranger; in fact, he was drawn to him. The man waded out, grabbed the fragile craft and pulled him towards the shore.

"That was most kind of you, good sire," Henry said politely, and the man bowed with courtly manners and smiled. He was a handsome and there was something disarming about him that Henry liked, so he smiled back. Intrigued as to why the man was standing in the water up to his knees, wearing the longest pair of boots he had ever seen and carrying what looked like a large net of sorts, Henry had a question.

"May I ask what you might doing, if that is not too inquisitive of me?"

The man looked pensive and then replied that he was fishing, surely it was obvious.

"Well, not to me, for I am not from these parts, but it looks interesting. Have you caught much?"

"You are full of questions, aren't you, son? In fact, I have caught a shad and a few twait. Are you hungry? We will be having dinner soon, and since you seem to have lost your friends, you are welcome to come ashore and eat with us."

Henry was immediately on the defensive. "Who is 'us' exactly?"

The man put his hands up in a gesture of peace. "Just me and my missus, son. We live in that cabin over there. You are more than welcome, but I am not pressing you." Saying that, he backed away, slowly rising from the river and onto the bank.

"Actually, I could eat a horse, I am so hungry," admitted the boy as he tried to climb out of the fragile coracle, which upturned and threw him into the water. This mishap eased the tension that new acquaintances sometimes create and the two of them laughed. The kind man offered Henry a hand and pulled him up again. They then lifted the light coracle out of the water and left it under a hedge.

"It'll be safe there: the wind won't take it and neither will any man, for few people ever come down this way. Do you come from far? Do you have any news of the world?"

Henry fell into step with his new friend as they walked up a narrow track towards the black outline of a small cabin that could be seen ahead.

Further upstream, Jack and Balthazar had noticed that Henry was gone. After a struggle they managed to leave the wave, which was finally losing its power, and paddled to firm ground. Looking at the rope, it was obvious that Henry had cut himself free.

"Well I never…" said Jack in disbelief.

"I think your friend not want us with him for more," suggested Balthazar.

"That's not like Henry. What have you done to upset him?"

Jack glared at Balthazar, still not able to reconcile himself to the fact that he had saved his life. He did not like the boy; he was too handsome for a start.

"I did nothing. We were friendly. I think we need go look for him. But which side of river I don't know." Balthazar did not relish being alone with the grumpy Jack.

Jack realized that this was a dilemma: if Henry did not want them to be with him, was it worth looking for him anyway? "Perhaps we ought to carry on until we find a bridge and wait there. He might come to it to cross over. It is a slim chance, but it is that or go back on our tracks."

"I think to find Charles like we planned is good," suggested Balthazar as another idea.

He was full of ideas, thought Jack, but what would Henry want him to do? "Let's sit here for a while and have something to eat," he suggested, for he was beginning to get hungry and he could not think straight.

For once, Balthazar agreed that this was a good idea, and the two boys sat down on the edge of the river together. A sort of truce held between them as they opened the last of the food taken from the sea-dogs' camp and began to fill themselves with bread, salted beef and cheese, all washed down with a swig of beer. That cheered them up somewhat, and within a short while the two of them started to chat and feel less antagonistic towards each other.

Just as Jack and Balthazar were tucking into their supplies, Henry, who had been introduced to his new friends as Emma and Ned, sat with them at a small table in the tiniest cabin he had ever seen, eating freshly cooked twait fillets. He recognised the shad that had been caught, for it was a fish that he often enjoyed at court. But the twait were small and bony. They were tasty, though, and he ate up every scrap, skin and all, and wiped the plate clean with a slice of brown bread. Henry had never had such delicious bread in his life, with country butter spread thickly on it, and he told Emma that this was the best food he had ever tasted.

"Well, you must have had a rough life if you think simple food like this is good," Emma laughed, but Henry noticed that she looked pleased.

The cabin was enchanting, especially after having lived in a cage in a damp cave for the last two days. There was a large hearth with a fire blazing in it made mostly of driftwood and sods of dried turf, which Henry had heard about but never seen before, and he found the peaty aroma was not displeasing. There was a cot bed made of pallets of wood, two chairs and a stool. Henry was sitting on the three-legged stool, which had caught his attention, for as Ned explained, with only three legs, the stool would sit firmly on any rough floor. Henry liked the simplicity of this innovation. Design had always fascinated him, the design of boats and ships most of all. Even the tiny coracle and how one could (eventually) control it with one oar and carry it over one's head was ingenious minimalism.

There was only one window, in the front wall by the door. There was no glass in the window, for glass was for the rich, not the poor. There were shutters that kept the wind and the rain out, which were now closed, it being dark outside. The gables were solid stone, rough fieldstone, not cut stone like he was used to in all the castles and manors where he had lived. It made for a bumpy wall with niches where knick-knacks could be placed, although this poor couple had no knick-knacks. The floor was earth, beaten down with a mix of bull's blood in it, so Ned explained, an invention of the Romans that helped prevent the damp from rising. There was one tallow candle on the table around which they sat, but after dinner Ned blew this out to save it for another day. The three companions pulled their chairs around the fire and Ned cooked sweet chestnuts on a flat pan in the flames.

"Okay, young man. Now we have filled our bellies and shared our bread, I think that it is time for you to tell us what you were doing alone in a boat no bigger than a nutshell and clearly far from home."

Ned had a way of looking at Henry that reminded him of someone, although he could not think who. "I believe that you had trouble with those sea-dogs and that you were able to escape their clutches, for I know where they live and I heard that deafening explosion last night. But there is more to this, isn't there?"

Henry felt such a strong tie to this kind, open-hearted man who had given him shelter for the night that he could not lie to him. "Sir, if you want to hear a long story full of intrigue and despair, I will tell you my tale. But I am worried that you will think me delusional, that you will not believe me. The problem is that I cannot prove it, as I have lost all my possessions, other than this lovely ring that my sister gave me."

Henry pulled the chain out from behind the neck of his shirt to produce the gold wavy ring, the only possession he had that linked him to his past. He was not expecting Ned to believe his story, even with this ring, which was obviously finely wrought. However, much to his surprise, Ned froze. He stared at it as if it were more than just a fine-looking ring.

"Where did you get that?" he asked the boy before him, almost accusingly.

"I told you, it was given to me by my sister, Margaret. It once belonged to our aunt Cecily."

Ned stood up and ran his hands though his lion-like mane, thought for a while and sat back down again. "I know that ring... I mean, uh..."

Emma, who had begun to twist a handkerchief nervously in her hands, gave Ned a warning look. "What he means, lad, is that we know that *design* of ring. It's the symbol of the River Goddess. But we want none of *that* nonsense here. Do we?" She glanced from Henry to her husband.

Henry was puzzled by what Emma said and how she reacted, almost recoiling into the shadows, so he tucked the ring away again. "I didn't mean to upset you, Emma, honestly."

Henry was now at a loss as to what to tell the couple. Jack had warned him before not to admit who he truly was, so he decided to tread carefully and cut his story short.

"It is like this. I am the son of a... a nobleman who lives at court where he serves our King. My brother lives in Ludlow, at the castle there, and I have some urgent information for him, as there is a plot to... harm him and only I can persuade him that this is so. I was travelling with my friend when a mad man thought I had stolen a pony, which I hadn't, and while running away from him I jumped a hedge and landed in the river and I am afraid... that... I... killed my... pony." Henry surprised himself, for his eyes began to sting.

Ned noticed this and took over to give the boy time to recover. "That must have been awful. So, you must have floated down the river and landed on the beach where the Morgan gang make camp. You know, I thought I saw a body floating in the river only a few days ago, but I couldn't be sure – it might have been a log, and I had no way of getting across. You see, I can't swim."

Henry was surprised. "But what if you fall in the river when you are fishing?"

Ned smiled. "Well, we fishing folk believe that it is better to drown quickly than suffer."

Henry did not agree. Master Skelton had taught them all to swim from a very young age and it had saved Henry's life once when he fell into the moat at Eltham Palace. He dared not say so and upset his hosts again, not after their reaction to the 'river ring,' so he kept on with his tale.

"Yes, you say you know the Morgan gang. Well, they are total villains and wanted to sell me as a *slave*. *Me*, a pr… well, practically a child." Henry was finding it hard not to tell the full story to his kind hosts. But he kept his guard up. "I tried to get them to let me go, or at least to ransom me, but to no avail. Luckily, my friends came to rescue me and we killed all the pirates and…"

"You *what*?" Now it was Ned's turn to be surprised. "They are the most feared group of criminals this land has ever known and you killed them?"

Henry fidgeted. It did all seem a little far-fetched.

"You see, my friend Jack, my whipping boy…. i mean…"

Ned laughed. "You have a whipping boy? Your father must be a powerful nobleman for you to have such a luxury. My father—"

"Ned," Emma cut in, pulling a face at her husband.

Ned went red. Henry noticed this. As much as he was keeping from the truth, he now guessed that this humble fisherman was being equally evasive about something in his life. Henry could not put his finger on it, but he thought he detected the hint of an educated accent in Ned's voice. "What I was going to say was that my father told me that only royalty and the greatest of noblemen employ whipping boys for their sons."

Emma relaxed and sat back in her chair.

Henry was feeling awkward. He wanted to tell his new friends the truth but felt a veil of deception clouding the air. Who were these people and why had they reacted so strangely to his river ring?

"Well, as I said, Jack had something from his father, a packet of stuff used with cannons. We… no, *I* threw it in the pirates' fire and it exploded like nothing I have ever seen before. When I recovered from the force of the explosion, most of the pirates were wounded or dead. It was like a scene from hell. I hated it… so much blood…"

Henry stared into the fire. With everything happening so fast, he had not had time to think about some of what he had seen. Now images appeared before him and his hands began to shake. "I… I…"

Ned could see the boy's distress. "Well, it is getting late. You can tell us the rest of your story tomorrow. But it seems to me that you have some good friends, young man. I am surprised you left them on the river like that after they rescued you and all, but you must have had your reasons."

Henry was still at a loss as to why he had so recklessly cut himself away from his friends. "I… I… don't know really. I felt I must do this journey on my own."

Ned laughed. "You can if you like. It is not far to Ludlow from here and we can set you on your way after breakfast tomorrow. But it is a long walk, so I suggest you go to sleep now." He stood, stretched his arms behind his head and yawned. "Time for bed, Emma."

Emma stood up and stretched her back, hands on her hips, revealing a small swell to her belly, a telltale sign that she was a few months pregnant.

"Come now." Emma sounded like Henry's mother. "I will make you a cot to lie on by the fire, and we will be sleeping over there, on the bed, so you are safe for the night."

Before long, Henry was lying on a mattress made of an old sack filled with sheep's wool. It was the roughest bed he had ever lain on, but after his recent accommodation in the cave, it was luxurious. He closed his eyes and whispered a prayer to God for having helped him find refuge with these kind people, then lay still, facing towards the fire.

Emma, who felt sorry for the lost child, pulled a blanket over him and gently tucked it around his body. Kneeling beside him, she leant and kissed him on the cheek before rising and making their own bed.

"Do you think he is one of your lot?" she asked Ned quietly.

"He looks remarkably like me and my brother when we were young, but I can't be sure. That was definitely one of our family rings. All the girls had them."

"Shhh. He might hear you. I don't want him ever to know who you are. Understand?"

Ned, who for the first time since he had left the Tower felt homesick, nodded obediently. If Henry ever discovered his real identity, it would open a whole world of problems that he and his pregnant wife did not need.

"I agree, my love. We will send him on his way tomorrow. The chances are he is just a nobleman's son, like he said, and has nothing to do with us. We will let sleeping dogs lie. Goodnight."

"Goodnight, dear heart."

By the fire, Henry, who had only closed his eyes to give Emma and her husband some privacy in which to undress, had heard the whispered conversation, and he went to sleep wondering why the fisherman was so fascinated by this river ring and had questioned whether he was one of their 'lot'.

❦

Jack and Balthazar's precarious relationship was deteriorating once again. They had eaten, but each wanted to go in a different direction to the other. Balthazar felt a sort of comfort in returning closer to where he had come from, Worcester, where they might bump into Charles. Jack, perhaps out of loyalty to Henry but perhaps by way of arguing with Balthazar, wanted to head towards Ludlow in the hope that either they found Henry along the way or they reached Ludlow in time to be there for him if he needed help.

"Charles has said we meet and go together," Balthazar much preferred the company of Charles than that of Jack.

"Henry needs us, or will, and is ahead of us," Jack reminded his companion.

"We only guess," was the reply.

The debate continued until Balthazar could take no more. "You bloody foreigner!" he cried. "Why not take your stupid *Jacky* self to Hell!"

This made Jack laugh more than he had wanted. "You call me a foreigner and you are a bloody Frenchman? Do you know what we English did to your French?"

"You massacre us, but we cut your fingers off, you dog turd!"

This was one insult too far for Jack, whose father had been in the French wars.

"I take that insult as a challenge," he said, Throwing down the bread he was eating as he had no glove to challenge the French boy with.

Within seconds, the two boys charged at each other and grabbing one another by the lapel, or whatever clothes would substitute for the same, they grappled as it started to rain, not that this dampened their fury at each other.

At first, Balthazar had the upper hand, being an experienced fighter, but Jack was no shrinking violet. After a few minutes, his low centre of gravity and his sheer determination gave him the better hand.

"Get off my… manhood!" shouted Balthazar in an uncomfortable moment when Jack had slipped and fallen on a place no man wishes to tread.

"Sorry, that was an accident," he replied and then started to laugh. "I cannot believe that I am apologising to a French git for treading on his privates!"

Balthazar, who was out of breath and, to be honest, out of any reason to fight the only friend that he had left in the world, sat down laughing.

"You are a… fat-arsed foreigner, you… stupid… dog!" was all he could say in between his panting and laughter.

The two boys calmed down as they sat in the rain until Balthazar had the idea of turning their two coracles upside down to use as shelters. They propped one side of each boat up on branches, so that they could still see each other, and then, curling up, said goodnight and fell asleep.

Charles was enjoying travelling with John and Margot. Margot seemed to have matured in the last few weeks. She was blossoming. Never a pretty child, she now had a glow to her that was promising. He even found that he was beginning to flirt with her. This did not escape John's attention. The problem of his charge's budding womanhood had been a weight on his shoulders from the start. Now he was worn down from protecting her from herself and from others.

"Charles," he said trying to distract the young man. "It is important that we concentrate on the matter in hand. When will we reach Ludlow and where is Henry?"

Charles did his best to answer. "Well, Ludlow is about ten hours' ride on a good day, and as for Henry, at this stage I have no idea. The boy is an enigma."

Charles had hit on the truth. All three companions fell into their own private reverie as to how Henry had changed over the last few days, or weeks, however long it had been. It seemed like forever.

Charles could not believe that Henry had gone on ahead without him. John Skelton, meanwhile, could not believe that this adventurous yet naive child had seemingly managed to survive in the open world without his care and had travelled halfway across England in a ridiculous disguise. He could not decide whether he would hug him once he found him or box his ears. He was also somewhat concerned that Henry was now in the company of a questionable character, a pirate boy of all things. What might he learn from such a nefarious individual? He wanted to interview the French child as soon as he caught up with them.

Margot was just pleased that Henry was alive and Jack was too. Jack had managed to stick to her brother like glue when Charles seemed to have been distracted by a woman, yet again. Charles had told her about Rosalind and how he had offered to take her back home on Bottom. This, Margot concluded, was an irresponsible decision, considering that Henry now had no adult to take care of him. As the three of them rode along in the rain, having slept in a roadside inn that night, they kept a lookout for three young boys who they hoped had managed to land eventually. They imagined they would be walking along the road, for want of a better way to get to Ludlow.

※

As it was, there were two boys walking along the road that morning. Balthazar and Jack had agreed to head towards Ludlow in the hope that they might meet one of their group of friends along the way. It was a miserable walk with sacks on their backs, the coracles having been discarded by the riverbank as going upstream had proved too difficult in the unstable boats without the aid of the great wave.

A burgeoning companionship was forming between the two children, and Jack was fascinated by Balthazar's tales of piracy and all the places he had seen. It turned out that after living with the sea-dogs for four years, he could hardly remember his parents, other than the terrible day when Captain Morgan had run a sword through his father's heart. Red blood had soaked into his shirt like an island, growing larger as he lay on the deck of the ship. Balthazar did not say much about that day but preferred to tell Jack tales of how they used to chase other ships and board them. They took prisoners and booty, making their money this way, trading with foreign folk in exotic seaside towns on this shore or that. Balthazar had seen some wonderful places, not that he could recall their names, and he explained how there were countries where everyone had dark skin and most wore strange costumes or funny hats like towels wrapped around their heads. He had eaten fruits with milk inside that was sweet, like honey, but whose outer shell was hairy like a pig's back. He had eaten eight-legged sea creatures that were like spiders with suckers on their legs, and he had seen pink birds, like swans only on stilt-like legs, that flew in massive flocks overhead and walked around in the water, catching fish.

This all sounded so exciting to poor Jack, who had only been on one journey in his life before this one, and that was from Lancaster to Eltham. But Balthazar was interested in his life too and asked question after question about his mother, his little brother and his home. Balthazar had missed having a family and a family home. He was fascinated by Jack's descriptions of how they celebrated Christmas together or how they helped the farmworkers collect apples in the autumn or hay from the fields. This all seemed as exotic to Balthazar as his tales of travelling abroad did to Jack, and so Jack enjoyed embellishing his descriptions to give the boy a strong idea of what it was to grow up in a family. The more he spoke about his old life, the more Jack missed it, so after a while he changed the subject.

"You know, life at Eltham is wonderful too, and Henry says that once we have saved Arthur, we can go home, and you can come and live with us," he mentioned.

Balthazar looked hopeful. "Do you think Henry wants me to live with you? I think he forgot."

"Oh, Henry never forgets. If he invited you to come and live with us, nothing can stop you from doing so, for everyone does what Henry wants. All the adults adore him, you know. He is like a little king at Eltham. Even Master Skelton gives into him much of the time."

Then Jack had to explain who Master Skelton was, and Margot and Mary. Balthazar was extremely interested in meeting any girls. He went quiet for a while as he wondered about them, for there were not any girls among the seadogs. Jack understood that sometimes not to talk was as good as talking, and so the two companions fell into step with each other, side by side, as they both withdrew into their own private reveries.

Jack was thinking about Lydia, whom he had not spoken about, for by keeping her to himself, he had found an inner strength with which to keep going. At the thought of her, Jack felt his eyes sting with emotion. He was determined to get through this ordeal, to reach Ludlow and help Henry, so that afterwards they could go home and perhaps she would keep her promise to visit him.

As he walked along like a somnambuilst, Jack dreamt he was riding along in the wagon by her side, holding the reins while she sat there, smiled at him and let him kiss her cheek. His thoughts were so vivid that he imagined he could even hear the jangling of the horses' harnesses and the clip-clop of their many hooves… and that bloody tin whistle playing Henry's tune so badly. That tune? He could hear that tune!

Stopping to turn around, Jack could clearly see the most wonderful sight he could possibly imagine. There, emerging from the rain, was the distinct form of the troupe of performers, headed by Lorenzo, coming straight towards them.

"Lorenzo, hey, Lorenzo!" shouted Jack with tears in his eyes, overcome by emotion.

"Henry? Jack?" came the cry, and before they knew it, the two boys were surrounded by an excited crowd of actors and jugglers, quite overwhelming Balthazar, while Jack shook hands with Lorenzo and Lydia looked at him shyly.

"But where is Henry?" asked Lorenzo. "And who is this young man?"

Jack made the introductions and explained that Henry had left them only the day before but without their knowledge and that they were heading for Ludlow where they might find him.

Lorenzo welcomed Balthazar, like he would anyone who needed a friend, but he was most concerned about Henry.

"Climb aboard, boys. Find a space and get blankets to warm yourselves with, for you both look like drowned rats. We are heading to Ludlow. Come on, men, let's quicken our pace. Henry needs us!"

Climbing into the wagon with Lydia, Jack proudly introduced her to Balthazar. Balthazar was impressed by the relationship that Jack had with this girl. Jack, feeling proud of his Lydia and aware of the appreciation Balthazar had for her, and his connection with her, decided that the French boy was not so bad after all.

20

1st APRIL

While Ned went out to set some eeltraps, Henry sat by the fire in the cabin thinking about his brother, Arthur, and wondering if he was going to reach him in time. It was about a week since he had left home on a journey that should have only taken four days. This was not good. As for his disappearance from Eltham Palace, Margot could only have covered for him for a few days. There must be soldiers out looking for him now, and goodness only knew how his father would react on learning he had run away from home.

As the morning progressed, the rain slowed to a stop and the sky began to clear. Emma was outside, throwing some peelings to the pig, when a horseman came trotting up the road. With hands on her hips and the wind blowing loose strands of hair across her face, Emma looked a pretty picture of domesticity, not that the rider had any interest other than to question her.

"Good morning, miss," the man began. He was an odd-looking man, thought Emma, with a face like a overgrown baby, although his eyes told a different story. "I am looking for a young fugitive who has escaped the law by jumping into the river some way from here. Downstream it was, but he might have swum ashore and could be wandering about these parts. I have yet to catch him, if you have seen a boy walk by or climb out of the river?"

Even if Emma had not had Henry in her cabin at that very moment, there was something so unsavoury about the man that she would have been unwilling to help him in his enquiries.

"I am sorry, mister, but there is never anyone here except for me and my husband, and if we had seen anyone, we would have shooed them away, as we don't like trouble around here. Especially from foogitives." She swept her hair out of her face and stared directly at the horseman. Anyone else would have believed her, but this man was of a suspicious nature.

"And what have you got in that cabin, may I ask?" he demanded.

Emma kept staring him down. "Nothing but the few possessions we carried on our horse and our backs. We walked all the way from London and there was not much we could carry. You can see that from the state of our packhorse. He isn't up to much. But he and the pig, plus what's in the cabin, are all our worldly possessions."

The horseman, who Henry recognized as Fiddle by his voice, was about to ride away when he stopped. He then sniffed the air as if he could *smell* something was up. Henry, who had come to the window to watch Fiddle, panicked upon seeing the rider halt. In his haste to find somewhere to hide, Henry knocked a tin mug off the table. Fiddle heard the sound of the mug hitting the earth floor and jumped off his horse. He pushed his way past Emma and through the door, suspicious that there was a fugitive in there after all. Emma gasped in horror and covered her mouth with her hands.

It was miserably dark in the cabin and the state of the fire was such that when he opened the door, smoke filled the air. Fiddle coughed and spluttered.

"What was that noise?" he asked Emma, who was peering in behind him, expecting to see a terrified Henry about to be arrested, but he was nowhere to be seen.

"I didn't hear nothing, mister, but the logs are dying in the fire. Maybe they fell and that is why it is smoking. Or perhaps it was the cat?"

Cats were not common creatures, and some thought they indicated that the owner of the house they lived in was a witch. Fiddle hesitated. Most women feared him, but this one was defiant. He peered carefully around the place, prodding clothes with the end of his horsewhip.

In a corner was a large wooden barrel. Fiddle was about to lift the lid, but the smell coming from the barrel assailed his nostrils it was so putrid.

"What on earth do you keep in there?" Fiddle asked, backing away as his throat gagged.

"Rotting fish, sir. They have been dead for weeks. We use them as bait. We cannot leave the barrel outside, as the foxes get at it."

How revolting, the man thought. "Is there any way out of this place other than the door?" he asked, searching the floor for a trapdoor, then the rafters for a cowering fugitive.

"The only way I know out of here is in a coffin," Emma replied, a wry smile on her otherwise worn face. "The last tenant died of the sweating sickness. That is why we got the rent cheap."

Fiddle covered his nose with a handkerchief as he stumbled out of the door. "Well, keep an eye out for the boy, and if you find him, there is a reward of sixpence."

There, that should make her give him up, if she was sheltering the boy. Sixpence was a fortune to a wench like herself.

"Oh sir, for sixpence I will surely catch the little beggar and bring him in by his ear, surely I will." Emma smiled a cheeky smile, something that made the man recoil. Women were evil.

"And where is your husband, if you have one?" he retorted. There were men's clothes in the cabin, but she might be 'living in sin'.

"Out on the water, looking for foogitives," Emma laughed.

This rattled Fiddle, who climbed back onto his horse just as Ned was coming up the back lane. Fiddle did not see him, but Ned spotted the man on the horse, and felt a shudder run down his spine.

"You should watch your words, miss, or they will get you into trouble. I am on the King's business. I could get you thrown out of this hovel in a moment."

Fiddle turned his horse and headed back up the road at an indignant trot, never deigning to look behind him. The woman was a hussy. He would come back with a constable and get the place pulled apart, not that there was much to destroy. However, he would enjoy it.

Ned came up behind Emma and put his hands around her waist protectively.

"Who was that creep?" he asked. He had instinctively disliked the man, even from a distance. Somewhere in the back of his mind something niggled at him, like an itch.

"He was looking for the boy," Emma explained what had just happened. The two of them ran into the cabin to call Henry out from where he was hiding. "Henry, that man has gone. Where are you?"

There was a slight noise from a dark corner, where the barrel of fish bait sat. The lid lifted and the stench of rotting fish assailed their senses.

"Oh, my goodness!" Ned was finding the sight of a gutcovered

Henry extremely funny. "Jump out of there *at once* and go and wash yourself in the river. Be careful an eel doesn't eat you, though."

Henry was not amused. He needed help to get out of the barrel, having kicked the stool away when he climbed in. It was a terrible task and it took both Emma and Ned to extract him. By the end of it, they all needed to go to the river to wash, but although Ned and Emma were not too badly affected by the stink of rotting fish, it had permeated Henry's skin. He scrubbed himself using the remains of his shirt and jumped out of the frigid water.

"Come on inside," chuckled Ned. "You will need some new clothes now."

Within a short while Henry was in a new set of clothes: a rough old dark-green shirt tied at the waist with his pirate belt, a pair of pale-green winter leggings knitted in a rough wool that itched his legs, and a green woollen jacket that belonged to Emma so was not too large and fitted Henry nicely.

"Thank you, Emma. I love green," Henry grinned.

Ned also found him a green felt hat that almost went over his eyes. "You look like Robin Hood," he joked.

Henry cheered up on hearing this, for he loved the legend of Robin Hood, although Ned added that Henry did not smell like Robin Hood, more like a dead whale. This did not go down well with Henry. Ned patted him on the back and told him not to take it too harshly. At least the nasty agent had left without finding his hiding place.

After a light meal of bread and cheese, Ned turned to Emma, resolute as to what he must do.

"I don't like the cut of that man. I am going to go with Henry to Ludlow. He only a child and now he is wanted by the law. He will be much safer if he has a cover story. I will say that he is my son; he looks enough like me to get away with it. I could do with buying some provisions at the market in any case. It's tomorrow, and I can stay in an inn overnight."

Emma could see that there was no point in arguing.

Ned turned to Henry. "I don't think you ought to travel on your own if there are men out there looking for you. Especially such a vile man as that horseman."

Henry was so grateful he threw himself at Ned and hugged him. "Thank you so much, Ned. And thank you, Emma." He turned to Emma and bowed. "I will send him home to you as soon as we reach the town. I can take it from there. I…I know where my brother lives."

"Look after yourself, Henry, and come back on your way home, so we know you are safe. I hope you get to your brother and give him the message, so you can go back home. You must miss your family."

Emma turned to Ned. "Farewell, husband. Come back soon and keep out of trouble."

"I will be home within two days at the most. I love you." Ned kissed her lips gently.

Once the old packhorse was saddled up, Ned climbed carefully on and put his hand out for Henry, who jumped up behind. The horse staggered under the weight of the two of them, but soon found his feet and moved forward at a snail's pace. It was going to be a long and tedious journey but for the company of one another.

"Put your arms around me in case he stumbles again," Ned suggested.

Henry did as he was told and found that it was quite comforting holding on to the fisherman. There was something so familiar about Ned that Henry found himself snuggling into the man's back for comfort.

Ned noticed the boy leaning into him and smiled to himself.

"I am enjoying having you around, young Henry. I think that if my baby is a boy, I am going to call him Henry after you."

"I would like that," admitted Henry. "I am named after my father."

"Are you like him?"

"No, quite the opposite. My brother is like him in every way. I think that is why my father favours him so. He looks upon me as a wastrel."

Ned chuckled. "And are you one?"

Henry sounded indignant. "Of course not. I work hard at my lessons and I excel at everything I do. At least, they tell me so." He hesitated. "It's just that whatever I do doesn't seem to be enough. My father doesn't like me."

Ned thought about this. "I can't imagine that is true. If I was your father, I would be very proud of you. Travelling all this way with only a couple of friends to take an urgent message to your brother – it is both brave and selfless. You have put yourself in some pretty dangerous situations."

"That is exactly why my father would be angry with me. He calls me impetuous, reckless, impulsive."

Ned laughed again. "Again, are you?" Henry saw no reason to lie. "Yes."

The two friends rode in silence for a while. Ned knew that if he kept quiet, the thoughts going around in the boy's head would soon emerge.

"Ned?"

"Yes?"

"Why can't a father love his two sons equally? Why must he have a favourite?"

"Hmm. That is a tough question to answer. If you are being truthful when you say that you work hard and do well with your education, perhaps it is something else. Do you answer back when he talks to you?"

"He hardly ever talks to me."

"Do you misbehave?"

Henry thought of the mouse trick under the table. "Not often."

Ned came up with another reason, one Henry had never thought about before.

"When you say your brother is like him, does he look like him? Does he have the same colouring and mannerisms?"

Henry laughed. "Give him twenty years and you won't be able to tell them apart."

Ned then asked a pertinent question. "And who do you look like? Your mother?"

"Not my mother, she's a woman! But she says I look like her brothers when they were young. I never met them, for they died, but she always smiles when she tells me this. She says I remind her of them."

Ned felt a chill run down his spine again, but this time for a good reason.

"What did your brothers die from? The sweating sickness?"

Henry noticed the stiffness in Ned's spine. It surprised him, for he had been so relaxed only moments earlier. "I don't really know. She never talks about it. It is a forbidden subject."

Ned had already had his suspicions because of the river ring, but now he wondered if the boy riding behind him was the son of one of his sisters, one who had a ring. It could not be Cecily, for Henry had said she was his aunt. Ned did not know if his other sisters, of which there were many, were alive or had children. He did know that Elizabeth had married the King, and he also knew that the King's eldest son was reputed to be the image of his father. 'The little King' he had heard the prince mockingly called.

Henry kept thinking about the wavy ring and how Ned had reacted when he saw it and how Emma had asked if Henry was one of their 'lot'. One of their family?

"Ned?"

"Yes?"

"Tell me about my ring; you recognised it. You say it is a symbol of the River Goddess. Tell me about her."

Now that Ned was away from Emma, he felt able to expand on the subject.

"Melusina was a River Goddess of incredible grace and beauty.[38] The legend goes that she was swimming in the moonlight under the water of a fountain when a young knight came across her and fell in love with her immediately. She had hair as black as a raven's wing and skin as white as porcelain. The knight asked her to marry him, and she agreed, so long as he promised she could return to the fountain once every month to bathe in the moonlight undisturbed and unseen.

"The couple loved each other and had many children, but the knight was curious as to what his wife got up to when she went for her monthly swim. He was worried that she was meeting another man. So one day he followed her, only to see that in the water, her legs had turned into the tail of a fish, and he understood that his wife was no mortal, but a magical creature.

"When Melusina discovered that her husband had spied on her, she was furious and left, never to see him again. However, she never stopped loving him, and at the hour of his death, he heard her singing for him from the Other Side. It is said that when one of her children's children is close to death, you can hear her singing to welcome them to the afterlife. For they are all blessed with the magic of the River Goddess. Your ring is a sign that you and your family have the blood of the river running in your veins. This gives you an affinity with water and with magic, and perhaps a safe passage to the afterlife that mere mortals cannot claim. You are a lucky boy if this ring is truly your own."

Henry touched the ring that lay against his skin. It felt warm, almost unnaturally so, and his fingers tingled at the touch. Did the ring have a power of its own? Had it perhaps saved his life when he fell into the river? It was Henry's turn to shudder now with trepidation and wonder.

After a while Ned returned to their original subject. "It is my guess, young man, that the problem you have with your father is that you do not remind him of himself but of your mother's side of the family. Now, I do not know who your father is, or your mother, but if your mother is of the family that wears this ring, there will be a natural prejudice against her and her kind. It is believed that all the descendants of the River Goddess are more than mortal and perhaps a little dangerous… or even mad…"

Henry was shocked. "Mad? I am not mad."

Ned patted him on the leg. "Neither am I, young Henry. So, you are in good company. Now, let us not dwell on such things. I just wanted to point out to you that your father might be prejudiced against you because of your looks, not your character. I think you must just accept your lot and be happy that you have your mother's fine looks, or your uncles', for you are a handsome lad indeed."

Henry leant against Ned's back and reflected on what he had learnt. His mother's family had a water goddess with magic powers as its matriarch. If Ned recognised the ring, perhaps it was because he was of the same family?

"Ned, I understand everything now. Thank you. And I also know… I can feel it… that you are somehow of the same family as I. You are a descendant of the River Goddess too. That is why you recognised the ring. Don't tell me and don't deny it. You and your wife wish to remain anonymous, but please don't lie to me, for we are kin."

Henry could hardly breathe as he waited for Ned to deny this fact, but he did not.

Ned said nothing. He just patted Henry's leg. That was enough for Henry to know the truth. Sometimes words did not have to be spoken. He touched his ring again and it was still unusually warm. Henry experienced the most wonderful surge of love and affection for the man with whom he was riding. It was true that they looked remarkably like one another. Now it appeared that they shared the same magical blood. As absurd as it sounded, Henry knew it to be true because he could *feel it*... a warmth, as if he were by a fire or being hugged by his dear mother.

"I love my mother very much; in fact, I miss her," Henry murmured, speaking his thoughts aloud, and then, clinging on to Ned, he let his head rest against the man's back.

"I miss her too," Ned said quietly, for he did.

Silence fell between the two as they both allowed their private thoughts to settle in their minds. After a while, Henry spoke up to voice all he had considered.

"You have opened my eyes, Ned. All my life I have been trying to win my father's love and it has only caused me heartache and loneliness. I resented him for not loving me like he does my brother. He does not or cannot love me for I am not like him, I am like my mother and her family."

"Well spoken, Henry." Ned was satisfied. "I can see why you do so well with your learning. Your tutor must be very proud of you, for you are both quick to learn and intelligent enough to use what you have learnt to grasp ideas that others might never understand all their lives."

Henry gleamed with pride. It was as if a great weight had been lifted from his shoulders. But after the giddy heights of realisation came the fall.

"But then, who will love me?" he asked.

Ned heard the change in Henry's mood. "You are loved already by your mother, I am sure, and you are loved by those friends you left behind on the river. But also, you are loved by me, son."

The word 'son' slipped off Ned's tongue before he could stop it. His heart missed a beat, thinking he might have offended the child. But the effect was quite the opposite. Henry wrapped his arms right around Ned's waist and gave him a squeeze.

"Thank you, 'Father'. I know you are not my real father, but we can pretend for a day anyway. I heard you say to Emma it would be a good disguise. In an ideal world I would love a father like you. I don't think my father would mind my saying this, for I now understand he has no feelings for me at all and never will. I will look elsewhere for love from now on."

"I don't think you should deny your father his role in your life. You should still honour him."

Ned did not want the void between Henry and his father to become a chasm.

"You are right, Ned. And you are right that my friends deserve better from me. I left them without thinking of their safety, I just cut myself off. I acted in a selfish manner, and I am as surprised by this as you. I will make up for it when I see them again."

"Excellent!" Ned laughed. "Then for one day only you are my son and I am your father, and a very proud father I am. Come on, son, we don't want to be late!"

The energy in his words was so infectious that Grog whinnied and trotted for half a moment. "That's it, Grog, what a fine horse you are. There isn't a greater animal on earth."

"I wonder what happened to Virtue?" Henry mused once Grog had slowed back to his normal speed. He had already told Ned about Virtue and what a super little pony she was, but apart from that, he had not had time to think much about her until now. His last memory was of them both flying over the hedge with Fiddle chasing after them.

"Whatever happened to her, son, I hope and pray it was quick," Ned replied. He could not see how the pony could have survived such a jump as Henry had described.

Henry went silent for a while. He felt a terrible sense of loss unlike anything he had ever felt before. *If having someone close to you die makes you feel anything like this, I never want to lose anybody – not Arthur, not anybody. I feel as if a part of me has died inside along with Virtue.*

Virtue, who everyone had assumed was dead, had in fact survived the fall. After jumping over the hedge and parting ways with Henry, she was wounded badly: her legs were cut, as was her front shoulder. But she swam across the river all the same and managed, with the last of her strength, to climb up and into a copse of trees, where she felt safe.

After a while, she wandered into a field to eat some sweet spring grass. It was there that the shadow monk had come across her. He had seen the chase and witnessed the jump, and though he could not reach Henry, for he did not know how to swim, the shadow monk had made a point of rescuing the prince's courageous pony. In fact, when he had shot Captain Morgan through the heart, Virtue and his own pony, Star, were tied next to each other just a short distance from where he stood. The two ponies had taken to each other and were easy to handle together.

The shadow monk had been tailing Henry ever since he met him, first with evil intent, but over time with the belief that the boy had a role to play in his own life. Perhaps the strangely likeable boy would be able to rescue him from the silent sentence he had been dealt from a young age, when, taken from his parents, his tongue was removed, and his life devoted to the ways of an assassin.

Virtue was now much better. Her cuts had mended and there was no heat there. He had wrapped her legs in cobwebs to prevent infection. He had groomed her and stroked her and loved her. He now understood he could feel love. He had always loved Star but had not had a word to describe this feeling until now. Henry had shown him the way to his own heart. Which was why he had followed Henry up the river on the coracles, and had watched him cut himself away from his friends and then meet up with the man with the light. The shadow monk was drawn to the young prince in some way, as if he knew the boy would be his salvation.

The shadow monk wanted to approach Henry and give him back his pony, but he was wary that Henry might still see him as the enemy. He would understand if he did. This was a waiting game, and so he shadowed the man and boy on their old horse and kept a watchful eye on them. What he wanted most of all was to be accepted into Henry's world, just like he had seen Balthazar be embraced. He wanted that more than anything, but what he feared more than what he yearned for was rejection. All the time he waited for that perfect moment to approach the boy, the future was a possibility; once he had made that approach, he would have to suffer the consequences. It had to be the right moment, and so he would wait. Patience was something he had learned a long time ago.

21

Lady Margaret had told the King that Henry was missing. Luckily it seemed that Captain Cripps knew in which direction Henry was travelling. The King was impressed that the captain he favoured was proving to be so resourceful. He must have his own network of spies, or so the King thought. While he wondered what he should do about his missing son, Cripps stole a look at the old woman who nodded in acknowledgement with the slightest move of her head.

"Go and find my son. Bring him back to me and I will whip his arse. It is time he was treated like the knave he is turning out to be. I will have the skin off the backside of that whipping boy too, while I am at it. That's what he is there for."

The captain saluted, clicked his heels and left. As he marched out of the chamber, the King noticed that the man's uniform was new and wondered was he paying the man too much.

The King's men followed the route Lady Margeret had extracted from William, Henry's page and passed it on to Cripps. He had a plan.

Two days later, Cripps and his men were catching up with the missing prince. They had followed Henry's trail from Abingdon Abbey to Enstone, where they thought he had stayed in an inn, to Worcester Cathedral, where he had been seen by one of the monks; but after that, the boys had vanished. There was talk of a chase through the town and some child falling into the river, and so the troop had searched first one side and now the other. They had come across the oddest impromptu burial site, with three crosses, reminiscent of the three crosses at Jerusalem, by eight graves on a beach. They had dug one up and found a villain of some sort, with tattoos and missing teeth. He had been shot right through his heart with an arrow. Now they were searching the other side of the river and were in the woods. Captain Cripps was fired up, for not only was he looking for Prince Henry on behalf of the King, but he knew his new benefactor, Lady Margaret, would be relieved to have her favourite grandson back in safe hands once again. If he had no luck in finding the prince, at least he could go to Ludlow to make sure that the message, sent by pigeon a few days ago, had, in fact, arrived. Had he known he was going to have to come this way he would not have sent the message by pigeon, but such are the plans of mice and men... or old women and men in this case.

Fiddle had not yet given up. He was certain the horse thief was in the neighbourhood; he could almost *feel* him. It was strange — he was certain he was close to the little vermin at that hovel back by the river. He had felt him there too. He was good at such feelings; it was instinct. Now he was certain he was closing in again on the boy. When he found him he would string him up on the nearest tree, the little tyke. Patting the rope packed away in his saddlebag, Fiddle urged his horse onwards. He was heading towards a crossroads in the woods where all roads met, travelling in every direction. Beyond it was a bridge that led to Ludlow which all travellers wanting to reach the town must cross. That boy was as good as dead – he would not get the better of Thaddeus Fiddle.

The troop of yeomen were riding towards the bridge, as it was the only way to cross the river again, so they could do a sweep search of the other bank. They had been told of a band of actor performers travelling towards Ludlow and wondered if the prince might be travelling in disguise. Princes could be fanciful creatures at times, and Henry might have taken to dressing up and mingling with the artisans of the world. It would not be the first time. Cossetted royals sometimes became fey, with strange tastes.

Henry and Ned were plodding along on Grog, who was looking at the grass and wondering how he could get a bite to eat. Henry was thinking hard about who Ned might be and why he had the same river magic running through his veins and yet would not explain how or why. Perhaps he was an illegitimate son of one of the Queen's side of the family. Henry was ashamed to realise that he had never been given any information about his mother or her past life. She was the Queen, his mother, and that was all. He knew she was the daughter of Edward IV, his father's nemesis, but apart from that, he knew next to nothing.

Grog, who had begun to stumble every few minutes, had had enough.

"Come on, son, let's have a break for a while," suggested Ned.

The sun was at its zenith and about to descend, leaving a wintery chill behind it. The woods were bare and damp, even though the first few flowers of spring were trying to push their noses up out of the ground, primroses and violets. Henry noticed steam rising from the damp moss around their feet. He slipped down from Grog's back and Ned lithely dismounted after him. He was a fit man, Henry noticed, much fitter than the King and yet only a few years younger than him.

The two friends let the old horse nibble at what he could find while they stretched their legs, and then sat together to break some bread to eat with a slice of farmhouse cheese.

"So, son, what do you want to be when you grow up?" Ned asked.

"What would you like me to be, Father? A fisherman like you seems an enticing thought. Standing in the river with a large net catching twait."

"That would be a great life. Do you know how to tickle a trout?"

"I know how to in theory. My tutor told me, John."

Ned was impressed. "He must be a good tutor. But I will teach you how to do it when you come back from Ludlow. There is nothing like doing it for real. To put a fish into a trance by tickling its belly, so that you can then lift it out of the water."

"I would love that. I will call in to you on the way home. After I have seen my brother. Maybe I could bring him with me!"

Ned was not sure that this was such a good idea. "Maybe…" Without warning, the temperature dropped around them. "Did you feel that? There is a sudden chill, I don't like this place anymore," said Ned, who had risen and was brushing bits of debris off his breeches. "There is something unsettling about it. I must go and relieve myself, and then let's get going."

He walked off behind a tree.

Henry sat there feeling the same sense of foreboding he had felt in Woodstock Woods a week before. He was sure someone was watching him. He could feel his skin creep. He thought about the strange monk in black and wondered if he was still following him.

I don't like this place either, he thought, just as a horseman trotted into the glade.

"Halt," the man cried, "in the name of the King!"

It was that dreadful man Fiddle yet again. Fiddle walked his horse towards the boy with his sword drawn.

"I am arresting you in the name of the King for your crime of horse-stealing," he announced in an official-sounding voice. Henry stood up and put his hands on his hips, legs wide apart in a commanding manner. "Fiddle, you are a fool. I am not a horse thief, I am Prince Henry, son of the King."

Fiddle was shocked. "How do you know my name? Explain yourself."

Henry pulled off his hat. "I *am* Prince Henry, you idiot. You know me from Eltham Palace. You brought me the pony. It was my pony I was riding when you chased me into the river. I was nearly killed by your actions. I should have you thrown in prison for your deeds."

Two things happened at this point: Fiddle looked at the bare-headed, red-haired boy and realised he had made the most terrible mistake of his life, and at the same time, Ned walked out from behind a tree and challenged him.

"Why are you threatening my boy?" he barked at the man on the horse.

"He's not your boy, he is the King's son."

Ned looked at Henry, his suspicions now confirmed.

Henry looked at Ned, his eyebrow raised. "I am the King's son, Ned."

Ned thought it was not the right time to admit this to the nasty man. "Rubbish, you keep your mouth shut, son, and don't be having high and mighty ideas like that. I have told you often enough about your dreaming."

Henry's mouth opened as if to protest, but Ned just winked at him and turned to Fiddle.

"He is *my* son, you fool, and you touch one hair on his head and I will break your neck." Ned raised himself to his fullest height – formidable even to a man on a horse.

What happened next surprised Ned, who was used to facing down men in bars or on the dockside. Fiddle jumped off his horse and prostrated himself in front of Ned, lying before him on the earthen floor of the forest.

"Edward, oh Edward, is it really you? My little prince? My darling boy!"

Ned was stunned into silence. 'Don't you see? It's me, Thady."

Ned kept quiet while a flood of memories overflowed in his brain, then said, *"Thady?"*

Memories flashed past of his time in the Tower of London with Thady as his only 'friend'.

The three froze for a moment. Nobody knew what to do. Grog looked at the other horse and whinnied in a friendly manner. Fiddle's horse, Flyer, moved towards him tentatively, just as Henry moved towards Fiddle and persuaded him to rise to his knees at least.

"Oh my God! Edward – I have missed you for all these years. I have your ring, you know. Here it is – I want to give it back to you." Fiddle produced from his pocket the ruby ring he had taken from the unconscious man he had attacked in London.

Ned was even more confused, then worse, he was incensed. "You? It was you? You attacked me and robbed me the night of the royal wedding. It is *I* who should be arresting *you*, you thief."

Henry realised who Ned must be, if he know who Thady was. "I thought you might be one of my mother's brothers."

Ned looked at him. "I am not, Henry – for Emma's sake, I am Ned."

"But…" Fiddle was still speaking to anyone who would listen. "I was on the King's business when I broke into the house where you were situated. I was surprised by your entry into the room and I am sorry I hurt you. My dear boy, I have found you."

Ned looked at him with menace. "But you nearly killed me, and you *stole* from me."

"I was searching for documents, for… evidence, you must understand. I did not realise it then, but later I worked it out. You are my child, my little prince, my angel. I let you go, I let you drift away on the tide. I saved you from certain death in the Tower, don't you remember?"

What Fiddle was saying was incomprehensible to Ned. Thady was a distant memory. What had happened in his 'other life' was too much of a blur to recall. In time, he might have sorted out the emotions clanging around his head like hammers, but right now it was impossible.

His train of thought was interrupted by a troop of the King's yeomen, who arrived on the scene to see three figures in a clearing by the bridge.

Henry was still computing all the information that he had already guessed but was now confirmed. "If you are Prince Edward, you are my uncle. I *knew* it. We share the same blood. The same magic."

"Don't mention the magic, or we will both suffer, son," Ned warned Henry through his teeth. "They will never accept us for what we are. Be careful; cherish the magic, conceal it. We are the children of Mother River, Henry. She will look after you."

The troop of horsemen pulled their horses to a halt.

Henry turned to face them and his heart sank on guessing that they were out looking for himself.

"Halt, in the name of the King!" Captain Cripps commanded. "This is an unusual gathering."

Captain Cripps could see a man on his knees begging before a man who looked very like the rebel who had led the uprising in London only a week ago, while a wood elf, dressed in green, who smelt of fish, stood between them.

"Excuse me, but *I* speak in the name of the King," stated Fiddle, although he looked less confident in the face of a troop of soldiers. He rose from the ground and brushed himself down, feeling rather stupid for having been found on his knees in front of a peasant, for that was what Ned would seem, although Fiddle knew otherwise.

"Excuse me, sir, but I am the captain of the Yeoman Guards and *I* speak for the King, for I am under his direct orders." Cripps puffed out his chest.

Henry stood watching the two men, who were like dogs baring their teeth at each other.

"If you must know, I am taking this man and boy into custody," Fiddle said, deciding to try to bluff it out. "The rascal is a horse thief and this other man has been harbouring him. I believe them to be related to each other, but I am not quite sure. The boy stole one of the King's horses and I am the King's agent. You can leave this matter to me, thank you."

The captain of the guards looked skeptical. "Which is why you were down on your knees when we arrived, begging?" he sneered.

"I had a stone in my shoe." Fiddle lifted his nose in the air.

The soldiers' horses were fidgeting, the sound of their shiny bits and buckles tinkling in the otherwise quiet arena that the woodland made.

Cripps was distracted by a repugnant aroma. Addressing Henry, he asked, "Why do you smell so bad, son?"

Henry could think of nothing else to say but the truth.

"I hid in a barrel of fish this morning. I was hiding from this man, who has mistaken me for a common thief."

"Maybe you *are* one. Where is the horse you stole?" Cripps looked at the tired old packhorse, Grog. "Surely *that* is not one of the King's horses?" he laughed.

Now it was Ned's turn to speak. "No, that is my horse, paid for with honest money, sir." He sounded indignant.

Cripps laughed without malice. "And where did you buy him? The knacker's yard?"

Ned replied honestly, "Actually, yes. He is a good animal, although somewhat slow."

Captain Cripps kept looking at Ned. "Tell me, were you in London a few days ago?"

"Why would you think that?" Ned asked. "I am a fisherman, and this is my apprentice, as you can tell from the way he stinks. He is a hapless child and did not think before he leapt into a barrel of rotting fish. A simpleton at times."

"I am *sure* I saw you in London not two weeks ago, when I was escorting the King through the streets. It *was* you, I am certain; you were leading a rebellion against the King."

Captain Cripps turned to his men and gave an order: "Arrest that man and take the boy with him. There is something fishy going on here!"

As the men jumped down from their horses as one and grabbed Ned by the arms, Henry stepped backwards to avoid arrest.

"Actually," he said, stepping forward, "if we are going to debate the subject, *I* speak for the King, for I am Prince Henry, King Henry's son, and we are wasting valuable time when I am meant to be elsewhere. I have to rescue my brother, the Prince of Wales, from a plot to kill him!"

Henry pointed to Ned. "And *he* is my protector, my personal friend, and if you lay a hand on him, I will have you horsewhipped and in the stocks for a week as soon as we get home."

Cripps was not expecting this turn of events. "Is this some kind of April Fool's joke?"[39]

Henry glared at him. "Of course not, that is preposterous."

He noticed the man staring at him and looked down at his ludicrous green attire.

"I mean…" He did not know what to say.

Neither did the captain, but he was on duty and duty called. He was out searching for the King's son and the boy *did* look remarkably like the younger son of the King, but he was not dressed like a prince; nor did he smell like one. He decided to change the subject.

"And who, may I ask, is plotting to kill the Prince of Wales?"

Henry pointed at Fiddle and said, "He is!"

Now it was Fiddle's turn to be cornered, but instead he looked incredulous. "I am? No, no, no, that is a lie. I am spying on him, on the orders of her ladyship, the King's mother, Lady Margaret, but I would never harm him."

Captain Cripps looked at the wood elf, who did look very like Prince Henry, and then at the baby-faced man in riding clothes. Then he looked at Ned, who was still being held by the men-at-arms and who really *did* look like the pretender, a wanted man. This was a complex situation. He turned to Fiddle and spoke carefully.

"So, why do you think this boy a thief? Where is the horse you speak of?"

Fiddle was about to answer that he had no idea, and that the horse, which was in fact a pony, had most likely died in a fall, when there was the sound of advancing hooves. The group of adversaries looked to the trees to see a youth all dressed in black appear, riding a black pony with another beast in tow.

"*There* she is!" shouted Henry, full of wonder as his lost pony materialized before his eyes, looking very alive indeed. "Virtue!" he cried.

"There she is," exclaimed Fiddle, feeling foolish beyond belief, for if this child *was* Prince Henry, he had never stolen the pony, for it was *his* pony. But what did he say he was doing here? Rescuing Arthur from a plot to poison him, by himself? He was just *spying* on him.

The youth in black rode up to Henry and slowed down long enough to address him. "Bump!" he cried, the first word he had uttered in many years, and Henry, seeing a way out of the ridiculous stalemate he was in, leaped onto Virtue's back.

"Come on, Ned." He stretched a hand toward Ned to lift him onto Virtue's back.

"No, Henry. Run." Ned waved him away. "I will distract them. Now go!"

"I won't leave without you," Henry pleaded.

Ned ignored him. "I said go, son, *that* is an order!"

"Wum!" the shadow monk shouted at Ned, who leaped onto Fiddle's horse and fled in the opposite direction, knowing Grog was not going to help him reunite with his beloved Emma.

The soldiers did not know whether to go after Prince Henry or the pretender. Fiddle was looking around for his horse and soon realized he had been duped, for his horse had been stolen.

While the soldiers split up, some going after Henry and others after Ned, Fiddle sat on a fallen tree and broke down and cried. Never before had he been so close to happiness and then thrown into such despair.

After a while, he pulled himself together. He was sitting in a forest in the middle of a glade, and the place was beginning to feel haunted, with the last of the daylight filtering through the trees. Looking around, he noticed Grog, the only animal left. Grog looked at him. They had both been forgotten, considered worthless. Fiddle went up to the skin-and-bones horse and climbed onto his back. There was nothing to do other than walk the nag home at his own speed, a broken man on a broken horse. Why did the boy think he was a threat to Prince Arthur? He needed to talk to Grope.

22

Head down over his pony's neck, Henry had an awful feeling of déjà vu. Only a few days after 'the fall', he was being chased yet again. However now, instead of Fiddle, his father's elite guard were after him. The only positive was that he had been able to lead at least half of the soldiers away from Ned, who was racing off in the other direction. Henry was trying to think why the captain of the guard thought Ned was in London heading an uprising. Not that he had much time to think. He held on to his darling pony, praying Ned would get away and that the monk knew how to shake himself free of this band of men-at-arms.

The shadow monk had a trick up his sleeve. While he had been waiting for an opportunity to introduce himself to Henry, he had familiarised himself with the terrain of the area and its environs. He took the prince along one track then another, downhills and up steep inclines, until finally they reached an area up on a hillside where the forest had been damaged by a storm in the past. The trees stood at all angles, some horizontal they had to jump, while others made them duck.

"Bup!" the monk shouted, delighted with the voice he had found inside himself. Henry did as he was told and Virtue, as true as ever, found her way through the various obstacles.

This was more than could be said for the three soldiers, whose horses were too tall to get them under the fallen trees. One after the other he heard them crash into the timber and cry out, and after a few miles, the two ponies were the only creatures left racing through the woods.

Finally, they came out of the trees and onto a path. The shadow monk pulled the reins of his pony, slowing to a trot and then a walk. Once he had caught his breath, Henry pulled up beside him to thank him.

"I have no idea who you are, sir, but you have not only saved my pony, you have saved me, not once, but twice now. I thank you sincerely." He looked at the boy riding beside him with interest.

The boy looked back at him and grinned. "I am mor femb, bup I mo beap." He then opened his mouth to show the cruel truth behind his strange way of talking.

Henry was appalled. "Who did this barbaric act? We must punish them!"

The boy smiled and his eyes twinkled as he shook his head. "Mo, mo."

"Do you have a name I can call you?" he asked.

The shadow monk had already thought about this. He had a vague memory of his parents calling him Jim when he was young, before he was taken by the abbey.

"Bim."

"Bim. Unusual, but you are an unusual sort of boy. My name is Henry."

So it was that Bim and Henry became friends and together rode on to Ludlow. Henry wanted to know how Bim had found Virtue. By asking several questions that Bim could answer by nodding or shaking his head, he learned that Bim had been following him, on orders, but had decided to rebel against his master to join the prince. He had rescued Virtue after the fall and had been keeping an eye on Henry, to be of help. When he killed the pirate, he had done so with glee.

Henry had the chance to thank Bim again, this time for having shot the sea-dog captain so skilfully. "We would not have survived that day without you. I am in your debt, sir, and ask you to join my company of friends. There are quite a few of us now, although I abandoned them yesterday; I still do not know why. I had this overriding urge to finish this journey on my own. Little good it did me, other than meeting Ned and now meeting you."

With a feeling of comradeship, the two boys made their way to Ludlow, one boy in black robes that he had modified since deciding to leave the monastery, so he looked more like a gangly spider than a monk, the other in bright green like a grasshopper.

As night fell, they could see the lights of Ludlow shining in the distance. Henry wondered how he should enter the castle. This troubled him as he trotted onwards with Bim at his side.

Nobody was expecting a prince to arrive smelling most horribly of rotting fish. He had not been able to shake off the smell. It would need someone like John Skelton to make a concoction to overpower the aroma. He decided that however he presented himself to the castle guards, the terrible smell was going to bring attention to him, so the only thing he could do was ride right up and announce himself as the King's missing son. The King's yeoman had said they were out looking for him, so his father must know he was missing and the entire country would be on high alert. Henry shivered at the thought of the reception he might get the next time they met.

John Skelton, Margot, Charles and Rosalind arrived at Ludlow castled to be welcomed by William who had arrived just before them.

"William!" Margot's eyes lit up on seeing him once again and she threw her arms around him in the most unqueenly manner. For once, John Skelton said nothing. He was as pleased to see William safe and sound as she was. The feeling was mutual.

"Thank God you are here, John. Things are very serious and looking grave. We need your support, for Sir Richard and Lady Margaret Pole[40] are in pieces. As the chamberlain here at Ludlow, Sir Richard is directly responsible for Prince Arthur's health and safety. Now he is gravely ill and so is the princess."

This was grave news indeed. "Princess Katherine is also ill? How can that be?" asked John Skelton, wondering if the illness they had half-guessed might be poisoning might in fact be the sweating sickness instead.[41]

It turned out the princess had been eating the same meals as those prepared for the prince. The physicians had been treating them for the sweating sickness or a similar disease, but Skelton knew otherwise. The couple looked awful. They had lost a noticeable amount of weight and were as pale as alabaster. Skelton's dilemma was that he had only brought enough of the antidote potion to counteract the poisoning of one person. Once he had been persuaded by his sister that there was poison in his body and that of Princess Katherine, Arthur was causing trouble.

"I will not take the antidote unless Katherine is saved first."

Arthur was adamant and nearly choked trying to assert his will. They assented, if only to keep him alive a while longer, for he would surely die if he kept coughing and choking.

"Darling Arthur," the princess answered, "you are more crucial to the country than I, and women are stronger than men when it comes to pain and sickness. Look at how we bear children."

She blushed at saying this, for unknown to anyone else there, they were both still virgins. They had chosen to wait until Easter to consummate their love, so their child would be conceived on a holy day. It now looked as if they had left it too late.

"That is a point," Arthur said cleverly. "The princess might be with child." It was his turn to go red this time, for what he said was a lie and he had never lied before in his life. "Her life must be saved so our son can be born."

Arthur would hear no other argument and Katherine was given the potion while John and Margot chanted the charm they had learned by heart into her ears. The charm worked and immediately a light appeared to shine from her otherwise dull eyes. It reminded Margot of the light that had shone from the cauldron when the potion was made. She found this fascinating. Margot was becoming more and more interested in herbs and potions. She had always had a yearning to learn about medicine, but this potion-making was one step further into the mysterious world of alchemy. Her quick and inquisitive mind was making its own conclusions about what was and was not legitimate research. Having seen her own grandmother, Lady Margaret, dabbling in what could only have been the dark arts, Margot saw no reason why she could not learn a bit of white magic. She decided she was going to ask Master Skelton to widen her studies to include this discipline. That was in the future, once they had returned to Eltham. For now, she and Skelton should try to make more of the potion they had seen Thomas make.

"It is either that, or we will need to return to Worcester and ask Thomas to make us more. We could be back in a day if we rode all night long," Margot said urgently to Master Skelton.

Master Skelton was undecided. "I don't think we have time to return to Worcester, but do we have the ingredients? We never thought of taking extra with us."

Margot considered this. "The physicians might have some. They have gardens of herbs, don't they?"

This enthusiasm was why Skelton adored Margot; she never gave up, to her anything was possible, and as a result, she came up with the obvious where others were blinded by doubt.

"Of course!" he agreed, and soon the two of them were begging herbs from both the physicians and the staff of the kitchens. It was there they made another discovery. When asking for herbs from one of the kitchen staff, a young man who often had the task of chopping up herbs to rub on large slabs of meat before roasting or to mix with breadcrumbs to make a stuffing for pheasants or swans, had an idea.

"If you can't find the right ingredients, ask Thady. He has a friend who makes medicines at home. He makes the tonic we give the prince when he is not feeling well."

Margot recognised the name from the diaries and tugged at Skelton's sleeve.

"And where is this Thady now?" he asked the kitchen boy.

"I don't rightly know, for he went away for a few days. He disappears from time to time. Says his friend is quite poorly and he must look after him. I don't know what kind of friend he is. Seems a bit strange to me, two men sharing a room in an inn."

"What inn?" asked Margot and John at the same time. "The Bull. It's on Castle Street."

This was vital news to John and Margot, who guessed Thady was Fiddle and that his 'friend' was Grope. So, they were here in Ludlow and, via the kitchens, had access to the prince, through his food and now in a tonic. This would be a perfect opportunity to poison his food. They must find Fiddle, but first they had to try to make another dose of the charm potion.

"We could send the guards out to find him," suggested Margot.

Skelton was against this move. "We are not meant to be here and need to keep as low a profile as we can. It is already a strain on our hosts having us here without the King's knowledge. We cannot start causing mayhem. We must just save Arthur and disappear back home."

"After we have found Henry too," added Margot.

"After we have found Henry, of course, my dear," he replied.

Henry was not all that far away at all; in fact, he and his companion were riding up Castle Street on their two ponies. As he did not know the layout of the castle to use a discreet side entrance, he could only think of riding right up to the front gates and asking for access to his brother. All he had his ring as proof of who he was, his river ring, and hoped this would make up for the state he was in, dressed in his elfish apparel. Bim rode close to his side, looking this way and that to ensure his friend was safe.

It was dark and cold, and the ponies kept slipping on the cobbled surface of the road. The two boys were tired and hungry, Henry especially, but he would not have time to rest or eat once he got there.

As they walked up to the gates of the castle, two guards with halberds challenged them.

"Halt, who goes there?"

"Prince Henry, second son of the King." Henry spoke with as much authority as he could muster. The guard came up and shone a lantern in his face.

"You don't look much like a prince to me. You look more like a bleeding elf." The man was friendly, but unimpressed by the two lads who had ridden up to demand access, one in strange green clothes and the other in black rags.

Henry could only do one thing. "I am who I say I am, and I have urgent business here and need to see my brother, Prince Arthur. Here is a ring that belongs to my sister, Princess Margaret Tudor. It used to belong to our grandmother, wife of Henry IV. Please alert your mistress and steward of this castle, Lady Margaret Pole. Tell her I am here and am demanding entry." He handed the ring to the guard. "I will remember your face if the ring is lost," he added.

The tone of his voice made the guard stand up straight.

The boy exuded authority and sounded *very* royal.

"If you wait here, sire, I will go and see her myself. Your ring will be safe with me."

The guard walked off into the night, but his colleague stood in the gateway with his halberd across it in a way that still barred the boys from entry, unless they wanted to push forward and risk a fight.

Bim was feeling nervous. He could take out one or two men, no problem, but he had a horror of entering the castle and being surrounded by people he did not know. He touched Henry on the arm and indicated he would prefer to melt into the night for now. At first Henry tried to make him stay, but he soon gave in. It would be difficult for someone with no tongue to mix with the entourage of Prince Arthur, be it with the nobility or the servants.

"Bim, I understand, but I have nothing to give you to pay for you to stay in an inn. Here you could at least sleep in the stables if you felt uncomfortable in the castle itself."

Bim shook his head, waved farewell and slipped off into the night with his faithful pony. Within seconds it was as if he had never existed.

"Where is your friend?" asked the guard when he returned.

Henry had to think quickly. "His mother called him home."

The guard laughed. "I thought you were just a couple of muffins! So, he has gone, has he? You are in luck, though, as Lady Pole is coming to meet you herself. Be polite now, sir, as she is in a bit of a state this evening, between you and me. Things are not going well for her right now." The guard putout his hand, "And take your ring, son. It appears to open doors for you."

Henry did not have to wait for long before his 'Aunt' Margaret, cousin to his mother, who knew him from court, arrived at the gates in a fluster. "Oh, my goodness, Henry, what are you doing here?" She looked terrified, something he was not expecting.

Normally, his aunt was an elegant figure who swanned around at court, while her rather dull husband stayed in a corner, talking farming to whoever would listen to him. Theirs had been a marriage forced by politics, as most marriages were, and yet it was not an unhappy one.

Henry stood waiting and was beginning to feel like what he was: a ten-year-old boy out in the cold on a dark night, missing his mother and feeling very young. His aunt looked surprised to see her young nephew at the gates without a complement of guards or any escort but did not try to reprimand him. It was as if her mind was on other things.

"I have come to see my brother. This is very urgent, but I am very pleased to see you, dear aunt." Tears of relief fell quietly down his face, and he wiped them away before she or anyone else might notice.

"Perhaps you would like a wash and a change of clothes first," his aunt suggested diplomatically. She had obviously caught a whiff of his fishy aroma.

"In a short while, maybe. I must see Arthur first. I have travelled many miles to talk to him."

His aunt looked dismayed and Henry was sure it was not because of the state of his dress. "If you say so, my dear. I am glad you are safe, now you are with us."

The distracted woman led Henry to the front door of the castle, where a groom took his pony, promising to look after her well and tend to her needs while Henry went indoors. Henry, having learnt to look after his pony, was much more interested than he had ever been in her welfare, especially after all she had been through.

Charles was discussing Fiddle with John and Margot when Henry was brought into the room.

"I tell you, it is for me to confront Fiddle and Grope, for I owe them one. Grope was particularly hostile towards me when I last visited The Bull. I have a debt to pay him." He was just about to tell them what had happened when Henry arrived.

"Oh, Henry!" Margot bounced over to hug and kiss him, although she soon stopped. "Goodness! You smell awful, Henry!"

John was next. First, he shook him by the hand and then he hugged him. "Thank goodness you are still alive. I could murder you for being such a worry to me, you rascal."

Finally, Charles came up and patted Henry on the back. "You had me worried when you did not meet us at Worcester, but you look none the worse for it, other than… what are you wearing? You look like a leprechaun!"

Charles ruffled Henry's hair and then looked at him solemnly. "I am afraid your brother is not well; nor the princess. Thank God Princess Margot and Master Skelton decided to come too. They have brought an antidote to the poison, but they have not brought enough. Those demons Fiddle and Grope were up to no good after all. I am sorry I did not believe you, Henry. I will make amends. I am going to confront them and see if I cannot extract from them the antidote, or ingredients for what we need in order to save him."

Henry wanted to see his brother right away, but Skelton insisted he bathe first and dress in some clean clothes before he was allowed into the sickroom. He might have some vapours about his body that would add to the poisons invading the prince. By God, he smelt evil enough.

Henry was upset about this, but knew he would not get past John Skelton, and so, with Margot sticking to him like glue despite the fishy smell, Henry went off to find his aunt and accept her offer of a bath after all.

All the time he was washing, Margot filled him in on what she and John Skelton had been doing. She told him how they had met Thomas when in Worcester.

"Tell me about the charm and how it works. Can you make more?"

Margot was certain they could, if only they could find the right ingredients.

"By the way…" Henry had finished washing and was taking the river ring and its chain from around his neck. "Thanks for lending this to me, Margot. You must look after it well. It is… er… beautiful."

He handed the ring to Margot, even though in truth, he wanted to keep it. There was a connection between him and Ned with this ring, but it belonged to Margot. As he handed it to her, his mind wandered back to Ned. Had he made it safely away from the soldiers?

"Thank you for not selling it."

Henry was pulled out of his reverie. "What?"

Margot looked at him quizzically. "I said thank you for not selling my ring. I want to give it to Arthur, as a keepsake."

"Don't… I mean… keep it, sister. There is something special about it and Aunt Cecily gave it to you. It has… a power, a connection."

Margot looked at her brother sideways. "A 'power'? Henry, what are you talking about?"

Henry went red in the face and looked away. "Oh, it's nothing. I am being silly. It was just a fancy. Come on, let's go and find the others."

Forgetting Henry's strange words, Margot ran with him back to John Skelton, Henry feeling bad that he could not tell Margot about Ned. She would have loved to know about Ned and about Melusina, but he felt she was not quite old enough yet.

Bim sat on a wall right outside the castle. His pony was eating from a nosebag he had 'borrowed' from the stables of a near by inn. Although more at ease out in the open, he could not help but wonder what it would be like to live inside a castle. Henry had invited him to come and live at Eltham with him after all this was over. He had explained to Bim about his brother and how he needed to rescue him from an attempt to assassinate him. Bim knew a lot about poisons but little about antidotes. He had never needed to revive any of his victims and now brooded on the way he had been turned into a lethal executioner when he would much preferred to have become a doctor who saved lives with his knowledge rather than destroy them.

As he sat there, passing the time away before going to look for a dark corner in which to sleep for the night, Bim saw the silhouette of a dejected figure walking along the cobbled street, closely followed by a well-worn and dejected-looking animal. He recognised the tall, thin man who had accosted Henry in the woods. He was with the old horse that Henry had been riding before he gave his Virtue back. The man was not leading the horse; in fact, he was walking away from it, but the poor beast kept on following him. The man turned around abruptly.

"Look, I told you to go away. Bugger off. I am not going to be seen with a scraggy creature like you. I don't want you, I don't own you and I am certainly not going to pay to put you in a stable for the night."

Saying this, Fiddle abruptly punched the horse on the nose. That had the desired effect: the creature flinched, stepped backwards and came to a halt. Fiddle walked on and in through a door at the side of the inn from which Bim had just stolen the horse food. Bim had a love of animals that was quickly growing stronger. He felt empathy for the horse and so, once the cross man had disappeared, he walked up to the dazed animal and slowly put his hand on his shoulder.

"Bere bere," he spoke soothingly, "bom iv me."

Stroking the horse, he gently led him towards his own pony and let them snort and blow at each other while he found more food for Grog – for it was old Grog who had been so badly treated by Fiddle. That man was a bad man to punch a tired, hungry horse in the nose, thought Bim to himself. It was time he got his comeuppance.

Bim was getting hungry. He would soon have to find something to eat for himself, so after he had settled the horses, he took out his bow and his quiver of arrows from his backpack and went for a walk along the river. There were often birds coming to roost at this time of day. He crouched on a rock, keeping as still as a stone. Soon birds began to land, curlews and oystercatchers, picking at the mud around the edge of the water. Curlews were not that tasty, and nor were the oystercatchers, but they were better than nothing. Bim carefully drew an arrow from his pack, thinking, *I am a rock*, to suppress his thoughts and stop the birds from picking up his movements as he prepared for the kill.

I am a rock, I am as the earth, the stones – mindless, still, ancient and unmoving. He loved this form of meditation. The arrow was nocked, the bow lifted into position. The hapless birds pecked at slim pickings –

worms, beetles, tiny fishlike creatures that wriggled in the wet mud. Bim could hear the birds thinking to themselves, *I am going to eat you, I am going to eat you.* He could hear the worms: *Wriggle, wriggle, home I go.*

His arrow was up against his eye and his supple muscles were taut. He pulled back the arrow a tiny bit further, aiming. The curlew was in his sights when something caught his eye from above. A flash of shadow, a flutter of wings. It was a pigeon flying high in the sky, tired.

In a flash, Bim lifted his bow away from the curlew and up towards the pigeon before unleashing his arrow. With a shot of pain in the back of his head, he felt the arrow pierce right through the bird's chest. The bird was dead in an instant. The curlews and oystercatchers flew off in a panic when the bird hit the ground beside them. Bim shook his head, arched his shoulders and pulled himself out of his trance.

Within a few minutes, Bim had built a small fire on the beach and gutted the bird. Having eaten the heart while it was still warm, he skinned the pigeon with one artful movement. It was only then that he noticed the ring around one of its legs. It had one of those tiny vessels attached to it that carried messages. Out of curiosity, Bim opened it. There was a message, but Bim could not read. He looked at the writing quizzically.

Urgent. Change of plan. Call it off. LM.

It was very pretty writing, but it was of no concern to him. It might be important, but then again it might not. Nonchalantly, he tossed it on the fire and watched it burn. He then pierced the carcass of the bird with a stick that he had cut for this very purpose, and within a few minutes, he was enjoying the hot, sweet taste of fresh pigeon. A dish fit for a prince.

Charles and William had slipped back into spending all their time together like they did at court. They both disliked Grope and decided they should go and visit the scoundrel. John Skelton had written a list of the ingredients he was missing to complete the antidote and they were determined to find them. Having sharpened their swords and wetted their whistles with a few glasses of wine, they donned their jackets before striding with purpose down Castle Street to The Bull.

Inside, a smoky atmosphere greeted them, as the wood fire and low ceilings combined to make it a given that the chimney would smoke. A few regular customers were sitting at tables around the place, on stools or benches, playing cards or dominoes. The barmaid who had flirted with Charles the last time he had been there was handing out jugs of ale, her ample bosom as exposed as it had been when he first saw her. She looked towards the door when it opened and smiled when two dashing men came in from the dark, but when she recognised Charles, the smile was wiped off her face. Putting down the jug, she turned away and slipped through a side door. Charles and William followed.

They caught up with her in the kitchen.

"Where is Grope?" Charles asked, not wishing to beat around the bush.

The woman looked towards the door that led down to the cellar.

"Thank you." He nodded to her before swiftly opening the door and entering. It was dark in the cellar but for a light on a table where a rotund man was sitting, pouring liquid into a bottle. There was a large book on the table, a pestle and mortar, and some different coloured phials, some open, others untouched.

"I do not need you tonight, sweet Mirabella. I told you I am busy," he said before looking up and noticing Charles and William, both with their swords drawn.

Charles nimbly descended the stairs and held the sword to Grope's chest.

"It is time for us to settle a debt, I believe," Charles began. "The last time I was here, you sent me away with a flea in my ear. Well, this time I am prepared and will not take any chances. We know what you have been up to, sir, and we find you guilty of poisoning the Prince of Wales. We will not kill you if you can help us by providing the medicines we are so desperate to find in order to save his life. My orders are not to harm you if you cooperate."

William came forward and looked at the items on the table. There were dead mice among the detritus. It was an unsavoury sight, as they were either bloated or exuding liquid. The smell of death and suffering was unmistakable.

"This looks interesting, a book with compartments in it. I wonder what they hold?" He was about to pick up the book when Grope growled in an animalistic manner.

"Don't *ever* touch my book. It is not for mortals to play with," he warned.

Just at this point the door opened at the top of the stairs once again and in stumbled Fiddle, who had just walked back after his encounter with Henry in the woods. He was beside himself with anguish and hardly noticed the presence of Charles with a sword to Grope's heart.

"You made poison for the prince, not tonic," he accused his partner. "I have been poisoning the prince all these weeks when I thought I was helping him. How dare you do that to me after all these years?"

Fiddle practically fell down the stone steps and into the room. The lamplight lit up the scene of the three men standing around the table where the accused sat, thinking fast as he worked out how he could escape this situation.

"... A book with compartments in it. I wonder what they hold?"

"Come on Fiddle, you are as guilty as I am, in fact more so. What do you think was in the sweets you gave the dear princess in the Tower? Your 'little angels'? You would have killed them with kindness the way you were going, handing them dangerous sweets all the time. Edward's teeth even began to fall out… We would have been caught had I not come up with the idea of 'rescuing' them and getting their bodies out of the way. Imagine what they would have found at an autopsy."

Fiddle's eyes looked like they were going to pop out of his head. He had unwittingly been poisoning his little Edward, and Richard too. The veins on his neck bulged alarmingly along with his eyes. He threw himself down the stairs to attack his partner, but Grope was quicker. He stood up, ignoring the pointed blade at his chest and lifted his hands as if in surrender. "Fiddle, these men need my assistance to save Prince Arthur from dying. Let me put things to right."

Fiddle stopped in his tracks, and Grope continued, turning to Charles.

"If you allow me to call my assistant, I will happily help you in finding the ingredients you are looking for."

He sidled around and past Charles, who turned with him, his sword still held in a threatening manner. Grope walked to the bottom of the stairs and pulled a cord that was dangling there, and a bell rang up in the kitchen. Within minutes, Mirabelle came down the steps.

"I need you to come down here, my pretty thing. Come and help us find the things these men are looking for."

The girl came cautiously down the stairs, but once she was within an arm's reach of her lover, he grabbed her, using her body as protection, with his arm around her neck and his free hand now holding a knife. He pushed this against her side, making Mirabelle scream.

"If any of you move, the girl gets it in the stomach," he warned, and slowly he began working his way up the steps, manhandling the terrified waitress between himself and the other men.

"Do not hurt that woman," warned Charles, "or I will come after you and stick this blade through your heart, you scoundrel."

William was stunned, for he was not used to seeing blades bared in anger. He kept still, unsure of what he could do. Fiddle watched his partner in disbelief as the man reached the top of the stairs.

"You will find what you are looking for in the blue bottle," were his last words before he violently stuck the gutting knife into his lover's side, threw her down the stairs and disappeared.

The sound of a heavy bolt being locked from the outside was the last they heard of him.

Charles and William ran to help the woman, who had fallen the full length of the stairs like a rag doll and was now holding her stomach, blood beginning to seep through her fingers.

"Oh God, oh God!" William could not believe what was happening.

Charles took over the situation. "Take off your shirt and tear it into strips. Quick, man!" William did as he was told and within minutes Charles had bandaged up the woman's side.

"There, that will have to do for now. William, grab the book that's on the table and the blue bottle. Fiddle! Open the door, open the bloody door!"

Fiddle, who had stood still, staring at the door through which his long-time partner had just gone, leaving him behind, broke out of his reverie and ran up the stairs to begin banging on the door. Eventually, the landlord came and unlocked it.

"What are you doing in here?" he asked; then, on looking around and taking in the scene before him, he saw his wounded daughter.

"What has happened here? What dirty deed are you guilty of? Who did this?" he asked as he stumbled down the steps to rescue his darling. "Mirabelle, are you alright? Can you hear me?"

Charles pulled at William's sleeve, then bounded up the stairs, William right behind him, holding the book and the blue bottle. "Fiddle, you stay here and look after these good people. You are not a bad fellow. Do some good and help them."

Charles and William ran outside to see if they could catch up with the real villain, Grope, but he was nowhere to be found. He had left the building.

"Come, William, we must hurry back to the castle and give these things to John Skelton. With these ingredients he mightbe able he might be able to finish the charm he is making and save Arthur. There is no time to lose."

As they ran up the hill towards the castle gates, a figure dressed all in black stood in the shadows watching the doorof the inn.

Fiddle, who was truly distressed at his erstwhile partner leaving him, decided to check the bedroom they shared to see if Grope might not just be sulking there. But the room was bare and the man was gone, taking his money purse and valuables with him.

So, Fiddle ran out into the street to see if he could catch Grope trotting down the road on his pony, but he never sawa thing, for just as he stepped out into the night, a spidery black figure confronted him and punched him right in the nose. He was left writhing on the ground in agony while two horses hidden in the shadow watched on.

23

When Ned jumped onto Flyer in the woods, he knew stealing a horse would end with him in the stocks or worse; and worse it became. After a gallant chase pursued by Captain Cripps and his men, Ned met his fate when a tree that had fallen right across the path blocked his way. Flyer jumped and cleared the tree, but Ned jumped even higher and left contact with the horse, who, once free of his burden, ran off into the woodland ahead. Cripps and his men also jumped the tree, narrowly missing Ned, who was lying there, stunned and winded. Within moments the soldiers had reined in their horses and surrounded the dazed man, their swords drawn and pointing at his heart.

"I arrest you in the name of the King," Captain Cripps barked. "Again!"

As soon as he saw the soldiers pulling up to arrest him, Ned had popped the ruby ring returned to him by Fiddle into his mouth. It would not do for the ring to be found on his person, as it would link him to the Yorkists and their treasonous cause.

Cripps interrogated him. "What is your name and where do you live?"

"I am Meb Wiver and I wive nop far fom here, wiv my pebmamp wife, Emma. Fee wiw be wonwey and afraid wivoup me. Pweashe wep me go poo her fo fee know of my fape."

He spoke with some difficulty because of the ring in his mouth, but luckily, Cripps thought he had a speech impediment. Cripps wondered to himself why he had not noticed it before, but then there had been a lot going on a few moments ago, what with the King's agent and the wood elf.

Cripps was married himself and knew his young wife would be distraught if he ever disappeared without a word. He agreed Ned could lead them to the cabin, for it would also be an opportunity for them to corroborate his story. It seemed odd that a political rebel would one week be leading an uprising in London and the next be a fisherman on the edge of the River Severn over two hundred miles away. Perhaps he had a twin? The soldiers bound Ned's hands together and lifted him onto the back of one of the soldier's horses, after which he directed them to his cabin. Emma greeted them in tears.

"Ned, oh Ned, why are you with these soldiers?" Then, to the soldiers: "Why have you arrested my husband? Where are you taking him?" she asked defiantly.

Cripps looked at the woman with compassion. "We found this man in the woods with a child, or elf, in some conversation with another man who accused the elf-child of stealing a horse. Then, a man in black turned up, the boy ran off on another horse and this man took the other man's horse and ran away, so we gave chase, to both parties in fact. I have since lost some of my men, who have gone after the elf-child on the other horse. It is a criminal offence to steal a horse, you know. It is an offence that deserves punishment. We cannot have horse thieves running around the countryside, not in this day and age, miss."

Emma went down on her knees. "My husband is not some common horse thief. He is an honest fisherman. We live here in solitude. We do not want to break the law or get into any trouble. Please let him go. I am pregnant with our first child. How can I survive without him?"

Ned was distressed. "Pweashe, darwing. Whese men are onwy doing their wob. I am sure I will be fet fwee in a week or two. Ifn't vat fo, offifer?"

Emma wondered why Ned was speaking so oddly.

Captain Cripps was beginning to feel most uncomfortable for these were simple, loving people. "Look, we have to take him to answer for the crimes of which he is accused. I will send you word of how things go, of that I promise." Then he turned to one of his men and instructed him to remember the location of the cabin, for he would come back with a message in a few days' time.

"Pweave can I have a few quiet wordf wiv my dear wife before we go?" asked Ned.

Captain Cripps allowed the fisherman to dismount, though he would not unbind his hands, and the group of soldiers took themselves a discreet distance away, their horses huddling together while Ned ran to his wife, who hugged and kissed him.

"Darwing, they wiw sep me go. Vey muft wep me go, but in the meampime, ake div wing that if hidden in my mouf anb beep it umpiw Hemwy pomef bap, for I am fertaim tha the wiw, as thoon as he can. Give the wing to him."

Ned kissed his wife, a long, lingering kiss, while he pushed the ruby ring carefully from his mouth to hers. "Give it to Henry, and if I am not back, he will come and rescue me."

"But he is only a child; what can he do to help?" Emma whimpered.

"Trust me, my darling, he is a resourceful lad." Ned winked at her.

He walked back to his captors, and the troop of yeomen and their prisoner remounted and took off down the road for the long journey back to the Tower of London, a place poor Ned dreaded more than anywhere on earth.

In London, Lady Margaret was with her old friend Bishop Fisher, who had come to call on her, having received an urgent message from her asking for his immediate presence.

"My dear Lady Margaret, you are looking well. Are you fully recovered after your 'turn'?" The old lady really did look well, miraculously so. It was as if a great weight had been lifted off her shoulders.

"John, come here, come here." Lady Margaret could hardly wait to tell her oldest, dearest friend about her good fortune. But first she would have to confess to him the dark secret she had been hiding for years.

"Yes, my dear, what can I do for you?" Fisher was seldom called John by anyone, even Lady Margaret. He knew something momentous was about to happen. "Do you want me to hear your confession?"

"Of *course* I do! Why else would I ask you to come here so urgently?" the woman scoffed.

Feeling a little hurt by the tone of her voice, the bishop went to his bag and reverently took out his confessional stole, with all its fine embroidery, and carefully placed it around his neck. He enjoyed making Lady Margaret wait, so took his time, for she had shown him no courtesy, not even a cup of ale after his long journey.

Lady Margaret regretted having been so thoughtless. She knew Fisher well enough to realise she had upset him. "I am sorry, dear

Bishop, but I have something to confess that has been tearing me apart for years and I *must* ask for God's forgiveness. I *must* have absolution."

Lady Margaret went to sit in her favourite chair by the fireside. She was fidgeting like a nervous child, the Bishop noted as he settled into a chair opposite her. There was an embossed black box he had never seen before tucked down beside the woman's chair. He wondered if it had anything to do with the confession.

Over the next hour, Lady Margaret slowly poured her heart out to her confessor: of her struggle to keep her darling son safe during his childhood; of how she had married not one but two men solely for their protection, their both being loyal subjects of her enemy, the York king Edward; of how Edward had died unexpectedly and Richard, his younger brother, had taken control of the country, throwing the rightful heir, Prince Edward, and his brother into the Tower of London 'for their safety' before crowning himself. Then came the crux of the confession: how she had ordered her henchmen to do away with the two young princes trapped in the Tower, so her son would be one step closer to the English throne. This shocked poor old Fisher to the core.

"You did what?"

"You… have to understand," Lady Margaret pleaded on seeing the horrified expression on his face. "I did it for my son. Listen!"

Fisher listened.

"I didn't want to hurt the little princes, but they were Yorkists and they were in the way. It has been eating at me all these years. I did it for my son, *and* for dear Edmund. It was his *dying wish* that our son become King of England!"

Again, Fisher hardly knew what to say, but he tried, "God does have the power to forgive even the most heinous of crimes, but madam, you are testing him greatly."

"But you don't understand. I am telling you this now for it *never happened!*" shouted Lady Margaret, jumping out of her chair and stamping her foot like a spoilt child. "I am redeemed, for they *live*! Fiddle, that stupid man, for once did the right thing. He hadn't the heart to kill the princes and so he let them go. I have proof, I have *proof*, John. I am redeemed! Please forgive me for my sins now. Please. I need redemption. I need no longer die a condemned soul!"

Bishop Fisher was even more disgusted. So *that* was it. All these years, all the gold coin she had spent on religious establishments, universities and alms for the poor, all of these donations he had thought were done against the odd political misdemeanour, were to buy her way out of Hell for having committed *murder*. Worse than that, for the murder of innocent *babes*.

Ignoring the face of disgust on her confessor, Lady Margaret continued to talk, words flowing freely out of her mouth. A confession to beat all confessions.

"Bishop, matters get worse before they get better, though. Thinking myself condemned by my callous actions twenty years ago and knowing I would be supping with the Devil when I died, I made an even worse decision and recently ordered my men to dispose of young Arthur as well."

This time, Fisher was frozen, his mouth fallen open in horror.

Lady Margaret continued, for she had to finish telling her tale before her confessor walked out on her. Not that he could, for when he arrived, she had locked the door, just in case.

"Better to be hung for a sheep than a couple of lambs, even York lambs. Arthur does not seem capable of having children, possibly because he prefers the company of men. This I know, for the Spanish princess is not with child. We need children, heirs to the throne, lots of sons. So, I wanted Arthur gone, to make way for young Henry. Despicable of me, I agree, but the Tudors *must have sons!*"

"For God's sake, your ladyship, you cannot…" Fisher fell back into his chair, silent. The woman was a demon, a disciple of the Devil!

"I know, I know. But I thought I was lost to eternal *damnation*, and I was hearing voices in my head that were *egging* me on. You know that, for I came to you about them. You said I could not do wrong if I was visited by saints or angels. I heard voices… but then they stopped, they deserted me. Not that it matters, for my men have been ordered to stand down. You see, I have worked out that the pretender who is now out there plotting to take the crown, is the real Edward V. My stupid henchmen never killed the York princes. He let them go! Prince Arthur is safe too. I have not been responsible for anyone's death. I am clean, innocent, FREE! And if Arthur never has sons well, we will just have to make sure Henry never becomes a bishop. He is bound to sire many children and we don't want them to be bastards if they are to inherit the throne, do we?" This joke was a sad attempt at humouring her friend.

"You bloody old fool!" Fisher glared at his benefactor. "God may have to forgive you, but I never will. Now, let me get on with this confession and you just say your bloody Hail Marys and let me out of here. I am finished!"

Lady Margaret was shocked. Her friend was meant to rejoice with her and welcome her back into the fold. Yet he was *judging* her and finding her wanting.

"You are a callous and corrupt megalomaniac who has lost all sense of decency, but the irony of it all is that, thanks to your own servants and their humanity, you have done nothing wrong. I can hardly believe it!"

This made him laugh and laugh and laugh until he cried. At first, Lady Margaret was shocked, incensed even, but then, comprehending the enormity of what she had just disclosed and how wonderful it was to have finally confessed it, she began to laugh too, until tears came to her eyes.

❦

At Ludlow Castle, in the set of rooms they had been given upon their arrival, John and Margot were looking at the strange 'book' that Charles had confiscated from Grope. There were many substances of note neatly labelled in the small drawers, but none of them were what was needed for the charm. These were killing drugs, not healing ones. The two friends were beside themselves. John had searched the kitchens and only found a few things of help. Margot had ventured outside to see what she could find around the castle. Nettles were still in season and so was plantain. They were only missing a couple of other herbs and she refused to believe they could not be found.

"We could use the medicine in the bottle that Grope gave us," Margot had suggested earlier when Charles and William came back from The Bull with their booty.

"We do not know what it is or if Grope was telling the truth," John replied.

So it was that the blue bottle was set aside until a servant coming into the rooms to tidy them later, when Margot and John Skelton were with Prince Arthur in his bedchamber, cleared it away, taking it into the kitchens below.

❦

Much to Skelton's delight and surprise, within an hour Margot had returned with all the necessary ingredients. Taking a castle guard along as her escort, she had knocked on the doors of all the villagers, asking if one of the 'cunning folk' – the medicine men or women who lived in the community and dispensed herbal remedies – was in residence. She found an old woman with a toothless grin who was happy to help out and within minutes had produced the final ingredients.

Together with Skelton, Margot took over the large fire in the castle kitchens and put the herbs in a copper cooking pot. Coaxing each other's memory, they started to recreate the potion Thomas had made them. At first Skelton was concerned they might have forgotten the exact words of the charm. However, Margot had a great capacity to learn, and she was word-perfect.

When light seemed to emerge from the cooking pot alongwith the steam from the concoction, Margot squealed with delight. She could feel a tingling throughout her body, which must have been her excitement.

"It's working – look, John, look!"

"What? What can you see, Margot?"

Margot pointed at the light emanating from the cauldron. "Can you not see the light?"

John looked at the cauldron and then at his pupil. "No, what light."

Margot hesitated. "Nor the chanting faces? Oh… it must be me. It must be my silly imagination."

John smiled at her. "Whatever your imagination, you have a great talent here, I can see."

Within an hour they had succeeded in recreating the potion and they ran to the bedchamber.

"Arthur, we have more of the charm for you…" Margot stopped to shake her brother gently by the arm. "Arthur, we can save you; you must drink this."

Margot and John rushed to the bed and John lifted Arthur up as best he could while Margot spooned small amounts of the potion past his blue lips. Tears ran down her face while she repeated the charm again and again. John was crying too, not at the sight of Arthur, but upon seeing his dear, brave Margot wearing her hope as armour against such a state of despair. Together they repeated the charm again and again.

At last, Arthur seemed to look a little better. His lips turned from grey to ashen and then pink. His eyes began to glimmer with the telltale light that had shone from Katherine's eyes once the first potion worked.

"By God, I think we have done it!" Skelton cried. "Look!" Margot leaned forward to feel her brother's brow. His temperature was going back to normal. "Arthur? How do you feel?" she asked her brother tentatively.

"I hardly recognise the feeling, but I think I am well." Arthur looked surprised.

Margot threw her arms around him. "Oh Arthur, how wonderful!" Her tears were now uncontrollable, but as they were tears of relief, they were welcome as they fell on Arthur's bed.

He smiled weakly.

"Margot, if you were not already Queen of Scotland, I would hire you as my top physician. You too, Master Skelton. I cannot thank you enough. You have saved my life."

John Skelton patted Arthur's leg. "Well, the good news is that your wife is much better, and you seem to be on the mend as well. This is a miraculous cure, but I do not claim to know how it works. The ingredients, apart from the words spoken, are easy enough to find and are simple herbs, so I cannot understand how they have the power to combat the poisons given to you. It is a mystery to me, but I will accept its efficiency with grace."

Arthur laughed for the first time in days. "I am with you there,

John: let sleeping dogs lie. Did you say Henry was here? Can I see him?" Arthur wanted to thank his little brother for having risked his life to come and warn him of the men who were trying to kill him. Arthur was still skeptical of this accusation, but he wanted to see Henry anyway.

John took on the role of doctor. "I think you should rest for now and see Henry when you wake up. He is having a bath right now, for he arrived smelling most horribly of dead fish."

Again Arthur laughed, his humour coming back with his strength. "He is always getting into trouble, that boy. It is a wonder it is not I trying to rescue him! But you are right, John, I will sleep now. I am tired."

John and Margot rose from their place by the bedside. Arthur reached for his sister's hand. "Thank you, sweet sister, from the bottom of my heart." He gave her trembling hand a gentle kiss and smiled. "I will sleep now."

Arthur slept for over two hours and everyone had time to relax, catch a few moments' sleep and even eat some food. Henry was especially pleased about this, for it was nearly ten o'clock at night by the time he was clean enough to be allowed back into the royal apartments. He had not eaten since lunchtime, and even then it was only some bread and cheese. When Lady Pole sent a 'light meal' up to the apartment where John, Margot and now Henry were to sleep, Henry fell on it as if he had not eaten for a week. There was a roast chicken, some quail, a side of poached salmon in a cream sauce with capers, lovely soft white manchet bread, and a selection of fruit and cheese. There was also ale, red wine, a sweet white wine and some mead. John poured himself a goblet of sweet white wine. It was delicious and he allowed himself to close his eyes and thank the Lord for having saved

Prince Arthur as well as providing such restorative food.

Henry and Margot were in high spirits. Arthur was on the mend, and Margot felt proud that she had made her first potion and it had been of such great importance. Surely her father would consequently allow her to study medicines and white magic. Henry was happy, for now he could tell Arthur about his adventures and what he had gone through to get here, without all the delays being of consequence. Now he could look back on the last few days with pride. That it had taken him so long to arrive no longer mattered.

"Can I see Arthur now?" he asked Master Skelton, who had just come back from the prince's bedchamber.

"You can, Henry. He is asking for you. He is looking well, thank goodness. But don't tire him out by talking too much. Let him rest."

Henry ran through the castle to his brother's privy chamber, where a few doctors were collecting their bags and heading to their rooms for the night. It had been a long and traumatic day, but now the prince had been stabilised, they could relax, their position at court no longer under threat, and they could sleep soundly in their beds.

"Do not keep him for long," one of them instructed Henry. "He needs sleep."

Henry hardly listened. What would those old crows in their black robes know? It was Margot who had saved the day. Henry was proud to be a Tudor. He knocked on the door to Arthur's bedchamber and it opened. A guard looked out, and upon seeing the young prince, stepped aside.

"Could you wait outside, please?" asked Henry. He did not want the guard to hear any of his conversation with Arthur. It would do no good for the details of his journey to get around.

Once he was alone. Henry bounced over to the bed. "Arthur, oh Arthur, you look well indeed. We were all so worried about you!" he started and gave his brother a mostunprincely hug. There was nobody watching, so the younger brother in him came to the fore and he felt boisterous. Plonking himself down on the edge of the bed, Henry could not stop talking.

"It was I who realised Fiddle was a murderer, Arthur. I deciphered the diary and then saw his tattoo. Well, that's not quite true, as Jack helped me and Margot too. Charles was wonderful. We dressed in disguise, you know, and I was chased by Fiddle, who thought I was a thief, and I had to make a leap of faith over a hedge – Virtue was terrific – and then I was captured by sea-dogs and they were going to —"

Arthur took Henry's hand and squeezed it, stopping Henry's flow of nonsensical words. "Hello, little brother. It is good to see you."

Henry realized he had been insensitive in all his excitement. "Sorry, dear Arthur, hello. How are you feeling?" He really was pleased to see Arthur.

"I am much better now. Thank you for uncovering the plot against me. Fiddle will have to be caught, and his accomplice, but for now we must keep this plot secret as it involves our grandmother, though I can hardly believe that. We must not tell a soul. Do you understand? We can punish those men under some other charge. I have sent guards to go and find them; they will soon be under lock and key." Exhausted by this long speech, Arthur stopped to catch his breath.

Henry used this moment to ask something that had been on his mind. "Arthur, can I ask you something? Do you love Katherine?"

Arthur looked baffled. "Where has that come from, Henry? Of course I do! Do people say otherwise?"

"No, it is something I have been pondering. What it must be like to marry someone you don't know and who has been chosen for you. I mean, do you think Mother and Father love each other?"

Arthur laughed. "Henry, if you are worried about your own marriage, never fear. As a man of the Church, you are safe from the wiles of a woman."

"But I don't want to marry the Church. I want a wife, one I can love. That's why I ask you now: is it possible for love to grow?"

Arthur looked upon his little brother with great love and admiration. "Dear Henry, for you to be worrying about such things at your tender age shows great sensitivity – and sensitivity to your wife makes for a good husband. You never told me you didn't want to become a priest."

"You never asked," Henry replied. "Father just makes decisions, and we are supposed to do as he demands. It scares me. Do you love Katherine? Is it possible to love a stranger?"

This made Arthur chuckle, but not without humanity.

"Henry, to answer your question with the same level of gravity you ask it, yes, I do love Katherine, with all my heart. Not only is she beautiful, kind and sensitive, but she has a heart of pure gold. She loves England as much as I do and she wants to improve the conditions in which our subjects live, just as I do. We were strangers when the ceremony made us man and wife in the name of the law, but it is the time we have spent together since that has allowed our love to grow.

"Something Mother taught me is that one has choice in life, even in the most rigid of regimes in the name of duty. Yes, we might have our destinies arranged by others, but it is our choice how we tackle that destiny. We have the ability to make the best of what we are given, and it is how we do this that makes us who we are. When you grow up and take on your duties, ensure that you govern how those duties work for you, make them work in your favour, don't allow them to take hold of you and mould you. You have the choice. Never forget that, little brother.

Now, I love my Katherine, I would rather die than see her die before me; in fact, but for Margot and John, I would have done so gladly. I would sacrifice myself for her, for I know I would live on in her heart, in her words and deeds. She is the epitome of all that is good in my heart. We are one, she and I—We are one."

Henry was humbled by his brother's candid reply to the question.

"Arthur, next time you talk to Father, can you put in a word for me, please? I want to marry a woman and to feel the kind of love you have. I want to honour, adore her, and put her on a pedestal, so I can gaze upon her and feel loved in return."

Arthur thought for a moment. "Henry, if it is in my power, I will ensure you marry a woman as worthy as mine. Rest assured; I will tell Father the Church is not for you. Now, you must let me rest, for I am still weak. And I am thirsty. Could you please get me a drink before you go?"

"Of course, dear Arthur." Henry stood up and looked around for a pitcher of wine.

Arthur pointed to a dark corner of the room. "Over there.

They keep the drinks and medicines on the sideboard."

Henry went over to the oak sideboard and looked for some wine. There was an array of bottles, phials, pots, cups and beakers. The containers were empty, but for one, a blue bottle that had not yet been opened. A servant had found it in the kitchen earlier and, recognising it as the tonic that Prince Arthur often used, brought it up and had left it on the sideboard with some other drinks.

Henry pulled out the stopper and smelled the liquid within. *It must be some sort of fortified wine*, he thought, for it smelled sweet. He stuck his finger in and licked it. It had a refreshing, slightly minty but sweet taste. So, Henry dutifully poured out a cupful of the liquid and took it to Arthur, who thanked him and drank it all in one draught.

"Thank you, dear brother. I must go to sleep now. Goodnight and sleep well. We will talk more in the morning." Arthur smiled contentedly.

"Goodnight, Arthur. I love you."

"I love you too, little brother."

24

2nd APRIL

Henry awoke to the sound of panic around him. The room was lit with candles. John Skelton was pulling on his clothes while issuing orders.

"Wake the master physician, but not the others. They are a bunch of bloodsuckers, a waste of space. Bank up the fires. Bring some clean towels and hot water!"

"What's going on?" asked a sleepy Henry, rubbing his eyes. Margot was already up. "It's Arthur. He has taken a turn for the worse. Quick, Henry, we must be ready to help in whatever way we can."

"But he was fine last night." Henry was bemused. He had left Arthur only a few hours ago. What could have happened to him in the interim? Pulling on his clothes in a haphazard manner – or rather Arthur's clothes, which had been lent to him after his bath – Henry staggered after the others and into the privy chamber that led to the prince's bedchamber.

Already, there was a flurry of activity there. Servants were rushing to and fro with clean sheets, buckets of hot water, pillows, herbs and whatever Lady Pole had instructed them to fetch. Lady Pole was a chattering mess, her hair bunched up and unbrushed. Her husband was beside himself too, chewing his nails and looking one way then the other. Henry stood there in a daze. His brother had been well a few hours ago. What could possibly be wrong with him now?

John Skelton was talking with Lady Pole in the corner of the room. They were conferring about whether the two younger royals should be allowed to watch this scene of chaos or if it would be better to send them back to bed. There was little hope of sending the two children back to their rooms without a fight, and so they decided to let them stay.

Princess Katherine arrived, looking terrible, her eyes red from crying. She rushed past them into the prince's bedchamber and within seconds the master physician was sent out, followed by his attendants. He looked over at John Skelton and Lady Pole, his expression dour, and shook his head with sorrow.

❦

Princess Katherine was having a private conversation with Arthur, for he had something of great import to discuss with her. He knew now that he was dying, for he had reacted violently to the glass of tonic from the blue bottle soon after he had lain down to sleep. At first, it was just a rumbling in his guts, but after a while, the lining of his stomach felt like it was burning. Something was wrong. The prince managed to get up and walk to the sideboard, where he poured himself more of the tonic, for he recognized it as that when he saw the bottle. Having drained the last drops into the cup, Arthur drank deeply. He was hoping the tonic would do the trick. Only this time it doubled the pain in his stomach, and he was not even able to walk back to bed.

Instead, he fell to the floor, writhing in agony. That was when the guard who was outside the door burst in, having heard Arthur moaning. The guard saw the prince, picked him up and put him on the bed before raising the alarm throughout the castle.

What Arthur did not know was that the tonic in the blue bottle Henry had opened was the final dose Grope had prepared for him. His *coup de grâce*. Unlike the previous tonics kept in the signature blue bottles that gave relief to the patient or victim, this 'tonic' hit the victim's vital organs, eating them like acid until they failed. Worse still, this evil liquid had reacted with the potion Margot and John had made. There was now a toxic concoction of substances fighting a battle to the death in the prince's failing body. The consequence was that he was coughing up copious amounts of blood. Nobody knew what to do, and so Katherine had bravely gone in to sit beside her husband to give him what comfort she could.

Standing outside the bedchamber door, Margot could hear Katherine crying, "No, no, you can't possibly mean that!" and "You cannot ask that of me!"

Eventually, Katherine came out of the prince's private bedchamber crying into her handkerchief. She stopped and looked at Henry, who was wearing one of Arthur's favourite jackets. It fitted him perfectly and he looked very handsome in it, a gold silk coat with black velvet lapels, but to Katherine, who had just left her dying husband, it was a sight she could hardly stand to see. Ignoring Henry pointedly, she swept past him and asked John Skelton to instruct Henry to go in to see his brother. John spoke to a somewhat bemused Henry, who, seeing an unsettling look of horror in his sister-in-law's eyes, mustered all the strength he could find before walking into the room.

Inside Arthur's bedchamber it was all but dark, for Arthur had complained the candlelight was burning his eyes. The acrid smell of herbs thrown hastily onto the fire to ward off evil spirits was suffocating. Henry felt bile working its way up from his stomach, but the severity of the situation forced him to swallow it back down. He stood there to allow himself to adjust to the scene that lay before him. Henry stepped forward awkwardly, fighting his legs, which wanted to run back out of the room. He shuffled forward, a feeling of panic rising from his very soul. Stepping up to the bed, he looked at his brother and stopped dead, for Arthur was almost lifeless, his skin deathly pale. It was as if he was looking at a wax effigy of the prince, the kind made for the top of a coffin.

"Oh my God!" Henry croaked.

Arthur lay there like a sacrifice upon an altar, quite lifeless.

"Arthur, can you hear me?" Henry's eyes began to fill with tears. Arthur was dying. "Dearest brother, please tell me you can hear me."

Arthur stirred and his lids opened, but his eyes were distant and unfocused. He moved his hand, which lay outside his covers, with extreme effort and beckoned Henry to come to his side.

Henry knelt. "Oh my God, Arthur, what has happened to you? You were looking so well. Something has happened. Who has done this? I will wreak vengeance on the souls who have brought you so low!"

Arthur turned his head, although his eyes still wandered around without control, a most terrifying sight for Henry.

"No, Henry," Arthur whispered, "do not seek vengeance. What is done is done. Instead, let me speak with you now about something of great import. Send everyone out."

Henry was puzzled, for there was nobody else in the room. Arthur must be blind. Henry held his brother's hand. "I am here. We are alone. Talk to me."

Arthur was having palpitations. He knew these were his last moments. No heart, however strong, could survive this ordeal. He knew his life was at an end, but he also knew he had a great burden to pass on to his younger brother. He was fully aware that Henry was not the stuff kings were made of, so it was imperative he make him promise this one thing.

"Henry," he wheezed, gasping for breath. "I have only one thing to ask of you. Promise me you will do this for me?"

"Anything you ask of me will be my command. But please don't die. We need you; I need you. I want you to get better and become King. Please don't ask me to be King. I am too young and too foolish. A King has to be wise. You must not die!"

By now, Arthur's life blood was draining from his vital organs and he could barely keep himself alive. His breathing was shallow and his eyes were growing dim. He spoke so quietly Henry had to lean right into his face in order to hear him. The putrid smell of death made him feel sick once more. Arthur gasped a cough and choked, before recovering for long enough to speak to Henry one last time.

"Swear to me now... that you will marry... Katherine... and make her Queen of England, to rule... alongside you... to guide you when you are King... She will speak for me in all... things, for she knows my... mind. Promise me, Henry."

With an extraordinary show of strength, Arthur grasped Henry's hand until it hurt. Henry wanted to cry out in pain, but the look in Arthur's eyes was so intense, he nodded as quickly as he could. This was a dying man's wish and Henry was in no position to deny it.

"Dear Arthur, I promise on my life I will do as you ask."

"Say it to me... again. Raise your hand and... make a promise, with... God as your... witness." Arthur was determined to tie his brother into an oath he dare not break.

"Arthur" – Henry raised his right hand – "I promise, as God is my witness, I will marry your widow, Princess Katherine, and she will rule England at my side. She will be my Queen and will speak for you in all matters, so help me God!"

Arthur, upon hearing the sworn promise, let go of Henry's hand and sank back into his bed with a sigh. "Thank you, my dear brother. I trust you to do as you promised."

For a moment, the two brothers, who had seldom spent any time together to grow to love each other, were as one. Their two hearts beat in time and it gave Arthur a sense of peace, for he felt, no, *knew* his little brother, the silly one who nobody ever thought would come to anything, would do as he asked. With Katherine by his side, he would be a great king, and all the reforms Arthur had dreamt about would come to fruition. With an intensity that shocked him, Arthur glowed with love for young Henry.

"I love you... little brother.... Remember, don't... let your... destiny rule you... *Rule Your Destiny.*" he stressed, and then his last words came.

"Music, I... can... hear... inging...no, calling... It is beautiful... Henry... she is there, she has come for me. I am saved. Henry, there is a white... oh, I... love..."

Henry was unsure if Arthur was talking to him or to some other being or spirit who was calling to him from the some other place. Arthur was looking into the distance, smiling and calm. He seemed to have come to some sort of realisation. From his expression, Henry could see that Arthur was not scared of death, in fact, he appeared rather to embrace it. Arthur was not dying, he was being born into another life elsewhere. He looked so young and... happy. Henry was mesmerised. Was it God who Arthur was seeing? Did God truly show himself to the dying? Henry had to know.

"Arthur..."

Henry was about to ask his brother if there was someone coming for him when cruelly, the moment was shattered as with one last, violent spasm, Arthur's back arched and a strange sound came out of his mouth. Arthur died with a deflating sigh, his eyes losing all movement and glazing over within seconds. The magic had gone – evaporated – and Henry wondered if it had really been there. Did Arthur just reveal the truth about death and what lies beyond, or had Henry just imagined the last few minutes?

Had he seen God?

But then Arthur had heard music, singing, and he had used the word 'she'. Could there have been an angel? Memories of a legend Ned had told him the day before came to mind… Melusina. Was Melusina an angel, one of God's own? But that would make him the descendant of someone divine. Thoughts spun around in Henry's young mind and made him confused, while tears sprung from his eyes and ran down his face.

Flies having congregated around the gases that the dying emit hours before the heart finally gives up, began their morbid descent, the sound of their wings buzzing an ancient lament.

Henry was left to grieve. There had been two of them in the room and yet now he was most horribly alone. From an almost spiritual moment where he swore his heart was beating in rhythm with his brother's, Arthur had slipped away Henry had never felt so alone and so helpless in his life. Even when he was about to be sold as a slave, he had had Rosalind there with him. Now the room was empty, but for the husk of his brother's soul, a soul that had fled, leaving Henry behind on earth as it rose towards Heaven.

There being nothing left to do, he allowed himself to break down. It was more than crying, so different to the tears of a little boy who had scuffed his knees on the ground, or who had been told off, or had his favourite toy taken from him. These were tears of sorrow, of pain, of love, of love lost and thus of total despair. As the tears flowed, his sobs became uncontrollable and morphed into a howl the likes of which the men standing outside had never heard before. A howl coming from a place unknown to mere mortals, accompanied by the soothing sound of a woman's voice singing the most serene yet mournful song, which nobody but Henry could hear.

On hearing Henry's state of delirium, John Skelton burst into the room, unable to bear it any longer. He knew Arthur must have died. He ran to the bed, looking down on the scene before him, and his eyes welled up like they had not since he was a small child himself. Pulling himself together, John Skelton put his arms gently around Henry.

"Come now, Henry. It is time to let go and to allow others to come and pay their last respects to your brave brother. Come with me and we will find a quiet place for you to rest after your long journey."

"But I don't want to leave him. I will never see him again, will I?"

At first the boy would not let go. But John Skelton gently pried his hands away from his brother's body, now growing colder by the moment, and pulled Henry towards himself. Henry sat up and looked one last time at Arthur, who was staring, unseeing, into the distance. Skelton leaned over and put his hands on the dead prince's eyelids to gently close them, letting him rest in peace.

"Come on, Henry, it is time to go." Saying this, John Skelton guided Henry, helping him stand and turn away from the scene of death before him. Henry turned into the warmth of John Skelton's robes and hid his face. He did not want the other people to know he had been crying, so he allowed his beloved tutor to guide him out of the room and back to their apartments.

Katherine was then led into the room to see her husband. Without the luxury of being alone with him, she showed no grief but walked up to him, gently lifted his pale hand and kissed it reverently. Her tears were silent as she gazed upon his deathly face, so full of peace at last. A face she had grown to love with all her heart, yet now he was gone from her, cruelly taken in the prime of his youth, a man on the cusp of adulthood with so many plans, dreams and desires he had yet to share with her in full.

"Please prepare my husband for me," she whispered to her attendants, her voice almost gone, and then with great dignity she walked away from all her hopes and dreams. There was something she had to do, for she had promised Arthur, much as it shocked her. She must go and talk to Henry about Arthur's dying wish, about her needing to marry him to ensure she became Queen of England. That way she could go ahead with all of the progressive plans and ideas she and Arthur had so often talked about. Katherine composed herself and then went to visit Henry in his private chamber.

"But I *can't* marry you!" Henry was still in shock. Arthur was hardly cold, yet Katherine was sitting at his side, holding his hand and telling him it was Arthur's wish that they marry. How could anyone think of such worldly matters when his brother was not even buried? Did she not care for him?

Henry's heart was breaking like it had been thrown over a cliff and had fallen onto frigid rocks.

"Henry, you made a promise. It will not be straight away. I understand you are still a child, although an extremely brave and capable one, as you have proved on your journey here to try to save Arthur." She smiled at the innocence of the boy who had burst in only a few hours ago, so sure he had achieved his goal by coming to warn Arthur of a plot to murder him. "For the love of your brother, you must do as he asked. Please."

Henry was numb with disbelief. "But I am only *ten years old!*" He looked up at Katherine with confused and pleading eyes. It was then he saw the anguish in her expression and checked himself for being so selfish. Katherine was in agony and this conversation was as disturbing to her as it was to him. "But you will grow into a man one day, just as Arthur did, and I will look after you, and together we will rule just as Arthur and I would have done. He told me all his plans. I can help you, Henry, don't you see? I know how to rule, for I have grown up preparing myself to become the Queen of this country ever since I was a babe. It will work out, I promise you."

Henry just stared at her, and she doubted that he had even heard her words. The boy was lost, stunned, driven to a place where he no longer saw or felt.

"Please, Henry, let us just accept the future and leave it aside for now. You are a very brave, loyal brother and I will do all I can to help you grieve for your loss. But for now, I will leave you to rest."

Unable to comfort the child anymore, the princess gathered her robes, gracefully rose and left the room. She could take no more of being a nursemaid to Henry when she needed her own nurse, Elvira, to come and comfort her. Katherine was desolate, exhausted – and humiliated by her husband's dying wish. She would have been better off dying alongside Arthur, the love of her life. She was as horrified at marrying Henry as he was, but for her it was a necessity, to retain her status as the future Queen of England. For the young boy, the idea of marriage at all was incomprehensible. He would need time.

25

John Skelton arranged for Prince Henry and his friends to leave at once, with Charles, Rosalind (who had not settled at court as one of Katherine's maids after all), Balthazar, Jack and Bim as their escorts.

Before they left, John Skelton spoke to Lady Margaret Pole. "You are going to have to quell any talk of poisoning among the courtiers. It is imperative that it be thought that the prince died of some illness. He and the princess suffered from the same sickness – possibly the sweating sickness, nobody can be sure – but she recovered. It was a tragedy, not a crime."

Lady Margaret Pole nodded her head in affirmation while wringing her hands. She could hardly speak for fear of her life being in jeopardy for allowing the prince to die when in her care.

"Now, don't you worry. We can keep this crime to ourselves. The perpetrators have fled. Burn everything, burn all the records of recent life here at the castle. Allow an accidental fire to occur in your office. That will not only create a distraction but will allow for any doctor's records to be lost. I do not like to take such actions, but this is for the safety of the realm. Understand?"

What Skelton meant was that it was for the safety of Lady Pole and her husband, both of whom could be sentenced to death for slacking in their royal duties.[1]. Lady Pole sighed and nodded her head. She curtsied low to Skelton, something a lady would not normally do to a mere tutor. He smiled a kind smile and, putting his hand to her face, wiped away a tear.

"You did your best. This was not your fault, dear. This was 'death by misadventure'."

Lorenzo and his troupe, who had arrived with Jack and Balthazar during all the chaos of Arthur's illness, offered to travel with Henry, Skelton and their friends for some of the way, suggesting Henry disguise himself as one of the actors so nobody recognized him. Henry liked this idea, as did Jack, who could be close to Lydia once again. Now he was back with Lydia, Jack had returned to his usual good humour and was getting along well with Balthazar.

Henry borrowed some clothes from Lorenzo's wardrobe of costumes. "I think I will wear this," he announced, finding a costume for the actor who played the part of Robin Hood in one of their plays.

"You are a man of habit." Jack grinned like a fool. He was fast creating for himself a role of general buffoon and entertainer, more so perhaps since he had been with the troupe.

After putting on the costume, Henry took out a pennywhistle John Skelton had brought for him to play a wistful melody he made up on the spur of the moment and it seemed to soothe him. The others sat around him and listened, enjoying the gift the prince had for turning his raw emotions into seemingly effortless yet heart-rending melodies.

John Skelton bade farewell to Katherine.

"I am sure the King will send for you soon. He will not want to leave you here in Ludlow Castle. He surely will want you to come to the court to be looked after by your friends and relatives. He will understand you must be in a terrible state, having lost your dear Arthur."

Katherine looked pale and nervous. "I do not know what will happen to me now. It will be many years before Henry is old enough to marry. Four years or more. What will I do in the meantime? Will they send me home to Spain? I would dearly love to see my mother and father again, for I miss them terribly."

Skelton had no idea. "I am sure the Queen will provide a place for you by her side. You are a 'dowager princess' now, you know. It is a formal title, and you will be provided with a decent income and a place of your own, for you and your courtiers, at the very least."

The princess smiled a wan smile. "Do you really think so? Then I must prepare myself and begin to pack my belongings." Katherine threw her arms around John and cried into his shoulder. "Oh, John, I am so afraid. I so miss my darling Arthur!"

John Skelton hardly knew how to respond, so he held her close and rubbed her back, then patted it gently, as if she were a baby in his arms.

"There, there, my dear. Arthur might be dead, but he will never leave you. He gave you instructions on how to move on from here. Just do as he asked you, however hard it might seem right now. Remember this: if ever you really miss him and need his advice, just listen and he will whisper in your ear, for he is your guardian angel now and will never leave you. Trust me on this, for I know. I lost my father when I was young, but he is still with me every day, and whenever I see something that reminds me of him, it is a great comfort to me, even now. When I see something that would make him laugh, I laugh with him, sometimes until tears of laughter run down my face, not sadness."

It was easy enough for the troupe of actors to slip out of the castle without drawing much interest, for everyone was running around hysterically, the news of the death of Prince Arthur having caused a general state of panic. There were rumours the prince had died of the sweating sickness, which put the fear of God into everyone who had been near him, from the servants to the doctors and physicians and the priest who had read the last rites to the dying teenager. Others mentioned it was possible Arthur had been poisoned, but this was quickly hushed up, and one poor child who was spreading this story was told unless he kept quiet, he would have his ears cut off.

Henry insisted before they returned to Worcester that he and his friends call in on the humble hut where he had met Ned and Emma. He had not told anyone who Ned really was, but instead explained that this fisherman and his wife had gone out of their way to help him and he wanted to ensure they were both safe and sound. There was also the matter of returning Grog, who was in Bim's care and who looked half the age he had before. Bim had a wonderful way with horses, both Charles and Henry had noticed.

Emma came out of her hut and saw the strange sight of a caravan of people all dressed in colourful clothing coming down the footpath. She was most alarmed and was ready to shoo them away with her broom, but then Henry rode up on a pretty pony.

"Look, Emma," he cried, "Virtue survived the fall; she is fine."

When Henry jumped down off his pony, Emma made the effort to pat the pony's coat and admire her. Henry noticed Emma was in distress and her eyes were red from crying.

"Where is Ned?" he asked her. He had requested of his friends that they hold back so he could have a private conversation with Emma.

"They took him away, Henry, to London, to the Tower. They said he stole a horse, and you stole a horse. I didn't really understand, but I am so glad you are alright. Ned told me the soldiers were chasing you."

"Emma – you must tell me. Is Ned a royal prince? Thady called him Prince *Edward*. Is he my mother's brother? Is he still alive?"

Emma had tears in her eyes. "I told him not to tell you and he promised me he wouldn't."

"He didn't," Henry assured her, "but it would have been better had he done so. It has all been most confusing, and the soldiers said he was a pretender and they tried to arrest him."

"But I thought they were chasing after you?" Emma looked so flustered, Henry put his arms around her to comfort her, the bump in her tummy getting in the way.

"They were, but Ned acted as a decoy and led many of them away from me." Henry was distraught upon thinking of his uncle locked back up in the place from which he had escaped as a child. "But the Tower of all places. We must find a way of getting him out of there, for it will destroy him to be back there after all these years."

Emma explained that the soldiers had allowed Ned to come and see her before he was taken away to the Tower. She put her hand in her pocket and handed Henry the ring.

"Ned told me to give it to you and you would know what to do with it."

Henry was bemused as to what he was meant to do, but he took it and tucked it away in a pocket. "I will do whatever is in my power to rescue Ned, I promise."

Emma then asked about Arthur, and Henry broke the news that his brother had died. "Emma, I have to go back home, as now I am going to become the Prince of Wales, which means I will have a much different life. Maybe my father will send me to Ludlow Castle, like he did Arthur, in which case I will send for you to come and visit, or even live with me.

"One last thing." He held Emma's hand and then, looking back at the gathering of friends who were waiting for him at a polite distance, he beckoned Rosalind over. Charles followed.

"This is my friend Rosalind. She has nowhere to go, for a bad man burned her house down. Would you allow her to stay and be your companion? She needs a friend as much as you do right now and she has come into a bit of money, so she can easily pay her way."

Emma was delighted to have a companion and the two women shook hands.

"Oh my," Rosalind said, looking at Emma's rough hands. "The first thing I am going to do is make you some gloves to protect your beautiful hands in this cold weather."

Henry smiled at Charles, for he could see their idea of introducing the two women was going to work. Then Charles gestured that he wanted to talk to Rosalind alone. Henry diplomatically took Emma to meet John and all the others while Charles said goodbye to Rosalind.

"Rosalind, I want you to take this." He pulled his dagger from his belt. "Keep it near you at all times and don't be frightened to use it." He looked into her eyes.

"Why, thank you, kind sir," she teased him. "But I am saddened if this is a parting gift and I will never see you again."

"Of course you will, you fool." Charles laughed kindly. "I will return as soon as my 'babysitting' duties are over."

It was Rosalind's turn to give something to Charles. "I only have this to give you," she said shyly, producing a small walnut shell from her pocket. It had a silver hinge and a clasp. Charles looked at it in surprise.

"Open it." She gave him the walnut and Charles carefully opened it to find, unfurling, the most delicate pair of kid gloves. They were a bit small for him, or so he thought.

"They will stretch," Emma explained. "I made them to qualify as a master glovemaker. It is the test we have to pass: to make a pair of gloves that will fit inside a walnut. They are tougher than they look and will fit you."

Charles thought them the prettiest things he had ever seen. Before he knew it, he had taken her in his arms, kissing her gently at first but then passionately on the mouth.

Stunned, Rosalind stepped back, as did Charles. "I am sorry. I mean, I didn't mean to, I didn't want to… well, I did want to, but not in that way…" he blustered.

Rosalind blushed and looked at him shyly. "I didn't mind."

Charles grinned. "Neither did I, for sure. I will come back as soon as I can," he promised. "For I would like to try that again."

Rosalind gave him a wicked glance that he had not expected. "So would I."

"Come on, Charles," called Henry, who had witnessed the moment and could see he would lose his friend and protector if he left him there any longer.

Charles ran back to the horse he was riding, who was being held by Bim, before turning and waving farewell to the two girls, who were now standing together, Emma teasing Rosalind.

"Goodbye, stay safe, come back soon."

"Farewell, friends."

Henry had tied Virtue to a wagon and was riding inside with his friends for a while. He was tired and hoped to forget his recent sorrows for a while by playing his pennywhistle once again, the other children singing along to the music. Each time the wheels of the wagon hit a stone, the children were all thrown up into the air and there was much merriment; even Henry laughed for a while. It was good for the prince to have such a distraction from the reality of what had just occurred, and the enormity of what Arthur's death meant for the future. It is one of the wonders of the world that none of us can be sad all the time.

Lorenzo, who was riding his fine piebald horse, trotted up to join John Skelton for a moment. "You know, I had a premonition Henry would become the next King of England. I had no idea who he was when we first met, but his future was already written in the stones, for when we were up at the stone circle, he saw a sign he would become a king one day. He is young and what has just happened will affect him, but I believe in the boy. I am certain he will become a great and much-loved monarch."

John considered what he had just heard. "I have been the tutor of this child for many years now and I have always known he was destined for great things. I grieve that this elevation to heir to the throne has come about in such a tragic way, but he would have been wasted elsewhere. Thank you for telling me this information, for it makes me even more confident that the boy is bound for greatness."

As for Henry, he felt anything other than great. He had failed in his quest, so had failed as a knight; but worse, he had let down his brother. He had failed in saving Arthur from the evil plot to murder him. All he could do now was stick to the promise he had made his dying brother:

to marry Katherine, the Spanish princess. He was in a shock at this Henry had nothing against Katherine, but neither did he love her.

Jack saw that Henry had sunk into a black mood and tried his best to distract him. "Come on, Henry. You have to pull yourself out of your darkness."

Jack placed himself next to his friend and whittled away at a piece of wood. He was making a love-spoon for Lydia, a traditional way of showing affection for your intended. It was not a very elegant spoon as of yet, but he was young and had plenty of time to practise. Henry appreciated the silence, but after a while he spoke.

"Jack, I let Arthur down. If I hadn't fallen into the river and wasted all that time being captured, I could have saved him."

Jack considered whether it was time to speak or not and chose to remain quiet There was silence for a while and then Henry continued.

"But what is done is done. I tried my best and I failed, so now I have to deal with the consequences, don't I?"

"Yes," Jack assured him, for now Henry had seen the light, he felt it prudent to encourage him. "Now is the time to look to yourself, Henry, for you are a good prince. You have many unique qualities that make you an outstanding character. I have witnessed you grow into a formidable young man on this journey, and anyway, you will have many good councillors who will advise you when you are king."

Henry chuckled. "Jack, you are most likely the only councillor I will ever need!" He turned to his friend. "I don't want to become king, Jack; I don't want to have to run the country. Arthur was trained for the role, but I know nothing about politics. It bores me. Father spends all day with his councillors and never has any fun. I want to be a knight and fight battles."

Jack put a brave face on it and bolstered him up. "Come on, Henry, you know you can do it. John Skelton will be at your side, and maybe you can still be a knight in battle? We can go and fight the French."

Balthazar looked up at him in surprise at this.

"Or maybe the Spanish?"

Henry, who was now engaged to a Spanish princess, looked at him disapprovingly.

"Or the Scots?"

Margot was Queen of Scotland.

"Jack, do shut up!" exclaimed Henry, and the atmosphere lightened once again as the group of children laughed, Jack the loudest.

The next day, Lorenzo and his troupe said their goodbyes to Prince Henry and his entourage, for they were heading down south to a town where they had arranged to put on a performance, whereas John Skelton and his royal charges were riding on in the direction of Oxford. There was much hugging and the odd kiss, mainly between Jack and Lydia, who was crying, but with promises for the future and many a meeting within the year, the two parties went their own ways.

That evening, the diminished party, which included Henry, Jack, Bim, Balthazar, Charles, William, John and Margot, were sitting around a campfire eating a dinner Balthazar had provided and cooked – pigeon stew.

"This is delicious," said Margot, who loved her food and was picking at bones and sucking them in a most unladylike manner.

"Margaret!" John only ever used Margot's full name when he was telling her off.

"Sorry, but it really is delicious!" she felt justified in admitting.

"Ips bewifus," agreed Bim.

Bim had been accepted into the coterie of friends that was forming, almost by osmosis, around Henry. By using signs language, Bim had told the whole story of his life, including why he had tried to kidnap Henry back in Enstone and had ended up tied to a tree by Henry and Jack. This caused some merriment before Jack had a revelation.

"I have just realised it. You and I look so like one another you could be James, my lost brother."

Henry understood what he meant. "Jack, do you mean to say we have found your brother after all, like we said we would?"

"Well, he looks like me and he is about the same age - and he remembers being called Jim, which is James just like Jack is." With this, Jack went and sat by Bim with his arm around him. There was no doubt that they looked exceedingly like brothers.

Bim beamed. Whether he was a brother to this boy or not, the boy wanted him to be his brother, and this made him feel loved. Love was so new to the young teenager that he felt raw with emotion and tears fell down his face.

"Come on, Bim," laughed Jack, "it can't be that bad being related to me?"

There was a great cheer from everyone as they gathered around Bim and Jack to congratulate them on finding each other.

"We have nothing to prove it, for the moment, but in time we could talk to my... I mean our parents and see if they accept you might be Jim and also what... has ... er happened.. to you."

Henry spoke up on cue. "And until then, you are more than welcome to live with me at Eltham Palace as my friend and bodyguard. Better still, you could be Master of the Horse."

"With me, *bien sur*," added Balthazar, who was also to become Henry's personal bodyguard. "My name is Protector of King, so you have it 'in a nutshell', *non*?"

John Skelton watched on, happy to see Henry among such good friends. He would need them over the next few years, for he had a huge task ahead, that of preparing to become the next King of England. It was a lot for a ten year old to face up to at such short notice.

When they passed through Worcester, John took Henry to meet the odd man who owned the shop with all the hats and herbs. Thomas Northfield was his name, or so he told Henry when they met this time around. Henry wanted to thank the old man for saving his life that day and asked him to tell his story.

Thomas gave a quick account of his life. "I was a monk here in the monastery at Worcester many years ago, but they caught me studying books kept in the library that were of a restricted nature, locked away from prying eyes. I had persuaded the old librarian to open the doors to the bookshelves on alchemy, magic and prophesy among other ancient crafts. These were books confiscated from the druids and witches of old, and I became fascinated by the old ways. For this I was defrocked, back in 1432[2]. I set up here and ever since I have done what I can to keep an eye on young scoundrels like you.

"There was no time for a formal introduction when we first met, but I am glad you are safe with your friends once again. Did you find your brother? Of course you did. But he died, I know. It was bound to happen."

The old man rambled on until Henry thought he must be quite mad. Then, without warning, he took Henry by the hand. "Henry, you are understandably alarmed by your new situation, but you should not be so. You were born to be a king and you will be the greatest king

England has ever known. You will go down in history and people will write books about you. I know this, as I see it in the heavens and in your eyes. But you must listen to your wife, Katherine. You must allow her to advise you and rule by your side. Do this and you will succeed in becoming the greatest king ever; ignore her and you will become a tyrant. Mark my words and etch them into your soul. Arthur will live on in you and your wife, and England will thrive. God bless you, child."

By evening the group had closed in on the castle where the knight lived, the one who had stolen Charles's horse in a card game. It was time for Charles to take his revenge. He had been plotting this moment and asked for volunteers to join him.

"I will come with you," said William.

"Me too!" Balthazar felt he owed Charles his life and this was a way of paying him back for saving them all that day on the beach.

"I am in too," said Jack, who was happy to enter any adventure that promised a bit of fun. Bim, who was now with Jack all the time, gave a thumbs-up sign.

John Skelton looked at Henry, who had not said a word. "Come on, Henry, it would do you some good to take your mind off whatever it is you are brooding about." He patted Henry on the arm.

"I am not brooding." Henry replied, but he knew this was a lie.

Henry could not stop thinking about Arthur and Katherine and how things could have been different. He kept seeing Arthur's pleading eyes as he made him promise to marry Katherine. That must have been so hard for him to do, to give up the one woman he loved so dearly. He had sacrificed his life for her. He had sacrificed everything. He was also thinking about the words Arthur spoke before he died and the way he seemed relieved when he thought he saw someone waiting for him.

Who was it he had seen? A man, a woman? God, an angel? Or Melusina? Henry so wanted to ask Ned if their shared blood made them more magical than religious. He truly believed in God, but who saved his life when he fell in the river? Who saved Virtue? Surely the two of them should have drowned. Was it the greatness of God or the magic of Melusina that had stepped in and saved both him and his pony?

"I am not brooding, I am thinking."

The others all looked at him expectedly and Henry, who was sitting by the fire, poking at it with a stick, looked up. "What?" he asked, feeling he was being unjustly questioned. "Oh, alright. I will come too."

John Skelton smiled with relief. He had tried distracting Henry with questions, riddles and even some of his latest poetry, but the boy kept falling back into a dark place. This was not good for his health. They needed to reignite the spark inside him. The old Henry – Henry the mischievous child.

The plan was for the gang of friends to ride up silently to the castle and for the four boys, Henry, Jack, Bim and Balthazar, to create a diversion by lighting a fire against the outer walls of the compound, somewhere around the other side from where the entrance gates might be. While the inhabitants of the castle tried to put out the fire, Charles and William would find where the stables were and would call for Caesar, who was trained to come to his call. Charles only hoped the horse could break his way out of the stables. He was a strong animal. Then they would all run away as quickly as they could. A simple plan, so not much could go wrong. John Skelton would wait back at the campfire with Margot, but in case matters did get out of hand, they would be mounted and ready to leave as soon as the others returned with Caesar. John had explained to Margot this was not stealing, for the knight had cheated at cards when he won the beast in the first place.

"I am not sure if that argument would hold up in a court of law," Margot had stated, but she knew how much Charles loved his horse and so was prepared to keep her doubts to herself.

It was a dark and still night, with the stars shining brightly in the sky and a sickle moon slowly rising up over the horizon. The boys crept up to the castle through a thicket of overgrown shrubs. The area would have been cleared in the past, so that the castle guards could see any advancing enemy, but this knight was a lazy, disorganized man and had not kept the shrubs cut back. Tonight, he would regret this mistake, for not only did the boys manage to find a concealed route right up to the wall of the castle, but they had collected enough deadwood to light a decent fire. Jack also had a tiny package in his pocket, although he was more respectful of it now he knew the impact it would have on the calm of the night air.

"Can you see Charles?" Henry asked.

"Yes," whispered Balthazar, who had very keen vision.

"He is over there in the trees."

"Right then, let's light this fire."

Henry struck a light with his flint and striker, and it soon lit the charcloth they had brought with them, wrapped up in some sheep's wool. This fed the sparks, which turned into a flame. The boys carefully laid the flame into the pile of brushwood they had piled up against the castle walls and then placed some larger timbers on top of the brushwood pile.

"Now, run!" urged Jack, flinging the tiny packet into the flames, and the four boys ran like Hell itself was about to erupt, shouting "Fire, fire!" as they fled.

Hell did erupt in the form of a flash of such brightness it lit the whole night scene up like daylight and an explosion like cannon fire that startled all the birds in the trees. The servants of the knight came rushing and screaming out of the front doors of the buildings and into the inner courtyard in a state of mass hysterics and confusion.

Reaching the cover of the trees, the boys jumped onto their ponies and galloped to a point a mile up the road to wait for Charles and William.

Charles, meanwhile, jumped off the horse he was sharing with William and within the chaos of the castle, there was a whinnying sound in response. Charles called again and Caesar, who knew his true master was at hand, kicked and smashed his way out of the stables, knocking over the groom who oversaw his care. There was nothing the groom could do. Caesar reared, bit and kicked at anyone who was in his way and ran out into the courtyard. The front gates of the castle had just been opened, so that a group of men could investigate the source of the fire, and Caesar ran straight at the gap before anyone could stop him.

"Close the gates, you fool, and stop that horse!"

The knight, drunk and confused, ran about waving his arms. But it was too late, for the beautiful white destrier came out of the gates looking like a phantom in the light of the burning fire. He ran instinctively towards Charles, who kept whistling to guide him.

Charles leapt onto his bare back. He held on to the mane of his trusty beast and shouted, "Go, Caesar, fly like the wind."

Henry and his friends were ready to flee once Charles and William had caught up with them. They were listening to the sound of horses' hooves coming towards them at a fast pace.

"Here we go – there are more than two horses coming; we are in for a race!" cried Henry, just as Charles and William came up out of the darkness, Caesar sweating with effort and with no intention of stopping. "Charge!" Henry shouted, and the band of thieves dug their boots into their animals' sides to urge them to leap into action.

John Skelton and Margot were waiting on the side road, well prepared to be overtaken by their fleeing friends. They had decided they were not to be involved in the theft, for as a queen, Margot had to be innocent of any such shenanigans. They were to act like surprised strangers as this galloping mass of friendship came up the road and rushed past them, hotly pursued by an unknown number of angry, confused and disgruntled knights. The knights were no match for the spirited lads they were chasing, and John Skelton had a feeling they would soon give up and go back to their castle.

The last John saw of Henry that night was the boy riding at the head of this group of mismatched but loyal companions, shouting "For God and for England!" as he disappeared up the road, his dagger held tightly in his hand. Behind him rode his friends, charging after him and shouting in unison, "For God and for Henry!"

"For Bob am for Hemwy!" shouted Bim.

"Bob?" Margot and Skelton laughed, mainly with relief.

Somehow, John Skelton knew that Henry would eventually get over the death of his brother and his happy countenance would shine once again, and it would be thanks to the strength his new gang of friends had brought him. His friends would stand by his side and protect him. They would never let him down.

Once the group of men chasing the gang of thieves had passed by, already beginning to tire, John Skelton decided it was time to move. He had arranged to meet Henry and the others back at the inn where all their troubles had started, at Enstone in the inn called The River Crossing

"Come on, Margot, we have some catching up to do." He looked at his young charge, so unlike the Queen of Scotland, sitting on her pony with an impish grin and waiting expectantly.

"I thought you would never ask. You know how much I hate it when Henry is allowed to go ahead of me," she laughed, and spurring their fat little ponies on, they rode off together into the night, leaving a cloud of dust behind them.

Epilogue

The hapless messenger sent to tell the King that his son and heir had died rode non-stop for two days. He allowed himself only a moment's sleep, plus six changes of horse, to make the two-hundred-mile trip from Ludlow Castle to London. En route, he passed a troop of the King's men, who were escorting a prisoner towards the capital city. Although he recognized his old friend Captain Cripps, the messenger did not stop, for he had an urgent duty to attend to.

He galloped onwards, the dirt from the road splattering the newest horse he was riding, so that soon its flanks were as covered in mud and sweat as were his own clothes. After hours of riding, the exhausted messenger could hardly tell what was going on around him. The horses were all used to the route and all he had to do was cling on until they reached the outskirts of London, where he took control to steer his mount to the palace where the court was residing.

As he approached the outer walls of London, the wind was blowing hard. People rushed along the streets while holding their hats and coats to their bodies. The messenger came cantering up the road, his cloak flying behind him like wings. Pulling his horse to a halt, the man jumped to the ground, his tired legs nearly giving way under his weight, and forced himself to run up the stone steps, past the palace guards. Seeing that he was wearing the royal livery, so must have a message for the King, they waved him through, whereupon he staggered to the chambers of the Chancellor.

The messenger had been told that Bishop Warham and his colleagues would know how to break the terrible news to the monarch. The bishop decided that, as it was late, the King should rest in peace that night and be told in the morning for they knew that this news would devastate him or, even worse, it might destroy his mind completely.

Lady Margaret was also informed of Arthur's death. She was told by Bishop Warham and immediately agreed that the news should be delayed, to give her son one more night of peace before his world was destroyed. What she really wanted was a time in which to pull herself together and collect her thoughts. How could Arthur have died? She had sent Grope the instructions to *stop* the killing. Had he ignored her order? Had the man gone mad? Lady Margaret had to face the fact that maybe her order had not reached him in time. Captain Cripps had reported to her that the message had been sent by pigeon. He had even watched the bird fly off himself.

This was a disaster. It would be less of one had she not told anyone, for Lady Margaret knew that Fiddle and Grope were trustworthy, or at least they were as guilty as she and therefore would keep silent, but she had *confessed* to Bishop Fisher. He knew that she had ordered the killing of her grandson and now he had died. Would the bishop keep her confession to himself? He was obliged to, for confession was between God and herself, but he might crack. Worse than the fact that she had murdered someone was that all hope of salvation upon her death was gone. Lady Margaret fell to her knees and began pulling her hair out with madness.

Early the next morning, as the King was in the Star Chamber ready to attend the morning session with his Council, there came a knock on the chamber door and the royal chaplain asked for an audience in private. The King guessed that this was a request of some import, for the chaplain had never before asked for a private audience. Consequently, he asked his councillors to leave, which they did, their heads bowed for they already knew the subject of the conversation to come. Once the room was empty, the chaplain broke the news to the King that his dear, beloved son and heir, Prince Arthur of Wales, had died of some unknown fever three days earlier. The King buckled as if he had been kicked in the stomach. Out of his mouth came a wail that the chaplain later described as a sound from Hell itself, it was so unworldly.

"My son, no, no, NO." The King pounded his hands on the council table and collapsed into a chair before banging his forehead on the table to ease his pain. The bemused chaplain did not know what to do, for he was not good with emotions, these not being part of his ecclesiastical training. He ran to the door and asked the councillors, who were waiting outside, to call for the Queen.

The Queen arrived in a state of disarray. She had been dressing, and upon hearing of her husband's distress, had pushed her ladies-in-waiting away to run through the corridors to reach the King. Her hair was half brushed, flying behind her as she ran, and her clothes were crooked, but nobody noticed. It was as if her dishevelment of dress matched the horror of the moment, the news that his beloved son and heir, Prince Arthur, had died sweeping before her like a tidal wave.

The Queen burst into the Star Chamber to find her husband catatonic, his face still down on the table, in a world of his own. The chaplain was there, but he was like a statue of a saint, for he had not been dismissed and could think of nothing to do other than putting his hands together and praying.

"Oh, my darling, my dearest," the Queen began, dismissing the chaplain with a wave of her hand. She ran to her husband's side and held him close. The devastated monarch rose only to hide his face in her clothes against her belly. The Queen supported her husband in her arms, pulling him towards her as she would a small child. She had no time to grieve herself. That she would do later, once her duty as wife to the King was done.

"Husband, don't cry. Arthur would have hated you to be so distressed. Maybe the princess is pregnant and will bear him a son? If not, we have Henry."

At the mention of Prince Henry, the King wailed even louder. "Beth, dearest. We are done for, we are doomed," he cried. "Henry will never make a good king. The child is an imbecile, a nightmare. Katherine *must* be pregnant. Oh, poor, darling Arthur. My son, my pride and joy. My life."

"Darling," the Queen continued, "shall I call for your mother? Would you like her here to comfort you?"

Normally, the King would want his mother, even if he stubbed his toe. But this time it was different. He had changed. For the first time ever in the sixteen years of their marriage, the King wanted his wife, not his mother. He now saw the value in his wife's love, her sense of duty and her wisdom. He could hardly believe he had ever put his callous mother first.

"No, leave her be. I need you, my Beth. You are the only person who loved Arthur like I did. You were his mother. Oh God. What have I done that God would punish me so?"

The Queen - amazed that her husband, for the first time *ever*, had put her before his mother, had needed her rather than his mother, let her husband cry like a child into her dress. There was nothing else she could do, for the King was clinging on to her so tightly, she was fearful that if he let go, he would fall into oblivion.

Pulling herself upright and with the greatest effort, the Queen then spoke words that she had hoped never to say again but did so out of love for her grieving husband.

"We are young yet, my dear; we can have more children. We will have another son and you can train him like you did Arthur. Henry is happy to go into the Church, I am certain."

The Queen was not so certain about this, for Henry would surely not allow a younger sibling to steal his birthright, but it might calm the King down somewhat, she hoped.

The King stopped wailing. "We could, could we?" He looked up at his dishevelled yet beautiful wife with hope, grabbing her by her arms and shaking her.

"Yes, we could," she replied, while her spirits sank at the thought of childbirth. "But let us wait and see if the princess is with child first. Let us write to her and ask her to come to London, where we can look after her in her widowhood and comfort her. Poor girl. She is barely wed and now she is a widow."

The King, now that he had a plan, sat up, ready to compose a letter to the beautiful princess. "Get me a pen, dear wife. That is a good idea. Let us write to Princess Katherine."

As the Queen asked the guard to arrange for pen and paper to be brought to the King immediately, along with a good burgundy to lift his spirits, the King sat back and dreamt of the auburn-haired princess, round with a child in her belly, and his heart fluttered. What a beautiful creature the princess was, what a prize. She would produce a new Arthur, a brand-new Arthur, who could become the next King of England. The child was bound to be as talented and honourable as his dead father. Henry could be hidden away in a monastery and kept out of trouble, to be brought out only on saints' days to bless the congregation. He could even preside over his nephew's coronation, the nearest that young Henry would ever get to holding the crown.

In her private chamber, Lady Margaret was dressed and carefully coiffed, her hair off balance despite her best efforts, having been destroyed the evening before in her distress. She sat, composed and collected, awaiting the call from her son, the King. As soon as he heard of Arthur's death, he would surely call for her, his mother, his closest confidante. She had been through every possible outcome that might occur as a result of this terrible moment and had decided that Bishop Fisher would have to be 'disposed of' by Grope if she thought that there was any weakening of his loyalty towards her. She would dedicate another two hundred gold coins to his university, but if that did not buy confirmation of his loyalty, she would have to find a new confessor.

Lady Margaret had rationalized the awful event that had occurred, despite her instructions to the contrary, and had chosen the best route forward. Her strong tie with her son would be reaffirmed as they both comforted each other over their heir's demise. They would plan the education of Prince Henry and together would mould him into the new heir. To take Henry away from the Queen would also press a note of satisfaction in the old woman's tune, for the Queen was the young boy's favourite and Lady Margaret was a little jealous of this. Even the pony she had bought him had not swayed him. Perhaps she would buy Henry a new saddle, so that he could better practise his jousting. Now that was an idea.

Lady Margaret waited, but nobody came to call her. No messenger knocked on her door with a message from the King asking for her to come to him. Nobody came to comfort her at all.

All the while, from a hole in the oak panelling that lined the Star Chamber, a mouse regarded the scene before him: a mouse with a white tip to his tail and a withered front paw that he held up under his chin. That evil woman had nearly killed him when she took a swipe at him with the coal shovel. He would get his revenge on the old witch. In fact, things were already turning against her. Her days of power were over.

The mouse understood everything that was coming to pass, for he was a visionary. He was also a magician, a metamorph, a shapeshifter and a sorcerer. His name was Thomas Northfield in his latest human form (for even magician's die from time to time). The royal children had named him Sir Jasper in his other body, but he was used to being called all sorts of names. In times of old, he had been known as Myrddin, or Merlin. In those days he advised King Arthur who ruled from Camelot. When woken from his centuries long sleep to prepare for a new king, he had assumed it would be a new King Arthur he would advise, but that was not to be the case.

Thomas had been reborn to help Henry prepare for kingship. He was a wilful boy, erratic and compulsive. It would take all the wisdom and magic that Thomas could conjure, to keep him on the right path.

If Thomas succeeded, Henry would be magnicicant, he would become the great monarch of modern times, but if he failed - well, Henry was likely to become a monster. Thomas must ensure Henry married Katherine of Aragon, who had sense and loyalty and understood how to rule England. Without Katherine at his side to control his whimsical ways, King Henry would lose control. Power would go to his head. He would be like a firework that has lost its fixing and dashes around in an ever expanding and destructive circle. Thousands would die — tens of thousands. Yes, without his guidance and that of young Katherine, King Henry VIII would become no more than a callous and dreadful monster.

ENDNOTES

1. Princess Margaret (Margot) was engaged to marry James IV, King of Scotland
2. Tudors have puches, rather than pockets as such, in their clothing, but that I am using the word pocket throughout the novel as it is easier for descriptive purposes.
3. Charles Brandon was a womaniser all his life. He was a rare and natural charmer who all women adored, without being crass or chauvinistic about it. He truly saw beauty in every woman he seduced and tried to act in a chivalrous manner. He was, however, orphan with ambition in those days where one married to advance oneself, and he was certainly guilty of doing so later in life.
4. Both Arthur and Katherine were the descendants of Edward III. Her English blood gave Katherine blue eyes and auburn hair, unusual colouring for a Spaniard.
5. This censer, now replaced by an iron one, had fallen on several occasions, but this time it might have changed the course of English history had it killed the

princess.

6. Prince Henry is recorded as having danced that night to the delight of the wedding guests who cheered when hethrew off his jacket to move more freely.
7. The King decided that Prince Henry ought to train for a religious life to be of use to his older brother in the futureas an archbishop, but never able to rally supporters against him as a knight in a bid to take the crown. He was concerned that Henry would become a popular duke in later life if not harnessed by the Church.
8. A pretender is a claimant to an abolished throne or to a throne already occupied by somebody else. Their claim may or may not be legitimate, but they are still a threat tothe current monarch. Henry Tudor was a pretender himself, now he was King, he had to deal with those whocame to oppose him.
9. It is believed that the King did once have some hunting dogs hung in this manner as a demonstration of his power.
10. The royal coffers were almost empty when Henry Tudor became king, and he did spend a fortune on clothes. He also used two tax collectors, Richard Empson and Edmund Dudley to seize fines and taxes from the nobles.Fiddle and Grope are loosely based on these unpopular characters.
11. Henry Tudor was taken from his mother and grew up firstwith a York family and then on the run with his uncle, until he came to England and took the crown from Richard III at the age of 28. Effectively, he never

12. lived with his mother until he was crowned King.
13. Sea coal was a valuable commodity that was only used by royalty. All other fires were built using timber which smoked and was less efficient. It was called sea coal as itwas delivered around the coast by sea.
13. Lady Margaret was a very religious child who claimed tohave been spoken to by the spirit of St Nicholas, much like how Joan of Arc was spoken to by God.
14. John Blanke was a black musician in London in the early 16th century, who came to England as one of the African attendants of Katherine of Aragon. He is one of the earliest recorded black people in England after the Romanperiod. His name may be a reference to his skin colour, derived either from the word "black" or from the French word "blanc", meaning white.
15. Canon were such a new form of warfare and so innaccurate that they were used more as a distractiontactic than as serious weaponry.
16. The dissolution of the monestaries occurred from 1536 and 1541 and was when Henry VIII ordered the destruction of many monestaries, priories, abbeys and convents around England, taking their riches for the use of the Crown and selling off their lands.
17. To claim 'sanctuary' in a church was to claim protectionfrom punishment by the law. The fugitive was protectedby the Holy Roman Church while they were in the confines of the church. But they could not leave the building while in sanctuary.
18. Henry VIII was quite prim and proper, and this was theonly phrase he used for swearing. Oh, and monks

ENDNOTES

were not to eat meat during Lent, although the corrupt ones took little heed of therules of the Church when it came to food and drink.

19. John Fisher was hung, drawn and quartered by Henry VIIIin 1535 as a traitor. He was beheaded only days before Sir Thomas More, and their reasons for death were the same. Both devoutly Catholic men opposed the proposed annulment of King Henry VIII's marriage to Queen Katherine, and they vehemently argued that the King could not be named Supreme Head of the Church, for only the Catholic Pope had such holy power on earth.
20. This scene is poignant, bearing in mind what happens tothe Queen in later years.
21. Henry VII, Henry's father, spent an exciting time aged 14when he had to run away from Henry's maternal grandfather Edward IV. I will try to cover this in another novel.
22. 50% of children in Tudor times died before they reachedmaturity.
23. Jack is talking about Stonehenge.
24. Another pretender who was conquered by the King wassent to the kitchens as a servant by way of punishment, so that people would laugh at him.
25. Some historians believe that Richard Duke of Yorkescaped to Flanders.
26. During these times the monestaries were becoming morepowerful and as sheep farming was so lucrative, they evickted entire villages to turn the land into grazing. This left many families out in the cold,

ENDNOTES

wandering around the courntryside looking for somewhere to live and to work.

27. John Fisher did not become Bishop of Rochester until 1504 but it suits the plot, so forgive me for bending the facts.

28. In 2015 the grave of a high-status woman of around 25 years of age was found near to the Rollright Stones. Buried with her were a long-handled copper alloy skillet lying to the left of the head. Such skillets – which are closely modelled on the Roman *trulleum*, used in handwashing rituals – are rare: only around seven other examples are known. Perhaps she was the witch?

29. Itriyya - is, of course, spaghetti, which came from the Arabian lands into Sicaly and then Italy as early as the 7th century a.d.

30. This windmill on stilts is no longer next to the Rollright Stones but was as described at the time of the Tudors.

31. Henry VIII was a prodigious musician and wrote a number of pieces, now lost.

32. Pirates, in particular Welsh pirates, were common enough in Tudor times. Sometimes the second son of a landowner, or someone who had fallen foul of the law, the Welsh were among the most notorious of all pirates through the ages, including Captain Morgan, born in 1635. Perhaps he was a descendant of our captain.

33. It has always intrigued me that of all the people who became close to Henry VIII, only Charles Brandon was not executed and died a natural death. I wonder

if there was something he did early in their friendship that made Henry trust him with his life?

34. Sabrina, or the Severn Bore is it is more commonly called, is a natural phenomenon where the sea's current fights against the flow of the River Severn, creating a tidal wave that reaches well up into the river. It happens at intervals that can be noted by the moon and so predicted. These days people travel from far and wide to surf on the Bore with surfboards and canoes.
35. Henry VIII was said to have sent a present to an unknownwoman on the occasion of her marriage.
36. There are copies of the Nine Herb charm still inexistance.
37. The Nine Herbs charm is a recorded antidote against poison used since early times and is written here in full.
38. Melusina is a mythological water goddess and the founder of the House of Luxembourg whose tragic love story andmagical legacy had a dramatic impact on her female descendants, particularly Jacquetta of Luxemburg and Elizabeth Woodville, mother of the Queen (thus Henry'smaternal grandmother). Some say that Elizabeth Woodville used her magical powers to bewitch Edward IV into going against all royal convention and marrying her, a widow and a commoner. Melusina sang to her estranged husband as he was dying, to enable him to find her in the spirit world. It is said that her descendants would hear her singing when dying, or when a family member was soon to die.

ENDNOTES

39. In 1508, French poet Eloy d'Amerval referred to a poisson d'avril (April fool, literally "April's fish"), possibly the first reference to the celebration in writing. Some writers suggest that April Fools' originated in the Middle Ages. It would seem then that the idea of the April Fool's jokewas around well before this first recorded reference.

40. Richard and Margaret Pole were courtiers who had beengiven the position of running Ludlow Castle during Arthur's life there. Lady Margaret was a first cousin of theQueen and had been married to Sir Richard by order of the King, who wanted her married to someone with Tudor loyalties.

41. It was never known what illness Prince Arthur and hiswife were suffering from.

42. The history books all say that both Arthur and Katherine were sick but she recovered. They do not know what illness killed him. Some say it was a form of cancer, but then how come Katherine was also ill? Otheres say it wasthe sweating sickness or a similar disease. There is no reasonwhy it could not have been poison but there is no evidence either.

43. The irony of this is that HenryVIII did execute Margaret Pole many years later, when she was 67. The executioner made a botch of the job and had to use ten blows to cut off her head, and some say she was screaming and struggling to run from him all the time. It must have beenthe most terrible death.

44. To enter the guild of glovemakers this was the test. Analmost impossible one for us to believe

today.
45. Thomas Northfield is exactly as described – an historicalcharacter who was defrocked for showing an interest in magical books held in the abbey where he resided. I know nothing more about him other than what he hasjust revealed, but he makes for a great magician.

Acknowledgments

Although I have already dedicated this novel to my husband, SHAUN, who has missed out on meals at times while I was writing, I must thank him again for his endurance and support. I also want to thank my sons, WOODY and RON, and the LOST BOYS (too many to mention) who spent much of their teenage years around at my house, devouring fantasy volumes with such appetite that it made me wonder if I could write a fantasy-style series using historic facts. I have drawn a lot of inspiration from these young men and women when creating my heroes – I hope they forgive me.

Another young man who needs a special mention is BALTHAZAR, upon whom my Balthazar is based. He is a French boy who comes to the village where I live on his holidays. He is so charming and friendly - and is always playing with swords in the street. He bows with chivalric grace whenever we meet. He inspired the character in the book. I hope he likes him.

Next, I bow to LORENZO, a talented artist who has spent many months illustrating this novel, even though he lives on the other side of the world, and we only correspond via the internet. Thank you to NATALIE and JACKSON for the introduction.

ACKNOWLEDGMENTS

Thank you to the highly successful author, MARGARET GEORGE, who's novel, "The Autobiography of Henry VIII," captured my imagination and inspired me to write a YA version of Henry's life as I loved her book so much. Her novel is compelling and diligent in its research.

Then there is the writing group that kicked off what was a vague ambition to write a book about the childhood of Henry VIII, so thank you to ROB - our tutor and guide, WENDY, JENNY and the others who I met there. Thanks especially to LESLEY, who read the manuscript and loved it so much that she injected much needed confidence into my writing soul. A massive thank you to my darling sister, JESSICA, who read the first draft (never show anyone your first draft!) and survived. Beta readers come nest, EVANGELINE and LIZELLE, and other kind readers like my Number 1, NANCY, my second great support, SALLY, then LORNA, my cousins GEORGE and DOONE, early victims of my 'testing process' who read a longer version of the novel and survived. Thank you to JACKIE who also read the manuscript and gave me a boost. Thanks to the many others who tried and failed to get back to me, and those who did and helped correct errors in my research, ZAK who works at Hampton Court deserves a special mention. To TRINA, who although we have yet to meet, has become a massive supporter, JO CARR, my childhood friend - thanks for your help and encouragement and good luck with your new book. Thank you also to PHIL. who grew up in Ludlow and told me that the inn The Bull, still in existence, was there in the 16th Century.

The next person to whom I am indebted is ANN O'CONNOR, the direct descendent of James Worsley, the whipping boy of Henry VIII. As a friend of ours in France, it was only by chance that I discovered she had the key to my novel, for up until then I had created

ACKNOWLEDGMENTS

at whipping boy without knowing his real identity. I hope Ann approves of my depiction of her illustrious ancestor.

Finally, I want to thank friends like JAAP from the BAR'BICANE, the best bar in SW France, and lovely LAUREN, who has helped me so much with the images of Prince Henry, SHELLY and MAGNUS (a.k.A Alexander) and MARY, who have supported me during moments of doubt and who have always been there for me, to rekindle flagging hopes only to have to listen to my enthusiastic rantings. They have given advice, and support and have told me never to give up.

I must also thank everyone who supported my KICKSTARTER campaign, both friends and family, then people who took a chance who have never met me. Thank you. Too many to name, I am eternally grateful to you all and when Book Two comes out, you will be given first refusal of any limited-edition copies. That, I promise.

Oh, and a big thank you to IGGY POP who has unwittingly contributed the theme music to this novel, keeping my spirits high and my creativity flowing to the beat of his primal, raw, powerful music. His honesty intelligence, and economy of words to create poetry that touches genius, puts my overwriting in its place.

Bena Stutchbury

March 2022

About The Artist

Lorenzo Sparascio was born in Tricase, a small town in the south of Italy, in 1994. He went through art studies at the Academy of Fine Arts at Lecce, and after which he chose to leave Italy to go on an adventure. During his trip from Italy to France on a vintage motorcycle, he met Bena, who asked him to illustrate her novel. Lorenzo's journey has now ended in Tasmania, via Alice Springs, Australia, where he is about to take on his second book illustration project for another author.

About The Author

Born in 1961, Bena Stutchbury spent her childhood riding the South Downs on horseback and her adulthood restoring Irish castles. She has sailed in the Tall Ships Race, been a dispatch rider in London and never grew up. With a lifelong yearning to write a novel, it was only recently that the story came to her – that of the childhood of Henry VIII. He was not always the fat old man we imagine when his name is mentioned and this series, which follows Henry until his coronation aged eighteen, gives the young Henry a voice.

www.benastutchbury.com

Printed in Great Britain
by Amazon